SAVIORS

SAVIORS

PAUL EGGERS

Harcourt Brace & Company

New York   San Diego   London

Requests for permission to make copies of any part of the work
should be mailed to: Permissions Department,
Harcourt Brace & Company, 6277 Sea Harbor Drive,
Orlando, Florida 32887-6777.

The author wishes to thank the *Sonora Review* and *Quarterly West*
for their support in publishing short stories that, substantially
revised, became part of *Saviors*.

Library of Congress Cataloging-in-Publication Data
Eggers, Paul.
Saviors/Paul Eggers.—1st ed.
p.   cm.
ISBN 0-15-100351-3
I. Title.
PS3555.G34S28   1998
813'.54—dc21   98-15452

Designed by Lydia D'moch
Printed in the United States of America
First edition
A C E F D B

For Ellen

Acknowledgments

I'd like to thank Marly Swick, Gerry Shapiro, Judith Slater, Lee Martin, and John McNally for their support and superb writerly advice during the drafting of this book, as well as for their friendship. For their faith in the manuscript, and for their perseverance and skill, I'd like to thank my editor, Walter Bode, and my agent, Kip Kotzen. And for helping me keep my Malaysian past alive for so many years, I'd like to thank Mike Kendellan, Doug Michell, Tom Petocz, Selvaratham, and Joseph Stimpfl.

SAVIORS

Prologue

SENTIMENTALITY, SAID NGUYEN VAN TRINH, was the Vietnamese sickness. He had a story to illustrate his point, though over time the events of his own life made him bury the words deep in his chest. The story was simple. Back in Vietnam, in the Quang Tri reeducation camp, he was allowed a bamboo sleeping mat to himself twice a month. Those nights, he unrolled the mat just outside the storage closet, where the cooking pots were piled, to better see the firm, certain line of the longhouse ridgepole. What was the proverb? "The strong man folds his arms; the wise man shuts his mouth." That was what the ridgepole said to him; it gave him the strength to live. So twice a month he stared at the ridgepole until the moonlight bathed the room in a chalky light and the bird spiders began to lower, dropping as if by parachute to the floor and scuttling over to the cooking pots, where they sometimes stroked their abdomens and detached giant egg sacs that seemed to Trinh's eyes to glow like distant balls of white-hot phosphorus. His friends, Nguoc and Vu, both telephone operators from his old unit, did not think of the nightly visitations in military terms. They were sentimentalists. They said their hearts were those spiders. What they meant was their love was delicate as a spider's sac of young. They would bleed for it. They would feed it with their lives.

Twice a month, Trinh woke his friends by flattening the phosphorescent balls with his sandal. He told them he had killed centipedes. He wasn't cruel. He had no wish to mock his friends. He just knew that sentimentalism was like a disease. It weakened you. It made you susceptible to all manner of spirits and paralysis.

Of course Nguoc and Vu later died—their heads were diseased, they were dreamy as clouds. Trinh lived to flee his ancestral home, his *que huong,* with his only child, his widowed daughter, Chi. A boy, his nephew Duoc, was aboard as well. They left in Year Four—1979, four years after the fall of Saigon—on a crowded wooden boat, the *Binh Huat,* and skirted the Thai coast, sailing south all the way to Malaysian waters, to the Bidong Island Refugee Camp, thirty kilometers offshore from the mainland city of Kuala Trengganu. When the *Binh Huat* arrived, foundering on the camp's Zone C coral, you could smell what had happened, even before camp security waded out with stretchers. It was never clear when the Thai pirates had boarded. No one pressed the issue. Trinh, Trinh with his nasty wound, had no memory of the attack. He was fortunate to have lived. The boy was too young to give a coherent account. Chi was found laid out in the hold, with the others.

Her death was what made him bury his story deep in his chest. Her death was what gave him the Vietnamese sickness, and now the sickness was killing him.

On Bidong, it was difficult not to think like a sentimentalist. Every day the loudspeakers played Vietnamese folk songs and announced arrivals and departures. No one knew how many boat people—boat people! even the American term was sentimental—no one knew exactly how many people were there, waiting on the tiny island for the Americans or the French or the Australians to shuttle them out. The relief workers said thirty thousand, but they always rounded up, to get more funding.

Thirty thousand. Decency, Trinh said, demanded a specific number. So he kept a private tally of all the young women. With every new face, his heart raced; his hands would move, fingers trembling, poised as if for seduction. He had to stop after a week. He had begun to imagine Chi in their strangers' clothes, Chi carrying a basket of cuttlefish, perhaps bored, slapping a fly away from her nose. If decency demanded a specific number, then what if, say, number 317 could trade places with her—some girl with a blank face, a betel-nut chewer, a skinny moonflower with hands like bark? What if he could have Chi back? He imagined ocean, a clean, blue horizon, without mess: the betel-nut chewer would drop swiftly, her face full of surprise, lungs flapping like balloons, the singsong voice of the water in her ears. *Breathe me,* the voice would say, and she would. Once, touching a girl on the arm, he said the words out loud. He knew he said them only when he saw her expression. Then he had to turn away, to hide his face. His sickness shamed him. It had turned him ghoulish.

He had heard that sentimentality let his countrymen endure their history. Perhaps that was true. The air in the camp was putrid, heady with the gases from the sewage canals that ran through the camp, and in the evening, the rats emerged from their burrows and began to squeal and shimmy up the sapling posts in the refugee huts. Then the Malay Task Force guards walked their rounds, spitting and hacking, and their flashlights shined right and left, like headlights on runaway cars. They were looking for women. The old people would look away, rubbing eucalyptus oil on their arms. What else could they do? How else could they endure? The old people would nod, saying the night smelled like the Chinese carnivals back in Vietnam, in the Delta, back when the French marched smartly through the streets with tassels dangling from their hats.

In those days, at the mid-autumn festivals, people said, before the water spirit and the land spirit began their seasonal battle out in the *padi*, you could see magicians glowing in the orange light of paper lanterns. The magicians wore pointed Siamese hats and turned bean-curd dumplings into dragonfly wings and blood-red petals, then led the crowds to a porcelain table where a tiny man peering through a microscope cut a rice grain into a hundred pieces. The tiny man waved his customers over and had them press their eyes to the microscope lens to see that the miraculous tiny specks of rice were swimming on the specimen slide. "They're alive," the tiny man said. "Cut a grain of rice into pieces, and you'll see. They're looking for each other." People smiled and chuckled. The schoolteachers among them knew the tiny man had swirled the solution with a toothpick and the specimens were riding in currents, but it was wonderful to imagine the chopped-up rice as families broken apart, swimming the ocean in search of loved ones. It was wonderful to imagine, and so that was what the schoolteachers did, and everyone slept that night quiet and peaceful as toads.

So beautiful, to be a sentimentalist. The old people, they floated on a silver string between the past and the present. They drifted in the air, light as kites, and at night they watched the fires die down and barely

stirred when rats squealed in the huts and ran out the sugar-bag doors
with mouthfuls of cabbage or skin.

They were dangerous, these sentimentalists.

His first actual sight of the camp, or so the social workers told him, had
been the dense wall of garbage, high as a man's waist, spread in mashed
layers the length of the Zone C beach, all the way from the shale abut-
ment at one end of the beach to the base of the Zone F hill at the other
end. At the time, he was said to be drifting in and out of consciousness,
severely sunburned, a slit running from the top of his head to his chin.
He was lifted roughly from the boat by his swollen ankles and bright
red arms by two Vietnamese men with special white badges who stared
at his blistering body and said to no one in particular that he shouldn't
have left in such a small boat in October.

What he remembered was a solid crust of yellow-green pineapple
husks, swirling brown cabbage, and twisted red Marlboro cartons,
under which he glimpsed strips of cloth and blue tarp winding in and
out like ribbons, and glistening, creamy pockets of white and yellow;
and just under the surface, he saw the silvery glints of aluminum, di-
aphanous claw membranes, tiny alabaster bones and cartilage, speckled
grayfish skin, and lengths of pink yarn, all supported by foundations of
crumbly gray and brown whose makeup over time had grown impossible to determine. He was carried through a path in the wall of garbage,
but because he had been infected, because he had the Vietnamese
sickness, his mind did not see what his eyes saw. He nearly cried out,
for so constant in texture were the layers, so unexpected in delicacy and
color, that the gummy bubble of air hanging over the beach seemed
suddenly not rancid but sweet, and the bloated cloud of bluebottles descending on garbage and human alike seemed the languorous, tickly
black down of fluffy store-bought pillows.

There, to either side, was layer after layer, grown to enormous size,
of his daughter's gaily colored wedding cake made years ago by a famous Saigon chef, the cake Chi's new husband had wheeled in himself
on a trolley cart to demonstrate for his bride the extravagance of his
love. In her lace dress and misty veil and gold tear-shaped jewelry, Chi
had looked so beautiful and new that even when she offered him a slice
of cake on a paper plate he did not trust himself to speak for fear of
bursting into tears of joy. He nodded his head and sat stiffly in his chair,

and when she knelt at his feet and placed her hand on his to guide his fingers over the red plastic fork, she whispered in his ear that she was grateful for his happiness because he was her father and had always treated her well and had never before eaten cake. She placed the morsel on his tongue, and his hand trembled with excitement in hers, for he had not expected to hear her declaration, or to feel the huge square dissolve so quickly in his mouth, or to hear his new son-in-law clap American soldiers on the back and cheer at his chewing, or to see his sister wipe at his shirt with the lace-fringed handkerchief she kept in a box with her jewelry. And when each mouthful of the rich cake slid down his throat, he moaned with pleasure and weepy astonishment that he should be sitting in a white metal chair with his plate on a table-cloth in a room at the best restaurant in the district, where Americans in shiny blue uniforms applauded and his sister from Phan Tiet clucked her tongue and fussed with his shirt and columns of light laced through the window and onto the small golden hand of his beautiful Chi, who fed him cake with a red plastic fork.

So it was that on the Zone C beach Trinh thrust his head toward the wall of garbage and opened his mouth. He felt his body slip from the grasp of the men wearing special white badges, and when his head touched the sand he clawed at the ground and lunged into the wall, sinking his teeth into the layers of green and pink before him. He chewed, he felt it on his tongue, and then he swallowed, tasting in the layers something so sweet that even one of the men wearing a special white badge could not pry open his mouth to scrape out what he was eating.

When later he lay in a long line of bunks that he recognized as being in a hospital, he tapped the gauze strips wrapped like a helmet around his head. He clucked his tongue. He listened. He heard the shuffling of sandals along the wood floor, the tinny scrape of metal pans, the soft Delta accents. Off to the right, ever so clearly, he heard a voice exclaim loudly over the size of a white nurse who had apparently lumbered past. It was Duoc. His nephew Duoc. The boy was nine and already coarse as a dog.

"Chi," Trinh said, pressing his fingers into the gauze. "Chi." He listened. He heard a ceiling fan. "Chi," he said. He heard a chainsaw far away, and he heard someone complain about a swollen arm. He heard a plastic bag full of liquid drop to the floor. He heard the ocean nearby.

And then his head was full of birds, and the birds were squawking and pulling at his eyes and his ears, and he tossed on his side and quite by accident pulled out a plastic tube that had been inserted into his arm. He thrashed around, balling his hands into fists. He pounded his bed sheet. A Vietnamese woman wearing a white T-shirt and loose black pants ran to his bunk and told him to lie still. She looked at him sternly, fiddling with a drip bottle connected to the tube that had fallen from his arm.

"*Ngu di,*" she said. "Sleep."

Trinh stared. The set of her mouth, the wispy hairs that moved around her throat, the graceful curve of her nose—all looked like Chi's. He held his arms out stiffly, as if to receive a package, and with a moan so loud it caused the nurse to step away, he rolled onto his stomach and shut his eyes and rocked his head back and forth. The nurse leaned over and whispered into his ear that she was sorry to hear about his daughter, but when loved ones died it made sense to rest.

So he did. When he awoke, he smelled the garbage on his breath.

For days he was content to stare at the ceiling fan whirring overhead and eat rice gruel served in a blue plastic bowl by a pretty girl from Binh Tuy province. As the fan blades moved, he thought of Chi's hair flapping in the wind aboard the boat. He pictured the boat on the Gulf of Siam. How long did they drift? Two weeks? Three? He wasn't sure. He saw himself sitting on a bench in the storage hold. Chi was beside him. Nephew Duoc sat on the opposite bench. The boy smelled. Trinh had taken him along—a burden, a hateful, screaming child— only as a favor to his sister. He remembered shouting at Duoc not to drink all their water. He remembered the boy stealing a cup from Chi's hand and pouring it down his throat. Why had he ever agreed to take him? He had slapped the boy, cursed him; and then he comforted Chi, stroking her hair, and told her the captain would bring them more water soon. He remembered showing the captain, a silk merchant, how to read the French compass. He remembered standing in a line of men, pulling a rope coiled around the generator. He had cheered when the motor stuttered with the sound of firecrackers. He remembered the ocean lunging at the hull. The water seeped through the planks and tickled their toes; at night, it licked their ears and bathed their eyes. He remembered the boat tilting. In the morning, Thais in a high-keeled boat came to save them. The Thais secured a line to their railing. They gave his shipmates a clamp for the bilge line. They clasped their hands together and touched their heads in greeting.

Then there was nothing. Just buzzing, like dragonflies hovering. Buzzing, and then her beautiful cake.

When the gauze strips came off, he was issued a camp ID from the Malay Task Force guards and stood in line every day with everyone else to receive packets of rations. The rice was full of stones and weevils; the salt was wet; the cans of peas no one would touch for fear of getting diarrhea. He shared his rations with Duoc, who, over his objections, had been assigned to live with him in Zone A. Together they slept in a lean-to of corrugated tin and blue plastic tarp, and they wore black running shorts selected by the Zone A Vietnamese administration chief. Occasionally Duoc brought in onions or mosquito coils. He quietly placed the items by the fire pit where they sat in the morning to boil water. Trinh did not know where Duoc got the supplies. He supposed the boy stole them. He did not ask. He knew only that the onions filled the shelter with a smell far more pleasant than the latrines in neighboring Zone B.

Every morning Trinh scooped the rat droppings from the dirt floor with a palm frond. He made rice in the fire pit and gave Duoc half, then took the blue plastic bowls to the Zone A beach, where he dunked them into the ocean and scraped them clean. He wrote long letters to the resettlement delegations on wispy blue paper, detailing his hate for communists. He wrote poems in the margins of newspapers, tearing them out and staring, then folding the strips into his pocket. He listened for the hourly chimes that rang from the loudspeakers hung in the trees. At the tenth chime he walked down the footpath to the Social Services division office, where white women wearing shirts that read *UNHCR* talked to him for half an hour. Each day they wrote question marks on tiny yellow stickers and pressed them onto the pages of his record file. The next day another white woman would read the yellow stickers and take them off.

The tiny boats continued to pile onto the beaches, and the men with special white badges lifted the bodies onto the beach and grabbed the arms of those who could walk until the lilting sounds of Vietnamese rose like small birds over the roar of the ocean. The refugees made shelters of branches and tarp and stood in lines for rations of rice and cabbage and processed chicken. There were so many arrivals, the island was rumored to be sinking under their weight. The refugees stripped Zone B of its underbrush, leaving a naked orange gouge that stretched from the beachfront to the water tower. The garbage on the Zone C beach had grown so immense that the rat specialist brought in from Hong Kong announced with much head-shaking from the bow of the UN speedboat that the rat population was threatened only by heart disease. The rats were becoming obese, he said. More relief workers came, and the Malay Task Force contingent doubled overnight. The loudspeakers blared music and English lessons and announcements from morning to night.

Trinh wanted only to work. When he worked, his body ached and his skin felt tough as hide and his mind was clear as sky. He heard that Mr. Hong's construction division was short of men. He helped build a dock from the planks that had been stripped off the hundreds of boats littering the beaches, jutting from the sand like giant black cheroots. He carried wood. He hammered nails in the walls of the new schools and the administration building. He hefted plastic pipes on his back. He dug trenches and pulled on a chain to lower a black water-storage tank into a hole. He put up plank frames for latrines, though many of his neighbors still preferred to use the slit trench behind the cemetery. At night, he unfolded strips of newsprint and stared at the poems he had scribbled in the margins, and in the glow of the fire-pit embers he wrote more and folded them into his pocket and licked the ink off his fingers so no one would know he had been writing.

He worked hard, and because he worked so hard he was chosen to work in the hospital, which had recently been outfitted with kerosene lamps and donated hospital beds from the *Isle de Lumiere,* a French hospital ship that anchored offshore. On Sundays he rose early with the white hospital staff to place diseased organs and amputated limbs into plastic bags that he then dumped into the ocean from the back of the water barge that brought supplies once a week.

At the beginning of the monsoon season, trouble started in the community center. Equipment began to disappear. And so he watched with great interest one evening as a Swedish social worker pointed her long finger at his friend Miss Hang, whom she accused of hiding sewing bobbins from the Chinese women in Zone F. Miss Hang denied the charge and feared she would be reported to the Malaysian police, who would cancel her interview with the American refugee delegation. Her mother and father were in Texas, and in her fear she could only say the word *Texas* over and over. When the Swede shook her head and held up a sewing bobbin, Miss Hang began to rock and moan and shiver violently, much to the confusion of the Swedish social worker, who began to cry in sympathy. Miss Hang went down on all fours. Her shiny polyester shirt glistened like a shell. Trinh felt a sudden whooshing in his head. He had to turn away. He closed his eyes to stop from seeing; he pounded his ears to stop from hearing; he bit his tongue to stop from speaking. He ran outside and saw in the brilliant sunset the same beautiful magenta and blue and ribboned gold and whites and greens he had seen on his daughter's wedding cake many years ago.

He folded his arms and walked to his shelter. He slept. When he awoke, it was night. Duoc lay sleeping by the entrance. Trinh stared at the boy, then turned and quietly changed his clothes. He then rushed to his nephew and shook him hard. Duoc shouted. Trinh clamped his hand around the boy's wrist and jerked him up. He threw aside the sugar bag door and forced Duoc outside. The cigarettes of young men lit up the camp like thousands of fireflies, and Duoc, seeing his uncle's face briefly in the faint light, squirmed in his grasp and began to cry. Trinh had on his very best white shirt, which he had ironed and creased himself just last week, by placing heated rocks in a can. He wore flip-flops and his only pair of socks, which he almost never wore. Socks were impractical and hot, but he kept the pair anyway because they had come in a package from the UN, and they were soft as a girl's hand pressed to his cheek. The two stepped onto the smooth basalt in front of their shelter and walked past a woman skinning a rat that had been skewered on a branch. They took the muddy trail that took them down the hill, into the main camp. They came to a wider footpath and hurried past the shelters, a jumble of blue and gray, some two stories high, as rickety and ingenious as monstrous houses of cards, then took the bald scalloped trail that led up the side of Religion Hill. The loudspeakers blared Paul Anka, then "The Tennessee Waltz," and the smell of cloves and oil soaked into their pores. They walked past the market, then past the barbed-wire bales that nipped at the backs of the cigarette sellers and the toothless old women who fingered joss sticks and running shorts piled high on desks donated by Malaysian schoolchildren in Kuala Trengganu.

In Trinh's pocket were the poems he had written, and a shiny black comb that was his only remaining possession from his boat journey from Vietnam. This he now removed from his pocket and raked firmly along the cheek of young Duoc, leaving a flaring red line that caused the boy to put his fingers to his face and stop making noise. Now silent, they continued past a Swede and an American sitting on the bright yellow porch of a bungalow in the staff compound, intent on a board game, then past a group of bare-chested boys floating boats carved from Clorox bottles in the sewer, which before the monsoons had moved more than a thousand pounds of shit from Zone A to Zone D each day before clogging up at the narrow, lichen-filled passage in Zone E and forcing the Vietnamese Sanitation Division men to use long hook poles to move the sewage along. Far from the sewer, at the top of the steep Zone F hill, the highest point on the island, were stands of coconut trees that grew so close together that the palms seemed to blot the sun from the sky, turning the ground so dark that children would drop to their knees to pretend they were anteaters trapped in a cave or rabbits hiding from the clouds that towered like mountains over the ocean and drenched the whole island in rain. Nguyen Van Trinh and his nephew Duoc walked into the coconut stands, past the giant white carving of a sail, past the Buddha carved by a famous Saigon artist, past the English classroom where the blackboard had been stolen by men believed to have later drowned in a homemade fishing boat. Trinh, diseased, enraged by the Vietnamese sickness, selected a tree. He swore at Duoc and shook his fist in the boy's face, and with threats and curses forced his nephew up into the tree, which the boy climbed with the ease of a monkey. He yelled at the boy to climb to the top, to the point where the palm fronds blocked out the sky, and he told him to shake the tree as hard as he could. Trinh circled underneath shouting, "Again, again," staring up at the tree, trying to see the coconut husk that would come tumbling down and hemorrhage his skull. When at last the men with special white badges responded to the siren wails of the boy, they found the poems in Trinh's pocket and showed them to the white people and the Malays. Power is greater than love, the Vietnamese said, translating slowly. Each poem was the same. Power is greater than love, power is greater than love, power is greater than love.

Allies and Strangers

1

The east coast of Malaysia was well into its six-month wet season, but the city of Kuala Trengganu had yet to see a hard rain, even though July had come and gone and the Kuala Trengganu soccer club had disbanded for the year. The humidity was so bad that you couldn't even ride in a trishaw without sticking to the seat. In the afternoon, people passed vials of eucalyptus oil under their noses. Malay men sat in roadside coffee stalls, flapping their pillbox *songkat* hats like fans; their children pressed cool tin silverware against their cheeks. At night the fruit hawkers stopped by the river to dump their tainted pineapple skewers, lumpy with flies so bloated and slow they settled on the fruit and drowned. Business was bad, so the hawkers pushed their heavy carts home, complaining to the Hindu night watchmen who lay in cots outside the stores and sucked on packets of soybean milk to help them sleep. Later, in the houses along the roadside, you could hear the sounds of exhaustion: the pedicab drivers wheezed by their bathing wells; their wives fanned old sarongs over sleeping Ibrahims and Hanizahs and thumb-sucking Abdullahs, then lay with their husbands on floor mats, dabbing sweat beads with T-shirts bearing the names of American universities.

Every day Reuben Gill of the United Nations High Commission for Refugees, Kuala Trengganu branch, awoke covered in a sheen of sweat and rose like a man climbing from a pool, eyes blinking, one hand placed high on his nightstand, hefting his considerable weight from the mattress. His body left a sweaty imprint on the sheets, and after plucking the drowned mosquitoes from the matted hair on his arms and chest, he filled the room with Malay curses that floated out the window slats and into the curious ears of children trudging off to school. He could not now, breathing as through a hose, imagine the delusion that had led him into trading his Peace Corps lean-to in the jungles of Kelantan State—six years in the jungle, six glorious years!—for employment with the Kuala Trengganu branch office of UNHCR. Just temporary, he had been told, upon signing the papers: you'll be out on Bidong soon. Talk, talk, talk. Then more talk. For ten months. Who would have imagined that a man who had spent six years slogging through mucky swamps, clearing brush, would now be stuck behind a desk, straining to draw a proper breath? It did not seem possible. Not for Reuben Gill, Malaysiaphile. Not for a Peace Corps jungle junkie. Not for a man so large in a country so small. He could lift gigantic loads: wheelbarrows of gravel, refrigerators, the back end of a car once. Even in his special-order Big Man Formal Wear from Singapore, he scared the bejeezus out of people on the street. The Malays said his mottled skin looked like dog belly; the Indians saw reptilian features in his hooded, narrow eyes; the Chinese called his wiry red hair monkey fur.

Every day he sat in a chair in the UN office, perfumed from head to foot by the potted bougainvillea in the corner, wheezing. *Nee-nah. Nee-nah.* Asthma, the office staff said. But they didn't know shit from shinola. For six years in the outback, his lungs had been strong as bellows. If there had been someone for him to write home to, he would have written that he was now wrestling with powerful natural forces. His symptoms were frightening. He would pound his chest; he would gasp, swear he tasted salt on his lips, roll his eyes heavenward. Oxygen trickled in as if through a straw. Sometimes there was nothing, just open-mouthed suffocation. In the aftermath, his face glistened with a sheen, and a Peace Corps doctor, dropping in one day for a visit, had medically certified the blockage in his esophagus and given him a prescription.

But he had no one to write home to back in Tucson, Arizona, not after nearly seven years of watching letters from home turn into aerograms and the aerograms turn into postcards and the postcards turn into nothing. What he had down the hall were little white lawyers and immigration spooks. What he had next door was Doctor Philip Johansson, head of the Kuala Trengganu UNHCR office, in charge of all local mainland UN operations. And Doctor Johansson, he knew, thought him a blowhard and a lout.

Reuben was at that moment standing inside his office, clenching and unclenching his fists in front of Doctor Johansson, who had dropped by unexpectedly. Reuben leaned against the door as if to prevent the doctor from leaving. "I mean it," said Reuben. "If I don't get a transfer, I'm going to kill someone. It's just talk, talk, talk around here. All those yaps wide open and noise coming out. I need Bidong. I deserve it. You know it."

"As staff liaison," said Doctor Johansson, "murder would reflect badly on your record." The doctor opened the file folder in his hands, then quickly shut it. He smiled.

"I'm not kidding," said Reuben.

"Well," said Doctor Johansson. "I'd just turn the air-con on high. This humidity is driving me nuts too. You have to be patient. No guarantees, but maybe next time around your transfer will come through."

"Next time around is two months," said Reuben.

"I'm well aware of that," said the doctor.

"But Gurmit Singh goes to Bidong. Fools get sent ahead of me."

"You know Gurmit's a special case. You know the Malaysians wanted a Malaysian running Admin. You know how delicate the situation is."

"Sure," said Reuben. "That's right. You're only head of UN Ops here. You can't possibly use any influence with the Malaysians. You can't possibly talk to Siew Hon Lee."

The doctor sighed.

"You act like it's not your decision. You act like Siew Hon Lee's got a pair of scissors aimed at your balls."

"That's enough," said Doctor Johansson. "I won't be talked to like that."

"Come on," said Reuben. "I know how this organization works. Staff liaison, remember? Siew Hon Lee controls MRCS, you control here. You put in a good word with her, and I can get out of your hair. Now don't tell me to put a lid on it. I can't help how I am. You know my . . ." He wouldn't say it. The doctor would just snort.

"Your title? Yes, I do. The Biggest White Man in Kuala Trengganu."

"So what? I won't apologize for it. I've got nothing to be ashamed of." He stopped to gather breath. His lungs felt fibrous, his throat sore. "Talk, talk, talk," he said. "All these yaps going off in my face. It's too much. You hear me?" He cracked his knuckles. Bidong Island was out there, out past the harbor, past the seawall, thirty kilometers into the South China Sea. Out there. That was where he belonged.

"Look at you," said the doctor. "You're sweating. You look terrible. Are you having trouble breathing? Your asthma's acting up, isn't it? All that smoking and drinking you do. Isn't it possible that you drive yourself a bit too hard after hours? Think about it seriously a moment, will you? There's no air-con on Bidong, you know."

"This again!" said Reuben. "We're not talking about air conditioning. Come on. We're talking about *doing* something. Getting your hands dirty."

"Yes," said the doctor. He pressed the file folder against his chest. "Kicking some ass, right?" He opened the file folder in his lap and seemed about to speak. But then he closed the folder and made for the door. "You really ought to watch it. You make it so difficult for me to tell you things."

The doctor slapped the file folder. "We need to talk about . . . No. Forget it." He shook the folder at Reuben. "No, not now. I'm going to leave now. I just want to remind you of the party tonight, *chez moi.* Please make an appearance. It's a very big deal, as you know. Tell Manley too, would you? I hear he's in town."

"Manley," said Reuben. "He's always in town. He spends more time here than on Bidong."

"Yes," said the doctor. "So you've told me. Yet he gets posted to the island months ago and you're still stuck here. It's a sad story we're all familiar with. Just be patient."

"Who else knows shit from shinola around here?" said Reuben. "Who else belongs there? One name. Just give me one name."

The doctor lingered at the door. His face took on a preoccupied look, as if he were just remembering something very important. "All right," he said. He closed the door. "All right, since you bring it up. We'll talk now. You're not going to like it." He opened his file folder and withdrew a thin sheet of official stationery. "I'll give you a name." He scanned the sheet. "That woman . . . you saw the cable on her recently. Due any day now, et cetera. The English teacher."

"Not Porkpie what's-her-name. The one from Chicago."

"Bobbi Porkpie Sortini," said the doctor. "She's due at Subang International tomorrow, and I've got to tell you, her file looks very good. She was in the Peace Corps in the Philippines, you know. Anyway, the country director in Manila said she was so good the Filipinos put her on national TV once."

"I hope you're joking. Filipino national TV? This is the litmus test these days?"

"I'm sorry," said the doctor. "Siew Hon Lee was sweet over her application. Bidong needs more English teachers *desperately*. As in yesterday."

"What you're telling me is she's going to Bidong. Now."

"Such a face you're pulling!"

Reuben stood. He grabbed the desk with both hands. "What you're telling me is someone who hasn't even set foot in Malaysia is going to Bidong. My place. Bidong. That's what you're telling me."

"Now, listen. It's not definite that she's going there immediately. There's orientation and Task Force clearance still to come. Most likely."

"She's going to Bidong. Ahead of me."

"Well." The doctor looked at the official stationery again. He frowned. "*Ahead of* is relative, isn't it? It's not like there's a master list. But most likely, yes, she'll be there before you. I'm sorry. I really am."

"This new person is going ahead of me," Reuben said, sitting down. He felt his throat close, the first salty hints on his lips. "Your hands were tied, naturally. There's nothing you could have done."

"I hope that's not an accusation, Reuben," said the doctor. "I did the best I could, all right? Siew Hon Lee is well aware you're overdue for a transfer. She just plain doesn't like you. But you know that. This isn't news."

"News is what people do or don't do, isn't it?" said Reuben. He pulled the desk drawer open, then slammed it shut. He felt fluid in his lungs. "News isn't something that just happens. Someone pulls the strings. Then it happens." He opened his mouth and gulped down air.

"I'll ignore that comment," said the doctor. "I want to walk out this door thinking you're being very good about all this. I want to walk out saying, 'Thank you for not making an issue out of it.' So I'm going to walk out this door, and that's exactly what I'm going to do. So thank you for not making an issue out of it. Really. Thank you. And please try to come to the party tonight." Then he was out the door.

Gurmit Singh, Bidong's new Malaysian Red Crescent Society administration chief, was having trouble finding his bearings. That horrible

Reuben Gill had actually sworn at him on the dock in Kuala Treng-ganu—so baffling, that man, so rude—and now, freshly arrived on Bidong, his legs still wobbly from the boat journey over, two women stood before him, demanding he fill out a form he did not wish to fill out. He wanted to resist them, but he felt helpless to refuse. What with the smell, the bluebottles hovering outside, the loudspeaker racket: it was difficult to focus. Even the trip from the mainland had been un-settling. He was crop-haired and small, and the boat captain had pinched his arm and pronounced him too skinny to be a real Sikh.

Gurmit sat frowning and confused. The form on his desk was red, and next to it lay a folder stuffed with other red forms. "How can?" he said. He leaned forward, as if through dint of concentration to make the form go away. He wore a dazzling white safari suit, purchased in Kuala Trengganu with advance pay from his new position. His pockets were full of jackfruit and plastic baggies—who knew the food situation on Bidong?—and around his neck was an ornamental Sikh dagger, no big-ger than a key, given to him by his father.

"Can," said the Malay clerk. Her name was Norizalina. Beside her sat Sally Hindermann, a teacher-slash-jack-of-all-trades with the UN. At least so she had introduced herself on the Zone C dock.

"Lucky boy," said Sally. She played with the straps of her overalls. "Your first executive decision. Admin's never been my cup of tea. You know?"

"I cannot fill out," said Gurmit, rapping his finger on the form.

"Can-*lah,*" said Norizalina.

"You can," said Sally. "Unless you want the hospital staff over here calling for your head. They say . . . what's his name again?"

"Nguyen Van Trinh," said Norizalina.

"They say his body's been stinking up the hospital for days. The Vietnamese nurses had to throw lime on him."

"Terrible," said Gurmit.

"Right. So we've got to put him under. For health reasons if noth-ing else. Now I've already told you the only way to get coffin wood is to fill this out." She laid her hand on the form. "Fill it out and have the skipper take it back to the mainland. Nobody in Kuala Trengganu moves without it."

"There is another way?" Gurmit asked.

"*Tidak*," said Norizalina firmly. "No."

"It's just a form," said Sally. "History of Deceased. That's all. Nothing unsavory."

"I am thinking unsavory," said Gurmit.

"Then where are you going to get the wood, Gurmit?" said Sally. "The boats have already been stripped. We can't fell any trees. Not since your government decreed us liable for property."

"Is a prison camp," said Norizalina. "Illegal aliens, yes?"

"Yes," said Gurmit. "I am aware."

"And Construction tells me they're out of plywood," said Sally. "So."

"But we are knowing nothing of Nguyen Van Trinh?" said Gurmit.

"Not a damn thing," said Sally. She stirred. "I'm sorry. That didn't come out right. But you've got to realize a lot of the suicides here are like that. They've been traumatized at sea. Sometimes they . . . I don't know, *disappear* when they arrive. Like there's no one there, you know?"

"No ID with the body-*lah*," said Norizalina. "No one come forward with informations. Task Force cannot find records. His nephew too shock. He not speaking now."

"So," said Sally.

"Can do," said Norizalina, tapping the form.

"I'll tell you what," said Sally. "We'll leave you to your decision. But I just don't see what else you can do. It's got to be done. You know, *I'd* be doing it if you hadn't arrived. It's about time we got an Admin chief. I was worried they were going to send that Reuben Gill person."

"If me, I would filling out the form, too," said Norizalina. "Must do. No other way."

The women turned and shuffled out the door. They didn't wave going down the steps. Nor did he. The air was suddenly stifling. Gurmit fiddled with the top button of his safari suit, then shrugged. He could hear singsongy Vietnamese spoken outside, and somewhere in the distance a chainsaw started up. There didn't seem to be any noise coming from the dock, except for the revving of the boat engine. He heard crackling nearby, and then the sound of guitars and singing. It was "Proud Mary," blaring from a point just behind him, overhead. He looked up. Through a hole cut in the ceiling, in the corner, two cables dangled to the floor and into a patchwork of duct tape by the door.

He placed one hand on the History of Deceased form and the other on the bulging folder and felt the noise vibrate through his shirt. The wall planks were buzzing to the beat, stirring dust, and heat seemed to rise in waves from the floorboards.

He had to have air. He leaned back and fiddled with the louver handle on the window frame, then stuck his nose through the open slats. Young women in flowered pajamas were milling around the Zone C garbage dump, putting cloth to their noses. Vietnamese boys ran in the sand, straining like swimmers, and a Malay Task Force guard on the dock steps waved his truncheon like a broom, shooing people away. A great cloud of diesel smoke issued from the back of the supply boat, bringing the boat captain out of the pilothouse. The man began pounding a screwdriver against a metal box outside the door. A bullhorn lay on the deck, atop wicker baskets of brown cabbage. Bluebottles shimmered over the cargo.

Gurmit pictured himself back in Kuala Trengganu, sitting in a crumbling Chinese theater, tilting his head at the screen, sweating, just chewing durian gum and watching. Like a bloody schoolboy, he thought. Always the bloody schoolboy. Just watching things pass by, frame by frame. He felt something like panic, though it wasn't panic. It was something raging and feverish, something that made him want to throw the form to the floor and wag his finger at Sally and Norizalina and run along the beach and slap the Viets and the guards and tell everyone to start over.

"Bloody hell," he said. He sat quietly a moment, hands spread over the History of Deceased form. Then he reached into the folder and extracted another form from the middle of the stack. The form was a man's. A burn victim, dead since April. Gurmit scanned the sheet quickly. The information would do. He laid the two forms side by side. He began. Word for word, he copied the burn victim's information onto Nguyen Van Trinh's form. Date of birth, family affiliation, employment, province: all lies. But the women were right. Nguyen Van Trinh had to be put in a box. The Kuala Trengganu office could ship the coffin wood out in half a day. Not that an hour here or there made much difference. In a few minutes Nguyen Van Trinh would never even have existed.

He completed the form. He sat. He looked out the window, composing his face.

2

Already the humidity was so bad that the stone walls of the open-air Ooi Boong Suey Restaurant were sweating gray drops into the noodle caldrons. The regulars didn't feel like breakfast anyway. The old Malays near the entrance took turns spitting into a silver tureen by the table; they had saucers of hot tea in front of them and sat on the edge of their chairs, as far from the slick vinyl upholstery as they could scoot, wiping their hands on their hiked-up sarongs. In the back by the soft drink freezer, a Chinese boy rocked on his heels, stripped to black running shorts, and rolled a cold bottle of Orange Crush over his face. Outside, the lorries and motorbikes roared past, leaving wreaths of exhaust in their wake. An Indian woman on the boardwalk took off her sandal and scraped the bottom of her foot against the boardwalk ledge.

None of it held much interest for Reuben, or for Manley Hutchinson, seated across the table. Reuben was fingering a large manila envelope, staring glumly at the contents. He wiggled the ceramic table to get his companion's attention. "This ain't right," he said. He paused, hoping by leaving the rest unsaid to encourage Manley's participation. Manley only nodded, shaking his long blond hair that hung perilously close to his bowl. But at least he was an ally from way back, a former Peace Corps volunteer. At least Manley's was a familiar, if tiny, face.

"There's nothing right about this," Reuben said.

"I hear you," Manley said. He opened his mouth and blinked, as if interrupted from meditation.

Reuben shook his head. Even Manley's presence was not right. Reuben stared at the man's ravaged, pockmarked skin, at his blinking eyes, his slight, schoolboy frame. He asked himself how such a man had made it to Bidong ahead of him. Manley taught English, even though the difference between *should have gone* and *should of went* eluded him. Reuben pictured the day Manley got his camp pass: Manley had held it in his teeth and run on all fours, like a dog; he had yelped; he had pretended to hump Reuben's leg. Later, they went to Cowboy Lim's to celebrate. But even then, just before Manley got falling-down drunk, he was shouting out elaborate plans for hitching rides back and forth on the camp supply boat, just to make sure he'd be able to spend plenty of nights in Kuala Trengganu carousing with his old Peace Corps pal.

"You know what I should do," said Reuben. "I'll tell you what I should do. I should just take this envelope and throw the whole damn thing into the fire." He whacked the envelope against the table top.

Manley held his face over his breakfast bowl, nodding rhythmically, in what seemed to Reuben a gesture of sarcasm. Inside the envelope were pages of contracts, insurance information, and, paper-clipped to the top of her résumé, a green camp pass for Bidong Island. The camp pass was for Bobbi Porkpie Sortini. The black-and-white passport photo stapled to the camp pass was inconclusive: a generous, perhaps overly wide mouth, smiling without conviction; straight hair, light-colored, falling to her shoulders; the possibility of freckles; a small, flat nose with wide nostrils. Her eyes were decidedly middle class: doelike and alert, overtly pleasant. Overall, she did not give a bad impression. On the other hand, it was her face, not his, on the camp pass.

How remarkable that in the span of a half hour, this woman's name should have come tumbling out of both the doctor's and Manley's yaps. And now there was her envelope. He fingered it again and contemplated action. Just tear it up, that's what he ought to do. Burn it. If only any of that would make her disappear. What the hell kind of name was Bobbi Porkpie Sortini anyway? Who calls herself Porkpie, in a Muslim country no less? He ran the risk, he realized, of being unfair, of judgment without due process. Her only fault might be a certain precocious earnestness, her hair in a bun, a habit of clapping her hands together when excited, a tendency to say *pooh*. But wasn't that bad enough? Another fool in the refugee business? He ground his thumb into her photo. She was still there.

He reviewed the events of the past half hour slowly, critically, probing the improbabilities, recalling statements, hoping through careful examination to prove his memory a liar. The doctor had laid a bombshell on him, all right. Had he taken it well? No, he had not. He had doubled over, clawing for air. He had punched his air conditioner and kicked his desk. He had puffed on a black Thai cigar until he hacked up phlegm. Then he left the building, away from the air conditioning and dusty reams of paper.

He had walked quickly, across the street to the Ooi Boong Suey Restaurant, where the smell was of sweet elephant palm, and there he had spotted Manley hunched over a bowl, reviewing the contents of a large manila envelope. "Reuben," Manley had said, lifting his head. His face blossomed. He waved the envelope. "Have I got news for you!" His story tumbled out. He had dropped by the Task Force office that morning, he said, to get his camp pass renewed. There he met the new English teacher. She was sitting across from some clerk, explaining how her travel itinerary had been scrambled. She was in Kuala Trengganu early. No one had met her at the bus station, so she had flagged down a trishaw and hightailed it to the Task Force office.

Big deal, Reuben said. She was probably wired from the trip up. Anyone can flag down a trishaw. It don't prove nothing.

Hey, can I continue? Manley said.

He did. He said he decided to give her a dose of Kuala Trengganu life: he told her to put up at Cowboy Lim's Resthouse, not the Hotel Kuala Trengganu. The Hotel Kuala Trengganu was for wimps, he said, not former Peace Corps volunteers. She asked a few questions about Bidong—How many Vietnamese are there now? Is there disease? What text do you use for English lessons?—but she was tired, she said. It had been a long trip. Manley had decided to be gallant. He told her to go on ahead to Cowboy Lim's. He would take it upon himself to collect her paperwork when Task Force was finished; he would put it in an envelope and drop by the next day and give her the camp pass.

What little Manley had left to tell then dribbled out of his mouth like bubbles. One of the Task Force clerks had run out to the street and flagged down a taxi; she thanked Manley and the clerk; she left.

And now here was her envelope, plopped on the table by Manley's own hand.

Ridiculous. But all true, all infuriating.

The two men sat near the entrance of the restaurant, which like all the Chinese restaurants in Kuala Trengganu looked like a garage: crumbling green stone on three sides, a raised metal accordion curtain facing the street. Manley ate his noodles like he'd never seen silverware before. He clamped down on the spoon. He gobbled the strands furiously, with a look of strained concentration, dropping bits of noodle and cabbage on the floor.

Manley looked up from his bowl. "You think she fucks?" he asked brightly. "I bet she does. She liked the idea of me dropping by tomorrow."

"Manley," Reuben said. "I don't want her on Bidong. Focus."

Manley started fiddling with his hair.

"Oh, Christ," said Reuben. "Don't start with that hair business again. Don't start acting put-upon. Focus."

"Hey," said Manley. "I'm just combing my locks, man."

"Right. I'm telling you, Manley, I'm going to crack heads. I am. I don't care how much Johansson and Siew Hon Lee don't like me."

"Siew Hon Lee?" said Manley. "Our Lady of the Sweet and Sour, Mostly Sour? Hey, you know, she comes out to Bidong last week and says, 'Mr. Manley, I hear you have been drinking alcohol in defiance of Task Force regulations. I give you a warning this time-*lah,* but oh my goodness don't you let me hear this again.' Hey, then she starts wagging her finger at me, and this big crowd of Viets shows up to watch, and she starts speaking Cantonese to them. They all start laughing, which is OK with me, I really don't care, but then I swear this happened, you can ask Stan, he saw it, I swear she kicks sand at me when she's walking away. Bitch. What's her problem?"

"She knows you know me," said Reuben. "Put two and two together."

Manley chewed contemplatively. He nodded, then lifted up his glass of ice water. "*Air batu,*" he said to the owner's son, hovering nearby.

"You wan' wadduh?" the boy said, pointing to Manley's glass.

Manley repeated himself in Malay, jiggling the glass.

"Wadduh? Yes?" asked the boy, looking at Reuben for confirmation.

"Here," said Manley, thrusting the glass at the boy. "Yes. I want water. I want water with ice. I said it right. *Air batu.* I know how to say it. Didn't I, Reuben? I said it right."

"You speak Malay like a white boy," Reuben said. "What'd you do in Peace Corps, anyway? Sit around eating chili dogs at the Raffles?" He grabbed the envelope again and ran his finger over the picture of Bobbi Porkpie Sortini.

"Hey, I know what you're doing," said Manley, resuming his lunch. The boy hustled back, splashing ice water on the cement floor. "You're sitting there looking for things to hang her with. Hey, you haven't even met her. She was *fine*. I'm telling you, man, *fine*. You're sitting there assassinating her character. You're an assassin, Reuben."

"Shut up."

"Hey," said Manley. He began pushing his hair back, and then went back to his noodles.

"Stop saying 'hey' all the time. The Viets ought to teach *you* English."

Manley looked up, then looked back down at his bowl.

"Bobbi Porkpie Sortini," said Reuben. "A fool's name."

"You don't have any sympathy for anyone, do you?" said Manley. He held his spoon like a stick and pointed it at Reuben.

"There's where you're wrong," Reuben said. "Sympathy's overrated if that's all you got to offer. Then it's not sympathy at all. Sympathy's something else. What you're talking about is hot air. Sympathy, the *real* stuff, that's always attached to something else. There's action behind it. Action. No action, it's just garbage. Now I've told you before, and I'll tell you again. There's shit and then there's shinola. You can guess what I think of goo-goo eyes at a basketful of puppies. And that's what you're talking about, isn't it? It makes me sick."

"OK," said Manley. "OK." He put his spoon back into his bowl. "How about if I told you Gurmit looks like he's ready to pack it in? No one likes him. He's not a bad guy. Are you saying you don't feel sorry for him at all?"

"Sorry is irrelevant. From where I sit, sorry or not sorry doesn't make any difference. There's nothing I can do about it. What makes a difference is what Gurmit does or doesn't do. And I'll tell you, the problem is what he does." He pointed his spoon at Manley. "He wants to put the 'gee' back in 'refugee.' He's a choirboy. What he needs is a backbone."

"Like you, huh?" said Manley, grinning.

"Manley, I'm just going to say this once." Reuben pulled himself back from the table. He arched his eyebrows. His voice was rumbly and deep. "If you know shit from shinola, you know how to fill in the blanks. There are three kinds of white people on Bidong, aren't there?"

"Brits, Americans, and Aussies," said Manley.

"No! Where's your imagination? Losers, true believers, and jungle junkies. I, for one, am a jungle junkie. Now what do you say about someone who hasn't even been to Malaysia and calls herself Porkpie?"

"You tell me," said Manley.

"There you go. That's why you're not a jungle junkie."

"Hey."

"You got to know what's what and stick your neck out sometimes. You got to say, 'I think she's a loser,' or whatever you think she is."

"She's a loser," said Manley. "You bet."

"In spades. You just wait and see."

"And she's going to Bidong ahead of you," said Manley.

"I didn't say I wasn't jealous. I'm just saying she's a loser." He looked at Manley, but Manley didn't look back. Reuben stared out the entrance. He saw wispy cooking fires climbing into the sky. He could see them trailing off and disappearing, swallowed in the humidity. Just like that. Like someone had come along and snuffed out a candle with a thumb and forefinger. Where once there had been something, now there was nothing. He had to look away.

"Manley," Reuben said suddenly. "I'm not taking this lying down." He snorted. "There's a party tonight at Johansson's, and you and me are going. No one keeps down a jungle junkie."

"Hey, that's right, Big Bro."

"That's damn right. I just need me a plan."

Gurmit Singh was given a small plywood office built on stilts to rise above the monsoon mud. The floor slats had been hurriedly pounded together, and in the gaps he saw the inquisitive, upturned faces of openmouthed Vietnamese children. When he moved, the faces moved with him. They yammered loudly to their mothers and fathers lounging in their burlap shelters, reporting the dramas unfolding inches above them. From his first week, lines of Vietnamese petitioners, accompanied by self-appointed translators, quietly jammed the steps in the early morning and filed in. He was exhausted. The refugees wore him down with pleading. They softened him with weeping. They enticed him with lascivious bribes. They wanted interviews with Western delegations, for resettlement. They wanted cooking pots in Zone C, running shorts in Zone F. They wanted Mr. Huang removed as Vietnamese chief of Zone A.

Later in the morning the white relief workers would knife through the crowd of petitioners outside his door. Howdy, they would say, and when they did the children under the floorboards would begin to chatter excitedly. The white people would stand, circling like tigers, or drop with a thud onto the low bench in front of the desk. They told him they weren't there to tell him his job, and they made sure he understood this point by thumping their index fingers on the desktop and staring him straight in the eye. They demanded more rations for the refugees, more plastic tarp, more extensive responsibilities, better lines of communication. They warned that they didn't give a hooey who was running the show, that Task Force Chief Ahmed Buttinski, or whatever his name was, better keep his paws off Miss Duong, or Dung, or Jung, they weren't sure how to pronounce it. In the afternoons the Malay Task Force police sauntered in, clothed in sarongs, sometimes with ancient carbines slung across their shoulders. They queried him for information on thieving Chinese Tongs and psychotic ex-ARVN Ranger Scouts and troublemaking white bastards. They frowned at his decision to provide lumber for Zone A while Zone B still needed a supply depot. They derided him for cleaning out the processed chicken in Zone F to give to the new arrivals in Zone C. In the early evening, just as the sky exploded with color and the beaches filled with loungers, he would hunch over the wireless to report to the mainland officials. They spoke sharply into his earpiece: Where are the tuberculosis clearance sheets for the Canadian group-*lah*? Why haven't you transferred the burn case to the Kuala Trengannu hospital-*lah*? Why aren't the cabbage baskets on the supply boat-*lah*? Who are you to give a camp pass to the Swedish-whore journalist-*lah*?

By dinner his mind blistered with doubt and worry. He had too much to do, and he made too many mistakes. The Vietnamese manipulated him. The police looked down on him. The whites walked over him. The UN officials berated him. He was alone. And then he would rise from his desk and throw down a candy sweet to the children gathered under the floor, shuffling the candy over to a gap with his sandal. Opening the door, he would find himself surrounded by petitioners. A great cry would go up, and refugees would thrust documents in his face.

"Later," he would say, waving them away, "I'll get to you all. I promise." He would walk past the police barracks and shout hello to the sleepy-eyed Malays; then he would walk down the main footpath and shout hello to the sullen Vietnamese hunkered in their burlap and plastic huts.

As he walked he thought of food, but he could not eat with the Malay Task Force police, for he reported to the UN and Malaysian Red Crescent officials on the mainland, not to the Malaysian Prison Systems. And he could not eat with the refugees because they barely had enough to feed themselves. So he would walk down to the staff eating hut, where the white people ate meals at a huge wooden table covered with a red-and-white checkered plastic tablecloth. "Hellooo, Gurmit!" they would say. "How's the paper pusher today?" He would smile and attempt to follow their rapid-fire jokes. He would tell them his problems, and they would nod and press him for details about the police and the Vietnamese, then pat his back and tell him he should get out of the office more because he was in a *refugee camp,* for crying out loud, and the real work, the satisfying stuff, was out among the Viets, not cooped up in that hot box he called an office. The teachers related how Mr. Nyouc, a star intermediate English student, had distracted a guard while they sneaked into the Task Force storehouse to steal notebooks for their classes. The engineers talked about leading lightning raids with their Vietnamese camp-generator team deep into the UN speedboat depot: oil barrel spotted, oil barrel requisitioned, oil barrel *in use.* The social workers revealed that they had just that day orchestrated a heist of canned milk for their weaning mothers in Zone F from the black market in Zone C.

The stories made Gurmit weak. Why couldn't they wait? He had just arrived on the island. He could make things work, if only he were given the time. He issued feeble protests and was met with withering glares. One day they lectured him in terrifying, unfamiliar tones: "Do you think this is about *paperwork*? There are people out there *in need*. We *have* what they need. We *need* to get it to them. We need to do it *now*."

Gurmit listened politely. He told them he understood, but that they must think of the future. They must consider the long-term effects. Establish order first. Go slow and steady, for if they didn't mind his telling them so, Task Force and Doctor Johansson in Kuala Trengganu and even the director of UNV and the sub-officers of UNHCR thought the camp staff too—well, yes, he would say it—too independent.

"That's very Asian," said the teacher.

The social worker pointed out that Orientals had a much different sense of time than they were used to. The engineer asked if Kronos were a Hindu god, or just Greek.

"I am a Sikh," said Gurmit. "I am not Hindu."

"So where's your turban?" asked the engineer.

"Bullshit," said the teacher. "Sikhs don't wear turbans."

"I thought they carried knives," said the social worker. She asked Gurmit if he carried a knife. Her face was furrowed with worry.

Bloody hell, thought Gurmit. He plucked his fork off his plate and brandished it like a stiletto, waving it in the air. He decided to keep his problems to himself.

After dinner, he often returned to his office to complete refugee arrival forms. He found solace in the deserted office, after the refugees had to leave the administrative compound. A fluorescent tube burned over his head, and geckos slithered out from the wall slats to feast on mosquitoes and moths. He would lean back, listening to Vietnamese music screeching from the loudspeakers. Relax, he thought. Concentrate on the task at hand. Despair is for cowards. For assurance, he would stare at the glossy sheet above the doorjamb, where he had hammered an advertisement from an *India Today!* magazine. The caption at the bottom read "Captain Knows Best. We Sail, You Rest." Above it was a color photo of a human V-wedge, men and women arranged like migrating birds. At the ends were black cooks in starched high hats, and beaming brown stewards. In the middle danced a conga line of busty white women with golden hair that fell on their shoulders like shocks of wheat. Their arms were wrapped around Teutonic men in creased tropical shirts. At the front, where he belonged, stood a strapping, cropped-hair Sikh in naval attire. The picture invigorated Gurmit. The island inhabitants were not yet that disciplined V-wedge. The refugees were not yet those casual, secure travelers. The staff was not yet those steady, contented workers. And he was not yet that strapping, cropped-hair Sikh captain. But he would be. In his heart he knew he would. He would be the invisible hand steering the course. He would be the righteous leader.

In preparation for that day, he had placed a dignified white and black naval hat in his bottom desk drawer. When that day came—when order reigned—he would take the hat from his drawer, place it on his head, and parade around the camp. He would wear it to lunch. He would wear it on the dock when he stood to greet the UN delegations. The Malays and the refugees would not think it odd. They would envy his dry head during the monsoons.

The white people would laugh at first, but the fact that he wore the cap would be in their minds. Soon a group of whites would smile hugely when Gurmit, still in his cap, walked past the staff bungalows. "Gurmit, up here," one would say, and Gurmit would stride up the steps. A bottle of Johnnie Walker, black label, would appear, and one of the men would pour him a glass with a great show of stealth, overdramatizing the danger that the Task Force police, Muslims all, would enforce the silly no-liquor rule.

The palaver would start. First his host would yell down to a favorite refugee across the wire fence, an English speaker, probably some ravaged ex-bargirl with bad teeth. "Keep an eye out for the police," his host would say to the girl. "We're having a snort." And the girl would smile and yell back "OK, Mr. Bob," or Mr. Ralph, or Mr. Manley—it really made little difference who spoke, as long as the face was white—and having smiled and waved theatrically, the girl would make a grand show of carrying out her duties and bark out commands to a dozen nephews and sisters, who would fan out like miniature snipers, keeping low, in the shadows, in full sight of the white man, and watch for some passing sarong-clad Malay policeman on his way to the police bathing well. The white man would watch until his sentries were in position, and the play would draw to its final scene. The white man would wink to the girl, and the girl would giggle. He would pause, look out at the sky, then focus on Gurmit and raise his glass. Their glasses would meet and clink. The white man would raise an imaginary hat with his free hand and say, "Cheers, Captain."

When that moment came, Gurmit knew, all the white people would soon call him Captain, for the white people spoke with one voice. In a few more days the Malay police would also call him Captain, for the Malays feared the language of the white bastards and made it their own whenever they could. And then the Vietnamese would call him Captain, for the white people and the Malays spoke the language of power. All would call him Captain, for that is what he would be. All would see that he had brought order. All would see the camp running well, the supplies in place, the rations increased, the delegations whisking in and whisking out, the hospital finished, another school in Zone B. They would eat together, Malays and whites; the concertina wire would be torn from the police and staff compound and shipped to the mainland; and the refugees would squat contentedly in their huts, awaiting their orderly procession onto the idling UN boats, where they would sit in comfort and look out over the ocean, drawing ever closer to places where they would not disappear, name and body and life.

3

Cowboy Lim, owner of Cowboy Lim's Resthouse off Bungaraya
Road, knew a quotation from Jean-Paul Sartre: "Hell is other
people." He knew it primarily because his establishment at-
tracted a white clientele, mostly Australian backpackers. Reuben Gill
was white, of course, and he was in almost every night, but Reuben Gill
also called himself the Biggest White Man in Kuala Trengganu, which
meant he knew he was a monkey's ass, which in turn meant he actually
wasn't. The backpackers didn't know they were monkeys' asses, which
meant they actually were. From the second floor, the backpackers on
the street side looked out over the marquee of the Lido Cinema for a
spectacular view of the waterfront and the South China Sea; from the
alleyway side, they leaned over the railing and took pictures of hawkers
squatting in the dirt, stirring woks full of boiling oil and spattering bananas. As much as the view, the price made the backpackers wink
with satisfaction: at nine ringgit per night, twelve with air-con, the Resthouse was much cheaper than the four-story Hotel Kuala Trengganu,
and each room had a plastic line stretching from door to window for
guests who wished to wash and hang their laundry. The price appealed
to their sense of privation; the view, to their sense of entitlement. The
two were forever in conflict.

White people could be unpleasantly contradictory, and they made
innkeeping difficult. They were more infuriating than his own wife,
and Mrs. Lim could make him so mad with her sharp tongue that he
went for long walks almost every night to think of ways to silence her.
Sometimes the white people said they liked his cowboy hat, but then

they leaned close and winked and said, "Hey mate, but you don't wear it all the time, do you?" As if you couldn't be Chinese and wear American cowboy hats. As if, because you were Chinese, you had to harbor seething grudges against the Malay-run government and join so many secret societies you didn't have time to brush your hat. The white people wanted their Chinese to act Chinese. They wanted him to work like a dog, but they also wanted him to utter expansive truths. In fact, working like a dog brought you much closer to thinking like a dog than speaking like a philosopher, so the equation was much more complicated than the white people suspected. He was neither dog nor philosopher. He was Cowboy Lim, and he wore a cowboy hat, and he spent his evenings bickering with Mrs. Lim and drinking Remy Martin V.S.O.P. with Reuben Gill. If people didn't like it, that was fine with him.

His nephew Yap agreed. "White bastards-*lah*," he said, folding waxy towels piled atop the check-in desk. Nephew Yap had his own complaints. On weekends he was a waiter on the roof garden of the Hotel Kuala Trengganu, where the white relief workers from Bidong Island stayed on leave. In some ways, they were even worse than the backpackers. They said Bidong was in their blood, but according to Reuben Gill, they thought they had a better chance of getting laid by tourists if they advertised themselves as humanitarians. Perhaps Reuben Gill was right. If Bidong truly was in their blood, then they wouldn't spend fifty ringgit a night to stay in the Hotel Kuala Trengganu, which had tablecloths and central air. They sat drinking on the roof garden of the hotel, leaning back in their chairs and telling people they worked with refugees. Sometimes they stared into the ocean. At certain times of day, they said, if atmospheric conditions were ideal, one could sit on the hotel's roof and see a little smudge in the water, way off to the northeast. That smudge, they said, was Bidong Island. They were apparently the only ones who could see it. Whenever Nephew Yap or the Malay waiters squinted from the railing, they just got headaches.

"You can't see it?" the white people would crow. "Is that wish fulfillment talking, or you? There it is, right there. Bidong has more Vietnamese than this country has ever seen. Hey? Isn't that right?"

So it was with calculated gruffness that Cowboy Lim greeted the white woman who stood before him that morning at the check-in counter, holding a large green vinyl suitcase. She was sweating profusely, to his eyes grotesquely, in the apish manner of white people.

Even their females were hairy. The woman before him, not nearly as slim-waisted as a Chinese, rested two forearms on the check-in counter. She was filling out the Resthouse registration card. Her limbs were blotched with wispy golden hairs matted into tufts, like sea grass. He did a quick survey. She was alone, so she probably wasn't in Kuala Trengganu simply for tourism. She had no tan. That meant either that she had just arrived in Malaysia or that she wasn't here to lounge around topless on the beach all day. He peeked down, pretending to check the number of bags she carried. Her clean-shaven legs revealed her to be American.

"American?" he asked, accepting her registration card.

"Yes," she said, rifling through her cloth purse. "There's a passport in here somewhere, though I don't really see what the point of it is. Everyone seems to know I'm American, anyway." She stopped rifling and looked up at him. A Chinese cowboy! She resisted the temptation to laugh. "It's like I have *American* tattooed on me," she said. "Are you really such an expert on accents? Or do I have this look that says I'm trying to make a good impression so you won't hate me?"

"No," he said absently. "Is just guess." He pressed down on his hat, securing it firmly, frowning much too long at the registration card she had just filled out.

The gestures suggested to the woman that he might be lying as well as condemning himself for the lie. The act of placing hand to head was perhaps more psychologically revealing than most people realized. Lies were a form of assault, and like all assaults, they anticipated counter-strikes. If a lie had left his mouth, then his hand was unconsciously securing protection for the most vulnerable part of his body. His apparent fascination with her registration card was equally suspect. When one lied, the gaze of the victim was the most terrible punishment of all, since one was then either forced to reinforce the original lie by gazing back, assured and unblinking, or to acknowledge one's shame by avoiding the victim's gaze altogether. His actions suggested the latter. At any rate, his apparent shame canceled his apparent lie, if indeed he had lied. She decided to forgive whatever his trespass might have been. On the other hand, she had just ridden all night in a rattling bus, suffered the leering of hoodlums at the bus station, been talked at by that Manley person, and climbed a steep flight of stairs with a forty-pound vinyl suitcase in her hand. She amended: forgiveness was granted, but if this

Chinese man in the cowboy hat stood there too much longer frowning at her registration card, he would be guilty, unconscionably so, of exploiting her sense of personal largess.

"Passport," he said, sternly.

"Oh," she said. She opened her purse. "You know, I'm still curious how you knew I was American. I only ask because I have this theory that Americans try too hard to make everyone like them. All these little ambassadors running around making nice."

She lifted her purse to the light and rummaged with both hands. "It's a kind of preemptive strike, isn't it?" she said. "Trying to make people like you in preparation for smearing their names at the bar. Actually, it's a little frightening. At least the Germans have the honesty to just come out and be obnoxious. Though I have to say when I was in the Philippines, the German tourists were a little too honest. They seemed to be saying, 'I didn't hide my club, so be a good child and let me have a whack at you.' Well, *there* it is."

She pulled out the passport and shook it a few times. "There," she said, "I was in the Philippines for two years. You can see the stamp on the passport. Philippines." She held her passport up to him for inspection. "The less secure the country, the bigger the stamp. I say get rid of the stamps and just have everyone sign a card promising decency under threat of death. That's a lovely hat, by the way. I don't believe I've seen a Stetson in Malaysia."

He didn't seem to be listening. He wrote down the passport number, then surprised her by tipping his hat in acknowledgment of the compliment. "How long you stay?" he said.

"I'm not really sure, to tell you the truth. I'm going out soon to Bidong Island where the refugee camp is. I don't know when. There's a Mr. Manley who's going to bring my papers tonight or tomorrow. He says he knows you."

"Manley, yes," he said. "Sign please." He tapped the check-in ledger.

Nephew Yap, quietly folding towels, looked up quizzically.

"Manley," Cowboy Lim said, speaking to the boy. "Teacher who need teaching."

"Ah, Mr. Manley," said Nephew Yap. He looked at Porkpie with what seemed to her to be concern.

Cowboy Lim watched her sign in. He began laughing.

"What's funny?" she said.

"Your name. Bobbi Porkpie Sortini. *Babi* mean "pork" in Malay. Sound same, yes? Bobbi, *babi.* Your name Pork Pork Sortini. Very funny."

"I see," she said evenly. There was the possibility of aggression in the man's comment. "I'm not sure if you're laughing at a sexual connotation or the fact that this is a Muslim country. It *is* OK to say the word *Muslim* out loud here, isn't it? There isn't going to be some sudden hush in the room, is there?" She looked over at Nephew Yap, obscured by a teetering pile of towels, searching his face for signs of discomfort.

"I am not Muslim," said Cowboy Lim. "I am Cowboy Lim. Chinese John Wayne. Not Buddhist, not Christian. Free thinker." He rapped the side of his head several times with a forefinger.

"Good for you, Mr. Cowboy!" she said. "Now, as a free thinker you must realize that only the idiosyncratic has meaning. Bobbi Porkpie was the name given me by my mother. I go by Porkpie. It's as natural to me as your apparent *nom de l'hotel* is to you. I don't mean to be petty, Mr. Cowboy, but when you laugh at my name, you diminish the flesh and blood behind it, and this flesh and blood is a very tired traveler who has just spent the last twelve hours on the overnight from Singapore. How would you feel if you had been riding your little Chinese pony around all day and then heard someone laugh in your face because you were a Mr. Cowboy?"

There was silence for a moment, then Cowboy Lim's face signaled mirth: a lopsided grin, one eye gone droopy, head cocked to the side, as if felled by a stroke. "No offense, ma'am," he said pleasantly. "Nine dollar, please."

So she had misread him. Graciousness demanded her immediate surrender. "Pork Pork," she said, counting out the bills and handing them over. "Well, yes. I see the humor now. I'm just exhausted, that's all." He handed her a receipt, which she made a point of taking without reading. "Really," she said brightly. "It's funny." Cowboy Lim nodded.

She wanted so much to demonstrate her sincerity that she found herself convinced by her own words. Why, the joke *was* funny. Outrageously clever, even. She would have to relate it in a letter to someone. Perhaps dear Esmeralda in Manila would enjoy it. Or Theresa in Bataan. Perhaps, why yes, perhaps even Lyle, back in Chicago, though an attempt at communication would require ignoring why she divorced him in the first place. And then there would be that messy business of mentally relocating him from Hell, where she had assigned him to rot for a thousand years. He had hardly done his time. Only two years served, and already his image seemed accommodating enough for less sanguine fantasies. Perhaps she could relocate him temporarily, just to see how he fit in, to a different lobe, perhaps just behind the ears, bordering Purgatory but well above Eternal Damnation. It was exciting to contemplate. Perhaps two years in the Peace Corps had been better therapy than graduate school, after all.

"Have nice stay, ma'am," Cowboy Lim drawled, tipping his hat. He smiled.

"Thank you," she said, and smiled back. She picked up the enormous suitcase at her feet. Nephew Yap took the room key and jangled it in front of him, indicating that she should follow. She did, willing herself and her bag up the stairs, summoning reserves of strength she didn't know she still possessed. The boy hadn't offered to carry her luggage. She was so tired, she found his lapse of etiquette hilarious. How odd, she thought, that one's physical state should influence one's frame of mind so much. How odd that this dank, dark place should suddenly seem so welcoming. If Cowboy Lim's was anything like the small Chinese hotels in the Philippines, the night would be filled with phlegmy gurgling and short, muffled shrieks. In the morning, there would be the clop of wet sandals in the hallway, bare lightbulbs glaring overhead, a chorus of bodily purgations splatting down holes or onto the washroom floor. She paused, panting slightly, on the second-floor landing. Her escort looked around the corner, as if checking for thieves. The Resthouse reeked of poverty. Out the window she saw wet undergarments hanging from the courtyard balconies. There were dark stains on the wall, a radio blaring Hindi music somewhere, doors slamming across the courtyard. A fat man down the hall looked at her with undisguised interest. Her skin held forth the possibility of miscegenation. But that was what made Asia so attractive, did it not? There was a charge of electricity in the air, even in the midst of stupefying boredom. One's life could change in a moment.

The room set her into a brief fit of laughter: stained gray linoleum, dull green walls, a dusty ceiling fan, a four-poster bed so big she would have to walk sideways to get to the bathroom. Torn green drapes covered a row of windows. In one corner was a small wooden writing table discolored with water marks; in another was a silver spittoon and a green plastic wastebasket, side by side. The sight was marvelous, the very picture of failed, earnest practicality, charming in its seediness and lack of imagination.

"That mark on the wall there," said Porkpie, dropping her bag on the bed. "Is that really an arrow pointed toward Mecca? For prayers?"

It was.

"Priceless! It really is. Are there Christian rooms with an arrow pointing straight up? I suppose a Buddhist arrow would always be right in front of you wherever you looked. Mr. Cowboy might like one that turns into a question mark. But only if you touch it, of course, matter being supreme."

The boy stood blinking in front of her. His lips parted and closed, fishlike, as if attempting to speak.

"Oh, look what I've done now," Porkpie said. "You poor thing. That's one thing you might as well know about me. I'm not one of these tourists who goes ga-ga at the local standards. There's nothing holy about the way you do things here. Come to America some day, and you'll see there's nothing holy about my home either."

"Yes," the boy said softly, and began to walk backward toward the door. He stopped to flick the light switch off and on, nodding his head at Porkpie.

"I'm sure the lights work fine," said Porkpie, crossing her arms. "It's a beautiful room. I couldn't be happier. Thank you."

The boy grasped the doorknob and closed the door slowly. The last Porkpie saw of him was his hand in the hallway, waving bye. She sighed, sitting heavily on the bed. The mattress was hard. She lifted up a corner and saw the plywood board lying between mattress and boxspring. The board had been stamped with a notice of ownership, in red letters: "Property of Cowboy Lim Resthouse." The sight made her smile: where else in the world would you find a "property of" stamp on a plywood bed board? It was all so silly and so crass, you had to smile. Sitting in this impoverished room, lying on the mattress, exploring: you had the feeling you were a child playing inside a cardboard box. The filthy dark corners suggested mystery. The walls were deliciously rough and discolored, irresistible to the touch. The air was stale and faintly lurid, faintly tragic. It was the whole world reduced to a room-sized square, right in front of you, and if your heart didn't beat faster in it, you might as well be reading excruciatingly intelligent books with someone like Lyle at your side, shilly-shallying your life away.

There was still so much to do. She zipped open her bag and took out clothes. Sundresses on the hangers, formal-occasion stockings inside the underwear, then pumps and sandals under the bed. Overhead, a pair of amorous geckos humped in mechanical rapture on the ceiling. A moth beat itself against the fluorescent light. She paused, shaking her suitcase hand, massaging it with her other hand. From the bottom of the bag she withdrew small objects: a sheathed aborigine knife, smuggled past customs; a child's handloom, of Filipino origin, made from discarded combs; a dictionary of Latin phrases; and something she had purchased for a ringgit in a Malay restaurant—a mud wasp's nest the size of her palm, preserved in shellac and stuffed, the waiter said, with paraffin. It *is* a delightful collection, she thought: dilettantish in theme, sexually charged, perhaps even a bit hostile intellectually.

The loom and wasp's nest she put on top of the dictionary, setting them on the writing table. The knife she placed on the floor, within reaching distance. A woman alone didn't have to be stupid about exploration, no matter what the appeal of danger. She rose and sidled her way to the bathroom to wash her face. Outside, a clanging noise was rising above the diesel and motorcycle traffic. It echoed against the bathroom tile, as in a sound chamber. How long had the noise been there? There was simply too much demanding her attention. Sleep was called for. Sleep and only sleep. She filled the plastic bucket with water from the square water cistern and poured it over her head, giving herself over, for a long, luxurious moment, to the pleasures of the bucket bath: the baptismal whoosh, the loss of sight and sound, the idle speculation that the world outside has ceased to exist. Then there was that clanging noise again, like cymbals in an orchestra. She paused. It was insistent. There would be no sleep until she knew. She placed the bucket back into the cistern and held her sarong against her like a blanket. Her feet squeaked against the linoleum, trailing water.

At the window, she pulled aside the drapes and saw them: Chinese mourners wearing white sackcloth, trailing a funeral wagon. At the front of the line were two men clanging small gongs. She cranked the window latch, watching the glass frames open like a door. The moist hot air poured in. But there was something else as well. She had to step back. There were starlings, hundreds of them, shrieking and wheeling overhead. The gongs below—clang, clang! clang, clang!—were driving them crazy. How could she not have seen the birds before? Why, the sky was filled with starlings, and she hadn't noticed. She cupped her hand like a visor over her eyes and looked out. It was such a contradiction. Birds above, a funeral below. Poetry.

She wiped her nose on her sarong and looked at the reflection in the window. The ghostly figure was hers. She did not immediately recognize her face, though she knew it could be no one else's. Her mouth was slack, her expression distant. Her hair lay in slick braids against her shoulders, and she was pressing so tightly against the latch she could see her fingers quiver. She loosened her grasp. Her body was trembly. Holding the window just so, half open, she saw the small pulse in her wrist rise and fall. Her eyes gleamed in the angle of light like a cat's, and she could feel her breath come rapid and shallow. She heard herself. She was giggling. Hysteria, she thought. I must watch that. It was degrading: it revealed one as girlish and naive. So utterly, utterly to be avoided. The day had altogether been too much.

She knotted the sarong above her breasts and stepped back, collapsing on the bed. The mattress was hard as earth. The clanging came in through the window; the overhead fan hacked at the air; down the hall somebody was spitting. Despite everything, was this not more lovely than life with Lyle? Had the Peace Corps not been more lovely as well? She closed her eyes, recalling the bus ride up from Singapore, roaring around the blind curves. Sitting upright in her seat, watching the trucks come barreling the other way, imagining collision, she had summoned forth his image and found him merely pathetic. Such a change from the loathsome creature she had imagined a scant two years back in Chicago! Such a change even from rural Luzon, where she was able to summon but a single image of her former husband: quiet, bookish Lyle in the backyard, wearing swim trunks and tennis shoes. He hadn't known she was watching. He was mowing the grass. His face was contorted in a way she had never seen. He mowed the entire backyard, row by row, a half hour in the sun, screaming obscenities under the roar of the mower. And in the span of a single afternoon, she knew she could not live side by side with his secrets.

No, he did not deserve a thousand years in Hell. She would drop him a civil note. She would write her friends back in the Philippines. She would tell everyone about Kuala Trengganu, and then she would tell them about Bidong Island. *I'm on my way home,* she would say. *Via a refugee camp. How fitting!*

She slept. Just like that, the world fell black, the air silent. Her mind filled with a delicious dream, full and bursting with the Chicago wind, the view of Lake Michigan, the rattling of the El. She smelled lilacs; she was eating a bratwurst, munching then holding it out like a torch, high and triumphant. The dream was so delicious she did not want to stir when the knocking started at the door.

She rose.

It was Mr. Cowboy. He had a note from Manley. She took it dumbly, peering from behind the door, mindful of her sarong and wet hair. She remembered too late to thank Mr. Cowboy for bringing up the message from Manley. Wait, she said softly, but he was already trotting down the stairs. She read the note, then crumpled it into a ball. She walked to the bed and lay down, her eyes open and blinking. A party tonight, she thought. She needed a party tonight like she needed another night on the bus. Would no one just let her sleep?

"You're in a refugee camp, little bugger." The words, spoken by the British engineer, Ralph, still stung in Gurmit's ears. Bloody hell, of course he was in a refugee camp. That was why he wanted to leave. And that was why he now marched down the Zone C footpath with a damaged wooden plank from the staff eating hut. He carried it like a surfboard, under his armpit, striding purposefully back to his office. Behind him, his new refugee administrative assistant, Miss Phu from Zone F, jogged to keep up. He spat. Of all things to carry, a table plank. He would just as soon tack one of the red-and-white checkered plastic tablecloths over it and go about his business. He would just as soon forget what he had seen. But Ralph! How dare he. The engineer's words had left Gurmit with little choice. He was, in any event, legally justified in taking the board, for the operating orders of the Malaysian Prison Systems were quite specific: "Destruction of government property shall be reported to the administrative chief, who shall initiate a full investigation to determine culpability if the persons and causes responsible are not known." So that was just what he would do. The damaged plank from the staff eating table, property of the Malaysian Prison Systems, was now in his charge, to remain in his office until such time as the investigation was complete. Let the staff complain all they wanted.

The refugees on the footpath cleared out of his way. Miss Phu, still unable to match his pace, weaved from side to side to avoid being struck by the bobbing plank and explained as well as she could to curious pedestrians what Gurmit was carrying. Overhead, the sky rumbled. It was August, a full two months since Gurmit had arrived, and a light rain began to fall.

"Mr. Gurmit, you walk so fast," Miss Phu said. She held his clipboard with both hands, like a serving tray.

"Bloody hell," he said sharply. "Are we having a picnic? Come."

Miss Phu detected his impatience and loped after him, shifting the clipboard to her left in anticipation of Gurmit's wide turn. "Wah!" she giggled. "No picnic. Too much rain."

Gurmit cocked his head to the side and shouted over a list of new announcements issuing from the loudspeaker. "This is *Sikh* rain. You see?" He looked down at his white safari suit, now mottled with drops.

"Not sick, Mr. Gurmit."

Gurmit sighed. Why could he never get assistants who spoke good English? Since the beginning of the rains last week he and Miss Phu had established a code that allowed them to carry out business in secret: complaints from Vietnamese were yellow rain; from the Malay police, brown rain; from the staff, white rain. The least she could do was understand Sikh rain. The least she could do was try harder to understand him. But no. All she seemed to care about was singing. She hummed in his office, she pampered her throat with his tea, she practiced her scales when she should have been listening.

"No," he shouted back. "*Sikh*. Indian Sikh, like me. This is *my* rain. I'm complaining."

"Ahhh," shouted Miss Phu. "Very funny, Mr. Gurmit."

Gurmit had not meant it as a joke. Just minutes ago, his daily status meeting in the eating hut had dissolved into Sikh rain. The evidence under his arm had been just another plank in the table. Ralph had been just another UN relief worker. How could things have gone bad so quickly? He gave the board a whack against a palm tree by the joss-stick sellers. For two months he had wolfed down lunch and dinner in the eating hut, his roving fork just inches away from the gouges in the plank. He had thought nothing of the wood's imperfections, as the table was always covered with a red-and-white checkered plastic tablecloth held down with tacks. He and the staff all ate their cuttlefish and rice on plastic plates, resting their elbows on the greasy red-and-white covering. Occasionally someone would spill coffee or water, and when the liquid gathered in pools on the plank now tucked firmly under his arm, they simply moved their plates.

But when, at the conclusion of that morning's status meeting, Sally Hindermann knocked over her tea, Gurmit noticed something peculiar. He saw that the liquid arranged itself in the form of letters. He made out a *T,* an *N,* and possibly an *H.* He put his fingers on the thick plastic covering and pressed so hard that the tablecloth pulled against the tacks holding it. He announced that the gouges seemed to be letters.

"Alphabet soup!" cried Johann the radiologist.

"Spelling bee!" said Ralph.

Gurmit and the radiologist began to push the water jugs and coffee cups to one side to make room for their investigation. As they did, Miss Thi, the head of the Vietnamese kitchen ladies, began to bustle around them and move the water jugs and coffee cups back to their original positions. She snapped at her two assistants, who ran from the cooking fire behind the corrugated tin wall, and the three of them scurried to put metal cups over the center of the table. Gurmit and the radiologist drew back in surprise.

"What's wrong, Miss Thi?" asked Sally, lingering at the entrance. She cast a sharp look at Gurmit and the radiologist and, placing her arm around her friend Miss Thi, drew out from the woman that the grooves did indeed spell something. Miss Thi swore she had nothing to do with it. "It's OK, Miss Thi. No problem," said Sally. Gurmit smiled and nodded. "No problem," said the radiologist. Miss Thi appeared relieved. Speaking in Vietnamese, she told her assistants to unroll the tarp awning so that no passersby could see in. At the same time, Miss Thi helped Gurmit and the radiologist strip the tacks from the tablecloth. When they finished, they peeled off the covering and with much effort tossed the stiff plastic onto the dirt floor. The table plank in question was not even nailed to the frame. There before them, gouged into the plank, they saw the words *Nguyen Van Trinh* in perfectly carved letters almost half a foot high.

"That name," said Gurmit.

"The suicide, isn't he?" said Sally, pointing.

"That right," said Miss Thi. "That right. That right. I not do the cut. I not know who do the cut."

"That's OK, Miss Thi," said Sally. She held Miss Thi's hand. "No one's blaming you. No problem. Gurmit buried him, didn't you, Gurmit? If anyone knows who did this, Gurmit does."

"Did not," said Gurmit quickly.

"Meaning?" said Sally.

"Did not bury." He shook his head violently. "I am only signing paperwork, isn't it? Did not bury. Health Division is responsible to bury. You understand-*lah*? I did not bury."

"All right, already," said Sally.

"Only signing paperwork. You understand, yes? Other people are burying, isn't it?"

"So who was he?" said Johann.

"I'm afraid no one really knows," said Sally. "A name. The meta-refugee."

Ralph chuckled. "Here's something, mates," he said. "Bet you buggers have never seen this." He reached into his pocket and pulled out a lighter. Unscrewing the bottom, he held the lighter over the table and poured its fluid into one of the gouges. Pointing to the lightness of the stain, he pronounced the cutting to have taken place about a month ago.

Johann shook his head. He produced a curled shaving. "Much too supple," he said, squeezing it with his fingers. He believed it no more than a few days old.

The mechanic from Colorado disputed both claims. "Over here," he motioned, and pressed Sally's hands into the grooves to feel the texture of the grain. "*Nothing* that smooth," he said, "could be less than a year old."

"The cut *always* been there," said Miss Thi suddenly.

"Just poof, huh?" said Ralph. "Abracadabra. The Ur-cut."

"Always there," Miss Thi said. She hiccuped.

"Please," said Gurmit. "No more. You are upsetting Miss Thi."

"Yes, holy one," said Ralph. He salaamed in Gurmit's direction.

"You are making fun," Gurmit said.

Ralph raised his eyebrows. "I'm pointing out you're taking the high road again."

"I am not understanding why you say this," said Gurmit.

"Forget it."

"I'm telling you this is upsetting Miss Thi," said Gurmit.

"You're the one continuing this," said Ralph. "Look who's upsetting Miss Thi now." He pointed at her.

"Always there," Miss Thi said, then brought her hands to her face.

"Will you two shut up," said Sally.

"I am not taking the high road," said Gurmit. "If I am taking, then my job is to make an investigation." He pointed to the plank. "Find who has committed this crime, yes? But I am not doing. Do you see an investigation?"

"Come on, cowboys," said the mechanic from Colorado. "Time to saddle up and skedaddle." He stood at the entrance.

"What are you saying?" asked Gurmit. "I am not watching cowboys and Indians. What are you saying?"

"He's not saying anything," said Ralph. "Good God Almighty. I thought *Brits* were supposed to be uptight."

"So Malaysians are uptight," said Gurmit sharply.

"It was you I had more in mind," said Ralph.

"I'm sorry you think so. You say anything you want, isn't it?"

"You need a paperwork fix, mate. I'm sorry I came to the meeting at all."

"Please take this outside," said Sally.

"And now the meeting is silly," said Gurmit.

"You're in a *refugee camp*, little bugger," said Ralph. "Think about it."

Gurmit began to click his pen rapidly. "Is that where I am?" he said. He felt everyone's eyes on him. He heard someone snigger. "A refugee camp, hey?" he said.

"Oh, don't get angry, Gurmit," said Sally. "You sound like Reuben Gill."

"I am in a refugee camp," Gurmit snapped. He moved quickly. He lifted the plank and placed it under his armpit. "Then I am Administration Chief, isn't it? I am keeping this damaged property for evidence." He clutched his clipboard with his free hand and stepped outside. The board nearly rammed Miss Phu, who, singing a folk song to herself, wasn't watching where she was going.

Late that night Gurmit sat hunched over his typewriter, staring at the words he had just typed on his Preliminary Damage Report sheet. Against the wall leaned the plank, and there it would stay. That name. He could not bring himself to look at the gouges. Had he not finished with Nguyen Van Trinh? A most unpleasant business. But he could not simply be done with it by returning the table plank to its rightful place.

Just thinking about the consequences made his heart race. If he walked back to the eating hut with the plank, a crowd of Viets would follow. They would pester Miss Phu for information, and Miss Phu would say she didn't know why he was returning the plank. But, she would add, he had been angry when he brought it to his office. Ah, the crowd would say, and then they would rush into the hospital and the administrative offices to drag out English-speaking relatives who worked with the white people. The relatives would seek out Sally Hindermann and Ralph and ask why Mr. Gurmit was angry with them.

"Well," Ralph would say, "he's a twit."

"Well," Sally would say, "he's upset that he can't do his job."

"Ah," the relatives would say, smiling. "Poor Mr. Gurmit."

The relatives would ruin him. At night, when the generator shuddered to a stop and rats scrabbled from their holes and up the poles of the huts, the refugees hunkered around their cardboard beds, drinking tea from severed 7-Up cans. The relatives would tell the story of Mr. Gurmit and the plank. They would say he had been angry with the white people. He had been defeated. He was a twit Indian, an angry Indian. The words would hang in the air. In the morning, when he opened his office door, the children under the floorboards would call up and greet him. They would think his name had changed: Angry Mr. Gurmit, they would say, repeating the words they had heard. Twit Mr. Gurmit. Poor Mr. Gurmit. They would repeat the words over and over, not even knowing their meanings, and then Task Force Chief Ahmed would walk up the steps and open the door to tell him what he could not bear to hear: Gurmit, Ahmed would say, the white bastards are playing you for the fool.

Unbearable. He had to carry through with an investigation—at least the pretense of one. For if the plank-gouger were discovered . . . It was painful to contemplate. Task Force guards would roust the culprit from his hut and whack him around with a rattan and shave his head and lock him in the chicken coop for days. Gurmit shook his head violently back and forth, driving the images away. He would employ all of his advantages to prevent discovery from occurring. Surely they would be sufficient. Typing his name at the bottom of the report, he reviewed them once again. He signed the delegation interview request forms. He assigned ration allotments and allocated clothing supplies to the zone chiefs. All the Viets knew that. And surely no Viet would challenge his authority to refuse information regarding the culprit, or to bury it under mounds of paper. They understood how power worked. Silence was assured.

There was still one delicate task ahead. Island operating orders required two signatures on the Preliminary Damage Report sheet—his and the senior staff member's. Sally Hindermann. He drummed his index finger on the space bar. Well, he had certain advantages over her as well. Hanging on the doorknob was a brand new T-shirt that had been confiscated from a refugee in Zone D. Miss Sally, the Viet said, had given it to him. She had apparently just walked into Supply and taken it without permission. Mistake. Task Force Chief Ahmed would not be pleased to hear such news. He whacked the space bar a few times and typed her name. He cracked his knuckles. Yes. An investigation could be made to fail. It was assuredly possible. He ripped the sheet from the typewriter and secured it to his clipboard. The words looked bold and formidable. He nodded with satisfaction and then, after walking briskly to his bungalow, crawled into bed immediately and fell asleep.

The next morning Gurmit tacked a sign on his office door announcing in three languages that he would be out for the morning. In one hand was the T-shirt; in the other was the clipboard containing his Preliminary Damage Report. In marching down the footpath to the UN compound he could not help but stop several times to reread what he had written. "One table plank, Malaysian Red Crescent property (value: 5 ringgit), damaged; investigation initiated for purposes of determining cause and/or responsibility, per operating orders." His breath was shallow. The words now seemed so thin, so inadequate. The type was smudged. There was an unsightly crusted spot of Wite-Out by his name. He admitted to himself that he was feeling neither confident nor confrontational. But he recalled the words of the great Sikh warrior Murthabi Singh: "Praise the day you meet your enemy, for on that day you shall become a hero." The words of the great Murthabi Singh calmed him. His safari suit pocket bristled with pens; he brought the clipboard up to settle squarely against his breast. He praised the day.

Inside the compound were Miss Tu and Miss Chong, two Vietnamese English teachers at the Zone C school, bent over a red plastic tub, scrubbing the relief workers' clothes. A small drizzle started up. Sally was sitting on the porch of her yellow bungalow, eating. She looked out at the ocean with an air of contemplation, as though enraptured by an internal symphony.

"I have been thinking about the table," Gurmit said, stopping at the bottom step.

"How I envy your private life," said Sally.

"And I am carrying something you have given away," he said. He draped the T-shirt over his arm.

Sally looked at him blankly. "Thank you," she said. "Are you a waiter now?" She smiled broadly. "I'm joking, for God's sake. You have such a hangdog expression."

"So much to do today," he said. "Investigation."

"Then you have some sleuthing to do."

"That is why I stand in the rain to talk to you," said Gurmit.

"Is it raining? Poor Gurmit. You don't have to stand out there, you know."

"What I have to say is very brief. Can only stay a moment."

"You're not disturbing me at all," she said, and took another bite.

"No?" said Gurmit. He shook the T-shirt at her like a cape.

"You're not disturbing me."

"I am not disturbing you?" said Gurmit. He gave the T-shirt another shake.

"That T-shirt is very nice. Wouldn't it look better on someone's back?"

"Mr. Cho in Zone D says you gave it to him, isn't it?"

"What did he say exactly?" said Sally.

"He says you gave it to him."

"Are you sure?" said Sally. "I didn't give it to him for *him* to wear. I gave it to him for his *son* to wear. Who was wearing it?"

"That is not my point," said Gurmit. "This belongs in Supply."

"How long do you and Chief Ahmed intend to keep the shirts clean in Supply?"

"That is not what I am saying," said Gurmit.

"So take it back to Supply," said Sally. She speared another bite from her plate.

"You are eating fish," he said.

"It makes a wonderful breakfast."

"Sunfish?"

She swallowed. "Excellent detective work. Bite?"

Gurmit shook his head. "How are you having sunfish?" he asked. "None has come for weeks."

"Oh, Gurmit, really," she said sharply, and laid down her fork.

"You have received it from illegal fishing."

"That," she said, "is a beastly rule. How can you work with that Ahmed?"

"He did not make the rule," said Gurmit.

"Not us. Not the Viets."

"The head of Prison Systems," said Gurmit.

"Well, that explains it."

"You wish to register a complaint, isn't it?"

"Not if I have to talk to the head of Prison Systems."

"What is the nature of your hesitation?" said Gurmit.

"No hesitation," she said. "I just don't talk to those kinds of people."

Her hand twitched—in disgust, Gurmit supposed. Her bloody arrogance. He frowned. "Did you know six refugees are drowning from offshore fishing this year?"

"If they had more rations they wouldn't go fishing," Sally said.

"That is a different issue."

"It's the *same* issue, Gurmit. It's called food."

"I am knowing the word," said Gurmit.

"Yes. I apologize. Of course you do. All I know is that they go fishing no matter what rules your friends make. Did you know my Zone C blackboard was stolen last week? Again? They're turning it into a boat hull. They're probably fishing right now, out there." She waved her hand vaguely in the direction of the ocean.

"You are assuming so much," said Gurmit.

"And you're playing sheriff," said Sally, spearing another bite.

Gurmit charged up the stairs. "No fish," he said firmly, placing his clipboard on the bungalow railing. "That is the rule."

"If you'd care to wait," said Sally, brightening suddenly, "you'd see that I'm going to give the leftovers to Miss Tu and Miss Chong when they finish the washing." The two women looked up at the mention of their names and waved. Sally waved back. "And it is *so* delicious," Sally said.

"No fish, no T-shirts," Gurmit said, mopping rain from his forehead.

Sally folded her arms and looked straight into Gurmit's eyes.

"But I will close my eyes this time," Gurmit said. He closed his eyes in demonstration. "Ahmed is not needing to know of your transgressions."

"My transgressions. Oh, *tell* him. I don't care. He can try and kick me off the island all he wants."

"You do not mean that," said Gurmit.

"I suppose not," said Sally, folding her arms. "You know what your problem is?"

Gurmit busied himself with draping the T-shirt over the bungalow railing. He pretended not to hear her question. He pulled the cloth to flatten it, then laid the T-shirt over the wood to dry. He did not want to hear what Sally thought his problem was. He did not want to hear another word from her.

"I am needing your signature," he said, holding up the clipboard.

Sally took it. Gurmit then reached into his front pocket and placed a green pen on the table, by her plate of fish.

"Oh," said Sally, smiling. "Oh, oh, oh. Now I get it." She placed the clipboard on the table. "Gurmit see no evil," she said, cupping her eyes. "Gurmit hear no evil," she said, cupping her ears. "Gurmit speak no evil," she said, cupping her mouth. "But Gurmit get my signature. Yes? You won't tattle about the fish and the T-shirt if you get what you want."

"Is not like that," Gurmit said quickly, but even as he spoke his cheeks began to burn.

"All right then," said Sally. She scribbled her name in giant letters on the signatory line. She looked away when she had finished, as though resuming her internal symphony. She calmly rubbed her hands against her arms. "You can have something else, too," she said, leaping up and entering her bungalow.

Gurmit heard a drawer open, then heard it slam shut. She came out immediately with a large rattan basket. Setting it on the table, she took her plate of half-eaten fish and shook it firmly into the basket. Slick globs of flesh stuck to the sides of the plate. These she removed by deftly scraping her index finger over the plastic surface.

"You get my signature," she said, handing him the clipboard. "And you get a fish." She thrust the basket at his face, briefly shaking it like a tambourine. "And you get a T-shirt," she said, grabbing the cloth off the railing. "Now poof. Off with you."

Gurmit took it all: clipboard, basket, and T-shirt. He watched Sally turn and walk into her bungalow. Her hands were balled into fists, turning her knuckles the color of alabaster. His mouth opened, but he could think of nothing to say. And then he heard boys blowing palm fronds, trumpeting eight in the morning. So bloody loud, he thought. That was all he could think.

Days passed. The water barge made its weekly delivery; the rain let up. At dusk the generator in Zone C continued to sputter under its shed, and the Vietnamese mechanics handed their oily shirts over to the washer girls and yelled over the motor for their children to bring them packets of rice and fish sauce tied up in newspaper. Dragonflies settled on the shelters, and girls in white blouses giggled at their mothers and trapped the insects in jars. The debris of the day lay trampled on the footpaths: mangled cigarette packs, plastic bags, rubber bands, locks of hair around the outdoor barber chairs, the occasional rat-killing brick, a sandal here and there. And then it was night again, just like that, the darkness glowing with coals and cigarettes, the lights from the Task Force barracks and UN compound bright and tinkly as carnivals. In the staff eating hut, the kitchen ladies served bowls of squid and cabbage and fried okra, placing them gently in front of the white people, away from the sagging hole in the middle of the red-and-white checkered tablecloth, then returning with a giant caldron of steamed rice, which they held by the handles and dragged across the dirt floor on a wooden pallet attached to a rope.

Gurmit's seat was still empty. No one remarked on his absence. The staff joked about the sagging hole, moving their silverware about, playing shuffleboard games to see whose fork would come the closest to the edge. They drank coffee. They pressed the cool tin of the water cups to their foreheads. They ate with ravenous appetites, passing the bowls person to person, scraping their spoons against the metal, saying it sure would be nice if their table didn't look like a medieval map, where all the ships sailed into the pit at the end of the world.

Gurmit sat on a tree stump at the top of the Zone F hill, staring down at the dark water and the mushrooming rain clouds racing in from the mainland. With a pocket knife, he cut open a can bearing a picture of a smiling sardine. He ate. At his back was the Zone F primary school, all plastic tarp and saplings, where an English teacher should have been conducting a lesson, if only there were enough teachers to go around. He thought he could make out faint lights far to the west, on the horizon, where Kuala Trengganu would be, where beer-bellied Sikhs would ride their motorbikes through zones of chutney and cloves and turmeric. He inhaled deeply, breathing in the moist night air, nostrils flaring, and he pictured himself with them, riding the streets of the city, groggy from beer and a dinner of *pratha* and chicken, putt-putting down the middle of Bungaraya Road, by the tiny mosque, hooting at the Chinese shop girls clacking their heels on the walkways after a full day at the emporium.

The image had weight; it was fleshy and breathing, and it filled him with longing. He sat thinking about it later that night, sitting at his desk in the office, catching up on refugee arrival and departure forms. He had not been in the office for days. Miss Phu had simply carried folders over to his bungalow, waiting quietly while he stamped them or approved them or shook his head "no." He worked dreamily now, pausing long moments, wishing with all his heart he were off the island. The image seemed so real he stuck out his hand, fending off an imaginary waiter bearing smelly food. He sniffed. Then he called himself a fool. The odor was real. There, next to the plank, covered with his clipboard and report, was the basket Sally had given him. The half-eaten fish had turned rancid; the oil had stained the T-shirt; bits of flesh speckled the clipboard.

He stopped working. He tapped his pen on his desk. He looked around. "Ruin," he whispered.

Rats were beginning to drop to the roof and chew at the plywood walls. The fluorescent light was sputtering; geckos waited in stony anticipation, like refrigerator magnets, along the length of the tube. Ruin. The whole office: the *India Today!* magazines, the jackfruit rinds, the soft drink bottle on the bench. Dust balls roamed the corners, moving with the faint breeze rising from between the floorboards, and to his eyes they did not seem to be dust balls at all, but the swirling, gaseous matter of ruin.

When the overhead light crackled, he groaned loudly and only with great reluctance stood up on his chair to jiggle the tube back and forth, scattering geckos across the ceiling. The tube glowed in his hand. It crackled off and on, and there in the light, as he stood with his feet on the chair, he saw a shadow fluttering on the front wall, something jerking and huge, and in his tiredness he was so startled by the sight that he felt his knees buckle. He jumped to the floor, suddenly weak, and nearly toppled over. His heart began to race. He felt himself floating, buoyed in something warm and dense, and then he was on his knees, falling hard, and his eyes were stinging. He clutched the chair, and then he felt it: a pressure on his shoulders, something frantic and hot, like hands clawing.

He crawled to his desk and pulled open the bottom left drawer, fumbling under his captain's hat. He raised his hand from the drawer, clutching a blue squirt gun, and fired an arcing stream of Raid wildly over his shoulder.

Nothing. The pressure was gone. He was squatting on the floor in a room of wood and paper and air. Overhead, the geckos slithered to the corners. A cockroach appeared, scuttling toward him across the ceiling. He was alone. He settled into his chair, facing the front wall, and tipped back slowly. He smoothed the lapel of his jacket, humming, just to hear the sound of his own voice, and cradled the gun in his lap. He couldn't stop shaking. He sat awhile, rocking, eyes roaming the walls, and then he balled his hand into a fist and brought it down hard on the desk. He clenched his teeth together and rose. He raised the gun. He squirted insecticide at the T-shirt. He squirted the basket of fish, his clipboard, his report. His hand clutched the gun so tightly he heard the plastic crack. Liquid was bubbling down his wrist. He fumbled with the bottom drawer and yanked out his captain's hat. He squirted it. He threw the hat to the floor, and then he was at the plank, and he stared at the mutilation. Nguyen Van Trinh. The name was infuriating. He put his finger to the trigger. Insecticide spattered the letters, but when he saw the dark liquid trickle down the gouges he felt the hairs on his neck bristle against his collar, and he held his arms wide and cradled the plank, pressing it close to his chest, feeling the splinters sink into his hands as he stroked its back, again and again, whispering to the wood, "Forgive me, forgive me, forgive me."

4

Doctor Johansson was in the upstairs bathroom with his wife, Sharon, even as party guests wandered around downstairs asking where the hell the Johanssons were hiding. "I'm finished," he said, sitting on the edge of the tub. He sighed.

Sharon held him to her bosom. "If you don't want to tell me what's going on, that's all right," she said. "At least you see you're acting unreasonable. I'm here for you." She held him in her arms and rocked him.

"Fanizah," he said suddenly. "You know, that secretary? Fanizah forgot to mail all the invitations."

Sharon held him tighter and cooed into his ear. "Is that really so bad? We don't have enough room anyway. They're already spilling out onto the patio."

"You don't understand," he said, freeing himself. He stood. "She divided the invitations into two piles. White people and Malaysians. She mailed the white ones and goddamn didn't mail the Malaysian ones."

Sharon patted his arm. "So we'll run through the liquor faster," she said. "At least we won't be left with footprints on the toilet seat. You know, I hear even the prime minister prefers a squat john."

"This isn't a joke," said the doctor, miserably. "The Malaysians are going to take this as a huge insult. They'll crucify my budget proposal at the regional meeting. They'll be bitching all the way to the prime minister."

"Oh, my little doctor," said Sharon, kissing his ear. "My poor little M.D. Now is that really so bad? It's not like you're the one responsible for this tow-the-Viets-out-to-sea business. You're not the one that sent the Ranger battalion up here. I mean, I know they're going to toughen up their policy soon. But sweetie, come on, you're my little doctor. You're not responsible for all the horrible things."

The doctor looked at her miserably. "You see? Even you. I'm just a small fry. Don't you see? This is important. If Siew Hon Lee gets offended, there's no way we're getting out of this backwater. She's probably down there right now counting how many peanut noses are in the room."

Siew Hon Lee was at that moment sitting on the doctor's white leather couch by the open sliding door leading to the patio. Each time the front door opened, bringing in more heat and humidity from outside, she spread her silk Chinese fan and waved it in front of her face. The room was uncomfortably hot and sticky, even with the doctor's high ceilings and humming wall units. The house itself, however, she thought quite spectacular. The yard was walled in on all sides by decorative blue brick and wrought-iron railings, pointed at the ends to discourage intruders. In front were well-trimmed frangipani and the doctor's ubiquitous bougainvillea. The patio area was set on a small rise that sloped gently onto the kind of fine-stemmed grass found on exclusive Singapore sports fields. There were marble columns by the front door, parquet everywhere, and pleasing high arches between rooms. The doctor had decorated the walls sensibly: Chinese prints, Malay shadow-puppet graphics, giant Indian vases containing bamboo poles lashed together with garlands of dried bougainvillea.

Where was the doctor anyway? She had never seen so many white people in her life, but not one of them was the man she wished to talk to. Jack Kelly from the UN Development Programs was in the kitchen, hee-hawing with a blonde woman in flowered stockings. Mike Petocz was striding back and forth, shaking everyone's hand, bringing his huge nostrils to the cheeks of all the women and kissing them. Many had come without ties or button shirts; one even wore shorts and flip-flops. She looked down at her left hand to review her count. Yes, three was right. Three of her fingers were pointing straight out. Colonel Mansoor bin Abdullah had walked past with a curry puff. That made one. Doctor Lim Kok Cheong and Encik Rawli from Social Services had briefly hovered by the satay table and then gone off in search of sauce in which to dunk the meat skewers. That made three Malaysians. Only three.

She rose from the couch and stepped outside to the patio, fanning herself. There were only groups of white people, shrieking and drinking like the world was coming to an end. More white people were arriving at the front door, just letting themselves in. White people were running in from the kitchen, swigging beer. All these white people. An abacus couldn't keep track of their number. First the Vietnamese, now the white people. So few Malaysians. She really must have a word with the doctor. Where was he?

Porkpie arrived at Doctor Johansson's front door much more vivacious than she had thought possible. She believed herself to be in that state of travel exhaustion often confused with wakefulness. You shook and veered out of control, your mouth operated against your will, and just when you thought your head would fall into the punch bowl, you found yourself suddenly calm, moving your body around with the silken ease of a puppet master, your mind alert as a deer. The sensation was exhilarating, like hovering in a carnival ride high above the ground, poised to swoop down in a rattling cage that had been secured, you recalled too late, by some man you wouldn't have trusted to light your cigarette.

The exhilaration was as close as one could get to an out-of-body experience without compromising one's intelligence, though it did involve a degree of mental slippage. Even the fluttering it produced in her stomach had an intellectually pyrrhic quality: the cause was deduced, but the knowledge made one even more likely to give in to collapse. She paused, her foot pressing on the inlaid stone of the walkway, resisting the sensation she had of floating. Perhaps acquiescing to the social advantages to be gained by attending the party had not been such a good idea. What must be happening inside my body? she wondered. Those swollen frankfurter link intestines, the intricate bits of nose cartilage, the prickly little blood vessels: they would have their say soon enough, preferably after the party.

Yet there was undeniable, if brief, pleasure in giving oneself over completely to out-of-bodiness. She stepped off the walkway, pretending to admire the bougainvillea trimmed to resemble a refugee boat: a high keel; a pilot cabin; long tufts of grass, dramatically rising from a row of pots, brushing like waves against its branchy hull. This state of exhaustion, she thought, made one susceptible to illusion as well as epiphany. In the trishaw ride to Doctor Johansson's she was sure she had glimpsed that Manley person coming out of a noodle shop, accompanied by a giant redheaded fellow. The giant had yelled words, inasmuch as one could hear anything yelled over the motorcycles and blaring radios, that struck her ears as *I'm breathing now. I'm breathing good. Yeah.* Could such an event actually have happened? If he truly were having trouble breathing, then he wouldn't have been walking around in such awful humidity. And the giant's very presence was so incongruous, like something from a Salvador Dalí painting. She would have to ask Manley. Or perhaps the redheaded giant was also a UN worker, in which case she would seek him out inside.

"Porkpie!"

She turned, nearly twisting her ankle. It was that Manley person. He was grinning hideously, grasping a big bottle of Carlsberg beer around the stem. Behind him, coming from the open door, were the sounds of laughter and conversation. Someone turned up the volume on some Caribbean music.

"Hello, Manley," she said. "I was just admiring this topiary. It seems so . . . I don't know, so garish. Though I suppose I don't have much business at this point to pass judgment on other people's bad taste."

"Hey," said Manley. He took a swig. "Well, hey, come on in. They got tubs of this stuff." He lifted his Carlsberg as if it were game, recently shot. "But maybe you want hard stuff or wine," he said, tilting forward confidentially.

He seemed to be waiting for a response: eyes immobile, brow slightly arched, mouth in a pucker. Apparently, much rode on her choice of drink. Was there something peculiar to men that made them keen on data collection? They could take the most trivial habit or preference and treat it like an opposing team's batting average, something representative of performance. Does so and so drink? If so, what, and how much? How does her tongue rest in her mouth? Do her lips move much? Does she blink when she talks, or does she look straight at you? Poor sexual socialization was at the root of it. Men ruled by fantasy translated one's personal nuances, any of which derived from unfathomable causes, into fuckability.

"Beer is fine," she said. "Hard liquor makes me fart, don't ask me why."

Manley averted his gaze and began pushing back his hair with his hand. He nodded, in agreement or consideration she couldn't tell. He exhaled loudly, as if deflating. The nervous way he kept brushing back his hair, his slouch, the unfortunate texture of his skin was so pathetic she wanted to wrap her arms around him, if only he weren't so repulsive as well.

"Hey," he said suddenly. "You ought to meet everyone. There's one guy says he can't wait to meet you. I mean he about split a gut waiting to meet you. I got to introduce you to him."

"You wouldn't mean a large redhead, would you?"

"You met him?" Manley said, disappointed.

"No, no," said Porkpie, pulling at the washboard tuck on her dress. "I think I saw you two on the way over. How did you beat me here? You were walking."

Manley's eyes followed her hands to her dress, as if in assistance. "Pirate taxi," said Manley. He winked. "The cars aren't marked. You just gotta have a feel for who's driving to make a few extra ringgit. We flagged one down."

"Good for you!" said Porkpie. "You have a feel for the country. You know, I don't think I really ever understood the Philippines all that well. All those University of the Philippines kids plotting revolution in Shakey's Pizza parlors: Americans out, but take me with you. My Tagalog is just passable and my Spanish always started people laughing, so I did most of my talking in English. Of course, that was a bit unfair because I knew the ten-dollar words and they were stuck with the dollar words. But that's the attraction of teaching English overseas, isn't it? You always come off smarter, even if you're really not."

"Hey," said Manley. He took another swig of beer. "Teaching's not easy."

"No, of course not," said Porkpie. "That really isn't what I meant. I was just saying there's a linguistic basis for our feelings of presumed superiority. At times what people do seems so much less important than how they say it. Wasn't that part of our trouble in Vietnam? The Vietnamese who spoke English we believed. We just ignored the other ones."

"The commies," said Manley. His eyes narrowed.

Porkpie paused. "Well, yes," she said. "The communists, I suppose, and whoever else. Though you're right that political affiliation is reflected in language. Oh, I'm sorry." She touched Manley lightly on the arm. He was shoving his hair back with his hand. He wouldn't look her in the eye. "Commies, communists. I don't care. You say it one way, I say it another. You see? That's what I mean. You're worried I might be overly sensitive to how you say things."

"Hey," Manley said, still averting his gaze. "*Commie's* slang, that's all. It's like casual speech. I don't know what you're apologizing about."

"Oh, you're right. I just want to make sure you didn't think I was mocking you. I'm not. I'm just tired."

"Hey," he said. "I don't think that. I don't even know why you're saying that. Are you mocking me? I don't think you're mocking me. You're not mocking me. I don't even know why you're saying it."

She was quiet. He started taking big swigs, nearly going cross-eyed watching the bottle come to his lips.

"Hey," he said. He looked at her now. His voice took on a severe tone. "You go a few miles out in the *ulu*, you know you're not in Kansas anymore. *Ulu's* 'jungle.' No one speaks English out there. This ain't no Philippines."

Touchy, this Manley! Touchy and ludicrous, especially given that he spoke under the awning of such a magnificent house. Thus far Malaysia had nothing of the poverty she had seen in the Philippines, in rural Luzon. There, the women wore dresses sewn from burlap sacks. You could see the worms in the open latrines; her students said their grandparents had them bend over sometimes so they could scrape their behinds with spoons to draw out infestations.

Lyle had been like that, like Manley. She should have seen the signs. A neatly trimmed beard, a wardrobe of lumberjack shirts. Gave money to relief funds, but wouldn't shell out for a movie on the weekend. Wouldn't complain about her friends, but never opened his mouth around them. Wanted blow jobs in the car, but couldn't stand to have his penis touch the steering wheel. Said hurtful things, then claimed he was just joking, or just denied saying them. All that passive aggressiveness. What could one do with such men?

"Yes," said Porkpie. "I imagine 'Please pass my plate of pumpkin pie' stops at the city limits." She smiled.

Manley, to her surprise, simply nodded. His attention turned again to his beer, which he was gulping in enormous swigs. It was a celebration, she thought: this Manley thought she was *agreeing* with him. She began giggling. He was completely unconscious, he really was.

They stepped onto the walkway, and Manley bounded up the stairs to open the door. The sounds from inside tinkled in Porkpie's ears like tiny glass bells. The light made everyone's hair shine. All these people. They all seemed to have their mouths open at once, laughing or putting food and drink up to their faces. On the small table in the breezeway was a giant bowl filled to overflowing with curry puffs. And now standing in front of her was a smooth-faced Malay in a waiter's outfit, white shirt and bow tie. He held a tray over his head. He had something behind his back. He smiled hugely. He brought his arm out from hiding and thrust a big bottle of Anchor beer into her hand.

"Hi-yo!" the waiter said, shouting over the music. "I am Yusof. Welcome you. Very hot tonight. Oh so sticky. Welcome you."

Reuben sat drinking beer in a lawn chair out back, scouting the house for enemies. The count was at six confirmeds, various uncommitteds, and two allies, Manley and Yusof the waiter. Off to the right, by the utility shed, an old Malay man was fanning strips of skewered meat over a burning oil drum. The man was singing, accompanied in the choruses by a young boy who arranged the finished skewers into a pyramid shape on a silver tray. That singing. How could he hit on a course of action with all that racket?

He reached under the chair for another bottle, clinking his empty against his small cache of cold ones, which he had carried out in a box provided by Yusof. He opened one with his belt buckle, drank, then held the bottle up and squinted over it, as if lining up targets in a gun sight. The sliding glass patio door provided a partial view of three rooms, plus the hallway. There were assholes everywhere. Whooping laughter escaped the house when someone slid open the patio door to get a fresh meat skewer.

Reuben leaned forward, sensing commotion in the sitting room. There, entering from the hallway, was Doctor Johansson and his wife, Sharon. Everyone rushed over to them, slapping the doctor's shoulders like they hadn't seem him for years. The doctor had that washcloth look on his face, and his little soap bar tongue was sliding in and out. Something was upsetting him. Perhaps Manley could find out what it was. Manley was now on reconnaissance inside, charged with locating Porkpie. When he returned, he would have to be sent back to eavesdrop on the doctor.

Reuben balled his hands into fists and pressed them against the sides of his head. That singing. He couldn't think straight. Porkpie to

Bidong! He kept picturing her name on the camp pass, the arrogant, drop-dead loops of her signature on the forms.

Action was called for, but the choice of action was still elusive. Most likely it was too late to change the course of events. The wheels were already in motion. But he couldn't just sit there like a two-hundred-and-forty-pound rock. What could he do? Why was clarity suddenly so difficult? Back in the Peace Corps, there had been clarity in everything. Even, he thought, even in a good night's sleep. He rolled the bottle across his forehead and took another long swig. Nowadays a good night's sleep was like being unconscious. Back in the Peace Corps a good night's sleep meant the night was over and the day was about to begin. March through the Kelantanese swamps, stink up the air with a mosquito fogger, throw a few pamphlets on hygiene around, then do whatever the hell you wanted. The swamp swallowed up your footsteps, the mosquitoes returned, and the pamphlets got taken to the outhouse for wiping. You were on your own, you and miles of jungle. The sun went down, the moon came out, then the sun came up again. Clarity.

He tapped the bottle against the metal rim of the lawn chair. For a brief moment, he thought about throwing the bottle and seeing where it landed. There was that time back in the Peace Corps—was it in 1974? '75? Who knew?—there was that time he threw a bottle at a feeding water buffalo, just to see what would happen. The bottle hit the animal in the head. It collapsed. The Malays laughed. The Chinese laughed. The Indians laughed. He laughed. *Ta'apa*, they all said. *Ta'apa* meant a lot of things. It meant don't worry. It meant screw-ups are the way of the world, so don't get riled. It meant after you did something, you couldn't affect the consequences, so just sit back. That was the meaning he liked best. Just do something and sit back to see what happens. Throw the bottle and see where it hits. Once the bottle left your hands, you were as much a bystander as anyone else. Either the buffalo would get hit, or it wouldn't. Either it would get up, or it wouldn't. You made something happen, then it finished happening, then something else happened. In the end, the sun would still beat down and the rice would still be in your bowl and the swamp muck would still be on your shoes. That was clarity. A wonderful clarity. First rate.

But here he was drinking beer in a lawn chair, scouting the house for enemies and worrying about the doctor and wishing ill on a woman he had never met. There was nothing happening. Make something happen. First check out the terrain. Then act on your instincts, then . . . Nothing came. Three beers into the evening, and all he knew was that the Malaysians were few and far between. You would have thought the doctor might have invited more Malaysians. It was, after all, their country. Political disagreements be damned. He looked again. There was one. Siew Hon Lee, Our Lady of the Sweet and Sour, Mostly Sour, stood behind a solid wall of white people, on her tippy-toes, apparently trying to catch the doctor's eye. Her mouth was open, and she was waving around her silk fan. He imagined the garlicky smell of her breath, the feeling he got that she was always just arriving from a banquet. What was she saying? Everyone was talking at once. They didn't seem to be speaking any language at all, just buzzing their vocal cords, the way deaf-mutes might if suddenly possessed of hearing and speech. All their yaps were going.

One night back in the Peace Corps, he'd been walking on a jungle trail, the stars invisible, sky thatched with palm and branches. He was standing stock still, drinking water from a canteen. Something shrieked. He'd wanted to see what. He'd wanted the pieces put together, right in front of him. If the puzzle wasn't put together, your mind put it together on its own. All the branches started swaying, and the night seemed to flicker, and then you started seeing wavering, airy things, there a second, then gone. When your mind put the puzzle together on its own, the puzzle gave you the willies.

Here came Yusof the waiter, regal in his white shirt and bow tie. He was bearing a tray of gelatinous cakes. He was smiling. The cakes wiggled in the tray. For a moment, Reuben imagined them chattering.

"Yusof," said Reuben. He spoke in Malay. "Where are all the Malaysians?"

"Only Allah knows," said Yusof, in Malay. "All I see are white people. White people everywhere, even in the kitchen. I've tried for half an hour to get someone to take a Malaysian delicacy, but their stomachs are all too timid. I know you'll take one. Here."

Reuben stuffed one into his mouth. "Did you see any new white women in there?" he said. He took another cake and ate it. "I'm looking for one with straight brown hair. Wide mouth, like a Kelantanese kite. She might be with Manley."

"He came in with a woman I haven't seen before," said Yusof, speaking rapidly. "He was sticking closer to her than flies to an ele-phant's ass. Don't tell me she's his girlfriend. He's too ugly."

"Ugly yourself," said Reuben.

"Of course it's known that whites are ugly," said Yusof, speaking even more rapidly. "Don't you people ever take baths?"

Reuben drank. "Malays don't use soap," he said.

"Ah, very good," said Yusof. He snapped his fingers, indicating a quicker tempo. "You've got a baboon nose."

"You look like the son of a whore," said Reuben.

"You're covered in monkey hair," said Yusof.

"You're pig balls," said Reuben.

"Your parents raised you badly."

"Your parents are Chinese."

"Excellent!" said Yusof. He switched to Kelantanese dialect. "Your Malay is wonderful."

"I am honored," said Reuben, in Kelantanese.

Yusof smiled, offering another delicacy. Reuben ate. The exchange in Malay had been encouraging. Solidarity disguised as insult. A fine line, and a dangerous one. You couldn't walk it if you didn't know shit from shinola. You couldn't horse around like that if you weren't ready to show some backbone. He was already feeling better.

Reuben ate some more, then drained his bottle, and when he reached for another, Yusof excused himself and, holding his tray of gelatinous cakes high over his head, began walking toward the utility shed. Reuben popped the cap with his belt buckle. "Here's looking at you," he said in English, raising the bottle to Yusof's retreating form. Yusof continued walking, mumbling something in response, then crossed the doctor's miniature Zen rock garden to talk with the Malay man basting meat over the oil drum. The boy at the man's side started thrusting the tray of skewers at Yusof. Yusof refused it. How, Yusof asked, speaking Malay, could he be expected to carry two full trays in-side? The cakes were hard enough to balance as it was. The man bast-ing meat said he didn't want his son going into the house. And what's wrong with the house? asked Yusof. The *orang putehs*, the man said: the white people; he didn't want his boy exposed to all those white people. Yusof said no one would eat the boy. They're dirty, the man said, slap-ping his heart: in here. Dirty. Yusof shook his head. He laughed. He said the white people would only eat the boy if they didn't have enough meat, and if someone didn't carry the tray in soon they were going to get awfully hungry. The boy burst into tears.

Reuben leaped from his lawn chair. The bottle in his hand dropped to the grass. "Yusof," he shouted in Malay. "I'll carry the tray." He walked. He felt light, his head suddenly clear. At Reuben's approach, the boy put the tray on the ground and curled his fingers around one of his father's belt loops. Reuben smiled, wobbly with beer, attempting a benign look. The boy hid behind his father. His chin was quivering.

So something's going to happen, Reuben thought. I'm going to walk up to the house and go through the glass door and carry the tray inside. Something will happen. Manley's there. Porkpie. The doctor, Siew Hon Lee. Oh yeah. Come on.

He held the meat tray in front of him and followed Yusof up the grass slope to the sliding glass door. The patio table was ringed with empties and mounds of yellow rice. Couples strolled past, drinking and tittering. On the patio he nodded to Jack Kelly and Sheila Johnson. They nodded back. He walked to the sliding glass door. "Drunk," he heard Sheila whisper. Through the glass he heard the Stones. In front of a bookcase a bald man in a tie was staring into his tumbler, shaking his head. A woman in a batik skirt was squatting by the coffee table, slapping her hand on the teak surface, in time with the music. A man whose name he'd forgotten, an education specialist stationed in Kuala Lumpur, was wagging his finger at someone, his eyes closed. Someone dropped a napkin.

He watched Yusof slide open the glass door with his foot. The talking and laughing spilled out over him and down the grassy slope and into the air, all the way back to the oil drum, where the Malay boy suddenly began crying again.

Someone turned up the volume on *Goat's Head Soup* and everyone just began talking louder. In the living room the UN Development Programs contingent was milling around holding blue-embroidered napkins wrapped around long toothpicks, searching out the Chinese dim sum rumored to have been brought in from the table on the patio. The track lighting had been dimmed, so when they looked at the food on the plates and bowls, they had to stoop to see if they wanted it in their mouths. They were taking up too much room. "Coming through," said

Reuben, burdened with the tray. "Straighten up. Straighten up." But no one straightened up. No one moved. People were crowding in from the hallway.

A dance circle broke out behind him. An elbow was in his back. In front of him were two little white lawyers from the office, Francine from Minneapolis and Ed from Nevada. Francine was jiggling, making little dance motions with her head. "You got the hot legs?" she was shouting in Ed's ear. "You got the hot legs?" Ed was laughing and nodding his head, squeezing against the bookshelf to avoid being struck by Reuben's meat tray. There was no room to maneuver. Yusof hadn't waited. The waiter had held his tray of cakes high overhead and slipped through the UNDP contingent just before they began spreading out looking for dim sum. The damn meat tray. It was like a porch. With all these bodies to get past, Reuben had no choice but to edge along the wall, and now he was backed up against an Indian vase, bougainvillea tickling his neck. New guests walked through the living room, wearing funny T-shirts and waving everyone over to take a look at their chests. There was a bottleneck. He couldn't move. Not with the tray. The pyramid of skewers had collapsed. He cursed the meat and the tray.

"Hey," he said. He nudged Ed from Nevada on the shoulder with his tray. "Hold this, Ed."

"He doesn't *want* to hold it, Reuben," said Francine from Minneapolis.

"I'll drop it," said Reuben. "Hold it or I'll drop it."

"Don't drop it," said Ed.

Francine cupped her hands into a megaphone. "He doesn't want to hold it," she shouted.

"I'll drop it, Ed," said Reuben.

"Don't," said Ed. "Jesus."

"Hold it," said Reuben. "I gotta move. I can't move with this tray."

"*You* hold it," said Francine, slapping Reuben's leg. "It's your damn tray."

"Here it goes," said Reuben.

"Give it," said Ed, angrily. He curled his fingers around the handles.

Free, thought Reuben, relieving himself of his burden. He was pushing, laying his hands on people's shoulders and applying pressure. He spotted another enemy coming through the door. "Make a hole," he said, to no one in particular. He pushed. People moved. He felt his heart beating. He felt his face set itself into a scowl. He was ready. He was walking inside the house, towering over all these heads, looking, his mind sharp, hands clenching and unclenching, shoving. There was Manley, squatting in the doctor's study, surrounded by resettlement officers stationed down in Kuala Lumpur. Manley was fishing out beers from the ice tub. "There you go," Manley said, handing one up. "*Baby,* this water's cold. Man."

Reuben pushed his way closer. Manley had his eyes closed. He was swishing his hand around the ice tub.

"Sure it's cold," one of the men said. "You're holding your hand in too long." He squatted at the other side of the tub.

Reuben was almost there. He saw Manley open his eyes. "You want beer or don't you?" Manley said to the man. He swished his fingers around the water some more.

"You don't have to hold your hand in so long."

"Hey, you wanna do this?" said Manley.

"I can get it myself."

"Look, just hold your horses and I'll get you a beer. You want beer?"

"I want a beer," said the man. "Just don't hold your hand in so long."

"Just hold your horses, huh? I'm getting you beer. You want beer or not?"

"Manley," said Reuben. He stood over the two, hands on hips.

"Rube! Hey, hold your horses," said Manley. "I'm getting beer."

"He's holding his hand in too long," said the man, looking up.

"Manley," said Reuben again. "Where is she?" He kicked the tub.

"There," Manley said, lifting out a hand and shaking it. He pointed toward the kitchen.

So Reuben began pushing the other way. A woman said Malaysian police had refused to let a Vietnamese boat land on the beach near the town of Mersing. A man said the Malay fishermen hated the Vietnamese because their bodies contaminated the fish. No one was buying fish anymore, he said. Too many Vietnamese were drowning in Malaysian waters. All those bodies. They bloated so much they looked like horses. They washed onto shore with seaweed wrapped around their wrists and ankles. The police rifled their pockets. They stuck their hands down the girls' brassieres. He'd heard a story, an absolutely horrible story, he didn't know if it was true, where the police dragged the corpse of this young girl into a shed—

"Shut up," Reuben said. "No more. Shut up." He clapped a hand over the man's mouth.

People stared. Reuben pushed some more. Damn them. Damn all their talk. He pushed so hard he felt a hand push back. He heard complaining voices behind him. He pushed past Colonel Mansoor, who was licking his finger and rubbing it on a glass picture frame. He pushed past Siew Hon Lee. She almost fell. She struck at him with her fan.

He recognized Porkpie immediately. She had on a pink sundress. French resettlement interviewers were dancing by the stove, stomping their feet to the music and singing along in French. Porkpie stood by a wood counter eating a carrot stick, putting her left foot in and right foot out, doing the hokey-pokey. There was a line of snack bowls on the counter, and one hand hovered over it, as if in indecision. It was too much to bear. Going to Bidong! This dance, for shit's sake. Reuben walked over and shouted over the music.

"You Porkpie?"

She nodded, chewing. She seemed to be focusing on a distant point.

"You got a bad case of white girl's disease," he said.

She continued dancing, shaking her right foot all about. Then she looked at him sternly. "Put some *pants* on that comment, will you?" she shouted.

"This is the Stones," he said. "This isn't grade school."

"Put some pants on it," she repeated. "If you want to talk to me, put some pants on it."

"I said this isn't grade school."

She stopped. She cupped her hand and shouted up to him. "Are you actually commenting on my dancing?"

"Let's start there," Reuben said, frowning.

"All this Old Testament fury over my dancing?"

"I got my eyes open and this is what I see."

"All right, then," she said. "Of course it's the Stones, and the last time I was in grade school, white girl's disease got you a gold star. Now, if you must know, I was standing here looking at these bowls and thinking just how repulsive mayonnaise actually is. Are there gold stars for that? I don't think so. I was thinking of a little jingle I heard about may-onnaise and moving my feet to it. The Stones weren't playing a little jingle, were they? So there you go. I'll think what I think."

"You're going to Bidong, aren't you?"

"You know," she said, "I was going to introduce myself to you." She lashed his arm with the carrot strip, then dropped the vegetable on the floor. "You're Manley's friend. I saw you on the way over. But I can't say I care very much for your tone. So if you don't mind I think I'm going to end this conversation by saying I appreciate your interest, but until you can control your bile I'm going to have to consider you a hostile species."

Reuben stared, registering what he had heard. "Do you know shit from shinola or not?" he said.

"Oh, that's *wonderful*," she said. "Shit from shinola! You could be a poster child for *Guns & Ammo*. Where did you learn to speak like that?"

The resettlement interviewers had stopped dancing, and Reuben felt their eyes on his back. The Stones album ended. There was murmuring outside. The kitchen, he noticed, had a ceiling fan. Someone had tied a beer bottle to one of the blades, and it was twirling around and around. He needed a moment to think. She was smiling at him, not unkindly, her eyes focused firmly on his.

"You come in here . . ." he said, lowering his voice. He stopped to fold his arms, slapping his hands against his skin. "Look, you come in here, you start dancing like that, and you're going to Bidong. You think you're ready for Bidong? Just like that?"

The music started again. It was a Chinese group, singing a rock version of "Oh Susannah." Everyone was groaning again in the living room, shouting for a different record.

"I hate these do-nothing bands, don't you?" she said.

The volume went up. She leaned close and talked in a voice Reuben could barely hear.

She said, "You're so ugly, you're magnificent."

And then Francine from Minneapolis walked in, holding onto Siew Hon Lee's shoulder. "Oh my goodness," said Siew Hon Lee, folding her fan into a stick. "Yes, Porkpie. Hello. I am Siew Hon Lee, Malaysian Red Crescent Society. Yes, come into the living room."

"Please come," said Francine. She placed a hand on Porkpie's shoulder. She looked at Reuben hard. "Away from here. Not here. How about the living room."

"Girl talk," said Siew Hon Lee. "Just us."

"Us," said Francine.

"Girl talk!" said Porkpie. "Do you mind?" she said, turning to Reuben.

Siew Hon Lee looked up at Reuben in warning. Francine frowned. He shook his head. Together, the two women ushered Porkpie out of the kitchen, walking quickly, heels clacking on the linoleum.

It was very complicated. Had she meant he was physically disgusting? Abnormally so? But the way she said "magnificent": it seemed an expression of delight. He had felt the heat from her body, she was standing so close. She had smiled. Was it a compliment? Or maybe she was just so whacked out she didn't know what the hell she was saying.

"Hey," said Manley, whispering. "What are you doing? You're getting everyone mad. What's the idea?"

Yusof sidled over, carrying an armload of empties. He spoke in Malay. "Reuben," he said, "Siew Hon Lee is talking to her. Siew Hon Lee says you're giving the wrong impression. She says you're a mistake."

"What?" said Manley. "Speak English."

"Allah-*mak*!" said Yusof. "Why you cannot speak Malay?"

The three men stood by the service entrance to the kitchen. The Dumpster was already full of crushed paper plates and beer bottles, and a flip-flop with something smelly on it lay in an empty food bowl. Off in the distance, beyond a line of trees, Bungaraya Road still roared with life, the motorcycles racing at full throttle, beeping their horns. There was no breeze. The heat floated in the air, settling into their clothes. The men were sweating, breathing through their mouths.

"I don't care what she says," growled Reuben. "You got a smoke, Yusof?"

Yusof dumped the empties and pulled a cigarette out of his shirt pocket.

"Are you serious?" said Manley. "What do you mean, you don't care? How you getting to Bidong, huh?"

Yusof lit Reuben's cigarette. Reuben smoked. Oh, he had let things out of the box, all right. He sure as hell had. If Siew Hon Lee hated him before, what was she going to think now? And Johansson . . . He didn't want to think about it. What would a jungle junkie do?

What *would* a jungle junkie do?

What would he do?

"Hey, Big Bro," said Manley. "The Frog fags told me Porkpie held her own." He squatted down and threw a pebble into the sloping grass. "She's got the mouth, don't she?"

"Shut up, Manley," said Reuben. "It's not over. The box is open, that's all."

"What's that supposed to mean?" said Manley.

"*Diam!*" said Yusof. "Be quiet."

"That's right," said Reuben. "*Diam* for a second." He smoked some more. Yusof patted him on the shoulder and opened the door. Music drifted out, while Yusof wiped his feet on a straw mat. It was the Stones again. "Hi-yo," Yusof sighed, then stepped inside and closed the door.

Manley pitched pebbles into the grass and Reuben smoked, wiping the dewy evening air from his face. The cigarette burned bright, crackling in the paper. Nothing moved. The grass was dark as tar.

Just breathe, thought Reuben. He coughed, hacking fluid into the grass. His throat was closing.

"Asthma OK?" asked Manley.

"What do you do," said Reuben, straining to talk, "when you're in the bush and you're on this trail with nothing around and it's real dark, you can't see a damn thing, and you kick at something real hard and then all hell breaks loose? You start hearing monkeys and the branches are breaking and something's on your tail. What do you do, Manley?"

"Don't kick nothing in the first place," said Manley. He straightened and started tucking in his shirt.

"I'm serious. What do you do?"

"Hey, Peace Corps was then. This is now. Then ain't now. This is the UN. Different ball game."

"I'll tell you what you do," said Reuben. He hacked again onto the grass. His breath grew shallow. "You keep on going straight down the trail, that's what. You got no place else to go."

He threw his cigarette to the ground and opened the door. He heard the Stones, and he stepped back inside. Manley was right behind him, tucking in his shirt, and closed the door hard.

5

According to Francine, Reuben Gill, the self-proclaimed Biggest White Man in Kuala Trengganu and the biggest royal pain in the Southern Hemisphere, did not reflect the attitudes of anyone else in Kuala Trengganu. Siew Hon Lee had nodded in agreement so vigorously you would have thought someone was tweaking the spring in her neck. It was obvious there was a long history of grudge-holding among these people, and she for one was not about to be railroaded into an opinion not her own. Reuben Gill: bastard or contrarian? Was such a question really so simple?

Porkpie leaned back in the couch, Francine to her right, Siew Hon Lee to her left. A curry puff on a napkin lay balanced on her knees.

"And I'll tell you something else," said Francine, crossing her legs. She had big eyes and dense lashes, and she kept tilting her head down and tucking her tiny chin into her neck. In the dim light she reminded Porkpie of one of those aliens that UFO abductees kept insisting were creeping through their windows. "He goes to this horrible bar-slash-hotel called Cowboy Lim's," said Francine, "and then sometimes, later, he goes to this even more horrible place called the Bamboo Club. There's where he gets really nasty. He puts his big, grubby paws all over the hostesses. Did you know they have slits in their skirts so the scum can get their hands on them quicker?"

"Wah!" said Siew Hon Lee, and Porkpie turned to listen. "Do you know what is prostitution, Porkpie? We having it here even in Malaysia, and Mr. Reuben Gill has waved from the UN van to women known to be disgraceful. I am seeing this myself. On Bungaraya Road he has leaned out the window of the van and said such words that make me turn red."

"What words?" said Francine.

"Last month the van was at full stop outside the MRCS office. Do you know what is MRCS? Malaysian Red Crescent Society, yes? UN and MRCS, working together, yes? As I say, a woman of disgrace, Malay, I think—she was not Chinese-*lah*—knocked on his window. He rolled it down, and do you know what? Here is what he said. He said, 'How now, brown cow?'"

"Oh God," said Francine.

Porkpie laughed. "Oh, but it's like *music*. It . . . well, it describes and evokes at the same time," she said. "Form and function, all in one greeting. It's such a self-conscious phrase. It's so obscene it's not obscene."

"Please explain," said Siew Hon Lee.

"Yes," said Francine.

"Oh, you know," said Porkpie. "No one, I don't care who, commits an obscenity if they're conscious of it as an obscenity. Hitler, Pol Pot, Idi Amin. I don't care who . . . They all fooled themselves into thinking they were doing something noble. They fooled themselves because they were fundamentally unconscious. Combine that with power, and there you have obscenity. That's obscenity, right there. Power plus unconsciousness equals obscenity. It's like Einstein's formula. You could probably put it on a graph."

Siew Hon Lee snapped her fingers at someone across the room, trying to get the person's attention. Porkpie looked. All these people, all strangers. Out the sliding glass door, past the patio table, a man and boy were fanning an orange ball of flame hovering at the top of an oil drum.

"Anyway," Porkpie said, "look at 'How now, brown cow?' It's direct and obnoxious, but it's so aware of itself as direct and obnoxious it can't be obscene. I mean it seems such a conscious thing to say. I hear irony in it. Wit, too. Now I don't mean to be talking so long, but it's the combination of wit and irony that undercuts unsavoriness. Irony alone is just a way of being spiteful. Wit alone is just evasion. But put them together, and you've got something . . . I don't know, something beautiful."

She looked at her two companions. Siew Hon Lee was waving someone over. Francine was blinking.

"Oh, I'm losing my point, aren't I?" Porkpie said. "I do that when I'm tired."

"No, no," said Francine. "Please, go on."

"All right. My point," said Porkpie.

"Yes, I'm all ears," said Francine, leaning closer.

"Ears-*lah*," said Siew Hon Lee, bending one lobe forward with the handle of her fan.

"Well," said Porkpie. "I'll bet the Malay woman smiled, didn't she? I'll bet when he stuck his head out the window and said it, she didn't feel so horrible about her life. Because there's nothing funny about what she endures every night, but his statement made it funny without denying its horror. You might even say that by being obnoxious, he helped her bear her shame. He was bringing it out in the open and shearing off its claws. They were laughing in its face."

"Until nightfall anyway," said Francine, pointing her finger. "Until he crawled into the Bamboo Club."

"Well, yes," said Porkpie. "Presumably, they're both caught in something of a cycle."

"Your opinions are very generous," said Francine.

"I think *very* generous, yes?" said Siew Hon Lee.

"I don't think you could consider Reuben Gill a saint," said Francine.

"I don't know him," said Porkpie. "But I can say this. He had the power position in the van. He could have said anything. He could have pretended she was just a friend, and that would have embarrassed her. It sounds to me as though he acted well. I didn't say he was a saint, just that he's not unconscious."

"Well, he's definitely not a saint," said Francine.

"Oh, my goodness," said Siew Hon Lee. She waved again at whoever it was she wanted to come over. "The way he talked to you in the kitchen."

"Yes," said Porkpie. "He was rude. But he wasn't unconscious."

"He was *very* rude," said Francine.

"Very," said Siew Hon Lee.

"But not unconscious," said Porkpie. "It wasn't unconscious rudeness."

"*Very* rude," said Francine.

"Such a rude man," said Siew Hon Lee.

Porkpie nodded. All this proselytizing: it was so tribal. But that was what tribal peoples did with strangers, and that was what Siew Hon Lee and Francine were doing to her now. The Peace Corps had been tribal, and now it was becoming clear that refugee workers were as well. If tribal peoples didn't reject you outright, they tried to absorb you. Chitchat was not chitchat, questions were not questions, stories were not stories. Their worlds were so small and narrowly defined, so threatened by incursion, so fragile, they viewed strangers as either potential converts or enemies.

Sandwiched between Francine and Siew Hon Lee, Porkpie felt trapped. Her fingers trembled when she lifted them toward her curry puff, so she dropped her hand back in her lap. Of course she wanted these refugee workers to like her. Being alone in this new country, exhausted and friendless: it was unimaginable. But she wanted to be honest as well, and she honestly couldn't say whether this Reuben Gill was as monstrous as she was hearing. She had just met the man, for God's sake.

Siew Hon Lee stirred on the couch and began snapping her fingers again, motioning to a person in the hallway. Porkpie followed the woman's gaze. She saw a tall Indian man dressed completely in white. He was coming their way. His hair was slicked back, and he was holding two unopened bottles of Anchor beer, one in each hand. A bottle opener was tied loosely around his neck and dangled over his stomach.

"Gunand," Siew Hon Lee said. She waved him over.

"What are you doing?" she said. "Oh, excuse me. Porkpie, this is Gunand . . . eh? What is your last name? He is one of our Red Crescent drivers."

The man mumbled something Porkpie couldn't hear.

"Gunand," said Siew Hon Lee. "Why are you serving drinks? People can be getting their own beer."

"Is not a problem," said the man. "So many people here. Yusof cannot do everything himself."

"This is a *party*," she said. "You are not working for Doctor Johansson. A *party*. Do you know what is a party?"

"Yes. So wonderful," he said. He put down one of his unopened beers and pulled out a cheese cracker from one of the bowls on the table. His movements were jerky and uncertain. He nibbled the cheese cracker with unnatural bliss. He appeared to be demonstrating just how wonderful the party was.

"Gunand," said Siew Hon Lee, fanning herself. She leaned forward and whispered something into his ear.

"Oh, but I do not mind to help out," he said.

"You are not a *servant* here," said Siew Hon Lee.

The driver smiled. "I am only taking these bottles to outside."

Siew Hon Lee turned to Porkpie. "Do you know Malaysia has been under British domination for so long," she said. Gunand suddenly straightened, clutching his two unopened bottles, and sidled his way through a circle of people examining a coffee-table book.

"Oh my goodness," said Siew Hon Lee, turning again toward Gunand. She fanned furiously, reaching out with her other hand as if to grab him. But he was far across the room, and now he slid open the glass door to the patio and stepped out. She had a peculiar expression on her face when she turned back to Porkpie: eyes half open, features set in such neutrality Porkpie imagined for a moment the woman had completely deserted her body. "Excuse me, please," she said suddenly. She rose, blinking. "There is the doctor. I must speak to the doctor." Then she, too, was gone.

"Don't worry about her," said Francine, leaning forward confidentially. "Internal affairs."

Porkpie looked at her questioningly.

"She's miffed about something," said Francine. "Malaysians curl up when they're angry. Don't worry, it's not you."

"Why would I think . . . ," said Porkpie, but she didn't complete her thought because of the scene unfolding in front of her. Siew Hon Lee walked up to the doctor from behind and tapped him on the shoulder with her fan. She began talking, loud enough for them to hear occasional words. The doctor was nodding. He seemed ready to cry. He was steepling his hands by his chin, then putting them down, then steepling again. Porkpie watched his mouth move. *I am so sorry,* he was saying. He seemed to be repeating it.

"I forgot to say they explode sometimes," Francine whispered.

Siew Hon Lee was saying something about name tags. *Did the doctor wish for Malaysians to wear name tags.* That's what Siew Hon Lee was saying. The doctor had his eyes closed. He was rocking on his heels. He hung his head.

Francine nudged Porkpie. "I'll bet you wish someone would do that to Reuben Gill, don't you?" she said.

Porkpie looked at her. Francine was smiling sympathetically, tucking her chin to her neck, eyes roaming. Porkpie understood the question to be a real question. Francine was waiting for an answer. She wanted to know if she had a convert. She wanted to hear that Reuben Gill was horrid.

"I said I'll bet you wish someone would do a Siew Hon Lee number on Reuben, don't you?" Francine said.

Porkpie turned to face Francine. One had to be careful with tribal peoples. They were astounding proselytizers and ferocious enemies. There was no need to antagonize. But she was thinking about Reuben Gill's face, screwed up in pain and outrage in the kitchen. She was thinking about Siew Hon Lee's snapping fan, about how glad she was that it was not his face wincing before it.

She shrugged.

Francine patted her lightly on the shoulder. "That's OK," she whispered. "Don't worry. We'll keep him away from you."

If there was one thing worse than being thought ill of, it was being thought so well of that people couldn't imagine thinking ill of you. You always wanted the option of behaving badly, but that required an audience who assumed that behaving badly was in your repertoire. Else, you just appeared hysterical. It was clear that no one could imagine thinking ill of her. Yes, she had shrugged in answer to Francine's question. Was that reason to assume she was actually *afraid* of Reuben Gill, but too worried about appearing weak to say so?

Apparently.

The doctor and his wife, Sharon, had for the past half hour been her constant companions. She suspected conspiracy. Francine had rushed over to the doctor and Sharon and whispered something, and then the doctor and Sharon had rushed over to her with smiles to break the bank and made themselves her personal bookends. They wouldn't leave. Their eyes roamed the perimeter, and they shuttled people over in small groups to stick out their hands and shake.

Francine and Ed from Nevada kept coming over and smiling and asking how things were going. Fine, the doctor said each time, wrapping his arm around Porkpie's shoulder: our newcomer's doing fine. She felt ridiculous. She didn't need protection. On the other hand, the arm that kept circling around her shoulder belonged to Doctor Johansson, head of UN operations in Kuala Trengganu and her boss, and all the people he was introducing her to were terribly important to Bidong operations, or so she was told. The doctor was saying wonderful things about her: how she had taken the bull by the horns and bussed up from Singapore all night and found her way to the Task Force office with no one there to meet her. Why, she was just the type of teacher Bidong needed. And she was goddamn *competent,* something of an expert on the use of stick figure drawings in the classroom. Goddamn. A wonderful addition to Bidong.

"Whoa, wagon train," said the doctor, stopping at the entrance of his study. "Wagons back. Let's go."

Porkpie peered around him and saw Reuben Gill in the study, standing with a group of men hanging around the beer tub. Manley was there, too, in the corner, sitting in an overstuffed chair and eating from a bowl of popcorn. Reuben Gill was peeling the label off his bottle. At his feet was a pile of label peelings. He saw her and nodded. His face was slack, and he seemed to be breathing through his mouth. The little bags of skin under his eyes were full and oily, and his face was shiny. He was perspiring hugely.

"Really, Doctor Johansson," said Porkpie. "There's no need."

"Well, we don't want you to get the wrong impression," said the doctor, moving the group back up the hallway. He had his arm wrapped around Sharon. "We've got to think of our reputation." He laughed. "What if you went to Bidong and told everyone that the staff here is a bunch of louts? We can't have *that,* now can we?"

"Don't worry about louts," said Sharon, smiling. "We're the lout whackers."

Reuben Gill had already made several forays into the living room, where Porkpie and the Johanssons had stood in small circles, talking to various contingents. He had stormed around, his huge arms wrapped around himself, a puzzled look on his face. The doctor kept looking at him. Once, Reuben Gill had come forward, rushing up quickly, his eyes darting from person to person, and then he simply stopped. His nostrils flared, his jaw snapped shut like a trapdoor, and then he just stood with his hands in his pockets for a while, that puzzled look again coming over his face, and turned around and headed back toward the doctor's study. A few minutes later, Manley had come forward in an ambassadorial role. He attached himself to the outside of whatever group it was she was talking to, then sidled up and told her he had a message from Reuben. The message was a bit jumbly. *I hope you break your neck on Bidong. No hard feelings.*

"Lovely," she said. She told Manley to say that the sentiment was perfectly understandable.

It was almost eleven when everyone suddenly rushed the front door or pressed themselves against the window in the living room. A busload of new Peace Corps trainees pulled up, driven personally by Flip Sherman, the Peace Corps country director. And behind the busload of Peace Corps trainees was an MRCS van containing, Flip Sherman said, three Vietnamese refugees from Bidong. The van got lost on the way up, and Flip Sherman had led the way.

Everyone started whooping.

"I haven't even *seen* a refugee," said Francine. "All I get is paperwork."

"Jesus, oh Jesus," said Ed. "Refugees!"

The doctor said the refugees were a special surprise. He explained how earlier in the week he had made arrangements with Task Force on Bidong to allow a small group of Vietnamese to ride the camp supply boat in to town. He had a small presentation planned, nothing extravagant, just a little booster to underscore the importance of the upcoming regional meeting.

The sound of applause interrupted. The doctor looked into the hallway and saw Flip Sherman at the head of a line of trainees. The men had fresh haircuts and long-sleeved batik shirts; the women wore long dresses and sensible shoes.

"Excuse my French," said the doctor, leaning over to Sharon. "But oh shit. Flip brought cherries with him."

Siew Hon Lee walked quickly into the room, clearing her throat, fan spread over her blouse. "A word, doctor," she said.

"Now I know what you're going to say," said the doctor. He reached out with his hand and placed it on her shoulder. "They were invited because the director's a friend of mine. He didn't tell me he was going to bring a busload of Peace Corps trainees with him."

"Oh, my goodness," she said. "Peace Corpse."

"Just for future reference," the doctor said, "they like to call themselves Peace *Corps*. The *ps* in *corps* is silent."

"Is not my language, doctor," she said. "I was very happy going to Chinese-medium school. What can you say in Cantonese?"

"Nothing," said the doctor. "You're right. I apologize."

"Wah!" she said. There was accusation in her voice. "Even Peace Corpse are invited. But they are not working with refugees, isn't it? They are working only with Malaysians, not Vietnamese. Only Malaysians and UN are working with Vietnamese." She snapped her fan shut and waved it in the doctor's face like an elongated finger. "Look, so many. Oh my goodness. Not even working with refugees. My goodness. Oh, my goodness."

"Siew Hon," said the doctor, rubbing his forehead. "I am *so* sorry. I really am. It was just an awful mix-up with the invitations. Really. I love Malaysia. I love Malaysians."

"We drove all the way from Pasir Mas just to see you," said Flip Sherman loudly, spotting the doctor. He waved his arm in the direction of the new volunteers fanning out into the living room and patio. "I was telling these guys this is the tropics, not the Tropicana. Oo-eee! It's sticky out there tonight. At the hotel, Charles from Bakersfield here told me it's hotter than this in August back home."

He looked around and found Charles behind him. "So I said, 'Charles, why don't you step *outside* the hotel and tell me that?' Isn't that right, Charles? Why don't you step *outside* the hotel and tell me that? Different story then, huh?"

Charles grinned sheepishly. "I just need some liquid now," he said. "It's humid."

"It's a steam bath, Charles," said Flip Sherman. "This here is what we like to call the Malaysian steam bath. Just don't go taking your clothes off. But I've got to tell you, frankly, I've never seen it so bad."

"Boy, it's bad," said Charles. "I can hardly breathe."

Flip Sherman laughed. "Just be thankful we don't have you guys rappel off cliffs anymore. That's what we did when *I* was a volunteer. We actually rappeled down cliffs." He made scudding motions with his hand. "Now we just repel each other." He laughed. "Oo-eee! We just repel each *other* now. Isn't that right, Charles?"

"Sharon," said the doctor. "You make the introductions, will you? I've got a presentation to do. Excuse me, Siew Hon. Flip. I've got to go."

"Under*stood*!" said Flip Sherman, slapping the doctor's arm. "So, Sharon," he said, eyeing Porkpie. "Who do we have here?"

Sharon was watching her husband weave through the crowd. She apparently didn't hear the question. Charles, who had been pulling his sticky batik shirt away from his skin, stepped in front of Flip Sherman. "You're with UNHCR, aren't you?" said Charles, catching Porkpie's eye. "Man. Working with refugees. What's that like? Like *M*A*S*H* on TV?"

"I wouldn't think so," said Porkpie. "I imagine it's not quite so self-delusional. You know, like when you're clerking in some awful summer job and all these boring people keep telling you how wacky they are. I imagine being cheek to jowl with the Vietnamese makes you feel somewhat less caught up in your own psychodrama. Or maybe more, I don't know."

"Refugees," said Charles. "Man. Like Mother Teresa, huh?"

"I wouldn't think so," said Porkpie. "I'm no one's mommy."

"So I noticed," said Flip Sherman, looking her up and down. "So, really, Sharon. Who do we have here?"

In the other room, the doctor was clapping his hands and telling everyone to move back so the guests of honor could make it through the hallway. Yusof put down his tray and flipped on all the lights. Someone took the record off. Then the Vietnamese, two women and a man, walked up the steps and entered the hallway, proceeding slowly, followed by a Malay man in an MRCS T-shirt. The Vietnamese seemed nervous. They grinned constantly, revealing horrible teeth; their movements were stiff and timid. All three were small-boned and thin as children. They shuffled in their flip-flops. The women had on plain white blouses and shiny black pants. One was young and pretty; her hair was pulled back into a bun, held with a green barrette. The other was enormously wrinkled, an older woman. She had bad teeth. Her lips trembled when she shook people's hands. The man, perhaps the older woman's husband, was buck-toothed. Porkpie saw immediately that he wore donated clothes: a billowing red and white lumberjack shirt and green work pants. He made friendly grunts, but he did not shake hands because he was holding a rough plywood box, outfitted with hinges and a small clasp lock.

The doctor shooed people away from the middle of the living room and began directing those closest to him to make more room by stacking the rattan chairs. Someone on the patio slid open the glass door so the small crowd outside could press closer. A woman got up on the patio table to see over the line of people in front and began nibbling at something wrapped in tinfoil.

Porkpie felt Flip Sherman's knuckles in her back, guiding her through to the living room. The good spots were already claimed. She couldn't see the Vietnamese for all the people. At her side were Ed and Francine. They were arguing with Manley.

"Hey," Manley was saying. "Just give them a snort."

Ed was whispering. He said it wasn't that simple. Alcohol was, after all, banned on Bidong. Of course he *wanted* to offer alcohol to the Vietnamese, it would only be gracious to do so, but what would the Malaysians in the room think? Might they not view an offer of alcohol as tacit disapproval of their countrymen's policies?

"Hey," said Manley. "A beer's not going to kill anyone."

"Please don't," said Ed.

"Please don't what?"

"Please don't turn this into some kind of mawkish argument. The hardy Bidong volunteer versus the insensitive white shirt. It's such a sham."

"Hey, what's the deal?" said Manley.

"You're waiting for me to say that you don't see the big picture, and I'm not going to say that. You want to turn this some kind of poor-but-proud people's *jihad* against the mincing bureaucracy of the Kuala Trengganu office. I don't appreciate it. Why don't you tell Siew Hon Lee or any of our other host country nationals that you think our guests should have alcohol?"

Manley began pushing his hair back. Then there was a pair of big hands on his shoulders, pushing past. It was Reuben Gill. He did not have a puzzled look on his face. His shirt was soaked in sweat, and Porkpie thought she heard him wheeze. "They get alcohol," Reuben said. He sounded angry.

Ed closed his eyes. "Why don't you tell Siew Hon Lee or any . . ."

"Siew Hon," said Reuben loudly. "The Viets get a snort. Siew Hon. Siew Hon."

Porkpie looked where he was talking. Siew Hon Lee was standing with Colonel Mansoor, fanning herself. She couldn't hear. But Gunand was nearby, holding a beer. Reuben spoke loudly to him in Malay, and the man began pushing his way toward the Vietnamese, tapping people on the shoulders with the bottle opener that dangled from his neck.

"At least we agree on something," said Porkpie. "Graciousness needs to extend beyond political considerations, don't you think?"

Reuben pursed his lips in contemplation and nodded. "You get my message?" he said. He put a napkin to his mouth and coughed noisily, moistly, into the paper.

She nodded. "You sound terrible," she said. She yawned. "I'm so tired."

"My sinuses," he said, tapping his nose. His breathing was labored. "So, back in the kitchen," he said. "Nothing personal."

"No. Apology is unnecessary."

Porkpie felt a hand on her arm, but it was small and soft. It belonged to Sharon. "Well, *look* who's here," said Sharon, peering over Porkpie's head at Reuben. "Look at this. Porkpie, I'm so sorry. We got separated. Flip, will you look at who's here? One of your former volunteers."

"Well, I'll be damned," said Flip Sherman. "Reuben Gill." He stuck out his hand, but then the doctor walked in front of them, rapping a fork against a glass and calling for quiet. He had his arm around the Vietnamese man holding the plywood box. The two women trailed behind, giggling, holding small glasses of beer. The middle of the living room had been cleared out; people were pressed against the walls, forming a circle. The doctor and his guests stepped into the circle.

"All right, people," said Flip Sherman, clapping his hands. "Let's quiet down. You heard the man."

That clapping, thought Porkpie: like a man summoning a genie.

She giggled. How the mind played tricks in the late hours! Her body was sluggish and cold. She put her hands to her cheeks and rubbed. The skin felt thin as a bubble. The hair on her hand was sticking out. Someone offered an arm; she was leaning against it.

The doctor motioned for his guests to form a small line in the middle of the circle, the man with the box in middle. The doctor, patting their arms, stood to the left. He grinned. The Vietnamese grinned. The circle of people grinned. Everyone was grinning so much, all Porkpie saw was teeth.

The doctor gave his speech.

Siew Hon Lee gave hers.

The head of the French delegation followed with a prepared statement.

Jack Kelly from UNDP said a few words.

They all said a party was an excellent way to kick off the upcoming regional meeting. The new year would soon be upon them, and with the new year changes were of course inevitable and, dare they say, not unproblematic. It was important to work as a team, they said, to share a common vision and goal. They said that it seemed only fitting that tonight's party be called a People Working with People Party, since all around them, all around the living room and in the hallway and on the patio, was the flesh and blood behind the letterheads, the faces behind the names, the minds behind the policies, the *people,* for crying out loud, who soldiered on in circumstances less than ideal and got the job done.

Everyone applauded.

How could she be so tired?

The applause grew louder. The noise hurt her ears. What she heard was falling lumber. She put her hands on top of her head and ducked. Had she fallen? No. She was standing. They were all still in a circle and the speakers stood in the middle, opening their mouths and talking. It was hard to see. People were in the way, shoulders and heads, and the air around them was hot and wet. Someone's arm was around her waist, holding her up.

Still the speakers talked on. Why were they still giving speeches? There was a war in the South China Sea, she heard, rising in the lacy tops of the waves. Why, there was a woman, a seamstress from Quang Tri, who had chased off a boat of pirates in the Gulf of Siam, holding nothing but a lightbulb that had been painted green, like a grenade. And there were Dutch ships, and German, and a trawler manned only by Thai monks, ships laden with crackers and barrels of water, cruising the coastlines in howling storms, scanning the waves with searchlights, their air horns blowing when they spotted a boat in distress. And so much tenderness as well. There was a man who later died in the Bidong hospital, a man with blistering lips, squatting for weeks in a foundering boat and rocking his crying wife, telling her over and over her face was more beautiful than water.

"Porkpie," said Sharon. "Do you need to lie down?"

"I'm just tired," said Porkpie.

Then everyone applauded for the evening's special guests, Mr. Nguyen Van Duong, Miss Lin Thi Vo, and Mrs. Ha Thi Quy. Mr. Duong waved at the crowd while his two companions smiled. He had something in his box, said Miss Vo. She spoke wonderful English. Miss Vo and Mrs. Quy each put a hand on either end of the box and, as if on cue, lifted the lid. With their free hands they withdrew what looked to be something prickly and sharp. Two needles rose from the box. The needles looked like antennae. They were antennae, and they were climbing out of the box. Something was buzzing. Mr. Duong was grinning so hard his face was trembling. The women started blinking, yanking at the thing in the box. It was stuck. The thing wouldn't come out. And then she heard the buzzing again, a sweet and rhythmic buzzing, coming from the center of the circle, and the thing began to rise from the box.

"It's alive," said Porkpie. She pointed.

"A refugee boat," Francine said. "They're giving Johansson a model boat."

"Is that them humming?" said Ed.

"Yes," said Francine. "It's the old South Vietnamese national anthem."

Porkpie leaned forward. Two masts: she had seen two masts on a model boat. She looked at the women's mouths. The women were humming a song. Mr. Duong shook the box once, and then Mrs. Quy's hand brought out one end of the boat. Miss Vo said something in Vietnamese and tugged hard, bringing up the other end. Everyone started clapping. Mr. Duong placed the box on the floor, and with his hand cupping the hull of the boat, keeping it from falling, he began humming with the two women. The humming got louder.

"Sing it," someone said. "The words."

"It's a beautiful anthem," said Francine. "I wish I understood Vietnamese."

Miss Vo nodded and began to sing the words. Mr. Duong and Mrs. Quy giggled, then joined in.

The boat was almost two feet long. It shone in the light, burnished with shellac. Its planks were hand-carved. On the deck was a railing and a pilothouse; portholes had been filed with a waxy plastic; a string of pearl lights ran from aft to stern. The rudder and propeller moved.

Mr. Duong began giggling and thrust his hand into the pilothouse and pressed on a silver tube sticking up from a hole in the wood. A whirring sound came from inside the boat, and suddenly the pearl lights began to blink off and on. The boat shuddered a little, its two masts wriggling in the air.

"It's alive, isn't it?" said Porkpie.

But the whole place was erupting in laughter and applause. The white people and the Malaysians slapped their knees; the Vietnamese put their hands over their mouths and giggled; Doctor Johansson laughed so hard the boat began to jiggle in his arms. He held up his hands again for quiet.

"This is wonderful," he said. "Where do you find the *material* on Bidong? Wonderful craftsmanship. Look at this. The hull is made from coconut husks." He held the boat up for inspection. "I thank you. It's simply wonderful. Come on, now." He motioned at the crowd. "How about some applause?"

Everyone applauded.

"You know," said Doctor Johansson, holding up his hands again for quiet. "I've been told that one of our guests has a story that will touch us all. Is that right, Miss Vo?"

Miss Vo looked up.

"Wouldn't you say?" he said to Mr. Duong and Mrs. Quy.

"They do not speak English," said Miss Vo.

"Ah!" said the doctor. "Well, of all people, they should most certainly hear what I have to say. Will you act as translator, Miss Vo? Will you please tell your colleagues of our admiration for what you've done? I've been told that you're a brave, courageous woman. Please tell them this."

Miss Vo translated into Vietnamese. She told Mr. Duong and Mrs. Quy she was a brave, courageous woman. The people in the circle nodded. Mr. Duong and Mrs. Quy nodded.

"Tell them, too," he said, "that you're the type of woman the world can be proud of." He stood next to her, displaying her to the crowd with his hand. "You've faced many hardships to escape to freedom. You've faced Thai pirates at sea. Tell them this."

Miss Vo listened closely, then translated. "I'm the type of woman," she said in Vietnamese, "the world can be proud of." She looked at the floor as she spoke. People in the audience nodded. Mr. Duong and Mrs. Quy nodded.

"Your boat left with sixty-four people. You spent sixteen days and nights at sea. The water ran out on day ten. Please. Tell them."

She did.

"On day nine, the first pirate attack occurred. They took gold and water. They took your generator. Please tell them."

She did.

"When you arrived on Bidong none of you had any clothes. You held pieces of cardboard in front of you. Oh, my Lord. Cardboard. I don't need to go into the details. We can only imagine . . . Tell them. Tell them this."

"Enough!" said Reuben. "Zip it!"

People looked. The doctor continued to talk. Miss Vo continued to talk. But everyone had heard Reuben. Everyone had looked, and now they turned away, casting glances at each other, and looked back at the doctor and Miss Vo.

Ed grabbed Reuben by the arm and asked in a stage whisper what the big idea was. Reuben said the doctor was embarrassing her. Ed said he wasn't. Ed said the doctor was expressing the admiration they all felt for a fine woman. Reuben said one thing he would hate to say in front of everyone was that the doctor was a bonehead.

"You have no right," Ed whispered.

"Of course I have a right," said Reuben. "He's *embarrassing* her."

"Keep it down. You're a bully boy, that's all."

Reuben face was red, his mouth twisted. "You can't have people say that about themselves."

"Why not?" said Ed. "She *is* brave and courageous."

"That's not the point. The point is he was saying it."

"In actual fact," said Ed, "she was saying it."

"She was saying it because *he* was saying it," said Reuben.

"Keep it down," said Ed. "He sure couldn't say it in Vietnamese. He doesn't speak Vietnamese."

"No Viet would say something like that in public." Reuben was gasping.

"*She* did!" said Ed.

"Not . . . another . . . word," said the doctor. The doctor had stopped his speech. He stood at the edge of the circle, one hand raised, the other holding the boat.

"I have to say I agree with Reuben Gill," said Porkpie.

"Wah!" said Siew Hon Lee.

"I'm sorry," said Porkpie, touching Ed on the arm. "I really feel I should say something. She was embarrassed. It was such a burden for her to say these things."

The doctor looked at her hard.

Siew Hon Lee began fanning and crinkling her nose. "Oh, my goodness," she said. She was staring at Porkpie. "Please, Porkpie, do not be afraid of Reuben Gill." She spread the fan and held it out at arm's length, fanning it from side to side with quick, tight motions. Something in her voice, something in the muscular way she jerked her fan, made Porkpie wince. The woman wasn't fanning at all. She was erasing. She looked like someone tidying up a drawing with a large eraser. She was erasing Reuben from the room, rubbing with tight strokes, right through to the teakwood table behind him, through the blue tablecloth, and even through the floor on which he stood.

Flip Sherman began barking something in Malay and Reuben barked back. Manley started tugging on Reuben's arm. "Hey," he was saying. "Hey. Hey."

"Get out," said the doctor. "Right now. Out of this house."

Siew Hon Lee turned toward Gunand and grabbed the bottle opener hanging from his neck. "Give me that," she said in English. She started to pull, so Gunand looped his fingers around the string and tried to wriggle free, but Siew Hon Lee dragged him with her, and he had to shout to make her pause and let him untangle himself.

"Hey," said Manley. He grabbed Reuben by the back of his shirt, and people in the hallway flattened themselves against the walls as Reuben and Manley started for the door. Reuben was coughing so hard he hacked something onto the floor, and all Porkpie could see was Manley rushing out the door with his hand pulling on Reuben's shirt while Reuben doubled over and stumbled along behind him.

"White bastard-*lah*," said Siew Hon Lee. She wagged the bottle opener at the door.

"I'm so sorry," said Porkpie to the doctor. He wasn't listening. He had his arm around Sharon, the boat clutched to his chest, watching

Reuben and Manley go out the door. "I'm so sorry," she said again. "I really better be going."

She put her hand on Flip Sherman's shoulder and pushed past him, past Charles from Bakersfield, past Ed, past Siew Hon Lee, and when she caught up with Reuben and Manley she could still hear Flip Sherman yelling something in Malay, and she saw the bottle opener fly through the air and land in the fine-stemmed grass. Reuben was wheezing and coughing, leaning his head against Manley. She grabbed one of Reuben's arms and draped it across her shoulder. Manley grabbed the other arm and they ran down the walkway onto the pebbly street, all the way down to Bungaraya Road, where Manley flagged down a pirate taxi and yelled at the driver to take them to Cowboy Lim's Resthouse.

6

The Australian backpackers had been few and far between all night, so Cowboy Lim asked his wife to tend the bar while he walked around the block a few times. She didn't want to. She said she had a bucket of string beans to snap and only two hands to snap them with. He told her she could shell them behind the bar if she brought her two hands with her. And when, she asked, would her cowboy husband like her to clean the white people's toilets and sweep up their garbage from the floor? He reflected for a moment, yanking at the rim of his new gray Stetson, and said he thought tomorrow morning would be fine. She looked up from her bucket and told him she could not think of a better way to honor her cowboy and master than to clean out the toilets and sweep up the garbage and throw the whole mess into his hat. He frowned. He said the last time someone touched his hat, he made sure the man couldn't use chopsticks for a week. She told him she wasn't someone, she was his wife. He said so much the worse for her. She laughed. His martial arts, she said, were not nearly as fearsome as his snoring. He called her a lazy woman. She said he was a foolish rooster.

They winked at each other. Negotiations were short. The compromise was that he would walk around the block just once while she watched the bar. Upon his return, he would help snap the string beans, in exchange for maid service in the morning. So Mrs. Lim picked up the bar rag and sat on a stool behind the wood counter, snapping. She hummed Chinese opera and absently tossed bean ends at the genuine leather saddle hanging on the wall. An Australian backpacker guest in a tank top peeked his head through the upstairs banister and turned back around to his room; the ceiling fan chopped at the air; Mrs. Lim placed an incense stick at the family altar, up on a shelf by the storage room. The night was so quiet she heard a gecko fall from the ceiling. She smiled at her string beans.

When Porkpie came through the swinging door, all she saw was the bucket on the counter and the tiny woman behind it, dressed in all-day Chinese pajamas. Cowboy Lim was nowhere to be found. Porkpie hesitated at the counter, adjusting her eyes to the dim light.

Mrs. Lim mumbled, then smiled tightly. "Bar closed," she said, and went back to snapping.

"No, you see, I'm staying here," said Porkpie. "Room 4. And Reuben Gill and Manley Hutchinson are with me." She wondered if her voice betrayed excessive emotion. Reuben was breathing normally again outside, but she was still panting and shaken. There was always the danger of becoming excessively enamored of one's own sense of drama. One didn't wish to intrude on others' placidity. Of course intrusion was the quintessential American trait. On a global level, it stirred up all manner of confusion. Domestically, it suggested discontent. All those hyperactive men running around with tools, knocking down walls and fixing things. It seemed a form of hysteria.

Reuben came staggering in, his shirt wet and rumpled. His face glistened. Manley followed, his hand at the small of Reuben's back. Manley's hair hung in his face, but he wasn't pushing it back. He looked terrified. His eyes were darting around the room.

Reuben sat down heavily on a chair. Manley immediately began pacing, raising his fists to his tiny ears and boxing them.

"Beer, Mrs. Lim," said Reuben. "I've got to have beer."

"Oh man," said Manley, stopping at the bar. He slapped the counter, then began pacing again. "Oh man," he said in a high, pinched voice, slapping tables as he walked. "What did we do? Oh shit. Oh man. We're dead."

Mrs. Lim reached into the freezer and pulled out a large Tiger beer.

"Didn't I hear you say 'bar closed'?" said Porkpie.

"Bar closed, yes," said Mrs. Lim, wiping the bottom of the bottle with her rag. "Now bar open."

She handed the bottle to Porkpie and pointed to Reuben.

"It's been such a terrible evening . . . ," said Porkpie.

"Yes, yes," said Mrs. Lim. "Give Reuben beer."

Porkpie did, placing the bottle squarely in front of him. He just sat there staring at it. She was alarmed. His face was ashen and, under the fluorescent light, full of shadow. He moved so slowly toward the bottle that she thought at first he was bringing up his hand surreptitiously, poised to smash a fly.

"Could I trouble you for some hot tea?" she asked.

Mrs. Lim motioned to the shelves along the wall. "What tea you want?" she said rapping a shelf. Behind them, Reuben began guzzling noisily. The shelves were piled with products covered in dust: Fish-brand insect repellent, dart guns, Woodward's Celebrated Gripe Water, glass jars full of oily beans, plastic envelopes of tamarind and chutney, Dobi washing detergent, Essence of Chicken, Tung-Hai Fish Liver Oil, Sloan's Ointment, bottles of Butterfly Florida Water, packets of medicine for gastrointestinal disorders. At the bottom were uncovered bowls of dark cubes.

"I don't see any teas," said Porkpie.

"Here," said Mrs. Lim, pointing to the cubes in the bowls. "Chinese cube tea. Very nice." She picked up a cube and put it to Porkpie's nose. "Is sweet," she said.

Porkpie agreed, then watched Mrs. Lim put the cube into a cup of steaming water she poured from a battered red metal thermos. Mrs. Lim then grunted and brought her foot down hard, spilling hot water on the counter. An insect had apparently scurried along the floor.

"More beer," said Reuben, holding up his empty.

"Are you just going to sit there and drink yourself to death?" said Porkpie. She watched Mrs. Lim open the freezer and draw out another Tiger.

Reuben put his face into his hands.

"It's over," he said. He closed his eyes. "Bidong's gone."

"Reuben," said Manley, sitting on a stool at the far corner. "What if Johansson blames me?"

"Manley, he's not going to blame you," said Reuben. "You didn't do anything. It's me . . . Bidong's gone."

"Hey, what if Johansson's mad at me?" said Manley.

"Manley," said Reuben softly. But he didn't continue. His voice drifted off, and his eyes seemed to glaze over. Mrs. Lim walked to Reuben's table, and Reuben took the bottle and began drinking.

"You know," said Porkpie, watching. She sipped her tea. "I think you should be proud of what you said back there."

Reuben groaned. "I'm never getting out of here," he said. His voice was nearly inaudible. He closed his eyes again. "Bidong's gone."

"You shouldn't care," said Porkpie. "Bidong's just a place. So's Kuala Trengganu. You're still with UNHCR."

"Bidong's gone," he said. He reached into the air as if grabbing for something, and then his face crumpled up and his mouth dropped open. She heard him exhale, long and slow, and saw him sink back into the chair, and then his mouth sunk to the top of the bottle and he drank some more. At the far end of the bar, Manley had taken a chopstick from a jar. He was breaking the wood into pieces with his fingers and jabbing his forehead with the broken ends. "Oh man," he was whispering. "We're dead. Oh man."

When Cowboy Lim swung the doors open, he stood for a moment taking in the scene. He greeted Reuben loudly. He tipped his hat at Porkpie and picked up a string bean wrapper, which he threw at Manley. "White bastards!" he said, smiling broadly, and pulled out a chair at Reuben's table. He stood grinning, one foot on the chair, the other on the floor.

No one said a word.

"How you can put your foot dere?" said Mrs. Lim suddenly, waving the bar rag at the chair. "Is for sitting, not standing."

"I stand now," said Cowboy Lim. He was scowling. "I finish standing, then I sit. Beer here."

"You sit first. Then beer," said Mrs. Lim.

"Beer now," said Cowboy Lim. He rattled the chair with his boot.

"Cannot," said Mrs. Lim.

"Why cannot-*lah*?" said Cowboy Lim.

"No beer," said Mrs. Lim.

"What you mean, no beer? How can?" said Cowboy Lim.

Mrs. Lim opened the freezer door, revealing only rows of Orange Crush and soybean milk. "You see?" she said. "No beer."

"Why you not tell before?" said Cowboy Lim.

"Because your foot on the chair," said Mrs. Lim. "If your foot not on the chair, then I tell you."

"Allah-*mak!*" said Cowboy Lim. He sat down. "I sit now and is no beer. I put my foot on the chair and is no beer. Is no beer, so why I care what you say?"

"Is difference. You sitting now. Now I get beer."

"How can? Is no beer."

"Is beer. No old beer. Is new beer in storeroom. Just come today." She put down the bar rag and inched sideways along the narrow corridor behind the bar to the storeroom.

"Wah!" said Cowboy Lim.

"Wah yourself, Chinaman," said Reuben, softly. He said it without inflection, just staring at his bottle, and Cowboy Lim looked at him questioningly. Reuben sat there, slumped in his chair, sinking into his shirt. His big arms looked flabby, his eyes hooded and blank.

Porkpie had to look away. She put down her tea.

"Will you stop it, Reuben?" she said, talking with her back to him. "For God's sakes. You know, in the Philippines there are thousands of people who live on this giant garbage dump outside Manila. I mean it. They actually live on top of garbage, and every day they flock around the dump trucks that come in and sort through other people's messes. Even they don't carry on like this. Now, please. Stop it."

Manley looked up. A piece of chopstick wood was tangled in his hair. Reuben took his mouth away from his bottle.

"Porkpie," Reuben said. "Just close your yap and go to bed. No more."

"I've been meaning to ask you," she said, turning around to face him. She sipped her cup. "Are those really arms, or are they prosthetics? They're so masculine. Do you mow them?" She stood up and held out her hand, as if to touch him, then drew back. She sat down again. "Oh, I'm sorry," she said. "I shouldn't be so mean. This is difficult for all of us, isn't it? I'm so tired, I'm irritable. I've got to sleep. I almost hallucinated at the party. Really. It's just . . . all this sitting like a lump. Like you're some big potato bug. It's more depressing than I can say. And Manley, please don't stick those things in your head. If not for yourself, then for me."

"Shut up," said Manley.

Reuben drank. His eyes were closed, and he was rocking. Cowboy Lim sat stiffly in his chair, his arms folded, watching her.

"Good night," said Porkpie. She put down her tea. Mrs. Lim reached under the counter and gave her the room key. Porkpie squeezed it. She walked swiftly to the stairs, listening to her shoes clack against the wood steps. She concentrated on walking, one foot in front of another, trying hard not to look at anyone, and when she reached her room and opened the door, she heard Manley raising his voice and Mrs. Lim squawking something in Cantonese at Cowboy Lim, who was squawking something back. She could not hear Reuben. She stood at the door, listening. She heard everyone's voice but Reuben's, and then she heard a beer bottle being opened, its muffled explosion of air like a sigh, then the tinkling of the cap as it hit the floor. The cap would be his. The cap tinkled and tinkled, then just stopped. Just like that. It must have whirled like crazy. Then nothing. All that whirling and tinkling, then quiet as a potato bug. She felt her chin quiver. She stepped into her room and closed the door behind her.

At first, the sounds were unrecognizable: some words in Malay, shouted, then a squishing noise, as if someone were in a vat, turning grapes into wine. In the distance, motorcycles whined down the streets. She heard English. It was Manley's voice, pleading, and then she heard angry Cantonese. The noise was coming from below, outside. She pulled back the sheet. What time was it? It was still night; she could see the dark patches in the gaps between the drapes. She went to the window and twirled the latch open and stuck her head out.

There were figures below on the sidewalk. Five or six men, Malay, she thought, were gesturing and grunting toward the door of the Resthouse. Two wore white singlets; the others had their shirts unbuttoned down to their belts. Cowboy Lim was facing them, yelling, snapping his fingers, his arms poised in a martial arts stance. The men were lunging, taking a few steps forward, then retreating. One had something in his hand. It might have been a knife. Behind them was a line of giant concrete squares that covered the open sewer running down the street, wide as a drainage ditch. One of the blocks had been removed, and in the dark, open space she saw Manley from the waist up, his arms raised as if in supplication, standing in the huge drain.

"Hey, I didn't mean nothing," Manley was saying to the men. "Hey, no insult. Let me out. Please."

Then she heard roaring, and the doors of Cowboy Lim's swung open. Reuben came lumbering out, his mouth open, fists clenched, his head glowing in the fluorescent light over the doorway. He charged, and she saw him drive into one of the Malays and run the man into a motor scooter parked along the cobblestone. The scooter clattered onto the street, and the man fell on top of it, sprawling, the bottom of his singlet rolled to his chest.

She began to giggle. She watched Reuben stumble over the man, tripping over the handlebars of the scooter. The Malay man clutched his arm and began wailing. Reuben rose. He turned to the others, gladiatorial, his hair wild. He was roaring, and across the street a light went on. Porkpie closed her eyes. She couldn't stop giggling. She was giggling, and she didn't want anyone to see her leaning out of the window, half dressed, giggling at the struggle below.

She turned away. She heard grunting and footfalls. She heard him roar again. He was roaring so loud he sounded like white noise from a television, turned high as the knob would go. She sat on the bed and stripped off her sarong, dropping it to the floor. On the chair was her sundress, bunched up like a blanket. She slipped it on. Where were her flip-flops? One was under the bed, so she reached with her foot and pulled it out. Where was the other? She wouldn't bother with it. She had on one sandal, and that was enough. She lay back on the bed. She could feel her chest rising and falling rapidly, her nipples erect against the cloth. No. She could not go downstairs like this. She had to stop giggling. She closed her eyes. She heard the fan whirring overhead and felt the warmth of the bed. Outside, there was only roaring now, roaring and the sound of people running.

Calm. Be calm. She put her hand on her wrist and counted. Her pulse was going down.

When she opened her door, another door down the hallway opened. It was a man and woman, both white. Their faces were tight with worry.

"What's going on?" they asked. Their accents revealed them as Australian.

"Nothing," said Porkpie. "It's over now."

For a moment they all stood completely still, looking at the floor, trying to make out what was happening below. The downstairs door opened and closed. There were voices, quiet and businesslike. The three stood in the darkness, listening, occasionally looking at each other and shaking their heads. The Australian man began to rub the shoulders of the woman.

"I'm going down," said Porkpie. She could feel the Australians stare as she walked down the hallway, past their door, and paused at the top of the stairs. She almost tripped. The single flip-flop was throwing her balance, so she kicked the sandal off and began to creep down in her bare feet. She could hear the stairs creaking. She couldn't see; the air was still. The sensation was bathyspheric. With each step, she felt herself descending, one level at a time, drawing closer to the bottom. She held on to the railing with both hands, listening, trying to piece together the small noises rising up from under the whir of the overhead fan. She thought she heard a groan, but then there was nothing, and then the stair creaked. She continued down. The railing gave way to air, and her feet touched the rubber of the mat at the foot of the stairs. She bumped into a table. To her right, in the hallway leading past the bar, light streamed from an open door, a cozy soft glow, as if from a reading-room lamp. She could hear dripping and whispering. She walked to the door and looked in. There was Manley, standing by the sink, looking down, holding his shoes over a plastic bucket. His pants were wet up to his thighs, as if he'd been in a flood. Mrs. Lim was squatting before him, the bar rag in her hands, wiping his cuffs, a metal bowl at her side. The floor was wet. Dark, smelly wads lay scattered about.

"I was just joking them," said Manley.

His shoulders were shaking. He looked away and cupped his chin with his hand.

"No cry, Manley," Mrs. Lim whispered.

Porkpie closed the door softly. She wrapped her arms around herself and didn't move. It seemed indecent to walk away, but it seemed indecent to walk in, or to speak. She didn't know how long she stood like that, her hands snuggling her waist, rocking slightly, when she heard a clunk in the storeroom. She turned. The storeroom door was half open, but there was no light on. She could make out a table in the middle of the room, rising over cases of beer and soft drinks, and on the table there was the immense form of Reuben Gill, arms outstretched and dangling. She entered sideways, sidling through when the door struck a case of beer. Empty bottles lay on the floor. Reuben was stretched out, immobile, one pant leg rolled up to his knees, his sandals at odd angles on his feet. His hair was wet. She looked closely and saw that his eyes were closed. His nose was bleeding a bit, a piece of tissue hanging from one of his nostrils. A button was missing from his shirt; in the gap, she could see his stomach. The skin was pearly and white, the color of abalone. It seemed to glow. A long, rough patch on his knuckles was moist and dark, as if it had been sanded.

"Sleeping now," she heard.

It was Mrs. Lim. She was standing behind her, holding the metal bowl against her thigh.

"I was worried he might be dead," Porkpie whispered.

"No," said Mrs. Lim. "Sleeping now."

"Your husband?"

"He sleeping now. Not hurt."

Porkpie nodded. She could hear Manley sopping his pants in the bathroom. Reuben was breathing wonderfully, deeply. His nostrils flared. His stomach rose and fell in perfect rhythm.

Mrs. Lim leaned close. She was beaming. "Reuben very fierce," she said. "Like soldier."

Porkpie smiled.

She bent over him and held out her finger. She puzzled over what words to use as blessing, then touched him, as lightly as she could, on the forehead.

7

The UN van pulled up in front of Cowboy Lim's just after the Malay matrons had finished their morning shopping and filled the city's trishaws with the butchered legs of cows that they propped like lumber out the sides of the carriages. All the way home, the matrons sniffed the meat appraisingly, delighting in the odor, which at every street corner mixed briefly with the wood smoke and spice rising from the curry stalls. For hours the sounds of people performing their morning toilette had issued from the shop-house windows, and fat Chinese men in singlets threw buckets of water onto the raised platform sidewalks, washing yesterday's grime onto the cobblestones and into the sewer. The Indian cloth merchants piled bolts of red and purple and dazzling yellow onto wooden racks; sparrows, mistaking the cloth for wildflowers, swooped down from the eaves. Out on the Trengganu River, a small wooden ferry passed by, loaded with pigs. The Muslims in the fishing village on the east bank hooted good-naturedly at the Chinese pole man, who hooted back and made eating motions with his hands and rubbed his stomach.

The driver of the UN van was on his fifth Indonesian clove cigarette. He had to ring the buzzer to Cowboy Lim's several times, and in the time it took Mrs. Lim to open the swinging doors and unlock the metal accordion guard gate, the cloves had so numbed his lips that he could hardly get the words out. Mrs. Lim nodded sharply. Yes, she would accept a letter for Bobbi Porkpie Sortini. She accepted the envelope. Yes, yes, she would not fail to deliver the letter. Yes, yes, she was aware of the blood and broken glass on the cobblestones.

The driver paused. Excusing him very much, but did she also know the whereabouts of the big white man with monkey hair and his small white friend? Allah-*mak!* she snapped: What you think? They inside-*lah*. The driver shrugged. He reached into his jacket pocket and pulled out two more letters, which Mrs. Lim snatched from his hand.

Porkpie was sound asleep in her room, and Reuben was just then beginning to stumble around, knocking into bottles and rubbing his sore hand. Cowboy Lim came down the stairs, examining his hat, which had been battered in the events of the previous night. He punched at the air a few times, smiling, and assumed the karate position. It had been a glorious fight, and he described again to his wife how he and Reuben had stood shoulder to shoulder. The cowardly Malays had been routed. He would mop their blood from the sidewalk after coffee. Then he would sit with Reuben. He would let him know he was family. If UNHCR fired him, he could stay with them. Even if, as Reuben had said, termination would take months to carry out, Reuben would have a home with them if and when the day of termination arrived. As for Manley . . . well, Manley was a different case. Manley he would have to think about.

Mrs. Lim told him if he wanted to gossip in such a loud voice about Manley, he better gossip in Cantonese because Manley was in a room just upstairs. He had stayed the night, too, in Room 16. It wasn't fair, Cowboy Lim said, switching to Cantonese. Why should Manley have gotten Room 16, which had a large feather bed, while Reuben slept on a table in the storeroom? Mrs. Lim asked her husband to think. Who, she asked, did he think had the better night's rest? Reuben had slept the sleep of the victorious: couldn't her husband hear Manley whimpering to himself half the night? The man's pants were still hanging from a line in the downstairs bathroom. She quoted a saying her mother had taught: "Better to own a hovel than to visit a mansion."

Reuben entered the bar area with a sock wrapped around his sore hand. He recognized the blue UNHCR insignia on the envelopes immediately. He tore open his letter. His hands were trembling. He read, moving his eyes wildly about. Then he threw his arms into the air, triumphant, and fell to his knees, promising cigars. He read the letter out loud.

Dear Reuben:

I am sending this letter by messenger as an act of generosity—you understand this term, do you not?—which is to say that through this act you are not required to grace the UNHCR office today to be made aware of the decision Siew Hon Lee and I have reached regarding your future in refugee work. Nor will I be required to knock on your door to make you aware of it. Given the events of last night, I think that's more than fair, don't you?

I have been talking with Siew Hon Lee since seven this morning. I will not mince words with you, Reuben. We both find your behavior inexcusably boorish. If I may be allowed a more intimate observation, I find it disagreeably self-serving as well. Siew Hon Lee has led me to understand in no uncertain terms that you are now, officially, *persona non grata* in the MRCS and Task Force offices. She wishes me to relate her dismay at your behavior.

I cannot begin to describe to you the difficult position into which your behavior has placed me. It has been suggested that your services be terminated. I am not unsympathetic to these suggestions. Quite the contrary. Your behavior has undercut the trust and respect forged between MRCS and UNHCR. It is contrary to the notions of partnership Siew Hon Lee and I have attempted to forge, and you may be interested to know that the political repercussions from last night may quite possibly disrupt the spirit of teamwork that we still hope will mark the upcoming regional meeting. I wonder if this is having any effect on you. I wonder, really, if you have the slightest idea of how power works.

The poets say you can't separate the dancer from the dance. Administratively speaking, however, this is not true. With the full support of Siew Hon Lee, I am separating you, effective now, from the Kuala Trengganu offices of UNHCR and MRCS. We will continue dancing on our own, thank you very much.

However, as staff liaison, you are surely aware of the difficulties, both administrative and practical, in terminating the services of local-hire employees paid through the Geneva UNV office. The procedures are wonderfully byzantine. Incredibly—and I am working to have this changed, believe me—you are protected by certain provisions in your Geneva contract. As I say, this is not news to you. I mention this only to let you know where we stand. We stand miles apart. But I am watching you, Reuben. Make no mistake.

Given what I have said, perhaps you will find irony in what I am about to say. So be it. Effective immediately, and with the full support of Siew Hon Lee, I am reassigning you to Bidong Island. This is not, I repeat, this is not a regular rotation transfer. This is a reassignment in lieu of termination. Your status is probationary, contingent upon performance. I understand your mechanical and carpentry skills are excellent; therefore I am placing you under the direct supervision of our chief engineer on Bidong. I'm sending him a full report on you—do you understand? Full—and if I receive a peep about you from him, or from anyone else on Bidong for that matter, I will see to it personally that your termination of service be carried out, regardless of cost or time, even if I have to fly to Geneva myself.

May I be allowed an observation? Please listen. The penis and the anus are remarkable devices. But refugee work relies on the heart and the head. Let us say your contributions to this enterprise have been directed more south than north of the belt line. Let us also say that I expect your behavior to move in a northerly direction. I believe my point is clear.

You are to report in with Gurmit Singh on Bidong ASAP, meaning I want you on this morning's boat run. I'll have a driver on the dock present you with a Bidong camp pass. I understand that you don't have any personal effects in your office here, so I would prefer that you stay away from the Kuala Trengganu offices.

Sincerely,

Doctor Philip Johansson
Director, UNHCR, Kuala Trengganu branch

Reuben ran to the swinging doors and leaned his head out, bellowing good-bye.

Manley came down the stairs in a sarong, wondering loudly what the hell all the racket was about. He received the news, proclaimed it a miracle, shook Reuben's hand several times, then took his own envelope and went silently to the bathroom. He said he needed to retrieve his pants, but Reuben and the Lims knew that he wanted to read his letter in private. He came out smiling, his pants none the worse for wear. He held the letter aloft. Hey, he said. Hey. Doctor Johansson had thanked him, he said, for escorting Reuben from last night's party. He showed the letter around. Reuben shook his hand.

There was not really much to do before Porkpie came down except for Reuben and Manley to sniff the air and smack their lips theatrically at the Chinese pancakes that Mrs. Lim was now preparing. A celebration breakfast, said Cowboy Lim. He slapped Reuben and Manley on the back and herded them into the family kitchen, adjacent to the storeroom, where he put plates from Denmark onto the table and served chicory coffee. Mrs. Lim was whipping batter in a large plastic bowl. What she poured onto the griddle sizzled like rain. The men breathed the sweet charcoal smoke from the burner; they sat at the table and moved aside the shiny parts of a motorcycle engine. They drank their coffee with gusto, pausing to praise its aroma. Bidong! They couldn't stop smiling. They toasted to badminton, then to powdered aphrodisiacs. They toasted to weight lifting. They toasted to the Chinese National Action Party. They toasted to Reuben's sore hand, to Manley's pants, and to Cowboy Lim's hat. They toasted to Mrs. Lim's special Chinese pancakes, and she laughed so hard at their delight she almost knocked over her mixing bowl.

"What's going on here?" said Porkpie. She stood at the doorway, running her hands through her hair, yawning. She was still barefoot. Her feet were covered with tiny pebbles that lay about loose on the concrete floor. Reuben motioned her over. "Letter for you on the table," he said. She tore a small hole at one end of the envelope, then stuck her finger in and used it like a pencil to rip the envelope the rest of the way. She turned the envelope over and shook the letter into her hand. She read. The special pancakes were steaming on the burner, and Cowboy Lim ran to to the cupboard to get two more cups. He poured one for his wife and one for Porkpie, spilling coffee onto the saucers. Reuben and Manley were laughing and grinning and slapping the table with their hands. In the bar area, some Australian backpacker guests shouted "Hello, hello," but Cowboy Lim made a face and said they could wait.

"Well," said Porkpie, folding the letter. "I'm going to Bidong today with you two."

"Awright," said Manley, nodding.

"I've got a curious assignment, too," she said. "I'm supposed to talk to a Mr. Gurmit Singh and get him to put some table plank or the other back on a table." She frowned. "I'm a little baffled."

"The plank!" said Manley. "Hey, I'll tell you all about it. Everyone's pissed at Gurmit."

"Loyalty test," said Reuben.

"What do you mean?" asked Porkpie.

"Not now," said Reuben. "Chow time." Mrs. Lim was placing her special pancakes on a platter.

"Hey, later, Porkpie," said Manley. "Let's eat."

Cowboy Lim tapped the rim of the chair next to him, and Porkpie seated herself at the table. Sunlight poured through the cracks in the tin door and shimmered on the wet bricks of the piss drain that ran under the sink and into the alley. Outside, a cat was rooting through the Dumpster, clattering metal, and when Mrs. Lim brought over her special pancakes and a pair of tongs, she was humming Chinese opera. She sat, clucking, and her husband poured sweetened milk into her coffee. Reuben tapped a chopstick on the table. He cleared his throat. He pictured himself on the island, drinking water from a canteen. He pictured the Vietnamese in their undershirts, standing around, waiting. He pictured the mud on his feet, the tiny hands touching his hair, the pleading, musical voices, and in the distance, out along the beach, something like fire in the air.

"To Bidong," he said. There was silence for a moment, and then they all stood and drank deeply from their cups.

In the Middle of the Ocean

8

Candles, the Vietnamese petitioners said, had been burning in Gurmit's office all night.

That was not all. Late in the morning, when Miss Phu knocked and entered, he had stuck a twenty-ringgit note into her hand and sent her on a black market spring roll hunt. Mr. Gurmit had *touched* her, they said, thumbing their resettlement forms. His hand had lingered above her elbow, fraternally, to be sure, perhaps even therapeutically, since she had been complaining for days about stiffness, but still, his black fingers had been clearly visible on her sleeve. That wasn't the Mr. Gurmit they knew. His manner had been gracious, but his hair was lank and uncombed. His movements—jerky and quick, as if a harness were yanking his limbs—had suggested arousal, perhaps a Saigon bar girl waiting back in his bunk, but his white safari suit looked so worn, so slept-in and unappealing, that an early-morning seduction seemed out of the question. Besides, people said, it was Mr. Gurmit they were talking about. Mr. Gurmit was not a tiger. He was a possum.

The petitioners leaned over the compound wire.

"*Em,*" they said, "children," waving folders at the girls playing under the raised office floor. "What's Mr. Gurmit doing?" The girls stopped winding string around the thick bamboo stilts and peered between the gaps in the floorboard.

"Something's happening," a girl giggled. She wiped her nose.

"What?"

"It smells so sweet," she said, sniffing.

"Girl! You heard our question."

"Something *wonderful*," she said, and her face lit up.

If anyone had asked him, Gurmit would have agreed. He would have wrapped his arms around his questioner's shoulders and smiled so big his gums would have shown. Inside, he lifted stacks of files from a Milo box and flipped the sturdy cardboard over. The box was perfect. It would easily serve as a table. The stools were already in place, equidistant around the makeshift table, and after shifting the silverware, spoons to the right of forks, Gurmit reviewed with satisfaction the bounty of his morning's work. Only the fruit centerpiece—a yellowish giant mango surrounded by pineapple wedges—remained unworthy of compliment. The mango looked as if it had been poached; it was rumpled and impoverished. But no matter. The breakfast was sure to elicit praise from the two new relief workers.

Gurmit had, since dawn, found himself anticipating their arrival. What better proof of his awakening—awakening! Gurmit marveled; how mysterious the world—what better proof than to welcome the same man he had spent so much time avoiding back in Kuala Trengganu? What did he truly know of Reuben Gill? In brief encounters, he had answered the giant's rudeness only with silence. He had not given of himself. He had shown neither generosity nor kindness. But now . . . Within the hour, Reuben Gill would stare at the plentiful food and his huge, pinched face would open like an umbrella; he would lunge at the riches, and he would be grateful. And then there was the new English teacher—an American woman, the wireless said, before going silent. Was not a stranger but a friend unknown? She appeared in Gurmit's mind as vivid, unrelated images: a denim dress, horsey teeth, a freckled shoulder, hair frizzing in the heat. They were all the common signatures of American females, that and their ferocious insistence on drinking straight from the bottle. He pictured a leisurely hour, the three of them chewing, smacking their lips. Their mouths would be debris-laden, moist with fruit and coffee. Crumbs would stick to their shirts. Later, standing at the bottom of his steps, they would linger drowsily, rocking, their bellies warm and sloshy, and at the moment of leave-taking they would all lurch forward, gesturing for embrace.

Gurmit bumped a stool and apologized to it for his clumsiness. He felt now, with the Americans due any minute, as if he were floating, drifting like mist over the whole office, over his ceramic Sikh figurines and the sewage blueprints and the plastic and cardboard containers and all the scurrying bugs. He unlocked stashes of food, lifted boxes, sifted through clothes for a misplaced cup. His hands would not stay still. They touched everything. They stroked and clasped and squeezed. He raced around the office touching books, clothes, glass, food items, folders, all manner of things, clutching them in his hands, delighting in their shape and texture. A word came to him. *Love.* He stopped, resting his chin on the file box in his arms. The word seemed feverish and absurd, but when he rolled it over his lips, he felt its trembly consonants slide from his tongue, and he put the box down and brought his hands to his face. He touched his nose, then his eyes. He massaged his cheeks. He touched his sandals, he felt his toes.

He looked now at the plank. Yes. After all these weeks of confusion, after so much searching, how good it was to be certain. The night before—mere hours! how miraculous is life!—in the darkness, all had appeared as if bathed in light. Ask, and you shall be forgiven. Ask. And he had been forgiven, had he not? The plank splinters that pierced his skin had not hurt. The tears he had spilled had not been mere tears. The name he had pressed to his bosom had not been mere gouges in wood. Had he not felt this ocean inside him, surging against his bones? He had. And then he had known. Simply *known.* Certainty had entered his heart, and he knew what he had to do.

All night he had worked. Squinting by candlelight, he had swung a hammer and given praise. His labors had been fruitful. The beauteous plank leaned flush against the wall. A garland of pearl lights and black electrical wire framed the plank, floor to ceiling, and gracing its top, nearly seven feet off the floor, was a thicket of small colored bulbs. Candles, unlit, stood like miniature organ pipes at its base, waxed securely to a roll of tinfoil. He had labored long and well through the night, splicing electrical cord, ripping duct tape off decorative lights.

Everything, absolutely everything, now felt delightful. Like love, he thought. That was the sensation of love. If he was a fool, then he was foolish in the ways of the righteous, not foolish in the way of fools.

If only the breakfast plates were brighter. They were, perhaps, too functional, mere plastic disks gnawed by rats. He touched one. He stood back from the table, closing one eye, panning cameralike over the display, and discovered compensating strengths. The black market jar of Folger's Instant Crystals, which, for dramatic effect, he had placed between two bowls of hot-plate toast, gave an impression of extravagance. And there was a giant thermos of hot water, steaming comfort and plenitude. His tin of delicacies lay on his bunk, looted. From it, he had chosen a jar of Broderick's Own Marmalade—a childhood favorite, lumpy with orange rinds riding atop a yellowish pool—and a gaping tub of Vegemite, as well as a Dutch chocolate bar, broken into three equal sections. For silverware, he had rummaged through the side pockets of his travel bag and found his mother's gift of tiny silver spoons and a gilt-handled butter knife.

"Mr. Gurmit," said Miss Phu. She stood at the open doorway bearing a rolled newspaper. His spring roll was inside. "Where you want this?"

"Oh, Miss Phu," he said. "Look at this." He swept his arm, magicianlike, over the cardboard table, then touched the silverware and Vegemite and plastic bowls. Miss Phu's face, normally placid, blossomed with an encouraging grin. She had always walked a bit stiffly, typically Vietnamese, decorous and thin-limbed, but now, in the light of the open door, she appeared inviting as a vase of flowers. Her white blouse and shiny black pants were freshly washed, wrinkling delicately, and when she turned sideways, sidestepping a pile of folders, her small breasts and buttocks suggested to Gurmit mounds of heady, aromatic vegetation. He had to look away. Distraction would not do. The newcomers were arriving! The Americans! He put his hands in his pockets and jangled coins. "In," he said, motioning with his chin, and as she walked he blinked at the dry, warm breeze that crinkled the nipa palm outside into crepe streamers.

"Where you want?" she said again, holding forth the blotty newsprint.

"Just here. Please." His hands pressed out against his pants pockets, indicating the table. "And how is your singing practice? You can sing a song for me later?"

Miss Phu eyed him coolly. "Feeling good today, Mr. Gurmit?"

"Yes!" he said. The word sounded so vigorous, he withdrew his hands and began clapping. "Feeling so good," he said. "I am feeling like clapping. And music! I am not singing, you know, but you can sing for me? Oh, I know you are busy. Later, perhaps."

Miss Phu ignored him. "Spring roll with only vegetable. No chicken," she said. "How to find chicken, Mr. Gurmit?" She unwrapped the newsprint. The spring roll was dark with oil; a ragged clump of cabbage lay broken beside it. "So expensive," she said, "and no meat late in the morning." She reached into her blouse pocket. "Your change here," she said, and spread out coins on the table.

"Can keep," said Gurmit. He smiled, grabbing the spring roll. The oil: he let it run down his fingers. It was silky as milk. Warm.

"Very generous, Mr. Gurmit," she said. She swept the coins up with one efficient motion. "Terrible spring roll. Cabbage, onion, some green-flake only. Not enough good things."

"It is the idea, hey?" said Gurmit. He released the spring roll into a bowl and crushed the newsprint into a ball, wadding it pleasurably, languorously, then tossing the mess into the wastebasket. "Think grand!" he said. "A morsel to a starving man is a banquet." He picked up a napkin and wiped each erect finger slowly. "It is *up here,*" he said, tapping his head. "Up here where is the banquet. The real food is up here. Not down there on a table. Down there is only a reflection of up here. Spirit food, Miss Phu. That is what feeds us."

"Very funny, Mr. Gurmit," she said. "But Americans like food too much. Too fat." She pointed to the table. "They like food down there."

"Oh, you worry so much," said Gurmit. "They are my guests, isn't it? Two more Americans for Bidong, hey? They will like." He spread his hands wide. "There. All set. Beautiful."

"Beautiful, Mr. Gurmit."

But there was no time to admire the sight, to stand over the steaming coffee water and sidle close to Miss Phu's freshly washed blouse. Already he could hear Reuben Gill's rumbly hee-haw carried in the breeze and, like birds, the cries of *American* from the refugees outside. Underneath, beneath the floorboards, were tiny squeals. "Huy!" Gurmit shouted to the floor. "You kids. Americans coming. Better go see. Better run."

And then the Americans were at the door, Reuben Gill clomping up the steps, his blue jeans streaked with water. Miss Phu nodded, excusing herself. She stopped for a moment, staring at the giant white man, then ran swiftly down the stairs. "Gurmit," said Reuben loudly. "Yeah. Long time." His expression was benign. Behind him was a thin white woman in a brown sundress. Her face was streaming sweat. She held on to the back of Reuben's T-shirt; with her other hand she clutched a small clasp purse.

"Welcome," said Gurmit. "For you! A Bidong welcome."

"I'm Bobbi Porkpie Sortini," said the woman, wiping her forehead. "Everyone calls me Porkpie. How are you?"

They all shook hands. The newcomers' flesh was hot and moist. Porkpie's grip was papery and light. Reuben's huge hand swallowed his, and the giant's palm pressed against the plank splinters still lodged in his fingers. Gurmit moaned.

"I'm afraid I'm a bit out of sorts," said Porkpie, holding her purse to her stomach. "A touch of seasickness on the way over. I've never been one for Dramamine. The whole idea of it, I mean. It's a form of anesthesia. Like a lobotomy for the tummy. That kind of escape from discomfort seems to me worse than the discomfort."

"Escape!" snorted Reuben. "Take a couple of pills and you won't heave on your shoes."

"I did no such thing onto my shoes," said Porkpie.

"Come," said Gurmit. "Let us eat." He rapped the table.

"No, you didn't chunk on your shoes," said Reuben. He began laughing. "But you know what? You know what, Gurmit? She actually brought plastic baggies along. In her stupid purse. Jesus H in a trishaw."

"Oh, don't laugh," said Porkpie brightly.

"So much food on the table," said Gurmit.

"We're rounding Zone D," Reuben continued. "Manley's running around, woofing or something. The boat's bouncing, right? So I look over, and Porkpie here is doing the stomach grind by the railing. Then she gives the old heave-ho into a zip-lock. Doesn't even make a sound."

"Physiologically," said Porkpie, "retching is inherently silent. All that racket is unnecessary."

"You *hear* this?" said Reuben gleefully. He threw back his head.

"Hearing," said Gurmit, motioning toward the table. "But come and—"

"So then," said Reuben, "she *seals it up*—zippo!—and chucks the baggie overboard and starts waving bye-bye to it. Like, nice to have met you. So long. See you soon."

"You're blinded by appearances," Porkpie said. "It was an exercise in graciousness, that's all. Which seems to me far preferable to you and Manley fighting."

"We weren't fighting."

"Oh, what would you call it then? All that shoving on board."

"Let us eat!" said Gurmit, walking to the table.

"Manley called me 'Big Bro' again. I told you I don't like it."

"See, now look what you're doing," said Porkpie. "Here Gurmit has made us this lovely breakfast."

"We already chowed," said Reuben. He looked the food over. "Hell, I'll chow again."

"Thank you, Gurmit," said Porkpie. "This is very thoughtful."

There was in her tone, Gurmit thought, an echo of Hindi musicals: an exotic heroine strapped to the railway tracks, frantic and helpless, but then taking time out to sing to the audience. You knew she took only the song seriously. Breakfast, arguing, even train tracks: on screen, all were the same. All were nibbles at the heroine's elbow, a vague munching in her ears, the rattle of the world, and she could silence it all with a voice like clear mountain water.

Wonderful! The morning, the food, his guests—all were wonderful. They sat down, Gurmit rocking back on his stool, hands caressing the wood seat. He surveyed, pleased at what he saw: the fruity marmalade, the steamy coffee water, the spring roll perfumed with oil, the roll of Porkpie's shoulders as she scooted her chair forward, the porcine glint in Reuben Gill's eyes, the fork peeking out like a chick from the man's giant balled hands. Truly, as his father had said, Akal Purakh, the divinity, shimmered in all creation, in the smallest gesture, the lightest puff of wind. With his hands wrapped tightly around the steaming thermos, Gurmit felt the presence of the plank splinters in his fingers. The skin was infected. The tiny wounds seemed to flare, echoing the rhythm of his pulse. Were they not . . . yes, were they not alive as well, awash in living blood? He could not now assign the sensation in his fingers to the adolescent category *throbbing*. It was something else. It was his blood moving, in-out, in-out, a feathery kind of itching. It was like breathing. Sucking in. Sucking out. The tide of his own body.

The thought was so exciting that Gurmit felt his hands tremble. He poured the hot thermos water into the waiting cups. Some spilled. Reuben picked up a spoon and began stirring his cup, mixing in the Folger's, and when Gurmit looked down at his own cup, he saw his fingers gripping his spoon tightly. He stirred loudly. Spoons clacked. Cup water frothed. It was as if the toast and mango, the spring roll, the marmalade, these sweating, loud Americans—as if the essence of the room was drawing into the entryways of his body, whisked into gaping nostrils, his open mouth, the sucking pinpricks in his fingers. Even the jabbering of his guests seemed to swirl toward him, into him, creeping like fog over the bowls and fruit. *Gurmit,* he heard. *Gurmit.* He saw Reuben waving in his direction. *Hey,* said Reuben, *how about some Vegemite?* Gurmit passed the yellow tub. Reuben sank his butter knife in deeply. Porkpie sipped, pausing occasionally to chew. She had lots of excited questions. What English text is used? Is there cholera here? What are the classroom facilities like? How could one make oneself heard over the racket? Does Bidong always smell so terrible?

Reuben, too, was talking, waving his hands around, cramming whole pieces of toast into his mouth, as if gobbling pancakes. Shit, Gurmit, he was saying. Shit this, shinola that. He was booming. He cracked his knuckles and held up his spoon.

Love, Gurmit thought, tipping back in his chair. He moaned. Love, love, love . . .

"So you got lots of stuff here," Reuben said, wagging the spoon. "A real office, Gurmit. Desk, a wastebasket, goddamn paperwork. Don't you sweep in here? What's that on those folders? Mold?"

"I have to say," said Porkpie, making a face. "It has an odor."

"Mold smells," said Reuben. "Do some plumbing, you'll get used to it. But I'll tell you what"—and now he rapped the spoon on the table—"I've never seen something like that." He motioned with his chin to a point behind the desk. "I've never seen a plank dolled up like a Christmas tree."

Gurmit looked. His eyes, watery, focused on the plank.

"Reuben," said Porkpie, holding up a finger. "Please."

His guests were silent a moment. He saw their expressions. He followed their eyes, watched them take in the wires and bulbs near the ceiling, the candles on the floor. Reuben's stool creaked. Porkpie cocked her head. They were reaching a decision. He could feel it in the air. Outside, someone began clanging a pot.

Gurmit, exhaling, blinked mightily. He sensed what was coming, and he could not allow it. This sea, this ocean inside him: how quickly it changed. How quickly it demanded his attention. The newcomers, so invigorating a minute ago, so delightful, were changing before his eyes. They would argue and bully, and Reuben Gill would rise from his chair and yank the wires and bulbs from the plank.

"Let us not be divisive, please," said Gurmit softly. "Let us enjoy the company with which—"

"Who said anything about divisive?" said Reuben. "I'm telling you what I see. That's all."

"I did not mean to upset," Gurmit smiled. "Please allow me to butter your bread which is now cold."

"Stop it with this," said Reuben. He cupped his hand over his toast. "What's with the dulcet tones? What about *that*?" He pointed with his spoon at the plank.

"It is a table plank," said Gurmit suddenly. "From the eating hut. I am keeping for investigation. And more." He paused, listening to the sound of his words. They were reasonable. His voice projected confidence. "You have not heard, isn't it?"

Reuben grunted. "I've heard," he said.

Porkpie spoke sharply: "Reuben."

"I have taken this plank from the table," said Gurmit.

"I said I heard."

"I don't believe this is the time or the place," said Porkpie.

"The real table," said Gurmit. "From the eating hut. Not this box."

Porkpie laid her hand on Reuben's arm, stilling him. "Gurmit," she said, "I guess we're just wondering what the story is. At least I am."

"Why the lights?" said Reuben, wiping his mouth. "And what's that you've got there? Votive candles? Come on."

"I am honoring the man whose name you see in the wood," said Gurmit. He rose, then sat down again. He rubbed his hands together. "Nguyen Van Trinh. You see?" He pointed. "That is terrible, isn't it? Nguyen Van Trinh is dead. How are you knowing what he has suffered? We cannot . . . forget him. We cannot say this is only a plank of wood. You are seeing his name there? This is all that is left. Cannot say only wood. Cannot." He slapped the Milo box.

"Well, you can," said Reuben evenly. "Johansson wants this plank business taken care of. Now. Just put it back."

"Put back!" said Gurmit. "Cannot. You are knowing island operating orders. I quote—"

"Save it," Reuben said, waving his hand in dismissal.

Porkpie said, "Can we please stop with—"

"Yeah," Reuben said, "I know all about island operating orders.

'Find out who mutilated government property.' Something like that. 'Initiate a full investigation.' I don't care about them."

"Perhaps Gurmit does," said Porkpie.

"Don't start up," said Reuben.

"We're just talking about a silly piece of wood," said Porkpie.

"No!" said Gurmit. "Is not silly."

"You're right," said Porkpie quickly. "I apologize. I only meant why is this an issue at all? Of course it's not silly. You're honoring this poor dead man. I understand. I only meant shouldn't we focus on . . . I don't know, more pressing matters. Live people, for instance?"

"If you will listen please," said Gurmit. He held up his coffee cup. "I cannot return this plank. For several reasons which I have already told you."

"I'll be a dog-faced baboon," said Reuben. "Grrr-mit Singh."

"No baboons here," said Gurmit.

"I don't believe that's his meaning, Gurmit," said Porkpie.

"I am knowing what he means," Gurmit snapped. "Listen what I am meaning, hey? No baboons. Only good people here."

"Yes," said Porkpie. "And Doctor Johansson wants all of us good people to work together, and it seems to me that this plank might be creating a rift. This all seems so unnecessary, all this sniping and—"

"Don't mention Johansson," said Reuben, folding his arms. "Not in front of me. I'll tell you what, Gurmit. I'm here on probation. That's no secret."

"I have heard on the shortwave," said Gurmit.

"All right," said Reuben. He seemed angry. He picked up the thermos and set it back down hard on the Milo box. "All right then. I'm on a short leash, Gurmit—"

"You made it to Bidong," said Porkpie, patting the thermos. "Bidong. You're here."

"I'm on a short leash and you know it," Reuben said, straightening. He picked up the thermos again and pounded it against the box. "Now look. I'm not going back."

"No one is telling you," said Gurmit. He folded his arms.

"No," said Reuben, holding the thermos against his knee. "And Porkpie, you're under orders, aren't you? You're not in the clear either. Now, this plank business has got to end. Gurmit, just put the damn thing back where you got it. I hear the staff is pissed. It's simpler for you to put the wood back than calm down those goofballs. What's it going to be?"

Gurmit reached for the mango and cradled the fruit in his lap. He sensed the agitation in Reuben's voice. He rubbed the mango's skin and looked away, staring out the louver windows. All of Bidong was finishing breakfast: a man was coughing into a bucket; a girl was rubbing her gums with a bottle cap. In the distance, he heard a chainsaw whirring. He looked down at the mango and saw his thumbs pressed into the fruit, bruising its flesh into shapes that suggested eyes. The image was startling. This mango, this wrinkled, inadequate fruit: it lay cradled in his lap, bruising in his fingers. He stroked it.

"I am keeping the plank," said Gurmit.

"You're making this difficult," said Reuben.

The problem, Gurmit thought later, was that there had been no common cause, no clear avenue of consent. The meal had been a success in terms of sustenance, and even insofar as their disagreement over the plank had remained civil, he felt breakfast a worthy endeavor. Yet so much had been selfish and mean. He could still taste the marmalade, metallic and bitter. It was now ten o'clock in the morning, and the sun was so bright that from certain angles all you could see out the louver windows was a blinding sheet of white. The office smelled of warm fruit. The Milo box lay on its side.

"I am telling you," said Gurmit, snipping a roll of duct tape. "Breakfast is king. It is we people who are unworthy of receiving it. Steady this box, please, Miss Phu."

"How can you say?" said Miss Phu. She held the Milo box while Gurmit stuck tape over the hole in the cardboard. "After breakfast, then lunch. Delicious."

"Breakfast, you see, is breaking the fast, isn't it? Breakfast. That is what it means. A worthy idea. Now lunch. What is lunch? Nothing worthy there. Just food and piggery."

Miss Phu frowned, then poked the patched hole with her finger, testing. Together, they righted the Milo box and began filling it with folders. "Food and piggery is fine, Mr. Gurmit," she said. "So much better than this."

She meant cleaning up the office, surely—folders, boxes, dishes, all manner of food needed to be put back in place. But did she, cuttingly, also mean working alongside him? Did she, perhaps, refer to living on Bidong? So many possibilities . . . He looked over the box at her. She did not return his look. She was humming a folk song.

Did she, too, think him foolish? The thought—so small, so minor!—was more than he could bear. The Americans had been confusing enough. They had seemed immune to his offers of goodwill. Reuben, possibly attempting intimidation, had reached across the table and plucked the mango from his lap. The American had hacked at the fruit so savagely that he poked a hole in the Milo box. An accident, Reuben said, though the way he later carried on about how stupid it was to keep the plank suggested a reservoir of hostility that was uncomfortable to think about. The whole time, Reuben had gobbled the poor fruit; he had sucked the fibrous seed, a monstrous lollipop, and when he was finished, he just threw it down and swept it over to a gap in the floorboard, where it vanished, Gurmit believed, into the hands of waiting children.

Porkpie, for her part, at least had derided her companion for his manners. She giggled occasionally, a pleasant, songbird warble, but she kept referring to an awful smell. She had gagged on her bread once. She made faces and sniffed the air, though it wasn't clear why. Smoke from the new incinerator masked much of the smell wafting in from the Zone C garbage dump, and the sewage canals had of late been moving along smartly; the food was fresh. Yet when the Americans left, Porkpie, stopping at the foot of the stairs, complained of lingering stomach difficulties. And what, she said, waving her hand in front of her nose, was that terrible smell?

"Miss Phu," Gurmit said, sighing.

Miss Phu looked up from a pile of folders.

"I am wanting to know . . . ," he said.

"OK, Mr. Gurmit."

"Yes, OK. I am wanting just to know . . ."

"OK."

"Are you sure you are not minding to help me clean?" he said. He sat down in his desk chair.

"Mr. Gurmit! You are helping refugees. You do so much. All the time, so much work. And now . . . ," She pointed to the plank. "Look now. You do *this*."

Gurmit leaned forward, shoulders hunched. The tone of her voice was encouraging. "Did you know him?" he said.

She shook her head. She told him she had heard stories. His boat had been attacked on the voyage over. He had landed on the Zone C beach, in the garbage. She didn't know him, she said, but he was Vietnamese. And then she pressed her hand to her chest, over her heart. "You are good, Mr. Gurmit," she said.

"Well, I . . ." Gurmit turned away. "Thank you so much," he said softly. "I am joyous. Thank you." He heard the catch in his voice. He sat down, holding his arms. He felt himself tremble. He held folders, rubbing them slowly. Then he opened a desk drawer: pens, paper clips, MRCS rubber stamps, requisition forms, rubber bands—each found its way into his palms, soothing him, cool against his skin. He came to the bottom drawer: there was his captain's hat. So far he had to go! So far before he could wear it. He traced his finger along the bill, then returned it.

He opened the other drawer.

He scowled, as if sucking a lemon.

"Bloody hell," he said.

Miss Phu put down her box and walked over.

"Miss Phu," he said, slamming the drawer shut. "Miss Phu. I . . . would you please mind allowing me to clean? You have worked so hard."

"But Mr. Gurmit."

"Please," he said. He walked her to the door, holding her gently by the elbow, guiding. "Please," he said. She smiled at him, allowing herself to be guided, but at the doorway she did not turn around when she descended the steps. She walked backward, just watching him, a question on her face, and as he closed the door he heard her say good-bye in a voice that sounded like pleading.

He put his hands to his head, quiet a moment, then he opened the drawer again. There, atop a legal pad, was the Prison Systems operating orders pamphlet, opened to the passage he knew so well. "Destruction of government property shall be reported to the administrative chief, who shall initiate a full investigation to determine culpability if the persons and causes responsible are not known."

Something came over him then, something hot and uncontrollable, something that traveled along his spine like electricity, and he yanked the drawer from the desk and heaved it to the floor. He snatched the pamphlet from the drawer and began turning the pages. He turned them so hard he ripped one of the pages, and then he began turning the pages in the opposite direction. Surely there was something . . . one page. Where was it?

There. "Staff shall at all times undertake to regard illegal Vietnamese aliens with respect and thereby encourage cooperation among island inhabitants." He traced the sentence with his finger. Respect. He threw the pamphlet back into the drawer. Yes. Island orders were explicit. "Bloody hell," he said, and then he lifted the drawer and carried it with one arm out the door. He chased away the waiting petitioners. The children under the floorboards scrambled out after him. A drawer, they said in Vietnamese: he's stealing a drawer now. Gurmit heard them chant his name. He walked quickly down the footpath, and the children followed at a distance, blowing palm frond trumpets, dragging Clorox bottle boats. They shouted; kids from nearby huts came running out. The boys hit each each other with twigs; the girls held each other's hair and galloped.

But Gurmit was walking quickly, ignoring the growing crowd. He waved small bands of young men out of his way. He felt the sun on his neck, the loudspeakers whining. Soon he was running, leaping over palm roots, climbing, balancing himself with his free hand on the pebbly footpath winding up the Zone F hill. People shouted at him. They pointed. *He's stealing a drawer. Look. He has a drawer.* Gurmit heard their voices. He heard the bleating of the palm-frond trumpets. And still he ran, only now he was running up the Zone F hill, grunting with exertion. He stumbled over palm roots, and when he did, he heard the laughter behind him. He ran faster. He saw nothing, he said nothing. He nudged women out of the way, a whole line of them, young mothers carrying empty plastic buckets, picking their way down the hill, and when he had run far enough, the steep hill ended and the rough ground leveled and he was walking along a clearing. The primary school was to his left; to his right was a clear, flat stretch of ground ending in a rocky outcropping. There, the ground simply ended. The small cliff was dotted with mossy tufts. The rocks below were polished and wet. Gurmit looked out over the black band of the horizon, then at the crinkling waves pluming over the Zone C coral. The coral was studded with dark clots, and the green water washed over the clots and onto the fringes of the Zone C garbage dump, where the foam was gray and polluted. Gurmit sneezed. Nguyen Van Trinh had landed there. His boat had probably scraped the coral. He had probably staggered into the garbage, probably pushed his way through mounds of gauze and shit and sticky wrappers. In his mind's eye, Gurmit traced the man's path, saw him wading through the garbage, pushing through cans and glass and rolls of plastic big as waves, stumbling, his legs too numb to carry him forward.

"Mr. Gurmit, Mr. Gurmit," the children shouted. Gurmit did not turn around. He closed his eyes and held the drawer stiffly out in front of him, and then he shook it, and the pamphlet fluttered down the shale. He scraped the corners of the drawer with his finger, and then he shook his finger, and the dust floated down in a hazy ball. All that shame, gone. All his weakness. He looked. The drawer was empty. But even as Gurmit turned away, he heard the children shout in glee. They rushed past him and started to climb down the rocks, picking their way through the branches, testing footholds in the shale, scrambling after the contents of the drawer. Even as Gurmit shouted at them to stop, he saw children leap from an engine hull off Zone C and swim toward the pamphlet. He slapped his hands against his head, but the children were already yelling over the pluming waves. A boy slipped; he landed hard on an outcrop and began to cry. Stop, Gurmit shouted. Dangerous, he said. But everyone was laughing. They threw stones at each other to slow their competitors down. Gurmit saw a girl clutch her head. She began wailing. Gurmit, leaning, felt himself slipping. He had to grab a vine to stop from falling. He broke the skin on his knee. He felt his blood. Children, do not, he yelled, grabbing his leg, but the swimmers were already wading to the coral. They lifted the limp pages. Some boys laid claim to it. They yanked. No one would let go until it tore, and even then the children fought a little more before starting back up the cliff, bearing in their hands what Gurmit had thrown away, returning all the sopping wads, unrecognizable now, all that ruin, returning.

9

Reuben stood at the top of the Supply Office steps, keeping Porkpie company. Porkpie sat on the bottom step, cupping her hand over her nose. She looked terrible. Long, languid drops ran down her neck and cheek, and her dress was stained with sweat. All through Gurmit's breakfast she had complained about the odor, and now, nearly twenty minutes later, her complaining had turned into silent, stomach-clutching rocking.

Her reaction was difficult to understand. He was breathing in the wonderful foul air just fine. In fact, the dust and smoke that swirled into his leftover toast seemed to make the Vegemite topping taste even better. He chewed. The trail was so crowded that people clutched their bags and ration cartons to their chests. A boy wheeled, stopping to urinate against a palm tree; a fat woman, her eyes cloudy with cataracts, kneaded the back of a girl's T-shirt, squeezing the cloth as if it were dough. Everyone was yammering at the top of their lungs while, overhead, the loudspeakers yammered louder still, mingling with sewage gases and heat. And the shelters: they stretched like a wall mural, dense and colorful, down the length of the path, on either side, a patchwork of rags and cardboard and rusted tin, as far as Reuben could see. Bidong. The word meant something now. It pealed like a clear, deep bell, Bidong, Bidong, rumbling in a low jungle register. Just standing there on the Supply Office steps with Porkpie excited in Reuben a sudden, confused erection. Gummy with pleasure, it yawed and stammered, inching along in fits and starts, and as it pushed to his thigh, it paused, then started again, then lifted its head as if to cough out a question: *Mine? Mine?*

Ever since leaving Gurmit's office, Reuben had asked himself the question. The island was where he belonged, but he was not yet completely present on the island. Not present in the way that Reuben Gill, Bidong sub-engineer, needed to feel present. There was a leash around his neck, and he had to get it off. The world turned on meanness, but the insult implied in putting Reuben Gill on probation—him, of all people—was unbearable. Porkpie was in no condition to take care of this plank business. If he had the assignment, he'd settle it, and in a hurry. He was no fuckup. Oh no. The sooner everyone knew it, the better.

"There you are!"

The words were Sally Hindermann's. She was knifing through the crowd, dressed in a pair of denim overalls studded with brass-colored rivets; her blonde hair, tucked under a white painter's hat, was choked into a tight French braid that she yanked like a pull chain. They had met briefly on the Kuala Trengganu dock ten months ago, his first day with the UN office. She was not an encouraging sight.

"*Chao ong,*" she said, yanking. "Oops, wrong language. Hello, I mean." She put her hands on her knees and spoke from a crouch. "You must be Porkpie. You OK?"

"A little nausea," Porkpie said, smiling. "I'll be fine, really."

Reuben looked away. *Oops, wrong language.* An idiot.

Sally stood and caught Reuben's eye. He nodded.

"You're on probation, aren't you?" she said. She placed her hand over her mouth, mimicking embarrassment. "Sorry," she said. "That just slipped out. But hello, Reuben." She smiled broadly. "What's it been? Almost a year? I hear you're our new sub-engineer. For a long time, I hope." Her face was full of movement: her mouth kept breaking into a smile, then collapsing; her eyes seemed to flutter.

Reuben said, "How did you know about probation?"

Sally reached into one of the pockets of her overalls and pulled out a folded letter. "We all got copies this morning, dear," she said, and then announced a walking tour. Porkpie stood. She pronounced herself fit.

Reuben was not sure what to protest first. He wasn't a goddamn tourist, he said, and neither was Porkpie. And Johansson's letter was addressed to him, he said. But Sally already had Porkpie's elbow in her hand and was leading her down the trail, chattering loudly into her ear. Sally looked back at him once—*you too,* she mouthed, frowning—and then Porkpie looked back, her face ashen and tense, her lips puckered as if to say *please.* So he swore, squinted into the sun, then jumped off the steps and waded into the crowd, pushing his way toward the women. Children shrieked at the giant white stranger, and Sally, without turning around, took off her painter's hat and waved it like a plume, urging him forward. He wiped his forehead. He stumbled on a tree root. He fell into line behind them.

They walked single-file through the crowd, Reuben at the rear. They passed a water tower and black plastic pipes set on raised clamps. A smashed pilot wheel hung like a dart board from a tree. Children were playing a hopping game on a rusted boat hull resting atop what appeared to be burned lumber. Past the hull were tables set up along the sides of the pathway—the black market, Sally yelled—where hawkers had piled an amazing assortment of goods: nails, spools of wire, fishing tackle, soap, shampoo, Chinese talcum powder, jerricans of kerosene, joss sticks, pencils, aerograms, writing paper, Malaysian stamps, scissors, Nescafé, sacks of rice flour and curry powder, packs of cigarettes stacked to resemble boats, warm cans of Orange Crush and 7-Up, even a sinister-looking sewing machine with pearl inlays and an exposed rotor.

Reuben issued himself silent orders: Widen the footpath. Take out those trees. Bury the water pipe. Replace plastic fittings with copper.

Sally, walking point, was waving at things with her painter's hat. She kept turning her head and shouting over the noise.

"OK, facts," she said. "Bidong is in seven zones, A through G. Each zone has its own council, though there's a camp committee that oversees everything." She counted on her fingers: "Admin, Engineering, Sanitation, Social Services, Information and Culture, Security, and Supply." She stopped a moment, turning to Porkpie. "Are you up for hearing this?"

"I'm up," Porkpie nodded.

Sally smiled broadly. "Great," she said, and then she yanked on her French braid and continued walking. "More facts. The standard

UNHCR ration pack is nine hundred grams of rice, a tin of condensed milk, three tins of whatever, two packets of noodles, sugar, salt, and two small tea bags. Though just because it's standard doesn't mean that's what actually gets delivered. One pack gets distributed to each person over three years old, and has to last three days. Children under three get milk powder and dry biscuits. Fresh veggies and fish get delivered from time to time. Very big items here, believe me. Food scams aplenty. The diet's not sufficient in vitamins or proteins for children or old people, and the doctors say we're short on nearly everything. Hepatitis and TB are problems, and we've had cases of meningitis and typhoid. And then you have all the sea casualties."

"Sea casualties," said Porkpie.

Sally turned again and stopped. She waved with her painter's hat for the crowd to go around. "You know, casualties at sea. Pirate attacks. Mostly along the Thai coast. Frankly, our Bidong Task Force guards don't strike me as much better. They're the dregs." She looked around and made a face. "That Task Force Chief Ahmed is a pig."

"Better them than the Rangers," said Reuben. "They're an hour away."

Sally smiled so big her chin cheeks trembled. "Yes. Better them than the Malaysian Rangers. Then it would all be over, wouldn't it? The whole island, swept clean, everyone towed out to sea. That's why Year Five has us worried. Oh, sorry. Year Five: five years since the fall of Saigon. But, anyway, this is what? October? We've got three months. After that, I hear the Malaysians might get even nastier with the boat people. Right now, the Viets have to dodge the navy or they get towed back out to sea. We're just hoping the shoot-on-sight legislation doesn't pass. The situation's bad enough as it is."

Her smile receded. "Do you know what?" she said. "The Australians estimate that 50 percent of the boats never make it. They guess between one hundred thousand and two hundred thousand drowned or killed."

"I didn't know," said Porkpie.

Sally began nodding rapidly. "And it's just going to get worse. It might get better, too. We'll know in Year Five. There's really not much we can do except wait."

"I doubt it," said Reuben, pointing. His voice was sharper than he had intended. "Look at that roof. It's just palm leaves and branches. Those coconuts could crash right through."

Sally ignored him. "Here," she said, withdrawing a folded sheet of paper from one of her pockets. "You might find this useful." She unfolded the sheet and handed it to Porkpie. "I'm sorry, but I just have one."

"A map," said Porkpie.

Sally smiled. "I drew it myself." She tapped the sheet:

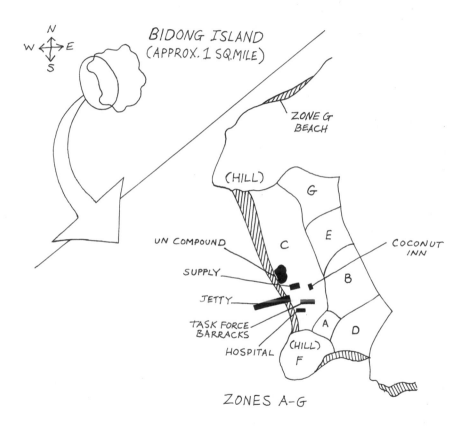

"We're in Zone C now," said Sally. Her finger traced a route. "And we're headed this way, toward this place called the Coconut Inn."

Porkpie nodded. She folded the map over once and placed it in her purse.

"Now come on," Sally said. She touched Porkpie's elbow and started down the trail again.

Reuben watched them go. He signaled to the people behind him to stop, then squeezed his way off the footpath. The walls of the shelter were crumpling under the frame of the roof, tilting outward like the sides of a box. A young woman in a white blouse lifted the cloth on the entryway and stuck her head out.

"You want," he said, touching the palm on the woman's roof, "I can board that roof up right now."

The woman shook her head. "No Eng'ish," she giggled.

"Never mind," he said. "Later. I'll come back. Reuben Gill, sub-engineer. Remember that. The big white man. The sub-engineer."

"Sub-engineer Reuben," said Porkpie, shielding her eyes with her hand. She had come back for him. The color had drained from her face. "There you are. We thought you'd been swallowed by the crowd. Come on now. Please."

She turned around, scouting for Sally, but their tour guide was well down the footpath, shaking hands with a man carrying a bundle of noodle wrappings.

"No talking heads," said Reuben. "No Sally-on-a-stick. Not now."

"This attitude," Porkpie said, shaking her head. "You're not being willful, you know. You're being hostile. We're new here. We've got to get along. Particularly you. You know you're under watch. Now please."

He scowled. Here's Willful, here's Hostile, snip, snip. If it weren't for her pained expression, he might have argued. He might even have called her good Green Beret material: quietly ferocious, full of herself, tireless. But the corners of her eyes trembled every time she took a breath. She was pale.

"You OK?" he said.

"The smell . . . I don't know. All these people. It's too much." But she wasn't waiting around. She looked away and moved her lips, talking to herself—*come on, come on,* she urged. She found an opening in the crowd and, pressing her purse to her breast, was carried away.

"Hey," he called after her, but then she was gone, vanished around a turn in the path into all those white T-shirts and brown legs and heads of black hair. He imagined her stumbling. He pictured himself reaching down and pulling her up, propping her against his shoulder. But there she was again, up ahead, smoothing her hair, waving for Sally to slow down.

So Reuben pushed on. He tramped over roots and plastic bags. Men in spotless white shirts were holding hands; girls with goiters the size of oranges shouted out to friends; and old women with blackened teeth and long hair tied into buns tottered along with burlap sacks in their hands. Porkpie was moving along swiftly, disappearing then reappearing. Sally was well out in front, standing off to the side of the path, occupied, talking to some man who had a bandage on his nose. As she talked, she was moving her head mechanically, scanning back and forth like a security camera, and every time she caught someone's eye she made them stop briefly and shake her hand. She saw Reuben looking. Smiling, she threw back her head and mouthed loud laughter. She pumped the hand of a passerby.

It was the kind of depressing theater he had seen during his first months in the Peace Corps: the Old Hand pretending for the newcomers. *I'm doing well. Can't you see? They love me.* A sham.

What did Porkpie think? Probably at that very moment she was thinking the same thing. Probably at that very moment she was dissecting Sally's frailty, just as he was. Probably she was thinking just like him. Border collie-ish, she would say. Pointlessly brisk.

Then they were with Sally. Their guide leaned against a cigarette seller's cart. Porkpie seemed to be moaning. Reuben looked her up and down. A vein near her ankle was pulsing.

"Hell," he said, greeting Sally. "Let's stop a moment."

Porkpie wiped her faced with her purse. She was panting. "I'm all right," she said, and then she touched Reuben's arm.

"You see over here," said Sally, shaking her hat like a tambourine. She seemed excited. "That's the water pipe. Careful now, when we go back in, we'll have to step over it."

The pipe was black plastic, big around as a volleyball. Reuben saw other exposed pipes farther ahead; the camp was covered with them.

"The pipe," said Sally. She paused. "It carries water."

"Christ," Reuben said.

"Oh, I'm sorry," Sally smiled. "I forgot you must know everything." And then she plunged Reuben and Porkpie back into the crowd, walking backward as she talked. People coming the opposite way yanked each other out of her way.

Porkpie elbowed Reuben. "Just ignore her," she whispered. "For your own good. OK?"

"Now over there," shouted Sally. "This is the Coconut Inn I was telling you about. It's the staff eating hut."

She shielded her eyes with her hand for a moment. "Oh, this is perfect," Sally said. "You came at a good time. You'll get to meet Ralph. He's in the Inn, playing chess."

"Chess," said Reuben. "You said chess."

"Maybe that sounds a little weird, unless you've actually been on Bidong. It's not really. Ralph's an absolute wizard at games. You ought to see him at Othello."

"Just a minute, please," said Porkpie. She bent forward, hands on her knees, and breathed deeply. Behind her, someone tripped.

"You get used to the smell," Sally said, rushing to her side. "I don't even notice it anymore." Sally reached into one of her pockets and pulled out a wad of tissues. "You might want to take a couple of these and breathe through them."

"Thank you," said Porkpie, taking the gift. She put the wad in her purse. "But, really, I've got to get used to it."

"*That's* the Bidong spirit," said Sally brightly. "Now come along. The Inn's just a bit farther. Follow me and there you are." She began marching again, swiveling her head and sticking out her hand to all who would shake it.

"The Bidong spirit," Reuben said. "My ass. She a den mother?" Porkpie nodded blankly. Her hair was matted in dark, curling tendrils. She looked as if she were ready to collapse.

The Inn was a tarp-covered porch, sealed off from the neighboring huts by a half wall of unpainted wood. There was a stack of lumber propped against the entrance. Sally opened the swing gate, and when Reuben walked in, still squinting from the sun, he was blinded momentarily in the deep shadows. It was like walking into a cave. He hit his head on a lantern tied to a beam and heard people laugh. "Hello, how you do?" said a Vietnamese woman. She was standing at the far wall, by the entrance of what appeared a dirt-floor kitchen, wiping her hands on a cloth. The kitchen was so dark that all he could see was a low flame under a huge silvery caldron. He felt Porkpie's hand on his arm; apparently she was blinded as well. He heard Sally greet somebody, and then, his sight recovering, Reuben saw the red-and-white plastic tablecloth over the now-famous table. The tablecloth sagged in the middle, where, he supposed, Gurmit had stolen the plank. "Hell," he said. It was just a table. Chessboards and pieces filled it, four on each side, and sitting on the benches behind them were Vietnamese men with carpenter's belts full of tools tied around their waists. The men were all frowning in concentration.

"Ralph," Sally said to a short white man stooping in front of one of the boards. He was skinny and wore glasses, and his wispy beard was flecked with what appeared to be wood shavings. He had on a busy long-sleeved shirt.

"Hey now," Ralph said, waving her off. "Just a minute. I've got these mates on the run." He went back to examining one of the boards, then reached out and snatched up a piece, moving it with a flourish to another square.

"He's playing a simultaneous," said Sally confidentially. "Eight players at once. The Viets taught him to play Chinese chess. He's repaying the favor by teaching a class on Western chess."

"That's . . . I don't know," said Porkpie, holding a wad of tissues to her nose. "That's really something."

"You got that right," Reuben mumbled. Porkpie began wandering around the Inn, a bit unsteady.

Ralph walked behind the man at the next board and studied the position. He nestled one arm in the crook of the other and stroked his beard.

"Hey now, missy," said Ralph, wagging his finger at Porkpie. "Careful now," he said. "Nixon's awake."

In the far corner, a rat circled a small wooden stake, sniffing. Pink raffia string was tied around its neck, securing it to the wood.

"I should explain," Sally whispered. "The Viets know Westerners love pets, so they got us one. We call it Nixon. The kitchen ladies got it for us. I mean, it's not like there's a pet store here. We don't want to hurt their feelings."

"Hey now," said Ralph. He looked at Reuben and Porkpie, then made a move at one board and went on to the next. "You're the new Yanks, that right? Mr. Large Fellow there, I've got a letter with your name on it. Just got it this half hour."

"The name's Reuben."

"Reuben. Right. Manley's friend, right? I've heard about you."

"Ralph," said Sally in a low voice. It sounded like a warning.

"Oh, yes, yes, yes," said Ralph, nodding. "A reputation's a funny thing. Won't hold it against you."

"No one will, Reuben," said Sally.

"What do you—" said Reuben, but Ralph cut him off.

"I got me a letter here from Doctor Johansson," the man said. He patted his shirt pocket. "Says you're the sub-engineer for the Sanitation Division. That's me. I'm the chief engineer. Bristol College degree."

"You the chief engineer?"

"Bugger me, yes," Ralph said.

"He's very intense," Sally whispered to Reuben.

"We'll be working together," said Ralph.

"That right?" said Reuben.

"It is. You know much about engineering? Got a Yank degree?" He made another move, and his opponent began pointing in consternation at a captured piece.

"No degree," said Reuben. "Experience. I get my hands dirty. Concrete, drywall, plumbing, carpentry. You name it."

"Concrete, drywall, plumbing, and carpentry," said Ralph. "There. I named it."

Reuben squinted.

"Says in my letter you're on probation," said Ralph. He looked up from one of his games, then moved a piece to another square. His opponent squealed. "Not that it makes any difference to me. Make any difference to you buggers?" He indicated his opponents.

"No, Mr. Ralph," one of them said, giggling.

Ralph said, "We just got back from a job. These mates are builders. Isn't that right?"

"Yes, Mr. Ralph." The builder reached out, his hand hovering over a pawn, and moved the piece one square forward.

Ralph turned to Reuben. "Just to let you know what's what."

"Shit on one hand, shinola on the other," said Reuben. "That's what's what."

Ralph didn't seem to be listening. He made a move and quickly moved on to the next board. His shirt, Reuben saw, was covered with cartoon dialogue bubbles.

"You like?" said Ralph, noting Reuben's interest. He pulled at his shirt. "Got this in Japan a ways back. Japanese English, hey?"

Reuben leaned close. *Taking beer in your wheel. Seven toes thank-you.*

"Oh now, Ralph," said Sally. "Look over here. Knight takes queen. You know you can't talk and play at the same time."

"Bugger," Ralph said absently. He studied the position.

"Play, play, play," Sally said, waving her hand. "It's almost lunchtime."

"Yes, madam Sally," said Ralph. "I'll be done shortly." He began stroking his beard again. "Did you tell them about our lovely little paradise here?"

"Ralph's quite the social critic," Sally said. "He thinks Bidong's a victory for predatory capitalism."

"Porkpie, you OK?" Reuben said.

Porkpie sat on a bench by the kitchen. One of the kitchen ladies, clucking, began to pet her.

"You go over the big hill, out that way"—Ralph waved his hand, indicating outside—"and that'll bring you to the northern beaches. That's where all the black marketeering goes on. The Malays boat over at night, and the entrepreneurs here hire longshoremen to carry goods back this way. Then the entrepreneurs hide the goods in their huts and sell them to the vendors. The prices get more outrageous the farther down the food chain you go. No money, you're in for a tough time."

"Yes," said Porkpie. She paused, collecting breath. "We passed their tables. I imagined that would be illegal. Task Force allows it?" She was dabbing her forehead with the tissue wad. *Tea?* one of the kitchen ladies asked her. *Want tea?*

"Oh, they do and they don't," said Sally. "Mostly they allow it since it's good for the local economy in Kuala Trengganu. But when they're mad at the Viets they confiscate everything and go around turning the tables over. It's a power game."

"You got influence with them?" said Reuben.

"Task Force is top dog here," Sally said. "You might want to file that away. Technically, Bidong is a prison camp. They can kick us out, you know."

"I know the policies, Sally," Reuben said sharply.

Sally looked at him coldly. Her eyes roamed his face.

"Man's on probation," said Ralph, pressing down on a pawn, "and he questions his elders." He slammed the piece forward one square. "Not that probation makes any difference to me. We're family here."

"You see," Sally said suddenly, "in Malaysia, only village boys become prison screws. Their English is really terrible. You might as well talk to your dog."

Reuben rapped the table hard. "You speak Malay?" he asked.

"I've been in Malaysia two years," said Ralph. "Not here. With British VSO, down in Johore State. Sally speaks the truth."

"You speak Malay?" Reuben asked.

Ralph looked down at his board. "Shh," he said, putting a finger to his lips. "Tough position here."

Porkpie, standing now, walked over to Reuben and put her hand on his arm. "Please don't," she whispered. "My stomach is in an uproar as it is. Just ignore them."

Reuben took a deep breath. Sally turned to watch Ralph make a move.

"Don't," said Porkpie. "Please."

So Reuben didn't.

"Do you want to see some photos?" asked Sally suddenly. She reached into a breast pocket and pulled out a small yellow album. "I've got some nice shots of people. Here. Lookie." She opened it. "Here's me holding a baby. They named her Bi Dong. Like Bidong Island, right? That's pretty common here. They name kids after places. People, too. I keep waiting for some baby Sallys. I sure do hear my name enough. All the time, it's 'Hello Miss Sally, hello Miss Sally.'" She smiled. She gazed out at the footpath, as if waiting for someone to call out to her. "That would be something, wouldn't it? People naming their kids after you?" She returned to her album, absently yanking her braid. "Oh, and here's one of me giving a ration bag to a zone chief."

"I think I'm going to be sick," said Porkpie, rubbing her stomach.

"Not the conversation, I hope," said Sally.

Porkpie shook her head and began rocking.

"Look," said Sally, holding the album up to Porkpie's face. "Here's one of me getting a model refugee boat from my teachers. I've got it in my room if you want to take a look."

"Oh Miss Sally," said Ralph. He seemed annoyed. "I'm trying to concentrate over here. Look where this mate put his rook."

Reuben stroked the tablecloth. He cracked his knuckles. He imagined, briefly, sweeping his hand across a board and sending the pieces flying. He turned to Porkpie. "You sure you're OK?" he said.

"I might . . . ," said Porkpie. She seemed to gag a little. She placed a tissue against her mouth. "Just a minute."

Miss Thi ran out from behind the tin screen and placed a plastic bucket at Porkpie's feet.

"Thank you," said Porkpie. "That's very kind."

"I've been here almost a year, you know," said Sally, peeling apart sticky pages. "Did I tell you that already?"

"She's team leader," said Ralph. He frowned at a pawn. "The old-timer here. So, team leader, how long did it take you to get used to the smell?"

Sally, smiling, looked at Porkpie rock over the bucket. A boy walked by, dragging a Clorox bottle attached to a string; the bottle had been cut into the shape of a boat. Someone heaved a brick over the far half wall, nearly hitting the rat, and Miss Thi ran out from the kitchen, yelling in Vietnamese at some running boys.

"Actually," said Sally, watching the boys run, "the smell never bothered me. I guess it takes a certain type." Then she looked at Reuben. "But not *too* certain. We're more . . . what would you say, Ralph?"

"Sensitized."

"Yes. Sensitized."

Reuben snorted.

"Breathing trouble, Reuben?" Sally said. "I heard asthma might be a problem with you. Let me know, and I can have them ship out some inhalers." She wagged her album at Reuben. "If you'd like to look, here's a nice shot of me on the Zone C beach. Want to see?"

Ralph snapped his fingers. "Hey now, Mr. Reuben. Take a gander over here. Lots of time for picture gawking. This is better." He moved a piece quickly. "Mate in two," he said gaily. He pointed at the board, and his opponent slapped his forehead and laughed.

"No, no," said Sally. "This is a good photo. Come look. This'll be good orientation for you both. There's always so much movement on Bidong, it's nice to look at a scene that'll just stay still on you. Photos give you such a sense of stability."

Reuben, rubbing Porkpie's shoulders, brushed a lank rope of hair from her cheek. He looked up. "She's not feeling well," he said.

"Oh, bugger," said Ralph. "You just missed a nice win over here. Rook down to the eighth rank, check, check, then checkmate. Lovely. But hey, Reuben Yank. Don't go getting the wrong idea. We work damn hard on Bidong."

"There's still a nice photo over here," said Sally, flipping the page back and forth.

"We work hard, we play hard," said Ralph. He scratched at his beard. "I'll show you. Miss Thi, would you fetch Mr. Vu for me?"

Miss Thi, wiping a spoon against a stick, called into the kitchen. A man wearing a Mets cap poked his head through the opening.

"Mr. Vu," said Ralph. "Who's the Vietnamese engineering chief?"

"I am the chief," said Mr. Vu.

"How many longhouses we got built now, hey? How many?"

"Three," the man said.

"Three. That's right. Bloody three. How come only three, hey?"

"Too much stealing, Mr. Ralph," said Mr. Vu.

"That's right, little mate. Too much stealing." He turned his attention to Reuben. "We order twenty boards, maybe fifteen come on the boat. Then it goes to Supply, and by the time we get it out to the construction site, it's down to ten. Did you see that stack of lumber outside? Yesterday there was double that amount. These carpenter buggers here will steal you blind, then play a rotten game of chess. Isn't that right, carpenter mates?"

The men laughed. One began nodding, then another spoke sharply to him in Vietnamese.

Reuben said, "I didn't say you weren't doing your job, Ralph."

"No, that's right," said Ralph. "Pawn takes bishop, by the way." He tapped a square on one of the boards, and his opponent began laughing. "Trouble is, who you going to blame, hey? These people have been through a lot. You going to box their ears, hey? For stealing?" He picked up a chess piece and pointed it at Reuben. "You going to get so bent out of shape you turn them over to Task Force?" He said it as if it were a challenge. "Those fucks will beat Holy Jesus out of them."

Everyone seemed to stiffen then. Miss Thi, lugging a basket of leafy vegetables from the kitchen, stopped in her tracks and stared at Mr. Vu, who looked away. Nixon squealed and stood briefly on its hind legs. Ralph was stroking his beard, but he was looking at Reuben, not at the boards, and his opponents, aware that the mood had changed, looked to Miss Thi, who spoke to them in hushed Vietnamese from across the room. They were all looking at Reuben. Sally held a picture against her cheek and stared. Ralph then crossed his arms. His head was tilted down, as if he were studying a position in one of the games, but his eyes were still on Reuben. *Tootle the horn,* his sleeve said. *Ripping the chocolate bar.*

"I'm here to work," said Reuben slowly. "I aim to stay."

"That's good," said Ralph. "I like that. Man's on probation, and he aims to stay. Good."

"We're all in this together," said Sally. "Isn't that right, Ralph?"

"Bugger me, yes. Probation make any difference to you, Mr. Vu?"

"No, Mr. Ralph."

"Well done, then," said Ralph. He raised his arm and walked to the end of the table. "Pawn up to king four," he said, pointing. "Makes no difference, Big Fellow Yank."

"Reuben, lookie this picture," said Sally. "It's Gurmit Singh. You know him, don't you?"

"The table thief," said Ralph. "You hear about this?" He rapped the table, then sank his hand into the sagging plastic tablecloth.

"I heard."

"You his friend?" asked Ralph.

Reuben said, "Friend or no friend's not my concern."

"Sure would like the table put back,'" said Ralph.

"You didn't look at Gurmit's picture," said Sally, waving her album.

"He shouldn't have taken it, you know," said Ralph.

"He even *looks* like a thief in this photo," said Sally.

Outside, the crowd bustled on, squawking and pushing, and Reuben, staring out over the half wall, was nearly blinded by the brightness of the day. There was a moist, swirling quality to the passersby, and watching them stream down the footpath, their faces energetic and strained, their movements precise, Reuben, rubbing his fingers along Porkpie's shoulder, had a momentary impulse to move his hands to her breasts. He did not, but in struggling with the impulse, in raising his hand to wipe sweat from her ear, it seemed to Reuben that the dark room had grown dry and small. He felt Ralph and Sally watching him. He felt their words buzz against him, crisp and light, like winged insects. He had to do something. He had to make his move.

He rose. He said, "If Gurmit took your plank, so what? Just nail another one to the table."

There was silence for a moment.

Ralph spoke. "I'm not talking to the little bugger. If he wants to talk to me, fine. I want an apology."

"It's not just about a plank," said Sally, closing her album. "It's the principle. He stole from our table."

"We're family here," said Ralph. "You can't steal from family."

"He just took it," said Sally. "Like a slap in the face."

"I want an apology from the little bugger," said Ralph. "If I just wanted a board put back in, I'd put a board back in. There's lumber outside. Plenty of hammers and nails on my carpenter mates here. But that's not the point."

"It's just a damn *table*," said Reuben. "Let's take care of it. Now."

"Yes," said Porkpie suddenly. She looked up from the bucket. "Please do solve this. I'd be grateful." She wiped her chin with a tissue.

There was pleading in her voice, a tone of mystified sweetness that was startling even to the Vietnamese chess players; they looked up from their boards and stared at the sweating white woman leaning over a plastic bucket. She dabbed her lips, then looked up at Reuben. Her expression said: I know what I just did. The Vietnamese were watching, perhaps not fully comprehending the rapid English, but knowing that a sick woman desired something from Sally and Ralph. The refugees would evaluate; they would talk, and the talk would spread from shelter to shelter. It was as if Porkpie had thrust Sally and Ralph onto a stage, had revealed the dark room as an intimate theater. Would their decision be cruel, or would they show kindness? One of the carpenters spoke in Vietnamese to Miss Thi, who answered with some urgency, then stood by the kitchen entrance, watching, drying a dish with a rag.

"We're team players here," said Ralph, glancing around.

"I'll bring Gurmit here," said Reuben. "Right now. Let's just hammer in something from that stack out there first. I'll bring him. He'll apologize. Guaranteed."

"You can't guarantee," said Sally weakly.

"He doesn't do it," said Reuben, "then his plank's going to show up missing and back here, anyway. He knows it. He doesn't, I'll make him aware."

"Please," said Porkpie. She lowered her head again. "Let's resolve this." Her voice was thick with fluid.

Ralph stood. He put his hands on his waist. He looked at his chess opponents, then down at the ground. "What say, Sally?"

Sally wouldn't look up. "Oh, I don't care," she said, waving her hand dismissively. "I just want an apology. In public."

Ralph nodded. "It's the principle of the thing, now isn't it?"

"So I say yes," said Sally. "Go ahead, Reuben. But you bring him here. Make good on your promise."

"I vote aye," said Ralph. "But only if you get the little bugger here."

Reuben moved quickly. He walked outside and sifted through the pile of lumber. He dragged a long board back in, and the chess players, without a word, scooped up their sets and pieces and yanked off the thumbtacks that held down the tablecloth. They shucked the covering onto the floor, and then Reuben, motioning for one of the men to give him a hammer and nails, placed the board into the space and hammered it in with a few quick strokes. "There," Reuben said. "Good as new. The problem has disappeared." He threw out his hands in imitation of a magician. "Poof. Vanished."

"Not quite," said Ralph, stroking his beard. "I want the little bugger here."

"Yes," said Sally. "We have a bargain."

Porkpie called to Reuben just as he opened the swing gate to leave. She said she needed air. She said she'd go with him. The office was on the way to the compound. If he would just walk slowly.

They passed the black market tables, the water tower, the smashed pilot wheel hanging from the tree. They didn't talk. Reuben led the way, clearing a path, while Porkpie held on to the back of his shirt. They stopped once, right in the middle of the trail, so that Porkpie could catch her breath. "I just wanted to say—" Reuben said, but she waved him off. She cupped a tissue over her nose. And then they were off, walking slowly, careful not to trip on any tree roots or depressions rutted into the ground. Reuben mumbled to himself, moving his lips, and his hair mushroomed in the breeze. His spine was tingling. He was so alert he was having trouble walking slowly, but Porkpie yanked on his shirt hard once or twice, and he eased his pace. His knuckles still hurt; his left knee was still warm, swollen from his fall on the street during the rout of the Malays. But the pain felt oddly reassuring. It made him feel strong. It made the image in his mind sharp and clear. He was picturing himself free. He was picturing Kuala Trengganu sinking. Block by block the crumbling shop houses were disappearing. The mosque fell; the monuments quaked and dropped into fissures the size of buses; the Lido lay under rubble; in the harbor district, circling dogs clacked over the still-trembling roof tiles of Chinese apartments. He felt the whole city sink, and as it sank he tilted his head this way and that, surprised at the sudden lurchings and the even more sudden collapses, watching as from an airplane the funneling of bricks and planks and homely food stalls into vast cleavages of earth and water. And then it was over. The ocean was glassy and smooth; the land was dark with furrows, the horizon clear and flat, and a dry, chaffing wind from the back of his mind whispered the city's obliteration. He thought: Bidong.

Porkpie turned onto a side path, toward the staff compound. She spoke to him through her tissue. She just needed some tea, she said. She just needed to lie down in her bunk. He waved, but he was already thinking of something else. He was thinking of Gurmit Singh, thinking of how the foolish little man would leap at his voice, and by the time he pushed his way through the crowd, placing his giant hands on people's shoulders and moving them out of the way, by the time he threw open Gurmit's office door, he had already pictured himself marching Gurmit down the path to the Coconut Inn and making him apologize. He saw Gurmit sitting at his chair. The man smelled of sea breeze; he was bandaging a cut on his leg; an empty drawer lay atop his desk, obscuring his expression. Reuben spoke sharply. He kicked at a bench. He spoke, and then he walked grimly to Gurmit's desk, his expression a frightful mask, ready to scare the man out of his chair, but what he saw stopped him in his tracks. Gurmit's face was radiant. Thanking you, said Gurmit: I will go with you, yes. Gurmit's voice broke; he took Reuben's hand and held it. I must apologize, isn't it? Gurmit asked. I must apologize, please. So guilty. So much I must apologize, yes. Thanking you for this, please. Yes. Thanking you.

10

Late that year the sky turned gray as ocean, and the rain fell in sheets and made the smell bloom like a plant. There was mud everywhere. The relief workers had tidy yellow bungalows, but no matter how often they swept the plywood floors, the ooze kept rising through the spaces between the slats and piling up around the door as if someone were slathering it on with a butter knife. People walked slower, and over in the camp hospital the doctors said the Vietnamese weighed a few pounds more than usual because everyone was just sitting around on their haunches and watching the rain come down. But people were also losing their tempers more, especially when children stood in the middle of the footpaths like their souls wouldn't budge from their bones and cried out for playmates back in Vietnam. The refugees were dreamy and on edge. They passed around news: Malaysian navy boats had fired on refugees off Kota Bharu; villagers had stoned new arrivals on a beach south of Kuala Trengganu; the battalion of Rangers stationed an hour away was conducting riot-control exercises. Husbands smoked clove cigarettes and played Chinese chess with armies fashioned from bottle caps. Wives rolled up the cuffs of their shiny black pants and spent hours teasing the mud from each other's hair with boar-bone combs.

In the UN compound, the relief workers were itching for leave time. There was mud in the oil canisters, and the generator kept breaking down. There was mud on the wire fence and between the bed sheets, and even in the toothpaste. One morning, Ralph said enough was enough, then walked down to the dock with his toothbrush still in his mouth and squirted his whole tube of Crest at the flatfish. Later, Johann the radiologist drank a mud ball that had somehow gotten into his Johnnie Walker bottle, and when Manley offered to punch him in the stomach to induce vomiting, Johann took it personally and they almost got into a fight.

All through the rains, Porkpie was jangly with newcomer's nerves. To calm herself, she let a fat Chinese man who claimed to be an acupuncturist stick needles into her elbow, and she stopped drinking coffee altogether. It was difficult to remember names and faces. The other relief workers seemed elusive, full-bodied and substantial inside the UN compound, then disappearing outside the compound gate, crab stepping through the mud, sealed inside their ponchos, then melding into the shelters and people and loudspeaker noise. She wasn't even completely sure how many relief workers there were. Inside the compound were ten bungalows, but she never saw ten white people together at the same time. The Bible thumpers, she heard, had been removed; the social worker, an Australian, was on extended leave; except for Johann, the Swedes working in the hospital kept to themselves. The Swedes even ate in the Coconut Inn at a later hour, what they called European time. She waved, and they waved back. They spoke in Swedish; they never joined in the board games at night.

Her bungalow, just behind Sally's, had two sets of frosted louvered windows, one set facing toward the ocean, the other overlooking the Zone C footpath, just yards from the wire fence separating the compound from the rest of the camp. She was always at the windows, turning the louver cranks one way, then the other. When she turned the cranks to the right, the window slats opened and noise and air filled the room, but then wasps flew in and crawled on her ears or rubbed their abdomens against the glue strips of her aerograms. When she turned the cranks to the left, the slats closed, but then the room turned hot as a crawl space and salt-crazed ants ran up her legs and arms to lick the sweat soaking through her underthings.

No matter which way she turned the cranks, she couldn't help staring at the Vietnamese outside. Her bungalow was built on enormous concrete pilings, so when she pressed her nose against the window slats, she saw the tops of the refugees' heads and, farther back, a ragged line of shelters that had been built so close together she at first thought she was looking at a wall. It was an unpleasant sensation, peering down as if from an elephant, moving about high and dry behind frosted glass while below people sank up to their knees in the earth. At all hours of the day, the crowds streamed by and churned up the mud until the footpath was lumpy with squishy black holes. They moved slow as dray animals. Their loads were always soggy, their clothes damp, and the mud was always sucking their flip-flops right off their feet.

They looked so pathetic, she was glad to see young men, their faces alert and open, lean against the wire fence during breaks in the rain and stare up at her windows as she folded blouses or combed her hair. Porkpie cranked her back windows open and shouted hello, which caused Sally to knock on her door. "Tell them to scat," said Sally, making shooing motions, but Porkpie just waved at the men. Fair was fair. If she could spy on them, then they should be able to spy back.

"Jesus, Porkpie, they're not children," said Sally.

"Of course they're not," said Porkpie, smiling at the men, but she was thinking how smooth their faces were. She recognized two of them. They addressed her as Miss Porkpie and favored haircuts that left them with cowlicks. At night they sang folk songs and rubbed camphor oil on their mothers' arms.

Sally put her hands on her hips. "They're hoping you'll undress," she said.

"Oh yes," said Porkpie. "Hope springs eternal." She had, in fact, already thought out the consequences of disrobing for them. Serving up one's corpus in the interest of charity: when she imagined the hoots and uproar that would be created by a peekaboo breast or thigh, she pronounced the notion misguided.

Sally frowned at her.

"Not that I'm going to do it," said Porkpie.

"Don't even think it," said Sally. She snapped the windows shut.

"I was simply speculating."

"I've shut the windows," said Sally, "and now I'm going to go outside and tell those men to go away." She turned abruptly and went out the door.

Later, in the Coconut Inn, the relief workers shook their heads at Sally's story.

"Porkpie," they said. "And that Reuben Gill. You can have 'em both."

"The worst yet."

The Six by Six Rule didn't seem to apply. The Six by Six Rule held that you spent your first six months on Bidong learning your ass from your elbow, and your last six months complaining that no one else knew their ass from their elbow. After that, your contract was up and the Viets gave you a model of a refugee boat and Doctor Johansson gave you an airplane ticket and took you out for a farewell dinner.

"Six by Six is for normal people," said Sally. "The arithmetic's different for these two."

"It's Zero by Twelve for Reuben Gill," said Ralph, pushing his glasses up his nose. "A diseased arse, that's what he is."

"If that's true," said Sally, "then it's Twelve by Zero for Porkpie. Alice through the Looking Glass for the whole year. Unless Year Five turns nasty. Then there won't be a whole year to think about."

If anyone had asked Porkpie for the numbers on Reuben Gill, she would have said x^2 by y^2 because Reuben was an equation at least as complicated as algebra. But no one asked her. And no one asked Reuben what he thought about Porkpie: the man was on probation and probably an acid commando or some other variety of militaristic undesirable, so one had to be careful. There was confirmation when Ralph, patrolling Zone C, pointed to Reuben's hands. "Mate," he said, "you've got calluses the size of tinned biscuits." There was no response. Reuben just kept on working, throwing out his tape measure like a fishing line. "Like tinned biscuits, mate," Ralph said. "Hey. Tinned biscuits, I said."

Then Reuben locked his tape measure, put his hand to his mouth, and chewed one of the calluses open. He spit the skin into a puddle. "Kind of stale for a biscuit," he said. The look in Reuben's eyes, Ralph said, had been so greedy and wild that a Vietnamese woman selling ramen noodles had ripped a package open and made him a bowl right on the spot.

"Reuben Gill?" said Sally. It was night, and the Scrabble boards were out. She looked up from her tile rack. "Just as I expected, that's what. Overbearing. Projector boy at the John Wayne Filmfest."

"Mr. Bloody Bugger You and You and You," said Ralph.

"But he's a worker," said Johann. "Isn't he?"

"I've seen his type before," said Sally. "They come and they go. They always end up more trouble than they're worth."

"But you ought to see him work," said Johann. "I can see him on Zone C from the radiology room. In Sweden, we have a saying. What is it in English? He is the person who gets the things done."

"Hey, hell yes," said Manley, putting down his *New Straits Times*. "That's my buddy, and I'll kick anyone's ass who says different."

"You see?" said Sally, motioning toward Manley. "Trouble already."

"What's that the Viets say?" said Ralph. "'If we kill each other, whom shall we live with?' There's been enough anger, hasn't there?" He pointed beyond the wire, where Vietnamese girls were watching the white people sit on the porch. "If it weren't for ass kickers, we wouldn't be here in the first place. There wouldn't be any boat people."

"Hey," said Manley. "I'm just saying he's my buddy."

"Peace, brothers," said Johann.

"Yes, peace," said Ralph. "I'm just saying he's on probation, that's all. I'm just saying, if he's like this on probation, what's he going to be like when he's not?"

"He ain't no Porkpie," said Manley. "That's all I'm saying."

"Well," said Sally. "There's where we can all agree." She picked four tiles from her rack and laid them on the board.

"Jesus," said Manley, shaking his head. "Porkpie."

"Porkpie," said Sally.

"Bugger me," said Ralph. "Porkpie."

It was too bad, people said, that Reuben couldn't be more like Porkpie, and Porkpie couldn't be more like Reuben. With Reuben, you shuddered; with Porkpie, you winced. Why, Porkpie couldn't even walk to the washing-up room without being precious. One morning, before the loudspeakers started, she walked across the compound dressed in a sarong, on her way to get herself a bucket bath. On the other side of the fence, children followed her progress, grabbing hold of the wire strands to pull themselves along when the muck grabbed their knees. They sneezed when she sneezed, and when she looked up to watch the light filter through the clouds and soak into the mud, they looked up too. She couldn't walk five steps without the ground swallowing her ankles, and every time she stopped to wipe the mud from her legs, the children stopped as well. She heard the bubbles sigh against her feet and burst apart with tiny, bright gasps. It was such a delightful sound, Porkpie said, that she had giggled when the children bent at the waist too, pretending to wipe away mud, then tilted their heads and remained stock-still, their ears hovering just inches over the footpath. She giggled even more when she stepped out of the washing-up room and saw them kneeling on all fours, pressing their ears to cardboard sheets laid flat on the mud.

At the Coconut Inn, Porkpie said aloud that if you walked to the washing-up room early enough, you could see children listening to the bubbles seep up through the mud. Imagine, she said: just imagine. *Pop,* she said, spreading her fingers wide. That's how the bubbles sounded. *Pop,* then *poof,* then *psss,* and then the light burst out.

Sally guffawed, and then she smiled. That's depression, she said. The kids sat like lumps because they were sick of sleeping on plastic and sinking into the ground. She had been on Bidong a long time, she said. The cardboard-sitters were nothing new. They were children who were sick of the rain and the smell and the mud lice biting their heads, and they put their ears to cardboard on the ground because the cardboard was cool and soft and muffled the racket from the loudspeakers.

Porkpie said nothing. She sat with her arms folded and thought over what Sally said. She sat through a round of gin rummy and didn't make a face even when Nixon started squealing.

The next day, a baby in Zone D fell from its hammock and almost drowned in a puddle. When Porkpie saw the crowd rushing the baby to the hospital, she had first thought they were carrying a tiny animal. The mud on its body was stiff as fur; one of its arms flailed like a tail, and the women rushed down the path with such fearful expressions that Porkpie thought someone had been bitten.

Outside the gate to the compound, Sally smiled when Porkpie told her about her mistake. Sally was carrying a bundle of bulging folders covered with tiny yellow stickers. They were the old administration forms of some of her adult students, she said. They had left just that morning for America.

"Take a look at the yellow stickers," said Sally, holding up the folders for inspection. "What do they say? Look close. It's all in pencil."

Porkpie looked. "RPM."

"What's it mean?"

"I wouldn't know. I just got here."

"Go on. Guess."

"Revolutions per minute," said Porkpie. "Though you're going to tell me that's wrong, aren't you?"

"Yes, I am."

"Well?"

"Well, I'm just making a small point."

"But what does RPM mean?"

"That's not my point. My point is that your eyes deceived you at the hospital. Now your eyes are deceiving you here. Animals aren't animals, and RPM isn't RPM. There's mud on everything. Just keep that in mind."

The statement was bewildering. "I think you've turned my story into something it's not," said Porkpie.

Sally cocked her head. "I was just making an observation. That's all."

"Oh," Porkpie said. She opened the gate and wiped her hand on the post. "Because I was curious, you know. You hear your words used against you, and you start to wonder."

"I'm sorry," said Sally, following Porkpie in. "I was just referring to teaching here." Sally looked at the towels on the clothesline and felt for dampness. "I was just talking about working here," she said, speaking into a towel. "Getting used to things. Being effective. Things like that." She turned suddenly. "You're such a *sensitive* type," she said. She put her hand on Porkpie's arm and walked her to her bungalow.

It seemed an easy thing for Sally to say: she had put herself in charge of the two schools in Zones C and D, where a team of carpenters had just last year built sturdy rooms that rested on stilts. Sally sloshed her way across flat ground, straddled a few water pipes, and within five minutes she was marching up the school steps. Manley had it nearly as easy. As second in seniority, at least among the three English teachers, he had put himself in charge of the schools in nearby Zones A and B, which, although they had no blackboards, at least had wooden floors and reinforced stilts.

Porkpie wondered if Manley and Sally had entered into some kind of pact. When Manley announced her posting, he had rudely pointed over her head. There, he said: enjoy the view. They had assigned her to the Zone F primary school, atop a forbiddingly steep hill, a stone's throw from the Zone F promontory. It hardly seemed a welcoming assignment, but Porkpie hadn't complained. Manley seemed to be making a point, but the point was so silly and mean she refused to grace it with an objection. He said she had to earn her stripes, but she felt what

he really meant was that she had to behave as if she could field-strip an
M-16 in thirty seconds flat.

Ever since she had sat next to him at dinner, he had grown posi-
tively hostile. Nixon had been acting up all through the meal, gnawing
at his leash, and when Porkpie turned, alarmed at the squealing, Manley gently poked her arm with his fork. Relax, he said. Nixon was tame:
in Kelantan State, back in the Peace Corps, he had seen a rat chew
Reuben's toenail.

"Tell me," she said. "For my own curiosity, what was he like back
then?"

All she got for an answer was that Reuben was his Big Bro. The
tone of his voice was clear: *Hands off.*

"I'm not picturing him naked, you know," she said. "I'm just asking
a question."

Manley frowned, then took out his wallet and, after fingering his
packets of Trojans suggestively, withdrew a dog-eared photo. The picture, he said, was taken when he and Reuben were in Peace Corps
training, down near the city of Seremban. It showed Reuben sitting in
an elaborate wicker chair, stuffing his mouth with what appeared to be
boiled eggs. Manley wouldn't let Porkpie hold the picture. He got
quiet. His expression softened when he looked at it with her, but even
in the half light of the Coconut Inn, you could see that his fingers were
trembling ever so slightly.

It was all rather embarrassing.

"Why . . . ," Porkpie said, and then she fell silent and completed
the sentence in her head: Why, Manley's smitten with him.

Manley looked her square in the face, and she swore she heard him
whisper, "No I'm not." He looked angry, but then one of the kitchen
ladies bumped the gas lantern, and in the sudden darkness she couldn't
see his expression. After that, he wouldn't sit by her at dinner. She worried he was grudge-holding, but whenever she caught his eye, hoping to
get him talking, he turned rude. He started belching in her presence.
He hadn't done that in Kuala Trengganu, but now he belched so much
that she suspected him of swallowing air just for that purpose. And she
began to notice the unpleasant habit he had of calling the Vietnamese
shelters "hootches."

It was difficult to believe that Sally approved of him. But it was
easy to see that neither one of them approved of her. Sally smiled too

much and kept looking into her eyes, as if expecting tears, and Manley just opened his little fish mouth and belched. They seemed to have little films running in their heads: the Hardy Volunteers, worldly and weary and a little impatient with the newcomer's adjustments. When she walked into Sally's bungalow for the weekly teachers' meetings, Sally and Manley would look at each other knowingly and start speaking in a language full of abbreviations and references that she couldn't follow.

"Got Mr. Huang's CDU for the A and G women's?" Sally might say.

"Hey," Manley would answer, "I seen where Miss Ng and Mr. Quang gave some serious JVA shit in KT."

At first Porkpie had giggled, but giggling just seemed to make Sally and Manley mad. She joined in.

"RPM," Porkpie said.

Sally didn't look up. "If you don't know what it means," she said, "then don't say it."

"Hey," said Manley. "Be here awhile. Then say it."

"You're making me feel . . . ," Porkpie stared at the floor. "I wish you would let me join in a little more."

No one said anything for a moment, but then Manley coughed and said that Bidong was no picnic. "This won't cut it," Sally added, reaching over and rubbing Porkpie's washboard-tuck sundress.

Porkpie protested that the dress had served her well in the Philippines. Manley shook his head and said that the only thing Bidong was like was Bidong, and then he looked at her feet and frowned.

"Beige flats," said Porkpie, following his eyes.

"Whatever," he said. "Only one who wears shoes like that is what's-her-toes." He snapped his fingers and looked at Sally. "That French delegation chick? The one with the braids?"

"Claudette," said Sally. "The FPRS delegation."

"Her," said Manley. He pushed back his hair and raised his eyebrows at Porkpie. "She comes out once a month and won't stay overnight."

"*Plus de* squealy things," said Sally, speaking in falsetto. "Too many rats."

"Too chickenshit, more like it," said Manley.

"Too Euroweenie," said Sally.

"Too prissy," said Manley, and then he lunged across his chair and ran his scuttling fingers up Porkpie's arm.

Porkpie slapped his hand away. She told them that her shoes had kicked more than one testicle in the Philippines, but that just started Manley snorting. When she left, Manley stuck his head out the door and shouted, "Good-bye, Lady Porkpie."

She picked her way through the compound, avoiding puddles, and sat on her porch, wiping her flats with a Kleenex. Over in the Task Force compound, the Malay guards held their prayer mats out the windows and shook them hard, then slapped the footprints and knee prints on the weave until clumps of dirt flew through the air. In back, she heard the Viets in their lean-tos swearing and scooping out the mud in plastic buckets and throwing it onto the footpaths. She slipped on her flats and peered around the corner. The men's pants were rolled to their thighs. The men held red plastic buckets, and they shoveled mud from the floors of their shelters. They shoveled and swore, but the muck kept seeping back in, and their toes squished in the liquid every time they leaned over to shovel some more.

She went inside and took out a bottle of Chinese perfume from her green vinyl travel bag. *Flower,* the label said. She squeezed the bottle. She stood and squirted some on herself, and then she squirted a wisp into the air. She breathed. She walked to each corner and squirted fine small clouds through the air, and then, standing by the back windows, she turned the window crank to the right and smelled the camp gust in, and started to cry.

After dinner, she talked to Reuben. During the day she hardly saw him at all, but come nighttime, when she sat outside on her bungalow porch, all she had to do was whisper hello to the geckos on the wall and Reuben would come bounding over out of the darkness and rest his arms on the railing. His belt buckle gleamed in the moonlight. "Thought I heard you," he'd say, and then they'd chat awhile and listen to the ocean washing in. He brought her gifts sometimes: an apple from New Zealand, a bar of Ghirardelli chocolate, an empty box of Dunhills to carry chalk in. "Here," he'd say, gruffly. "Brought you something." And then with no more fanfare than if he were handing over a wrench, he'd reach into his pocket and pull out a gift. It was pleasurable to imagine someone so large and sweaty giving himself over to domestic niceties. She pictured him lingering over the wicker baskets piled high on the supply boat, then picking out an object for her and stuffing it into his pants.

There was in human relations a mercantile aspect to even the finest, most delicate, interactions, and no matter how much you pleaded impoverishment, no matter how foaming and apoplectic your litigations, the ventricles of your heart opened and closed like a ledger book, *debit-credit, debit-credit,* and in the final reckoning, you paid your bills in blood. There was something both effortless and invigorating about the way they spoke to each other. Like undertow, she thought: like swimming in the ocean and feeling the current sweep you along.

"People could be more welcoming," she said.

"Just ignore them," he whispered. His throat was sore from yelling all day.

"It's hard to ignore," she said.

"You're Green Beret material, Porkpie," he said. His voice was seductive: a moist rumble, a vague suggestion of heat.

She looked at him blankly.

"I mean it," he said. He held his hands out in imitation of a balancing scale. "Here's shit, here's shinola. Which is which?"

"Please. If you're going for a Zen koan, you might think about elevating the subject a bit."

"Yes!" said Reuben. "There you are. That's it exactly. Sally and Manley would just tell me to shut up. Then I'd have to pop them one, wouldn't I? But you tell me to shut up without saying it. Swift, silent, and deadly. Just like a Green Beret."

"Well, thank you, Reuben. But if you don't mind, I'd prefer to have my résumé filled with civilian pursuits."

"I look at you, I see someone packing ammo."

"Please don't arm me with your eyes."

"You see? That's what I mean. A killer-diller."

"Oh, Reuben."

"Hard as nails."

"Thank you," she said. "That was a lovely gesture."

"Gesture, nothing. I told you what I think."

But she saw the way his eyes were moving, tracking her small movements, watching for changes in her expression. Her, a killer-diller: she started to giggle. He had told a lie, but a scrupulous one, a lie oafish and sincere, and all the more lovely because of its clumsiness.

It was still a lie the next morning, because she wanted nothing more than to fumble for aspirin under the loudspeakers and pinch her nose shut at the smell and wear her sundress and flats without Sally and Manley rolling their eyes.

And it remained a lie the next night, during a round of charades on Sally's porch. Porkpie shouted out *The Kama Sutra!*" when Manley acted out his word by thrusting his hips back and forth and rotating his hands, as if squeezing gigantic breasts. The way everyone reacted, Porkpie was worried she had blurted out an old locker combination. Manley froze. Sally closed her eyes and smiled, then leaned forward in her chair. Ralph, draped on the railing, suddenly got very quiet.

"See," Sally said. "When you play charades, you're supposed to choose really familiar books."

"*The Kama Sutra,*" Porkpie protested. "Oh, come on."

"Everyone has to be familiar with it," said Sally. "Or the game gets spoiled."

"Manley," said Porkpie. "*The Kama Sutra.* Is that too obscure?"

Manley slapped at a mosquito on his leg. "Hey, obscure comes to mind. What the hell is a Comma Suture? You can't use grammar books. You're supposed to use reading books." He stuck his finger out and started jabbing the air. "This is Bidong. This ain't Vassar or something." His lips parted, and a little belch came out.

"Like I said," said Sally, smiling. "Everyone's got to be familiar with it."

Ralph put his head down. All Porkpie could see of him was his hair. "What book were you doing, Manley?" he said, popping up. He was smiling. "I mean, no point in continuing this round, is there?"

"*Turn of the Screw,*" said Manley.

Porkpie slapped the arm of her chair and giggled. "Oh gosh," she said, putting her hand over her mouth. "Oh Manley. Really."

"Hey," he said. "I'm just getting casual. I play to relax."

"It's evening," said Ralph. "We relax."

"I sure get tired," said Sally. "I could be here for *two* years, and I'd get tired."

"Anyone else heard of Porkpie's clue?" asked Manley, nodding. He turned to Sally.

"You know," Sally said. "All this time I've been here, I've never heard it used for charades. Ralph, how about you?"

Ralph fiddled with his beard. "Let me think about that."

"I say it's obscure," said Manley, raising his hand. "Sally?"

"I'm in," she said. "O-B-S-cure." She raised her hand and looked at Ralph.

"Well, I don't think I've heard translations used before," Ralph said. "What say, Sally?"

"Why should they be used?" she said. "We're not out to impress each other."

"Right," said Ralph. "I guess that makes three." He raised his hand.

"Hey, three to one," said Manley. He had his hands on his hips. "What we got here is a majority."

Porkpie thought: two liars, one ignoramus. A majority.

The rest of the game, she kept things simple. *War and Peace,* she said defiantly. *Last of the Mohicans. Gone with the Wind.* Each time she spoke, she glanced around, daring anyone to exchange looks. Her score was terrible.

Ralph was her partner for a while, and once he laughed and said, "Hullo. Hullo. I hereby give you permission to help us out."

"Too little, too late," she said. She could hardly speak. Her throat felt as if it were coated in chalk dust.

"What's that, now?" he said, perplexed.

"Never mind," she said.

When the scores were tallied, Manley did a jig on the porch.

At ten, the generators shut down, and the fluorescent light on the porch buzzed and died. In the sudden darkness Porkpie found herself making a face and sticking her tongue out.

"Sorry," she said, rising to leave. She felt her way to the steps. "That wasn't very polite."

"Tut-tut," said Ralph. She heard him fumbling for his pipe. "Nothing personal. It wasn't a familiar book."

"Not that," she said. "I just made an unfortunate reflex gesture. I'm apologizing for it."

"Accepted," said Sally. "For whatever."

"Here's another gesture for you," Manley said.

She couldn't see it, but she didn't have to.

She wrote a letter to Lyle that night, scribbling onto the aerogram with an uncertain, looping hand. She had a cup of lemongrass tea on her desk, and her throat was so cottony and dry she grew impatient waiting for the drink to cool. She burned her tongue. Her gas lantern hissed, and its blinding patch of mantle was fiery and impertinent. *Dear Lyle,* the letter began, *It would be so much easier to write if you were dead, but if you're not, and if you're still in Chicago, I hope you're doing well.* A postcard to Lyle would have sufficed, but in staring at the blank, blue expanse of the aerogram, she was overcome with an urge to fill the space with civility.

It was not easy. Her head was swirling with cruel facts, facts she thought she had forgotten, facts that could burn a hole into Lyle's chest. The dome at the end of his penis leaked. His skin flaked like a pastry shell. The total calculated volume of his known marital ejaculations, in terms of pint-sized mason jars, was, at best, two and a quarter. But such facts were the servants of cruelty, and cruelty was, after all, that which made truth unbearable, and because unbearable, no longer true. She frowned. She poked her arm with her pen, recalling the flesh-rending arrows of Saint Theresa. She ground her teeth and pulled her hair, and then she scalded her finger in her cup of lemongrass tea, and she was ready to write. She shut her eyes tight and exhaled loudly, then reached over to the window crank and turned it to the right, and blew the facts clear out the window.

Bidong, she wrote, *is not at all what I expected.*

She held the aerogram up to the light, then put her pen down and looked around the room. It was bare as a nun's cell. The sheets on her bunk were neatly tucked into the corners of the mattress. By the door, her flats were gleaming, wiped clean by Kleenex. Except for clothes, she had hardly unpacked: her giant green vinyl bag lay by the wastebasket, under a shelf brimming with silverware, cups, and various teas.

She had no idea how to continue the letter. She crumpled it into a ball and threw it into the wastebasket. What had she expected Bidong to be? Nothing specific came to mind. Something sprawling. A place of transit. Limbo, maybe. Even now, she had no clear image of the island. The geography of a place, its patterns, its language: all worked their way into one's spirit slowly. You could live in a place for years, and its meanings might still be impenetrable as a row of bricks. When you were new to a place, what could you do but accept its surprises? You knew nothing. What could you do but keep looking and wait for the day when you would just be sitting in a chair or waving to someone, and all of a sudden your spirit would whisper into your ear: *You are in this place. You are here.*

Every morning, she woke early and sat up in her bunk, just listening, hoping her spirit would whisper into her ear. She heard the rain, and she heard the Vietnamese stirring behind her bungalow. After washing up, she heard the loudspeakers blare to life with the Malaysian national anthem, then the South Vietnamese national anthem. At seven o'clock, just as the lines were forming at the wells, she stepped out of her bungalow and into the rain and smell, and began her long walk to the Zone F primary school. It took her almost half an hour to reach her destination, and long before she arrived, she stopped listening for her spirit to whisper into her ear.

Every morning she tucked her lesson books and attendance sheets under her yellow slicker and pressed them like kittens to her stomach, then swayed down the crowded footpath until she came to the sewage canal, crossed at regular intervals by thin planks. Porkpie would stand in line behind the Vietnamese, waiting her turn, and study their sure-footed crossings. Her depth perception was suspect, her balance was never good, and loaded down with books and paper, she felt pregnant and wobbly. But every morning she stepped onto the plank and bobbed over the lumpy sewage. She felt the squeal caught in her throat shake all the way down to her feet. People murmured behind her, buzzing like flies. Naked children ran out of their huts, shouting things at her she didn't understand, and when the slick plank rocked with her weight, she thought she heard laughter. Once a rat had stood on its hind legs on the other side, just waiting, sniffing in her direction. And the smell—everywhere, the smell!—the smell rose like a bubble to the tops of the palms and stuck to her clothes. Even the rain stank. It plopped against her slicker and ran down her nose.

When she stepped over the ropes, her feet sank in the mud. "Where do you go?" people said. "What is your name?" But she couldn't turn to address them because she would trip in her flats and bring down plastic sheeting and people's drying laundry. The wood smoke stung her eyes, and sodden branches tumbled down from the trees, trailing spiky fronds. The Vietnamese darted around her. Through their wet shirts she saw the knotty rope of their spines. Sometimes she turned the wrong way and didn't know it until people ran up to her and pointed the other way. "Zone F," the Vietnamese said, jabbing the air. "F. F. Zone F." Somehow the whole camp knew where she was going.

Somehow they could distinguish between sheets of blue tarp that all looked the same to her.

Zone F began at the foot of a hill so steep that a work detail had hacked at the soil, all the way down to the tree roots, to give people better footing. She lengthened her stride to make the climb, humming hiking songs and clutching her books so tightly her fingers turned white. The path led around lean-tos built at impossible angles, and under the mud were mounds of brownish palm and crushed cans and shredded tarp that stuck to the soles of her shoes. In places, shelters leaned into the trail, forming archways over her head, and children swinging in hammocks reached down to touch her. Their parents seemed to be in light trances, moving so slowly that Porkpie wondered if they weren't stunned by the wood smoke curling out between the branches and tarp. People lived on top of each other, sometimes in shelters two stories high, and the women all had circles under their eyes and hefted giant, colicky babies around on their hips. On cold mornings, the adults squatted in circles around their fire pits and held their hands over the embers. They didn't say much. They snapped at their children. They rooted around the insides of battered boxes and heaps of crinkling tarp. "Good morning," Porkpie would say, summoning a smile. "Hello. Good morning." People smiled back at her. Sometimes they addressed her in Vietnamese. They seemed preoccupied, and in their expressions Porkpie thought she detected evaluation. *You,* the expressions said: *you can't even walk up a hill.*

Porkpie climbed on, pulling on sapling limbs to haul herself up. She looked for footholds in the flat rocks, leaning forward and probing with her free hand for tree roots. Sometimes she lost her balance. Sometimes she fell. Her lesson books would slip from under her slicker, and she would curse under her breath as the pages flapped like doves and tumbled down the slopes, coming to rest in muddy rivulets. Young men retrieved the books for her, running effortlessly up the trail to where she sat, bounding like gazelles, and she would be so embarrassed sitting in the mud waiting for the samaritans to arrive that when they thrust the books in her face she would fumble around in her pockets and hold out shiny new pencils for them to take. No one would. They just smiled, then motioned to a point over her head, guiding her vision to the thick black water pipe that marked the top of the hill. So she would brush herself off and pull at the hood of her slicker and start to climb again, stopping every few steps to mark her progress. It was hot inside the slicker, and her skin stuck to the material. Her lungs hurt. She breathed with her mouth open and let the smelly rain moisten her tongue. When the first joint of the water pipe came into view she yelped in relief: the top of the hill was only twenty more steps away. But the mud was slick and the underbrush too scraggly to pull, so she had to grab the nylon rope dangling from the water pipe and pull herself hand over hand to the top.

At the water pipe, Porkpie rested. She breathed so hard for the first few minutes that her voice sounded funny when she said hello. People looked at her with surprise.

"Why you crying?" one woman asked, grabbing hold of Porkpie's slicker. The woman peered out from under a palm leaf covering her head. The raindrops were fat and warm, and Porkpie felt them trickle down her collar.

"I'm not crying," said Porkpie. The words came out in gasps. "I'm out . . . I'm just out of breath."

The woman patted her arm. A man wearing a striped bellboy hat came by and said something in Vietnamese to the woman. His legs were muddy. The woman said something back. Then, presumably for Porkpie's benefit, she said in English, "She crying."

"No, I told you," said Porkpie, shifting books under her slicker. "I'm not crying." But it was no use. The woman left quickly, and the man nodded at her and said something soothing in Vietnamese. He raised one of his legs. He was barefoot.

"Yes," said Porkpie, pointing. "No shoes."

"You, you," the man said, laughing. He pointed at Porkpie's legs, and then she saw: her calves were covered with mud and leaves. Her knee was dimpled with pebbles, and below that were streaks of her own blood.

At the top of Zone F was a mud flat off to the right, as smooth and spacious as a gym floor; to the left, a dense stand of coconut trees. Her school was set in the middle, built on a small hump ravaged with tree roots and pebbly gullies. The cliff was exactly fifty-three paces across the mud flat, and the smell from the camp funneled up over the sides in gusts. Standing on the outcrop, Porkpie could see the gray expanse of ocean, long and wide as prairie; below, to her right, was the enormous wall of garbage that filled the Zone C beach; to her left, under-brush and slick rocks. The school wasn't much to look at. One wall was tin sheeting; the others, branches and tarp. It had a dirt floor. Next to the teachers' bench was a rough desk, loaded with donated items from Singapore: a small world globe, a stapler without a spring, a coffee cup reading PENINSULAR GAMES '72. Sugar bags had been sewn together into a drooping roof.

All day, Porkpie sat patiently on the teacher's bench, high atop the camp, waiting for something useful to do. In the dry season, she heard, the minute you turned your back, the children would raise the wall tarp to watch the sea beetles flutter in over the outcrop. You had to be strict in the dry season. You had to take the children by the hand and lead them back to their benches. But now hardly anyone came to class. The refugees didn't have umbrellas; the children were afraid of catching cold. Now the rain pounded like hooves, and the children sat all day in-side their lean-tos and shanties and wore play galoshes made from cig-arette cartons. Now in the evening, when Porkpie descended the hill, stepping gingerly, stumbling back to the UN compound, the rain fell so hard it bled through the crevices of her body and poked at her mouth and spattered her breasts, and when it was finished she had to wash off the mud that had squirted up her skirt. Now Porkpie heard that another boat from Vietnam had beached at Kuala Trengganu. Pirates, the young girls wailed: Thais in demon boats had boarded. Now by the glow of a fire pit, Porkpie saw a girl rock in a shelter, eyes puffy and red, her hand lodged deeply in her mouth: just rocking, ashes at her feet, just rocking and rocking, not making a sound, the air around her burning and black. Now Porkpie understood. *Rape, Pillage, Murder.* RPM. Now Bidong was racing gullies and dripping palm, and every morning when she started back up the hill, scouting for toeholds, testing vines, she squinted into the mud, searching for yesterday's footsteps, for a dropped pencil, for a torn textbook page, a familiar face, for anything that would whisper into her ears, *You are here.*

11

Reuben Gill, Bidong sub-engineer, probationary status, walked a fine line. Every morning he threw open his bungalow door, then gulped down mouthfuls of air and walked in his new rubber waders onto the Zone C beach, where he put his nose to the garbage like a chef smelling stew, hardly the behavior of a man with a history of asthma. "Lungs?" he'd say, puffing one of those horrible black Thai cigars. "Clean as a whistle. Clear as a bell." In the Coconut Inn he ate like a hog, shoveling in platefuls of meat and rice and oily green vegetables, then raising his sauce-flecked face and going on and on about his healthy sub-engineer appetite. On the beach, he flared his nostrils and made a point of breathing deeply, but of course that gave him an excuse to loom like some ridiculous white colossus and walk around with his chest puffed up.

Still, no one denied that he put in full days. The way he sloshed through the mud swinging his hammer and crowbar hours on end, it was a miracle he hadn't dropped dead after a week. He laid black plastic pipe, and the Vietnamese swore he ran his chainsaw with one hand. He could read rat-gnawed blueprints, hammer in Sheetrock nails with one powerful stroke, do eight hours of pipe fitting, welding, and roofing in four, and he could talk with fire in his eyes about the difference between concrete and cement. His first week, he had tossed off-loaded sacks of concrete back onto the supply boat. "Look like cement to you?" he said to a puzzled Ralph. Then he grabbed a staple gun and staple-punched threatening notes onto the sacks, which he ordered sent back immediately to the supplier in Kuala Trengganu. On the footpaths, he kept an eye out for people with scabs or lesions and sometimes he ambushed old men, hauling them off the path and squirting their infections with tubes of Swedish antiseptic cream that he carried in a pouch clipped to his belt. On days when the rain was bad, he clambered aboard the supply boat himself, since no one wanted to off-load in the rain, and with much grunting and swearing he heaved the ten-gallon jugs and two-by-fours onto the dock and lugged them on a cart to Supply. At dusk, he strapped rows of bricks to his back and carried them all the way to Zone G. He brooked no fools. Ralph said he heard from a reliable source that Reuben had actually yanked the hair of one of the crew chiefs when he found out that the chief had lied about knowing masonry.

Evenings, in the UN compound, you could see him drinking with Manley, sticking his big arms into Manley's blueprint tube, where hidden bottles of Mekong whiskey clinked together like mortar shells. Then, when the stars came out and the loudspeaker finally shut down, he would cock his head like a dog, listening hard, and sniff the air, and without warning he would jump off Manley's porch and stumble across the muddy compound to Porkpie's bungalow, where she sat outside, sipping tea. The two of them talked for hours in the darkness, blathering on in low tones, Reuben swaying on the porch railing, towering over her, talking in that growling way, Sally said, that large men use when they think their voice is a sexual organ. It made you sick, said Sally. He was so tall he spoke down into your scalp, and when he got done talking, Sally whispered, you had the feeling that he'd left a white, spunky puddle in your hair.

Reuben's bungalow was isolated, clear across the compound from Porkpie's, facing the beach on one side and the Task Force compound on the other. His room was small and bare; roofing tar plugged the spaces between the wall slats, forming vertical stripes that looked like bars. In one corner was a wobbling desk on which he laid his arm and scraped away dirt from his fingers with a pocketknife. In the other corner he stashed his tools—a claw hammer, a dowel, a plumb line, a small crowbar—and his duffel bag, lumpy with clothes and spare belt buckles. True enough, said Ralph: sometimes the duffel bag did look big as a sea lion, especially in the half light of dusk. But that didn't seem much of a justification for Reuben's behavior one evening. There they had been, said Ralph, just standing around, reviewing incinerator plans, disagreeing in a professional manner over the construction of a latrine, when Reuben suddenly snarled at the duffel bag, then dropped to his knees and sank his teeth into the fabric.

It was also true, said Sally, that he clomped around with his door wide open, pacing like an animal, half naked, walking from the window louvers to his bunk and back again, over and over, until you nearly screamed with the urge to toss some meat into his cage. You had to wonder what was going on in his head. Some nights you could see him sprawled atop his bunk, spilling over the sides, still fully clothed, his T-shirt stinky from the day's work. He farted shamelessly. Once he found a line of ants streaming up his porch and squashed them, every last one, with his thumb. Rats he killed with chilling mockery. Just as Manley was about to jump aboard the supply boat one day, off for an educational-supplies buying spree on the mainland, Reuben handed over a fistful of ringgit and told him to buy some spring traps. Upon Manley's return, Reuben paraded around the dock, rattling the shopping bag in everyone's face, then rattled his way back to his bungalow. There, he set to work, loading the traps with bits of Zone C garbage. He placed the traps under his bed, in the corners, over a small hole in the floorboards, everywhere. He even taped a couple to the window louvers. From that day forward, everyone woke to the sight of Reuben Gill doing his morning sweeping, pushing the mangled corpses out his door, draping around their twisted necks the remains of his mosquito coils that had smoldered with scent through the night and burned themselves into perfect wreaths of ash.

"Where's his sensibility?" asked Sally.

"A man like that," said Ralph. "A hard worker, OK. But a brute."

"He better not cross the line," said Sally.

"You put him in Soho or Times Square," said Ralph. "I'll tell you where he'd go. Straight for the pornography shops, that's where."

"There's one good thing," said Sally, raising her finger. "A man like that, you can read like a book. It's all there on the surface. Simple Simon."

"A beast," said Ralph. "Grunt, grunt."

There wasn't much more to say on the subject.

But they didn't sit with Reuben late at night on a bungalow porch. They didn't grow calm and sleepy listening to his words tumble out like a child's, awkward and braying and even oafishly sweet. Only Porkpie stared out with him at the dark rushing ocean, where naked boys dove off the boat hulls and bathed among the bluegills and angelfish. Only Porkpie saw him smile as the naked boys bathed, washing the day's mud away, pale in the bright warm moonlight, looking for the world like lovely amphibious creatures shucking their skins. She sat with him in the dark, holding a cup of tea, pleasantly sinking into her chair by minute degrees. His baritone vibrated in her ears. He swayed when he talked. Sometimes his voice was so low it seemed to hang in the air, lingering in her ears even after his lips had stopped moving.

"I got to sweat it out," he said.

"It? What's it?"

"It. Come on. It. Probation." The way he spoke, whispering, made the word ugly.

"Well, that's a commendable attitude. Grin and bear your burden, I suppose. Though I have to say—"

"No." He raised his voice. "*Sweat* it out. I'm not grinning and bearing nothing. I mean work so hard the damn word won't stick."

"Now calm down. The day's over. You're getting worked up again."

"No one does anything here," he said. "Everyone just waits around."

"Calm yourself, please."

"I am."

"Oh, but you aren't."

He sucked on his cigar awhile. "OK," he said. He brushed sand off the porch railing. "OK. I can handle it. I'm staying put."

But she could tell he was steaming. She could tell probation was eating him up.

One night, as they listened to angry Vietnamese voices somewhere behind them, beyond the wire, she touched his arm. The hair on his arm stuck straight up and curled around her fingers. He said something to her, but at first she didn't understand. Her head turned foggy, and through the fog she pieced together full sentences, word upon word, the sounds gaining weight and momentum the more he talked. She looked up at him in concern. Sometimes, he was saying, sometimes he woke in the middle of the night, fearing in the darkness that he was back in Kuala Trengganu, back in his office, dark now, black as a sepulcher, buried deep under the ground where he had put it. The sensation lasted only a moment, but it left him panicky and short of breath. In those moments, he said, he was not aware of time passing. He became a kind of furniture, static and immobile.

Then he scratched at his face. It was stupid, he said. Stupid and humiliating, and only after a snort of bedside Mekong could he bring himself on certain nights to contemplate what his eyes were seeing. He would walk over to his desk and open the drawer and stare. There was the letter from Doctor Johansson. Probation: the word was cum-heavy and evasive. It filled his head with unpleasant associations. Probe. Masturbation. It was a Peeping Tom at the window, a hungry eye at the keyhole. *Reuben Gill, hold perfectly still. That's it. That's it. Oh yeah.* He said the word had meanings for him that it wasn't meant to have. The word meant disappear. Vanish. It meant lying in a dark, empty office.

What he didn't tell Porkpie, because he still didn't believe it himself, was that he had bolted upright in his bunk one night, certain that he was covered not in a bed sheet but in the letter from Doctor Johansson, grown to monstrous size, the words coarse and fibrous against his skin. Nor did he say that his lungs suddenly clogged, or that his nostrils and throat seemed to shrivel, or that the air turned thick and soupy, or that then, falling to the floor, tumbling onto the snapping spring traps, yowling now in surprise and pain, he sensed the doctor all around him.

The Malays had their *hauntus* and their jinns, creatures comical in their horribleness. Malay ghosts shrieked and walked around holding their heads; they preyed on the adulterous and the unbelieving, and were driven away by reciting passages from the Koran. The doctor was not so easily dismissed, nor so discernible. He did not make his presence known like a pebble wedged in a shoe. He did not bite or howl or carry entrails or rattling chains. For that one terrible moment, the doctor was just outside Reuben's line of vision, something peripheral, a footstep tracked along the floor, a palm frond rustling, a fingerprint caught in the dust. Reuben rushed for the door, stumbling over the spring traps, falling once, his foot bleeding and pierced, and when he threw the door open and leaped off the steps, he swore he heard the doctor's whispered voice in the oncoming waves. He clenched his fists and listened. He ran forward a few steps. He scanned the wall of garbage on the Zone C beach. There was nothing. Just the night sky, the dark line of the compound wire, the water washing onto the beach, shimmering.

It was too crazy to say.

"What did you tell me before?" he asked Porkpie.

"When?"

"I don't know. A while back. About my title here."

"I believe I referred to the term *sub-engineer*. The way it sounds, you know? Down where the wriggly stuff lives."

"Yeah."

They listened to the waves. Palm fronds shook.

"Do me a favor?" he said.

"Certainly."

"Don't say 'the wriggly stuff' again. It gives me the willies."

You needed something you could hold in your hand, something you could plop on the table and say "stay," and it would. But Bidong wouldn't. Not his Bidong. Not on probation. Even with its glorious smell and rot and hissing back-alley intrigue, Bidong wriggled. One thing you learned from the jungle was an appreciation for clarity. Cut here, stop there, eat this, drink that, shut up. That was clear. Vomit brought rats, cum brought ants, shit brought flies. That was clear, too. The thing about the jungle was, the rules stayed the same. Familiarity did not breed contempt; familiarity *bred*, full stop. You knew the limits. You knew just how far you could push. Not like Bidong, not on probation anyway.

On Bidong, all he saw was people and junk, and then the people left, and then more people took their place and piled their junk on top of the old junk. It was chaos. Every morning when he woke up, he'd look around and see new faces. On any given day, ten Viets who knew all about jiggers and trowels and corner joists would leave, accepted by the Australians or Americans or French, and twenty new arrivals, nervous little men who knew only ginger roots and parsley, would replace them. People wouldn't even say good-bye. They'd just disappear. The supply boat left with departures, the boats from Vietnam came with arrivals; people kept collapsing on the dock; the blood vials kept filling up, case upon case of vials, shipped every week for testing to the hospital in Kuala Trengganu. There was nothing familiar about it.

The notice board in Zone C, the one listing recent departures and new arrivals, was always surrounded by a crowd, and the crowd cheered and pushed and sometimes cried. The island rumbled underfoot; even standing in the mud, you could feel a small vibration. Reuben wondered aloud if there were tunnels, but the looks people gave him convinced him to do his wondering quietly. At night, smoke from the cooking fires hung over the footpaths and formed human shapes. People would run out of their shelters, shouting, and beat pans to make the shapes go away. The sounds were eerie. The air was full of squawking loudspeaker racket and murmuring, singsongy sounds of complaint. Bidong: it wasn't Malaysia, not really, not the Malaysia he knew. It was not Vietnam, either, and it sure wasn't Tucson, Arizona.

Every time he thought he had the puzzle all put together, the pieces would start to wriggle, and then they'd plop to the floor and leave him with a hole. The Vietnamese stared at him, but it wasn't the stare he got in the Peace Corps, tramping into filthy jungle villages with his mosquito fogger. Back then, the stares gave him a sense of bounty; they were full of mirth and anticipation, and they held in reserve the possibility of expansion, either through friendship or a swift thrust of the kris into his gut. They were the stares of people who fed you and laughed in your face and gave you a mat to sleep on and told you to get the hell out if you pushed them too far. Those people, they owned the soil you walked on and tended the crops you waded through. But the Viets were wary and distant. They were maddeningly diffident.

Porkpie said of course they were. Look at it from the Vietnamese point of view: How could the refugees be sure the relief workers had no effect on their resettlement? When the delegations speedboated over from Kuala Trengganu, the Vietnamese leaned against the wire and strained to hear the conversations. Wouldn't it be be natural to wonder if their names were being added or deleted to private lists? It was entirely possible that a nod from a Ralph or a Reuben could get them on an airplane to America, where everyone was pink and rich and used thirty-two different words for types of corn. For all the Viets knew, one's destiny hung in the balance every time the white people engaged them in conversation. When one is a mouse, said Porkpie, one had to be clever when living with cats.

"I'm not the enemy," said Reuben.

"But you could be," Porkpie said. She snapped her fingers. "Just like that. That's the difference, isn't it? You can choose how you want to play it. They can't."

"Maybe," said Reuben, dropping cigar ash on the porch. He took a long puff. "But I say when a man's shown he's on your side, you owe him some trust."

"So it's that simple," said Porkpie.

"I didn't say that. Let's just say the weather sure ain't helping."

"Well, on that we can agree."

The rain and mud seemed to trigger all kinds of curious mental fugues in the refugees. His first week on the island, Reuben had watched as a solemn man in Zone C had limped up to him and with a look of great stealth opened a lacquered box filled with translucent lizard heads. Why the cripple showed them to him, he didn't know. Nor could he find out. The man talked to himself; he seemed fixated on Reuben's finger, and before he limped away, he lifted one of the heads from the box and rubbed it against Reuben's hand. There was another man who had greeted him in front of the UN compound by holding up a cardboard sign that read THE VIETNAMESE COMMUNISTS ARE LIARS FOR FIVE REASONS. Then the man's left eye started to blink so much he covered it with his sign. Reuben said: "Sorry, can't help you with Vietnam." Reuben had smiled, then opened the gate and left the man standing there. And on his way to the Coconut Inn one day, a woman with arms no thicker than bamboo staves had followed him, tugging on his sleeve. "My baby dead," she said in English, over and over. It was an unpleasant walk, and Reuben's sympathies had been aroused. But there was nothing he could do. The bamboo woman had looked right through him the whole time. Then another Vietnamese woman came rushing up and pulled her friend away, and the bamboo woman simply turned, docile as a puppy, and followed her friend into the crowd.

For the Viets, said Porkpie, there was a problem with time. They had no present. There was only the past and the future. Only the war and the sea behind them, a dream of leaving in front.

"It's terrible," she said, looking out past the compound's wire fence. Reuben nodded.

"It's like they're here, but not here. You know?"

Reuben stared out at the camp with her.

Here, but not here. He knew what she meant. He knew exactly. The words didn't wriggle a bit.

It seemed to Reuben that he was enclosed in a bubble. He stood outside the wire fence of the UN compound one day, watching the camp supply boat round the western side of the island, past the Zone C coral that had for weeks been crowded with boys who fished for bluegills and angel wings. The supply boat slowed, its engine clanking, and sailed past the wall of garbage on the Zone C beach. The shoreline was gauzy with flies, and back from the beach everyone was holding their nose, warding off the stench, though a crowd had already gathered by the steps of the wooden dock to watch the boat glide to the moorings. There were bare-backed men and shrieking girls in flowered pajamas; there were women with soft drink cans rolled in their hair like curlers; there were even black-toothed crones staring in silence, pausing on their way to the wall of garbage, where every day they shoveled stinking mounds into wicker baskets in exchange for bottles of fermented onions.

The day was clear, and all around the dock the water was a delicate lime green, still as a pond. Skipper Rahim, visible now in his pilot-house, sounded the air horn, and children from Zone B began wading out into the water, treading carefully over the coral, stopping every now and then to splash after sea worms and spiraling miniature jellyfish that they tossed into each other's hair. People were shouting. An amputee waved his crutch in the air. A white and tan pug, someone's Saigon pet, was hoisted into the air, barking crazily, its belly flecked with kernels of uncooked rice. Everywhere, people had their mouths wide open. They bellowed like opera stars, joking and shouting, pointing sometimes at the green-shirted Task Force guards and refugee longshoremen who stood on the dock behind a yellow line painted onto the planks. Women in mollusk-shaped hats waved from engine blocks; wading children squirted mouthfuls of water at the approaching boat. When the gunwale tires thumped against the moorings, the longshoremen threw boarding planks clattering onto the metal deck, and then the guards shouted "off-load, off-load" and banged their truncheons on the dock steps to keep the gawkers away, and the longshoremen shouted at each other, and the loudspeakers screeched out the Welcome Song.

Reuben frowned. All that noise, that action: it was so near. Why did it seem a hundred miles away? He began walking toward the dock. He surprised himself then. "Kiss me," he whispered. "Something kiss me." His voice sounded funny. Quavering.

He made his way up the dock stairs, nodded at the Malay in the Task Force guardhouse, then walked all the way to the end of the dock. He waved to Skipper Rahim, but the captain was busy shoving plastic honey buckets away from the pilothouse door. Longshoremen weaved and stumbled, keeping out of Reuben's way; a guard walked by with a metal whistle in his mouth, but didn't look up. Behind Reuben, commotion: stacks of lumber rippled onto the jetty; cans without labels fell with modest plops into the water.

He stood motionless, watching the longshoremen lift boxes onto their shoulders. No one spoke to him, no one looked. He turned and walked back, toward the dock steps, and when he passed the guardhouse, Reuben waved at the Malay. The man ignored him. Reuben paused. He thrust his hands into his pockets. He might as well have been in a movie house, watching Bidong flicker against a screen. Was it only weeks ago that he had first arrived, standing in exactly this same spot, right in front of the guardhouse, fumbling for his camp pass? That first day, the guard ran his finger along his new pass, then opened the check-in ledger and nodded at him. Children surrounded him. They craned their necks to see him write his name in the ledger. He signed with a flourish, then leaped down the rough steps to the beach, into the hot sand, the fish bones, the seaweed, the shards of cabbage and plastic. He yelled. His blood raced. He breathed fish sauce and coconut milk and hothouse air. He stepped over a cylinder head, a heap of claw membranes. Young girls, awestruck, were yanked out of his way, and he looked at the sweat beading on his arms and smiled. And then he waved to somebody white, a colleague—he couldn't remember who—someone trudging off to class with an attendance book or carrying a tube of blueprints, and he felt in his bones that his days would be wondrous.

Kiss me, he thought now, walking down the dock steps.

Sweat coated his face; nearby, soccer players sneaked glances; a line of departures headed for the airport in Kuala Lumpur rummaged through their belongings.

Kiss me.

A man trudged past, holding a muddy chainsaw; a woman stopped to roll her pants up to her knees.

Reuben stood on the muddy beach, enclosed in a bubble. All around him Bidong flitted by, shifting and indistinct, the forms weightless, the tide at his feet drifting and cold.

Kiss me.

But nothing did.

Manley approached, dragging his travel bag, just as the skipper revved the supply-boat engine, signaling for the longshoremen to hurry. The men were still off-loading lumber and tins of processed chicken. A large box next to the dock pill house fell into the water. The Task Force guards pointed accusing fingers at the Vietnamese; the Vietnamese shouted at each other.

"Off your asses," Reuben yelled. The anger in his voice startled him. Manley stared.

Reuben raised his arm, pointing, and saw that he was trembling. "Someone get that box," he shouted. Then he shouted even louder: "Now."

"Hey," Manley whispered.

Everyone was looking.

Reuben began to run. He ran through the mud as fast as he could, stepping high, and splashed into the water. He lifted the sinking box. He heaved it onto the dock, spilling cans across the dock planks. A longshoreman, bent under a load of sloshing jerricans, stuck out a foot and stopped a can from rolling over the side.

"That's it," Reuben shouted at the man. "*Do* something. *Feel* it."

Manley, squatting on the dock now, hovered over Reuben and gestured to him to calm down.

Reuben grabbed hold of a plank and hoisted himself up. He glistened; people pointed; foam was dripping down his pants.

"Hey, I'm leaving now," said Manley, stepping back. "To Kuala Trengganu," he said weakly. "Educational supplies." Skipper Rahim blew the air horn, signaling departure.

"Yeah?" said Reuben, his chest heaving. He wiped his face with his shirt and grabbed Manley's arm. He thought a moment. "You can get me something, too."

Manley returned on the afternoon run, laden with exercise booklets and boxes of colored chalk. Reuben was waiting. "Here," said Manley, shaking his head in disapproval. He handed over a small package. Reuben ripped off the wrapping with his teeth. Inside were business cards, printed in Vietnamese, English, and Malay. The cards read: *Bidong Island Sanitation Division. Shacks Built. Shit Hauled.*

"I don't know, Big Bro," said Manley, dropping a box of chalk. "You think Johansson's going to approve?"

"So I won't ask him."

"I don't know," said Manley. "Maybe that's too much, huh?"

"It's not too much."

"Probation, man. Hey, aren't you worried?"

"Hell with it."

"Careful, man," said Manley. "Hey, if it was me . . . I'd be worried."

"You're either here," said Reuben, waving the cards in Manley's face. "Or you aren't. Which one are you?"

He left Manley and walked to the Sanitation Division office, stooped under the doorway, then pushed aside the cloth door. Mr. Luc was sitting at the table, drawing on a blueprint with a pencil stuck into a protractor.

"Mr. Luc," said Reuben, putting the box on the table. "We're going to start getting serious around here." He slapped the box.

Mr. Luc was the refugee sanitation division chief. Back in Vietnam, before the communists came to power, he had taught structural engineering at the University of Da Lat. He was stoop-shouldered and graying, and his face was disfigured from a bullet that had passed through his jaw during the Tet Offensive of 1968. The bones had been reset hurriedly, giving him a pronounced, jutting underbite, and the skin around his mouth and neck was mottled and ridged, like a bad plaster job.

He looked at the cards on the table. He read one and frowned.

His jaw was hinged loosely to the rest of his face. He could, by thrusting out his chin and manipulating the muscles in his neck, detach the bone and rotate his jaw in a continuous, grinding circle. This he now did. The skin under his ear protruded as the bone unhinged, then slowly deflated as his jaw rotated and returned to its original position, then out again.

It was a signal. It meant: I'm thinking, Mr. Reuben.

Reuben pulled a card from the box and shook it. "Getting serious," he said. "No discussion."

Early the next morning, Reuben, accompanied by Mr. Luc, rounded up all the Vietnamese crew chiefs. He had them stand in a line, and then he walked down the line, Mr. Luc walking beside him, and stapled one of the cards to each man's shirt. There the cards stayed. One of the chiefs ripped the card off his shirt, but Reuben reached into the pouch attached to his belt and pulled out a needle and thread and sewed the card onto the man's pocket.

"I'm not your mommy and I'm not your daddy," said Reuben, pulling thread. "You understand my English, yeah?" The chiefs nodded. "All right, then. I'm not your uncle Ho Chi Minh, either. I build shacks and I haul shit. That's what we're here to do. Now you think about it. You want the goo-goo eyes, you go to the social workers. Think about it. You gotta *live* shacks. You gotta *live* shit. You don't, then you all might as well camp out on the damn beach."

The chiefs giggled to each other, a mirthless Vietnamese laugh, indicating uncertainty.

"What good's moping around?" Reuben said. The chiefs were mumbling to each other in Vietnamese.

Reuben said, "You don't go to San Francisco any faster sitting on your ass."

Mr. Luc stepped forward. "Mr. Reuben. I think maybe they do not like the cards."

Mr. Luc's jaw was rotating, but Reuben held up his hand. "Tough," he said. He felt great. He cracked his knuckles. He stapled one of the cards to his own shirt pocket. "There," he said, lifting the card like a flap. "You forget where you are, you take a look at your shirt, huh?" He smiled at Mr. Luc, but the man had already turned away, tapping his own stapled card. He was talking softly in Vietnamese to the crew chiefs. Reuben listened awhile; he heard them raise their voices, in protest he supposed, but it was already eight o'clock in the morning and there was still so much to do before lunch.

"I am guilty," said Gurmit.

"Who cares?" said Reuben. It had been drizzling outside all morning, and Reuben's hair was still leaking water down onto his face. He wiped his forehead, then held up the can of peas. The writing on the label was hard to see. The dim morning light was a faint pattern on the floor, and the overhead fluorescent light didn't seem to be working. "Ralph's waiting for me," Reuben said. "I just want to know if you've seen what's in the morning shipment. That's all. I didn't say you personally ordered the peas."

There was a maddening silence. Then Gurmit spoke: "I am guilty for that of which I am to blame."

Reuben squinted. His eyes were itching from all the paper dust floating around, and the office was so gloomy he wasn't sure if the dark spots on Gurmit's safari jacket were stains or shadow. In half an hour, the kitchen ladies would close up the Coconut Inn. If he hurried, he might make it in time for a hot thermos of sweetened Nescafé. Yet he was standing here, dripping rain, squeezing a can of peas in front of a man who let cobwebs grow between his ceiling rafters. There were thick file folders everywhere, mounds of them, and a row of gaping metal cabinet drawers lay open, bulging with crushed boxes and what appeared to be plates and silverware. Fluttering paper and plastic shards rustled between the spaces in the floorboards.

"Drop it," said Reuben. "You already apologized for the plank. I'm not here to take it."

"Thanking you."

"This conversation would go a lot quicker if I could see," said Reuben. He waved the can as if it were a flashlight.

"You are thinking the office is dark for the reason that the fluorescent tube is broken. And this morning is not so sunshiny with all this rain, isn't it?"

"I'll fix the tube. I'll stop by tomorrow."

"I have been negligent in reporting difficulties with the tube."

"Stop that."

"I am to blame, isn't it?"

"You're not guilty. The light went out. Period. You're not the damn Prince of Darkness. And you're not guilty about this either." He waved the peas again.

"Guilty," said Gurmit.

"Why don't you clean this mess up? How can you get anything done in here?"

"I am accepting your displeasure, for I—"

"Don't say it." Reuben held up his hand. "Not another word."

"Guilty."

"Like hell. Now look. Did you or did you not order a hundred cases of peas?"

Gurmit was silent.

"All right," said Reuben. "No. No, you did not order a hundred cases of peas. Don't make me do all the work here."

"The refugees cannot eat peas," said Gurmit. "Diarrhea."

"That's it. That's the problem. What I'm saying is, the requisition list at Supply says one hundred twenty cases of string beans came in this morning. But what I see is one hundred cases of peas. Exhibit A." He displayed the can, holding it by the rim. "I counted. A hundred cases."

"Shameful."

"Shameful is right. I know for a fact that . . . what's his name? Head of Supply?"

"Abdullah bin Ismail."

"Abdullah. Right. Now you can check, but I know for a fact that Abdullah's cousin in Kuala Trengganu owns Malaysian Produce and Vegetable. What does that tell you?"

"I am guilty."

Reuben banged the can against the desk. "I'm warning you, Gurmit. Just stop it. Now what that tells you is that when Abdullah's cousin makes a low bid to ship out green beans, three things happen. First, we don't get the crap we ordered. Second, we get different crap, but less of it. Third, cousin Abdullah turns a blind eye when the crap comes in, and everyone either gets the shits or builds walls out of canned peas. I've seen it with my own eyes. Zone D. Plus Abdullah gets a kickback. That's what this tells you."

"I am knowing nothing," Gurmit said in a tight voice. "Even this." He brought his hands up, then let them fall of their own weight onto his knees. He lowered his head. "Guilty."

There was a sound then. It came from somewhere around Gurmit's lowered face, about where the man's mouth would be: a sudden intake of air. A sob. Reuben waited. Gurmit wasn't making sense. It was like talking to a movie: no matter what you said, the action wasn't going to change. Gurmit's mewling little voice was still going to gather itself into a sob. His crumpled safari suit was still going to sag.

"That you making racket?" asked Reuben.

"For this I am guilty too. I am all the time making racket, and I—"

An image of what was left of the morning—a roof-raising in Zone B, water-tower repair in Zone D—swept across Reuben's eyes, dissolving in endless talk, and drained as into a whirlpool at the point just above Gurmit's chair. Reuben sighed. Gurmit was worthless. He would put the fear of the Lord into Abdullah by himself. Unbidden, a tremor of anticipation surged through Reuben's arm. He gripped the can of peas mightily, restraining his hand, imagining confrontation. He, Reuben Gill, Bidong sub-engineer, would stomp into Supply, bang the can of peas down on the man's desk, and demand to know what the hell was going on. Oh yes, he would. He was a hauler of shit and a builder of shacks, and a man like that, you didn't want to mess with, probation or not.

"All right," Reuben said. He placed the can on Gurmit's desk. "So you're guilty. I got things to do. Have it your way."

"And I have caused you so much trouble with the plank, isn't it?"

"Calm down."

"You have taken new wood and covered the hole in the table. I am grateful, you see, and you are repaid only with the silence of your colleagues. I am at fault for your inconveniences, and I—"

"Enough," Reuben said, turning to leave. "I'll bring a whip next time, all right?"

"For your rudeness I am guilty too," he heard behind him. "And I do not blame you for—"

Reuben slammed the door shut, and then he was back in the drizzle, facing Ralph. It was like coming out for a curtain call. An idle crowd lined the footpath, and behind them, a line of yellow-scarfed Bidong Boy Scouts, residents of the Unaccompanied Minors longhouse—all orphans, their families killed at sea—stood with their arms folded, lounging under the eaves of a row of shelters. There was a stir. "Mr. Reuben," someone shouted, and then Reuben walked down the steps, much to the delight of the crowd. The Bidong Scouts pointed. Women giggled. The stairs creaked under his weight.

"What's the holdup, Large Fellow Yank?" said Ralph. The brim of his cricket hat was drooping like a leaf; his white shorts were smudged, and his galoshes, a shiny brown pair from Singapore, were buckled tight against his calves. "I've been standing here in the *mua phun* longer than I care to remember."

"Gurmit," said Reuben, shaking his head. "The man's not *here*."

"All that time talking to an empty chair?"

"He's not here," Reuben said, pointing to the ground. "He's up here." Reuben pointed to his head and tapped it. "That's what he's guilty of. Too much moping around up here." He tapped his head again. "I could have shoved a skull in his face and called it peas. Wouldn't have made any difference." He held up the can. "Alas," he said, addressing the can. "Poor Yorkshire-brand pea."

"Now hold your tongue. They've a fine chess club in Yorkshire. I believe Harold Staunton moved about some there. He was unofficial world champion, you know."

"Hello."

"That was before they had officially sanctioned world championships. Actually, Staunton's an interesting figure. Old-world manners, political ambitions. A real gent's gent. You probably don't know this, but all the chess pieces used in tournaments these days look the same." He held up a finger. "And here's why. Because Harold Staunton pushed for uniformity in set design. I don't care where you play, the pieces all look alike now. He did a great service, believe me."

"Are *you* here?" Reuben said.

"Seven more months here than you, Large Fellow Yank."

"You're not here, are you?"

"Careful, now," said Ralph.

"You're guilty. Both of you."

"What's that, now? You're comparing me to our little Sikh chappie? You have me stand in the *mua phun* and draw a line straight from him to me?"

"No one asked you to stand outside, Ralph. You could have come in. And it's no *mua phun*. *Mua phun*'s a stinging rain, and it drives you crazy. This is a drizzle."

"Two points, mate." Ralph held up two fingers. "One," he said, lowering his forefinger, "I've nothing to say to our little plank snatcher. I don't care if he did apologize. He's a little twit, is what he is. And two . . ." He looked at his remaining pointing finger. "Oh, say now. That's what's known in the colonies as the bird, isn't it? My mistake, you know. Nothing personal. As I was saying, two, my second point: I've been on this bloody island long enough, which gives me every right to say *mua phun* if I want. I've been here longer than you, which means in all likelihood I'm not going to go off half-cocked and talking twaddle just because I'm standing in the middle of a freaking *mua phun*. Now come along." He started walking. "We've still got to get that pipe. I think I left it in my bungalow."

"*Rumah buruk disapu cat,*" said Reuben. He pulled out in front.

Ralph caught up. "I've no time for that now," he said, waving his hand dismissively.

"You don't know what I said, do you? I thought you said you'd lived in Malaysia. Well, that's a Malay proverb. It means 'A crappy house that's painted to look new.'"

"I've rather a lot to do today. I don't have time for showing off. And what's that card stapled to your shirt? Shacks built, shit hauled. What are you proving, hey?"

"This is what I do," said Reuben, fingering the card. "What do you do?"

Ralph didn't answer. The two men walked in silence a way. Their feet burped the mud. A man ran up and asked if they could cash a money order sent by his brother in California; a woman shouted out, "I want to go Canada"; a small boy sat in a box in the middle of the foot-path, crying.

They ignored them all.

"You know what I think?" Reuben said. "I don't think you speak Malay. I think Manley speaks Malay better than you. How come I've never seen you speak Malay to Ahmed? How come I've never seen you talk to Task Force?"

"Bugger me. Bloody savages. They're not worth talking to."

"They're here, aren't they?"

"Large Fellow Yank, those prison screws are arses."

"You listen to Sally too much. Of course they're asses. So what? They're here, right? Here. See 'em, smell 'em, feel 'em. That means they're here. If they're here, you got to deal with them."

"They're village-boy Malays. Put a gun in their hands, and they think they've got to use it."

"What do you know?"

"I know rural Malays. I worked five years in Kuala Lipis. I had to chase goats out of my building sites. I ate cold rice."

"That so?" Reuben said. They arrived at the gate to the UN compound, and when Reuben swung the gate open, the metal bar at the bottom sluiced through mud. "I worked in Bukit Serampang. That's the *ulu*. Big-time jungle. I slept in a shack. A rat bit my little toe off."

"The places I ate, they had cockroaches in the curry."

"You and your gut," said Reuben, ducking under a clothesline. "I went for weeks with rice balls and grasshoppers. I bought mosquito netting for my birthday."

"I had malaria."

"Had it! You ever get dengue fever? I did. Temperature of 105."

Ralph pulled down firmly on the brim of his hat. "Always with the mouth, aren't you?" he said, wiping his damp beard with his arm. "Mr. Large Fellow Yank of Bidong, probationary status no less, and he can't carry on a civil conversation. With the head engineer, no less. Not that I'd use that against you. No, no." He shook his head violently, and a volley of raindrops spattered Reuben's shirt. "Now that's enough," said Ralph, bounding up the steps of his bungalow. "For God's sake, let me at least enter my own room in peace. Are you coming in, or are you going to stand out in the *mua phun?*"

Reuben held up his hand. "Hold on. There's Mr. Luc." He pointed to the figure in a white button-down shirt and running shorts, jogging up to the gate.

"Mr. Luc," Reuben shouted, waving him in. "Over here. Yes, that's all right. Come on in."

Mr. Luc jogged over. "I have come to help you look for the pipe," he said. He held his thumb and forefinger wide apart, indicating the length of the plastic tubing still needed for the water tower.

"Excellent, Mr. Luc," said Ralph, opening the door to his room. "You can join in the search. I'm sure I left it in here somewhere. What's this? You've got one of those cards stapled to your pocket?"

"That's right," said Reuben. He looked at Ralph. "What about it?"

Ralph shrugged. "Nothing," he said. Then he spoke to Mr. Luc: "Come along now. In you go."

"Not so fast," said Reuben. He stopped Mr. Luc at the steps. "I've got a question for you. Mr. Luc: Is this a *mua phun* or just a drizzle?"

Mr. Luc began rotating his jaw.

"You can say *mua phun* or you can say drizzle," he said. "Whatever you like."

Ralph nodded vigorously. "There," he said, grabbing the doorknob firmly. "You see? Either way."

Reuben kicked his boots against the steps, dislodging clumps of mud, and as Ralph disappeared into the room, he turned to Mr. Luc. "Just between you and me," he said, lowering his voice, "which one is it?"

"Which you like?"

"I'm asking. Which one is it, really?"

"Anything you want, Mr. Reuben."

"Damn it. One's a *mua phun* and one's a drizzle. Which one's slicking your hair down? Right here, right now?"

"Some rain is *mua phun.* Some is drizzle. I cannot tell you more."

Reuben, hissing, scraped the soles of his boot against the steps. He searched Mr. Luc's face. The man stuck out his jaw.

"Now don't go grinding that thing again," said Reuben. "All I'm asking is whether—"

"Reuben," Ralph shouted from inside. "Stop harassing him a moment, can you? Come along, both of you."

Mr. Luc ran up the steps and kicked off his sandals, the Vietnamese prelude to entering living quarters. At the doorway, Mr. Luc wavered. Reuben saw the back of the man's head move: he was staring down at his bare feet. A gurgling sound followed, from deep in Mr. Luc's throat, as if words were being formed, then swallowed.

Reuben walked up the steps, still kicking mud from his boots, and saw Mr. Luc bring his left leg up, ballet style, and cradle his bare foot in his hands. The foot was caked with mud.

"Just walk in," Reuben whispered. "Ralph's a pig anyway. The floor's already muddy."

"Asians take off their shoes," said Ralph loudly, rummaging through his desk drawer. He didn't look up. "Or didn't you know that?"

Mr. Luc, standing on one leg, jammed his ankle tight against his crotch and began wiping his foot clean, rubbing it into the folds of his running shorts.

"I'm not talking about shoes," Reuben shouted into the room. Then, to Mr. Luc: "You're getting your shorts dirty. You don't need to do that."

Mr. Luc's face bristled with tiny movements, his features collapsing and rearranging themselves into fleeting portraits. He gurgled again. Whatever words he was swallowing were buried in his emerging jaw, which suddenly jutted forth like a sliding drawer.

Mr. Luc looked away. He deftly brought his other foot up to his crotch and wiped the mud onto the material.

His shorts were streaked now. He glanced up and followed Reuben's gaze back down to a thin strip of plastic that stuck out like a hair, glued to a clump just below his waistband. He pulled it off, and without another word walked into the room, moving stiffly, arms at his sides, his face once again under control.

"What's your card say?" said Reuben, tapping his own stapled pocket.

Mr. Luc giggled.

It had been an unpleasant display, watching Mr. Luc soil his own clothes just to enter Ralph's room. If you hauled shit and built shacks, you didn't worry about a few dirt clumps here and there. The hell with the Confucian Ideal of Right Relationship. The hell with Vietnamese manners. Bidong was its own country, and the sooner people learned that, the better. If Mr. Luc was a mouse and Ralph was a cat, then it was time the mouse stood up and put a bell around the Brit's neck.

"Just walk in next time," said Reuben, sharply.

"Hey now," said Ralph, looking up. "Don't tell my guests how to behave in my room. Isn't that right, Mr. Luc?"

Mr. Luc's jaw began rotating. He stood in the middle of the room, giggling.

The room looked like an animal's lair: plastic clotheslines, most of them empty, crisscrossed the room. The one nearest the door drooped with hangers bearing cartoon shirts from Japan. Reuben ducked. He slid the hangers to one side. *Tootle the horn,* a sleeve said. *Running my candy gum,* read a breast pocket. There, at the foot of the bunk, Ralph squatted over a heap of piping and fittings, and rocked on the heels of his boots, which shed a growing pile of pebbles and mud. Along the walls were opened boxes of metal pipes. In the corner, thin paperbacks filled a long bookshelf, jammed next to a small table covered with scraps of wrapping paper and a waxy, reddish ball the size of an orange.

"Mr. Luc," said Ralph urgently. He was holding a flywheel. "Don't, please."

Mr. Luc jerked his hand away from the red ball. He looked at his fingers, as if checking for burns.

"You got a pipe in there?" said Reuben, pointing to the ball.

"It's sealing wax," said Ralph. He looked at Reuben. "For mailing, right? If you want to mail large packages out of Malaysia, you can't wrap them in string. You knew that, right? You've got a package like so"—he dropped the flywheel and held his hands apart the space of a ruler—"about so big, and they won't let you use string. You can only use sealing wax. But you know that."

"Sealing wax," said Reuben.

"Sorry, Mr. Luc," said Ralph. "I didn't mean to snap at you."

"Not snapping," giggled Mr. Luc.

"Yes. Well. It's just I've been missing things from my room lately. Lots of light fingers on Bidong, right? You can't tell from looking at it, but when I bought that wax ball, it was twice the size."

"So you're saying people break into your room and steal wax," said Reuben.

"So you're saying you don't believe me. Fine. I can read your tone."

"And you use it on packages. No string."

"That's right."

"The whole package. Nothing but globs of wax?"

"That's right, Large Fellow Yank. No string. You can only use seal-ing wax. Bugger me. These Malaysians."

Over in the corner, Mr. Luc's jaw was rotating slowly. Surely the man could not think highly of Ralph. The Brit went on for hours about chess strategy and Union Rules Football, even about American eco-nomic policy. "See here, now," Ralph would say, fixing you with his gaze. "You Yanks have to ease up on tariffs." He was all squawk-squawk-squawk, a one-man Chinese opera, and at the end of the performance all you had was a headache from all the noise. He drew up grandiose plans for longhouses and latrines and then sat stroking his beard until he had a handful of hair. He kept forgetting to lock the storehouse, and he didn't keep track of the screwdrivers and mortar and bricks and lumber.

Surely Mr. Luc was secretly hee-hawing at the chief engineer. The Vietnamese penchant for contempt ran deep. Back in Vietnam, Mr. Luc said, he had kept a line of small stones on his desk when he taught; whenever some dull boy stammered in ignorance, he picked up a stone and sent it whistling in the boy's direction. Back in Vietnam, you didn't indulge your fantasies. You worked your fingers raw. You didn't live in an animal's lair and tell people you actually believed you weren't al-lowed to tie up your packages with string.

"Now mates," said Ralph, peering under his bunk. "Let's get orga-nized. Mr. Luc, how about you look over there." He pointed to a line of boxes by the front windows. "Large Fellow Yank, how about you poke around the bookshelf."

Reuben shoved a box out of his way and squatted. Tiny scraps of paper, markers, had been inserted into most of the paperbacks. He rubbed his finger along the titles: *Rubenstein's Best Games. The Fischer Years. The Dover Collection of Chess Combinations. Play the Blackmar-Deimer Gambit! The Art of the Endgame.* There were nothing but chess books, and in a shoebox next to the shelf was a notebook labeled *Bidong,* written in giant letters in Magic Marker. Reuben took off the lid. Inside was sheet after sheet of notebook paper, hundreds of sheets packed so tight that they rose from the box like bread swelling in an oven. He sifted through. They were all filled with penciled-in hieroglyphics, numbers and squiggles that he recognized as chess moves. Every single sheet. Hundreds of them.

"That's not your property," said Ralph. "Please don't look through that. It's pipe we're after."

"They're all yours," said Reuben. "You played all this chess on Bidong."

"That's right," Ralph said. "What of it?"

"And you wrote down all the moves."

"For study, mate."

Reuben shook his head. "Play chess all day. Study chess all night. On Bidong."

Mr. Luc, who had been rattling boxes of metal clasps, began humming loudly, in time to a Vietnamese folk song whining from the loudspeakers.

Ralph glanced over at Mr. Luc, then addressed Reuben: "Forget it," he said.

"You just said 'What of it?' Now you say 'Forget it.'"

"Forget it," Ralph said again, motioning with his head toward Mr. Luc.

"Don't tell me forget it. You brought it up."

Mr. Luc hummed louder, busily flapping the butterfly valve of a carburetor. There was something theatrical about his motions: his hand jerked back and forth, as if wracked with spasms. The valve kept clacking, faster and faster.

"Hey now, Reuben," said Ralph quickly. He looked around in the heap, and pulled out a small metal box. Screws hung from the bottom. "What do you suppose this is? Let's go out on the porch and have a look. Better light, yes?" His fingers were all over it.

"How am I supposed to see if you've got your hand all over it?"

"How about we have a look, hey?" Ralph said. "Outside. On the porch. Excuse us, Mr. Luc."

Mr. Luc nodded, then went back to his noisemaking.

Outside, Ralph held up the box.

Reuben looked down at the man. "It's a light socket," he said angrily. "Goddammit it, Ralph."

Ralph closed his hand around the socket. "Of course it's a bloody light socket," he whispered. Tiny veins were breaking out all over his face. "I wanted to talk to you," he said, talking into Reuben's chest. He hesitated. What he said came out in a hiss: "Not in front of the refugees. Not this bloody arguing. You want to argue in private, fine."

Ralph didn't move. His lips remained locked, positioned for hissing, though no more sound came out. Inside, Mr. Luc stood hunched over a box, singing badly now and clanging metal clasps together. He had turned his head, obscuring a view of his face. There was something perverse about the tableau—Ralph silent and grim, Mr. Luc making as much noise as a child—and the longer Reuben stood on the porch, looking first at Ralph, then at Mr. Luc, the more it became clear to him what was happening. These two men before him: they were playing out a drama that had nothing to do with getting the water tower repaired. They feared exposure. Ralph feared that Mr. Luc would think him a fool; Mr. Luc feared that Ralph would suspect him of thinking it. Each man was acting, pretending for the other.

He could not bear to look at either man any longer. His head was pounding; he felt his face turn hard. The morning had been too much. He grabbed Ralph's shoulder and shoved him. Ralph, startled, stumbled a few steps back. Then Ralph straightened and looked over at Mr. Luc, who glanced over his shoulder before going back to his singing.

Reuben could not think of the words to explain what he had done. He had done it, and now he had to get off the porch. That was all he could think. He turned and walked quickly down the steps.

"Hey now," Ralph called out. "You're out of control."

But Reuben kept on walking, pausing only to close the compound gate behind him. He walked past the Zone C beach, squishing through something white and creamy. His waders broke the crust, and brown, foamy water filled the holes. Off to the right, Viets stood in long lines, holding red plastic buckets, waiting for their chance at the water spout. He walked past the hospital and the Task Force compound. He walked fast, snapping his teeth in time with the rock music coming from the loudspeaker. People were clearing out of his way. He was walking just to walk, walking to let off steam, to feel his blood flow through his veins, to breathe. He was walking to Zone F, up to Porkpie's school, because if he walked up the steep Zone F hill, he'd be tired and sweaty and his hair would be wild and his legs would ache and he wouldn't have to picture Ralph and Mr. Luc playing around in each other's heads. He could hammer her blackboard straight or put in another bench. He had to do something. He had to sweat the anger out of him.

So he kept on walking. He stepped over water pipes. He let the tools lashed to his belt dig into his legs. He let the drizzle wet him down.

There were crowds by the black market tables, and he had to slow down. The tables, protected from the rain by tarps, teetered with cans of sweetened condensed milk and Thai shampoo. At one of the tables, a Task Force guard, shrouded in a rain slicker, fingered bottles of swollen beans that floated in green liquid. At the next table, a woman sat in a straight-back chair, selling squid dangling from sticks; farther down were boxes of clothes spilling out onto the footpath. Reuben, stopped now by the crowd, stared blankly at the Task Force man. The guard kept fingering the bottles of swollen beans, picking them up then going on to the next one. The guard said something then to the seller. The woman behind the table looked at the guard, then down at her wares, hardly moving her lips when the guard slipped one of the bottles into his slicker pocket and slowly moved on to the next table and started fingering the squid sticks.

"Pay," Reuben snapped, but the guard didn't look up.

Reuben approached the bean table. The woman was staring off at some distant point. Reuben pointed to the guard, then reached into his pocket, pulled out two Malaysian dollars and presented the woman with the money. "For him," Reuben said, pointing. The guard turned then. The woman smiled and put the money in her pocket. She began jabbering at passersby, nodding and smiling at Reuben, and the passersby jabbered back.

The guard looked at Reuben briefly, catching his eye, and threw a stick of squid into the mud. He reached over to the next table and tipped over a box of running shorts. Nobody moved. For a moment, all you could hear was the loudspeaker announcement; a chainsaw started up down the path. The guard stepped to the next table and knocked over some shampoo bottles. At the next table he took a box of clothes and dumped them, then flipped the table over. People scattered. The sellers leaped from their chairs and stepped back. From a distance, the guard looked at Reuben in challenge, then turned his back and continued down the path.

People were shouting. The sellers stepped into the mud and picked up their wares, pausing to wipe mud from the boxes. Some boys righted the table. "You," Reuben shouted at the guard, but the crowd pushed on, holding on to each other's shoulders, clutching their bags, stumbling at the clothes seller's table, where the seller was snapping fallen running shorts like capes and tossing them back into the box. No one looked at Reuben. The woman with the bottles of swollen beans stared intently at her bottles. The squid seller looked at the ground. Reuben, enraged, pushed into the crowd. He stopped. There was nothing he could do, but his blood was on fire. He had to do something. So he bent down and scooped up a handful of mud. He raised his hand over his head, then threw the mud down hard, back onto the footpath, where the mud splattered onto his legs.

He swore. He picked up another handful and threw it down hard, too. People gave him a wide berth, and he started walking again, wet, spattered with mud, tools clanking against his legs, and then he turned onto the side path that led up to Porkpie's school and walked as fast as he could up the steep hill.

12

The classroom was so dreary that Porkpie pictured herself as some burrowing animal sealed into a box. She sat at the teacher's desk, looking first at the long empty benches, then at the wall tarps, which every few seconds shook and crinkled from the ocean gusts swept up over the cliff. A band of gray sky glowed in the space between the ceiling slats and the walls, but the light seemed to evaporate before reaching the mud floor.

"Oh, Miss Phu," Porkpie said, surprised at the force with which she leaped from her chair. Her rain slicker dripped nearby, dangling from a nail pounded into a support beam. On her desk lay mimeographed copies of *English for You!* "I'm feeling a little antsy," she said. "You know 'antsy'? Like this." She stiffened, allowing the pent-up little tremblers to roll through her body. "Like you have ants crawling on you."

"Antsy," Miss Phu nodded. The woman was clear across the room, squatting by the entrance, where she was rocking a support pole back and forth. "Miss Porkpie, you do so much," she said, and then she rocked the neighboring pole as well. "We are so grateful."

Miss Phu nudged the pole with her knee. She seemed to be frowning, though frowning in itself meant nothing. She had been frowning inside the classroom all week, earnestly rocking the support poles, testing for looseness, then folding her arms and staring up at the sewn sugar bags that served as a ceiling.

"Now there you go again," said Porkpie, picking up her stack of English texts, then setting them down on the other side of the desk. "I'm not doing so much. Just waiting for students to show."

"Yes, Miss Porkpie. You do so much."

"I don't really. Please."

"Yes, Miss Porkpie."

There was clanking outside the back wall, then Vietnamese voices. "What was that?" Porkpie said. "You hear that? That can't be students coming."

"No, Miss Porkpie."

But Porkpie could not keep still. She ran to the back tarp and fumbled with the strap holding it in place. What could the refugees outside be up to? Her head was already full of titillating suspicions. Perhaps there was a rat pogrom in progress. Perhaps workmen were preparing a disposal pit, excavating freshly turned red clay. Maybe someone was scraping mud off a wheelbarrow hearse parked nearby.

She heard herself grunting, and then she saw her fingers lunge at the knot in the strap. Her fingers seemed to pull and yank of their own accord, and then in her mind's eye she saw the outcome: the tarp thrown aside, her greed satisfied. She would stare at the pile, at the patchy, raw bellies, the broken snouts, at the jellied pink eyes. Then more: the tattooed silversmiths, the diesel mechanics, all workmen now, clumsy pit diggers, all captured in decorative poses. Already she felt flickers of delight and horror distort her face, and behind the flickers, the approach of other, more powerful, impulses. A thrill would course up and down her spine. She would giggle. She would put her hand over her mouth, and the giggle would work its way through her fingers, out into the air, public and bleating, while her flanks rippled like horse-flesh. The workmen would look away, and then Miss Phu would lay a hand on her arm and look her straight in the eyes, and Porkpie would be so ashamed that her spirit would curl up and rise like a puff of smoke and whisper a curt good-bye into her ears.

So no. She willed her fingers still. She would not throw aside the tarp.

She jerked her hand away, and the wall strap fell with a small thump.

"What *are* they doing outside, Miss Phu?" Porkpie's arms flew up, then dropped back down. "Is there a work crew actually? . . . I was wondering if they're doing what I think they're doing."

Miss Phu sniffed. "They digging drain for rain outside." Then she shook another pole, mumbling to herself in Vietnamese.

Porkpie returned to her position on the teacher's bench. So she had been wrong. Again. So her imagination had proved itself yet one more time as vile and unworthy. UN Education Advisor: she was no such thing. She was tourist-souled, a voyeur with a title, that's what she was. She lugged books and writing tablets and pencils up that awful hill, then spent the rest of the day drying off and staring at the Vietnamese.

She looked over at Miss Phu, who was slowly working her way to the back of the classroom, eyeing the drooping ceiling and shaking the poles as she went. In the evenings, talking with friends, did Miss Phu mock her? Did she squat on a board and say, "Hello, I'm Porkpie. I don't know anything"? It was possible. It was also possible that Miss Phu didn't think about her at all, that Miss Phu simply put her on a level with coconut palm and water pipes, part of the material bounty of the island and therefore extraneous to evaluation. Whatever the case, Porkpie was certain that her sudden rush to the straps of the back wall hadn't raised her standing.

Miss Phu, jabbing a ceiling section with a stick, paused in her duties. "Do not worry, Miss Porkpie," she said. "Roof is OK."

"I'm not worried. I trust your judgment. I'm just antsy, that's all."

"But Miss Porkpie," smiled Miss Phu. "Just now, you running to the back. You trying to take down the wall. You wanting out. You thinking roof is coming down, yes Miss Porkpie?"

"Oh no. Really. I was just . . . I don't know. I was trying to get some answers, I suppose. Just trying to understand things."

Miss Phu, now working along the back wall, gave a post a tentative shake. "What you meaning, Miss Porkpie?" she said.

"I'm not making any sense, am I? Sorry."

Sorry. It was a familiar start to the morning. Sorry, sorry, sorry. She had been apologizing to Miss Phu all week. Ever since she had failed to recognize Miss Phu as someone she'd met, she had been saying how sorry she was. Yes, of course they had met earlier, in Gurmit's office, her first day on Bidong. Yes, of course Miss Phu was Gurmit's assistant. Of course the woman's name had sounded familiar. But last week, when Miss Phu first marched into the Zone F primary school, her wet hair had molded itself to her skull like a helmet, completely changing her appearance. And her clothes were different, the blouse soaked and pink rather than dry and white.

Not that Miss Phu was easy to forget. Far from it. Watching her now, admiring the woman's calm, expert appraisals of the support posts and ceiling, Porkpie recalled the impressive entrance Miss Phu had made last week. Miss Phu had run into the school, sweeping aside the clear plastic sheet hanging from the entrance, and after smiling broadly, she had made an announcement: She and a friend had arrived to teach the children. Then she turned her head and barked something in Vietnamese. In walked the friend, an older, fat woman who snickered nervously and made small bowing movements. The fat woman said in perfect English that she did not speak English and then fell into a snickering fit. Miss Phu looked at her friend crossly, then turned to Porkpie. The fat woman's name was Mrs. Lai, she said: Mrs. Lai, a new arrival, had just been assigned by the camp committee to teach in Zone F for ten hours a week.

Mazel tov, said Porkpie, but who are you? She was sorry as soon as she said it. Miss Phu's face crinkled, then fell, then restored itself in stony shock.

Sorry, sorry, sorry. Who could have guessed that the same woman who already worked long hours down in the Administration Office would volunteer her free time to teach? Up in the primary school no less, up where students were rare as sunshine? Who could have guessed that sweet-faced Miss Phu would of her own accord run back and forth up and down the Zone F hill?

Miss Phu, it turned out, was so tireless and efficient that Porkpie found herself wondering how the South Vietnamese could have lost the war. Miss Phu had been a primary schoolteacher in Vietnam, and she got on wonderfully with the Zone F children who occasionally wandered in, assigning them seats on the benches, wiping their dirty faces with palm fronds, training everyone to hold their legs straight out when dying rats, blind with poison, crawled in and staggered from bench to bench. With Miss Phu bustling around, Porkpie had little to do but reach over to her stack of pencils and writing tablets and count her supplies. The children stared at her, at the American, the giant, the long-nosed UN Education Advisor. Sometimes they made squealing runs her way and touched her hair, then raced back to their benches. Sometimes they looked in bewilderment and awe when English came out of her mouth. Sometimes they wondered aloud to Miss Phu if the white woman really did have a tail, as their grandmothers said.

Miss Phu seemed to be on familiar terms with all the children. For more than a year, she reported, she had lived near the bottom of the Zone F hill, where every night she sat behind a coffee can full of Malaysian 555 cigarettes that she sold by the stick. Taped to the can was a notice from the camp committee, written in both Vietnamese and English, that she thrust into the faces of all the mothers and fathers who bought from her. The English read: *Education is important for children! Enroll them in the free Bidong Island schools!*

If not for Miss Phu, Porkpie doubted whether any children at all would have stumbled in for lessons. The rains were just getting worse, and since few of the refugees had watches, and since Mr. Tan in the Loudspeaker Division had grown lax in tapping out the hour on his bamboo xylophone, it was difficult for parents to know when the classes started. Miss Phu said she made rounds of Zone F sometimes, herding together large, rowdy groups of children with the promise of presenting a real Malaysian nickel to whoever guessed the lucky number that was scribbled under the flap of a pack of cigarettes she carried in her pocket. To the assembled group, she told motivational stories about education: how a boy from Tuyen Duc province, a mechanic's son, had just last year graduated first in his class in Los Angeles; how if you memorized just one page of an English dictionary each night, you could be fluent inside of a year; how by sticking your feet into a tub of cold water, you could keep yourself awake and study through the night.

Miss Phu carried her slight shoulders with dignity. Though frayed, her clothes were always clean, and her hair was shiny and fashionably bobbed. The other refugees seemed to look up to her. Even fat Mrs. Lai, who collapsed at the slightest provocation into a snickering fit, was respectfully quiet when Miss Phu fulfilled her morning's inspirational duties by singing praise songs to education. *Come children, come children,* she would sing in Vietnamese, standing outside the school's entrance:

> *Come learn where the oriole flies*
> *Come learn where the oriole lives.*
> *Chickadees, katydids, macaws chirp*
> *But in your head the oriole flies*
> *In your heart the oriole lives*
> *Oh why? Oh why?*
> *Come children, come children, learn.*

Sometimes Mrs. Lai accompanied her, snickering at first, then growing solemn, banging a giant ladle in perfect time against the sides of a washtub. It was a wonderful sight to see and to hear, and a little sad as well. Miss Phu's voice was nasally and small, and though she sang as loud as she could, shouting the words down the hill, mouth wide open, her voice was quickly swallowed by the racket from the loudspeaker just outside the school, then lost in the rain and the mud and even the smell, which seemed to drift over the camp like fog.

Now, standing under the entrance, Miss Phu rubbed her fingers along the length of her throat. It was something of a routine with her: first she examined the structural integrity of the classroom, then she massaged her throat, pampering her vocal chords.

"Are you going to sing now, Miss Phu?" said Porkpie.

"Yes, Miss Porkpie," said Miss Phu, massaging. "I waiting for Mrs. Lai, but maybe she not coming. I singing myself." She smiled broadly.

"I wish I could join you. I wish I spoke Vietnamese."

"Yes, yes, Miss Porkpie. You do so much. We are so grateful."

Would Miss Phu never stop saying that? The statement seemed a kind of mantra with her. It was the sort of thing you said when you really weren't listening.

Porkpie sighed.

"You're so polite to me," she said then.

But as she spoke, the loudspeakers crackled outside and Freddy Fender blared to life. Miss Phu looked up in frustration. Porkpie offered Miss Phu her rain slicker, holding it out for her to take, but Miss Phu shook her head. She threw aside the clear plastic sheet hanging from the entrance and walked outside, stepping gingerly onto the cardboard sheets that served as a walkway. It was drizzling. The loudspeaker music was deafening, but Miss Phu, pausing only to yell at the workmen to stop adding to the racket, rolled up the cuffs of her pants, peered down the hill and began to sing.

Miss Phu was leaning forward, very nearly losing her balance and tumbling onto the muddy slope, and even from her position on the teacher's bench, Porkpie could see the veins rising on the woman's neck. All that effort . . . Her tinny voice sounded as if it were coming from a can. Between guitar riffs screeching from the loudspeaker, Porkpie heard a faint response, a man's voice floating over the tarp roofs, shouting back what sounded like encouragement. A moment later someone started clapping. Porkpie closed her eyes. If only more people could hear Miss Phu. If only her voice could carry all the way down the hill, where the shelters and lean-tos were thick as elephant grass, where the children squatted on cardboard and listened for hours to the bubbles pushing up through the mud.

"Dreaming, Miss Porkpie?" said Miss Phu, walking back in. The loudspeaker rang with ten chimes. Ten o'clock.

"Oh no," Porkpie said. "It's just so dark in here. Like a movie theater."

"Ah! Movie is better. Sometimes the dreaming too . . . how do you say?" She hugged her arms and shook.

"Nightmares. Scary dreams."

"Scary, yes. Thank you, Miss Porkpie. You can preparing the blackboard?"

Porkpie nodded. Ten o'clock was geography hour. If any students were going to come, they would arrive in a few minutes, before the rain got bad.

Porkpie pulled out a sponge from her purse, then Reuben's gift of the Dunhill pack containing three crumbling sticks of chalk. She stood in front of the blackboard, a framed sheet of blackened plywood, and began drawing with the chalk, dabbing residue from the board with the sponge.

She worked carefully. The blackboard hung from two long nails sticking out of support beams, and when she pressed too hard, the board wobbled. At the top she drew Vietnam; at the bottom, the refugee camp countries: Thailand, Singapore, Indonesia, and Malaysia. For Bidong, she drew an egg-shaped oval that was almost half the size of the Malaysian mainland. The children demanded it. In the textbook, the island was only a dot, which upset the students. The dot was so tiny, they were afraid to touch the page for fear of crushing it. "Too small!" they cried in Vietnamese, to Miss Phu. "What if a tidal wave comes? What if it sinks in the ocean?" And then they'd run back to their shelters and hold on to their mothers' legs all day.

"Thank you, Miss Porkpie," said Miss Phu, examining the drawings. She stood behind Porkpie. "You do so much."

"Oh, now," said Porkpie, putting the sponge down. "It's not even a good picture."

"Beautiful, Miss Porkpie."

In truth, it wasn't. The chalk outlines were smudged and powdery. The blackboard was so rough that there were gaps between the lines. She stepped back and shut one eye, evaluating. It was a dismal effort. The countries seemed squirmy and bloated. The Bidong drawing looked like scratch marks.

But there wasn't time to fix the pictures. Through the clear plastic sheet, Porkpie could see the hazy forms of young men sloshing up over the crest of the hill. They were carrying small girls, no bigger than sandbags, holding them by the armpits, swinging their stiff, resigned bundles side to side for balance, high over the mud. Three students. An average showing: two had shown up yesterday, five the day before that. Panting voices murmured outside, and just as Miss Phu shouted hellos toward the entrance, the loudspeaker crackled and a Vietnamese folk song filled the classroom.

Three tiny girls in all-day pajamas came running in, holding hands; they had chubby, round faces; their flip-flops were enormous. Behind them came a surprise: a tall boy, clearly older than the girls. Around his neck was the yellow scarf of the Bidong Boy Scouts. He was wearing a filthy button-down shirt and gray underpants. Apparently, he had walked up the hill on his own. His legs were muddy up to his knees.

Porkpie cupped her hand against Miss Phu's ear: "Isn't he a bit old for just underpants?"

"I know him a little, Miss Porkpie." Miss Phu tapped her head. "He living in Unaccompany . . . how do you say? Unaccompanied Minors longhouse. He crazy sometime."

Crazy. Miss Phu's English patois was coarse. Still, the word was chilling. This boy, this scabby-faced Bidong Boy Scout in underpants: he was alone, without family, a yellow-scarfed resident of the orphans' longhouse. What had happened to his parents? His brothers, sisters, cousins? Had their boat been ravaged? He had a watchful expression. His eyes hardly moved. Under his grimy sheet of skin, Porkpie wondered, what secrets lay sleeping?

The question made you want to do something. But what? She had nothing to offer. And if you had nothing to offer, thought Porkpie, then you had no right to ask the question, not when you slept in a dry, painted bungalow and kept buried in your travel bag the passport that shuttled you onto the UN speedboat. Porkpie dug her knuckles into her forehead, driving the question away. The boy sat on a bench behind the three girls and stared nervously at the plastic sheet draping the entrance. He had a perceptible twitch.

Miss Phu clapped her hands together and pointed at the chalk drawings on the blackboard. She snapped her fingers, demanding the boy's attention. It was the Vietnamese way: work hard, carry on, let time heal all wounds.

The girls began chanting the names of the countries, shouting out each time Miss Phu's pointing hand moved up or down the blackboard. The boy responded well. He blinked at first, as if waking from sleep, and chanted. But then he seemed to lose focus. He lost the rhythm of the chant; his shouts lagged behind the girls. Then he stopped.

Miss Phu began speaking to the boy, shouting over the loudspeaker and the chanting girls. The boy spoke up.

Miss Phu continued pointing, and even though the girls began chanting louder, she seemed more interested in carrying on a conversation with the boy.

She dropped her hand, and the chanting stopped. The boy was still speaking, and now the girls joined in as well, chattering all at once.

"He saying," said Miss Phu, turning to Porkpie. "Wah! All the children saying. Girls too. A demon coming. I do not know why they say it."

"I won't ask, Miss Phu."

"Now they waiting."

"Waiting for . . . ?"

"No class now because they not concentrating. We waiting for the person."

"The demon."

Miss Phu scowled. "The children say demon, Miss Porkpie. Is a person, I think. They scared too easy."

But in Miss Phu's breathy voice Porkpie detected uncertainty, which undercut the woman's defiant expression. The children were much easier to read. They were somber and wooden; they had turned their bodies toward the entrance. Porkpie put her hands on her hips. She listened. She listened all the way through a harried announcement in Vietnamese, something about a doctor, and then she heard. Someone really was coming. Under the loudspeaker noise, Porkpie heard squishing mud. It was coming from along the back wall. There was the sound of scraping, too, and then the squishing began to move forward, along the side wall. The children followed the noise, whispering in high voices as the sound neared the entrance.

A giant, muddy hand swept aside the plastic sheet.

"That's no demon," said Porkpie, nodding in greeting. "That's Mr. Reuben. He's just big, that's all. Hello, Mr. Reuben," she said cheerily. "Everyone, say hello."

"Porkpie," Reuben shouted, putting a hand over his ear. "You got enough racket around here?" He stooped down, both in demonstration of the noise and to avoid collision with the ceiling. "Who put a loud-speaker outside?" His rubber waders glistened with a skin of mud, and his hair was wild. The hammer looped around his belt rocked itself still. He was panting; his lips were flecked with mud.

"Reuben," said Porkpie. "You look awful."

Miss Phu turned to the children and addressed them. The boy shut his eyes. The girls squeezed each other's hands; one had her mouth open, but no sound came out.

"Hell," said Reuben, nostrils flaring. Even stooping, he brushed the ceiling with his hair. "Get this ceiling straightened out. I can do that." But then he simply stopped, breathing hard, his shoulders hunched.

"Is something the matter?" said Porkpie.

He didn't say anything. He wiped mud from his arm.

"We . . . ," said Porkpie. "Well, Miss Phu was just teaching a lesson."

"Miss Phu, yeah," he said. "Thought that was you." He nodded down at her in acknowledgment, but she was busy stroking the arm of one of the girls.

Shush, Miss Phu said to the girl. Shush now.

Reuben twirled his right hand around like a propeller, summoning words, then turned to Miss Phu. "Hey, tell them it's me. Mr. Reuben. The sub-engineer."

"Yes, Mr. Reuben," said Miss Phu quickly. She shushed the girl again.

"I was down at the black market," he said, turning to Porkpie. His face labored a moment, then his voice got loud. "This guard . . . I don't even know who it was. He took something and didn't pay. You hear me? He took something . . . I gave her the money . . . and then . . ."

He faltered. The girls pressed together, holding on to each other's hair. The boy in the underpants had risen. The boy walked over to Miss Phu and, kneeling, wrapped his arms around her legs, burying his face into the crook of her knees.

"Maybe this isn't a good time," Porkpie whispered.

They were silent a moment. Nobody moved. Miss Phu rocked the boy. Then the loudspeaker started up again. For once, Porkpie was glad to hear its scratchy whine.

"Son of a bitch," Reuben shouted, scowling at the noise.

"Please, Reuben. Maybe another time."

"No," he said. He walked to the blackboard and stopped. "I'm here. I'm talking now. You listen."

He pointed angrily, frowning at Porkpie. He turned around, clanking his tools against the desk, and in one motion he raised his fist and brought it down hard against the blackboard. The board shook. One end slipped from a nail and fell to the ground.

One of the girls started to wail.

"Miss Porkpie," said Miss Phu suddenly.

The noise from the loudspeaker seemed to wobble. The boy in the underpants began to rub his head into Miss Phu's legs.

"Oh, Miss Phu," said Porkpie. "Miss Phu."

Half of Bidong was smeared onto Reuben's fist. Porkpie put her hand on his arm, stilling him, but out of the corner of her eye, just before Miss Phu turned away, Porkpie saw the woman's face tighten and clamp shut. It was an expression Porkpie had seen before on the Vietnamese, though not on Miss Phu: the skin suddenly drawn taut, exaggerating the contours of the skull and jaw. She sensed Miss Phu flushing moisture and fat from her body, discarding everything that wasn't essential, as if in preparation for flight, while she drew the children close with a protective arm.

The image had a formal quality, like a Renaissance painting, all the figures arranged to draw the viewer's eye toward a certain point. It was almost as if the scene had been choreographed, the complex movements made fluid through rehearsal, arms and legs prearranged in exacting patterns, the yelping noises fine-tuned in front of mirrors. And perhaps they were. Horribly so. Who knew what they had faced on the high seas? There was in trauma a spiraling kind of repetition, the shout reborn as echo, the body's violation giving way to the mind's visitation. Perhaps that was what she was seeing. Repetition, echo, visitation. The mane of the beast, rolling onto the beaches in waves: the roaring, the liquid warm and foaming, then nothing, then the roaring again and again and again.

Porkpie said, "You have to leave now, Reuben." Reuben bent down, turning his ear to her, as if he hadn't heard.

"I said you have to leave," she said again. Miss Phu, draping her arm around the boy, motioned toward the entrance.

"I'll fix the blackboard," Reuben said, picking up the fallen corner.

Porkpie reached up and grabbed his head firmly with her hands. She whispered into his ear. When she stopped, he looked dazed. He put the blackboard down. He lifted a hand in the direction of Miss Phu, but then the boy in the underpants shrieked. "I didn't mean anything," Reuben said. His voice cracked. "It's me. Reuben Gill. I'm not . . . It's me. Bidong sub-engineer. I'm not a demon." He stumbled backward, as if struck by a blow. He turned to the entrance, hammer clinking against his belt. The clear plastic sheet crinkled, and he was gone.

By the time Miss Phu came back from lunch, the smell was so bad that Porkpie, out of fresh Kleenex, was using a discarded tissue as a breathing filter. The loudspeaker had been going for more than an hour, and now that the rain had started up again, beetles were scurrying under the tarp, seeking dry ground.

"Miss Phu," Porkpie said at last, but she couldn't think of how to continue.

Miss Phu hadn't heard her anyway. The noise was intolerable, but as soon as Porkpie cursed the loudspeaker under her breath, she berated herself for thinking the noise intolerable. She vowed to complain less about the racket, and the mud and the smell. She called herself horrid, though she knew her complaining to be limited to occasional outbursts of frustration. But self-recrimination seemed proper, an act of purification. As a practice, self-recrimination was vastly underrated. Giving yourself a tongue-lashing drove you to gauge your behavior more precisely. It suggested the existence of an overriding moral calculus, wherein emotional responses were measured against the external cause of the response. Responses greater than the cause were invalidated; equilibrium was established; unreasonableness was flagged as incorrect.

"You OK, Miss Porkpie?" said Miss Phu, shouting over the music. She was squatting by the wall, where for the past five minutes she had been examining entry holes along the base of the tarp, damming them up with mud.

"Oh, Miss Phu," Porkpie said brightly, but Miss Phu had already returned to her work. I'm sorry, Porkpie wanted to say. So very, very sorry.

But she did not say it. The words seemed childish and mean.

Miss Phu apparently didn't want to bring up what had happened, so neither would she. She would follow the woman's cue. She would pretend nothing had happened. That, too, was the Vietnamese way. Miss Phu, still damming up beetle holes, was working herself silly, molding mud bricks as if she were on the clock. If the whole wall collapsed, she would probably just shrug and start digging new post holes.

It was an attractive attitude, one that stirred Porkpie to rise briefly, standing in admiration of Miss Phu's resolve. And in standing, in feeling her muscles tighten, in flexing her belly against the tuck of her sundress, Porkpie breathed deeply, combatively, in what seemed to her solidarity with Miss Phu. She filled her lungs with the foul odor. Buck up, she thought. Yes. It seemed to her then, breathing, that her presence was trivial, her every precious concern perfumed with shame. She was a doe in the forest, an innocent. She breathed again, yipping at the smell, but she was gladdened by her discomfort. Buck up, she thought. Suffer this small indignity. In this tiny, pure way, learn. Breathe. Fight. Open your body to pollution.

Again she breathed.

She pictured the insides of her nose, recalling photographs of the bed of tiny follicles lining the nasal passages, a dense growth of microscopic fingers swaying to the rhythm of great unseen currents. Some type of seepage occurred, she knew, some intermingling of the body and natural gases, and the chemical reactions generated by the contact raced to the brain through electrical pulses, bearing complex codes. But that was not really much of an explanation, just overfed intellectualization, dense as rock. The brain was no more than an organ. Who was to say that this organ was the seat of knowledge?

The brain sat atop the body, blaring its superiority. It filtered input from the body's other organs, allowing one access to only a portion of one's actual experience. Did the brain's function not find its closest external parallel in political propaganda? The brain censored and shaped and made proclamations. It was the State, reproduced along biological lines. But that censored information . . . where did it go? What truths entered through the senses, only to be cast aside? What ghostly knowledge? When you sat inside a dark tarp shelter all day and stared at empty benches and heard a loudspeaker babble in a language you didn't understand, you were attuned to different frequencies, to different . . .

"I smell the demon," she said suddenly. "The beast."

She felt foolish as soon as she spoke. Miss Phu didn't hear her. She was outside, squatting by the entrance, pushing mud against the tarp. My gosh, Porkpie thought. What had she just said? She smelled no such thing. She was Bobbi Porkpie Sortini, and she was sitting on a bench.

She pinched herself until a satisfying welt formed on her arm.

The odor gusting up from the Zone C garbage had grown appalling, sweet and acrid and hot and rotting all at once, and Porkpie, sighing with resignation, grimly appealed to her brain to ward it off. But she had already scorned the organ, ridiculed its generosity and benign nature, and she felt the need to apologize. She pictured it lying inert inside her head, like a turtle drawn deep into its shell. She closed her eyes and gave silent praise for its powers. She tapped her head, knocking as if she were at a door and desired entry. She was rewarded. "Thank you," she mumbled, and she felt strong and clear-eyed again.

The world, she thought: it could swallow you up from the inside out. You could go mad trying to understand. You could go mad with thinking.

"You OK, Miss Porkpie?" asked Miss Phu. "OK, yes? You OK?"

"Yes," said Porkpie, smiling. "Just resting my eyes."

"Dreaming, Miss Porkpie?" Miss Phu asked. The rain thrummed against the tarp walls.

Porkpie looked at her intently. She saw now that Miss Phu's chin was bandaged.

"Miss Phu," said Porkpie. "What happened to your face?" She reached up to touch the bandage, but Miss Phu drew away.

"A mouse bites me," she said pleasantly. "When I eating my lunch."

But Porkpie had seen the island's giant rats. The camp hospital was full of patients with gauze-wrapped faces and limbs. A mouse, they all said, but at night you could hear people yelling in their huts.

"You OK, Miss Porkpie?" asked Miss Phu. She put her hands on her knees and bent down, as if addressing a child.

"Thank you, Miss Phu. Yes. Really. I'm sorry. Was I staring?"

"Not looking." Miss Phu paused. She seemed to be looking for a word. "You doing this," she said, and then she sniffed the air like a rabbit.

"Yes. Smelling a mouse, I suppose. A little, tiny mouse."

"Here," said Miss Phu. She reached into her blouse pocket and pulled out something very slowly. It was a Kleenex, folded tightly. She unfolded it quickly, then draped it over her palm.

"For breathing," Miss Phu said, holding the tissue out. "Putting on your nose."

Porkpie looked at the tissue a moment. "Oh, Miss Phu," she said. She accepted the gift. Miss Phu nodded briskly, and in the nod Porkpie thought she understood: Miss Phu forgave her. Her presence was accepted.

"You're very kind, Miss Phu," said Porkpie, stirring. "Thank you."

But Miss Phu was already at the entrance, fussing over a puddle that was leaking in from outside. Porkpie frowned. Taped to Miss Phu's left heel was fresh gauze; disinfectant had soaked through, leaving a purple stain.

She wondered: How could I not have seen it? How could I be so self-absorbed? She walked over and stood mutely behind Miss Phu, searching for something to say.

"Yes, Miss Porkpie?" Miss Phu tapped the plastic sheeting with her finger. Then she pointed at the puddle. "How you say?"

"Puddle," said Porkpie. The loudspeaker over the entrance crackled to life again; a voice started reading off a list of names in Vietnamese. "That's my first contribution all day," Porkpie shouted, but Miss Phu just smiled distractedly and bowed her head in concentration, listening.

Porkpie stood with Miss Phu awhile. Outside, the rain dropped off, then started again. The wall tarps rustled.

"Miss Phu," Porkpie said, but Miss Phu smiled again and held up her hand, listening to the names.

Porkpie returned to her bench. She held the tissue to her nose.

"I'm doing what I can," she said.

"Thank you, Miss Porkpie. You do so much. We are so grateful." The loudspeaker went silent. The rain began to fall again.

The rain fell and fell and the mud wriggled under its weight, and then Miss Phu's friend, Mrs. Lai, appeared at the entrance. She was carrying a large rusted pot over her head. She snickered a hello, then squatted with Miss Phu in front of a bench, examining the pot and scraping off the rust with a stick.

"Miss Porkpie," said Miss Phu, waving the stick. "I can borrowing?" Miss Phu pointed to Porkpie's slicker.

"Yes, of course. Please." Porkpie stood and handed the item over. "Leaving?"

"No, no," said Miss Phu. "For singing."

The two women walked outside, Miss Phu holding the stick, Mrs. Lai dragging the pot through the mud. They held the slicker over them as if it were an umbrella, and then Mrs. Lai took the stick from Miss Phu and gave the pot a few practice whacks. They looked at each other, counting silently. Then they burst into a praise song for education. Miss Phu lifted her head and sang; Mrs. Lai beat the pot in accompaniment. The sound the women made carried down the hill and then back up, buffeted by gusts. The loudspeaker started again—the speaker's voice was breathy and panicked—and then Miss Phu raised her voice, wincing with effort, but the loudspeaker drowned her out.

It seemed so heroic: the two women standing in the rain, singing songs no one could hear. If only their voices could carry farther. If only more people could hear them. If only . . .

Porkpie leaped from her bench. "You know what," she shouted. She slapped her lesson books in glee and ran out the entrance. The rain was warm on her face. "Miss Phu," she said. She wiped hair from her eyes. "Miss Phu."

She stood watching the women a moment, waiting for their song to finish. Mrs. Lai beat the pot furiously, marking the final flourish.

Miss Phu raised the tent of the rain slicker.

"I can help you, Miss Phu," Porkpie said.

"You do not speak Vietnamese, Miss Porkpie."

"No," said Porkpie. "That's right. But I can help you."

"Oh, you do so much, Miss Porkpie."

Mrs. Lai eased the pot down and sat on it.

"No, Miss Phu," Porkpie said, shaking her head.

"You are getting wet," said Miss Phu. She held the slicker high, inviting Porkpie to share it.

"Please don't bother about that," said Porkpie. She picked up the limp arm of her rain slicker and wiped her face. "Look. I've got an idea. How would you like your education song to reach all the way down this hill?" She swept her arm expansively toward the camp below. "All the way down, so the children can hear?"

Miss Phu scratched at the gauze strips on her chin. "Then," she said evenly, "you are very wonderful, Miss Porkpie."

Porkpie giggled. She held her arms out to hug Miss Phu, but Miss Phu looked at her coolly.

"Thank you, Miss Porkpie," she said. "But in Vietnam we are not hugging. Not nice in front of all the people."

But Porkpie wasn't bothered. She smiled so big her cheeks started to hurt.

When the rain let up, Porkpie slid and stumbled down the hill, and walked straight to the UN compound. She was still smiling. Yes. She would talk to Gurmit. He would get her what she needed, and then Miss Phu could be heard. She opened the gate. She entered her tidy yellow bungalow and changed her clothes and combed her hair and looked at herself in the mirror. She smiled and touched her face and sat alone for a long, long time because her spirit had whispered into her ear, *You are here.*

13

All afternoon she looked for Reuben, but apparently he didn't wish to be found. At Engineering, Ralph simply scowled when she asked for Reuben's whereabouts; at the Zone A school, Manley shrugged then turned on his heel. When at last Reuben showed up for dinner at the Coconut Inn, sliding quietly onto the end of the bench, Porkpie called out his name in greeting. He wouldn't look up. Without a word he began eating in a bad-dog kind of way, bending his head over his bowl and chewing quickly. She stared at him so intently that Manley leaned over and asked if she thought she was in an art museum. She laughed loudly; she made bright conversation and tossed a rice clump at Nixon; she stood up several times to help Miss Thi pour a yellowish soup into people's cups. Still Reuben wouldn't look her way. He sat well back on the bench, out of the lamplight. Once he turned around and spit something out, but there was no expression on his face, even when Miss Thi and the other kitchen ladies paraded the length of the table, holding forth a platter of cabbage that had been carved into the shape of a roast chicken.

"Good show, Miss Thi," said Johann, clapping.

"Yummy," said Sally, catching Miss Thi's eye. She held her by the arm. "Bravo, Miss Thi. It's a beautiful presentation."

Reuben didn't look at the platter, and he didn't narrow his eyes and glare at Johann or Sally. He pulled out a black cigar and whispered to Manley for a light. His speech seemed a bit slurred—from drinking, Porkpie suspected—and he held on to the match so long that he burned his fingers. He didn't flinch; he simply dropped the match and placed his cigar, unlit, on the table. Then he held up his hand and examined his fingernails. They were surprisingly long. One looked jagged, as if it had been torn. Just as Porkpie was about to comment, Reuben stood, then left the table and disappeared onto the footpath.

She ran after him. She caught a glimpse of him turning a corner, but he was walking so fast that she quickly found herself lost in the middle of the Zone D footpath, without a flashlight. She appealed for help. Outside the shelters were dozens of young men playing cards and smoking cigarettes. They must have seen him. "Mr. Reuben," she said, holding her arms out in exasperation. They all pointed with their cigarettes, lighting her path with small, orange embers, and one of them ran with her all the way to the Zone D beach, where she found him kneeling on one knee, passing his hand over the glistening mud.

"Reuben," she said, panting from the run. "I thought of how to help Miss Phu. Just forget about what happened up there today. Reuben, we can *help* her."

"Shh," he said. He passed his hand over the mud, tracing the air in slow, wide circles. He was frowning at the ground, and every so often he glanced at his hand, as if unsure of its location. Then his fingers started trembling, just twitching at first, then rolling violently, like a divining rod, and he suddenly plunged his arm into the brown crust of mud, working his way down, all the way up to his elbow, and in one grunting motion he pulled out a buried engine casing. He tossed the dripping metal aside as though it were a weed.

"What's this all about?" she said.

He held up his muddy hand and shook it. "I knew where the casing was. I didn't have to look."

She waited.

"I could sense where it was," he said.

"You just knew, is that it?"

His knee was slowly sinking deeper into the mud. He spoke softly: "There's something happening to me."

"Reuben, I can smell the liquor on your breath. Now come on."

"And look at this." He stuck his hand up to her face.

"Your hand."

"Look how long my fingernails are."

"I noticed at dinner."

"They weren't that long yesterday. Fingernails don't grow that fast."

"Reuben, stop this."

"Something's happening to me."

"It's the pressure of being here," she said. "Up in the primary school, I thought I smelled . . ." She decided not to say it.

He looked up at her. "What?"

She waved the question away. "I don't know what. I was just getting carried away. Like you are. So your fingernails are growing fast. So you found some junk. What is this all about?"

He groaned. His knees creaked when he rose. He turned away, stooping low, and walked a few steps, once again waving his hand over the mud. "Here," he said. She could see his hand shaking. He dropped to one knee and thrust his arm into the ground, yanking out a muddy locket.

"You see?" he said, wiping mud off the object. There was a pool of water forming around his knee. A dark stain was creeping up his pants. "This afternoon I found a ruler and a shoe. They must been buried in a foot of mud. I just put my hand in, and there they were. I tell you, something's happening to me."

"A parlor trick."

"It's not natural," he whispered.

"Now Reuben."

"I said it's not natural."

"Since when is anything about a refugee camp natural?"

He brought his hand up, level with his eyes, and started twisting the fingers around, studying them from different angles.

She put her hand on his shoulder. "Is this about what happened with Miss Phu? Just put it out of your mind. I've got a plan."

He held up his hand, gesturing *stop*.

She shook her head. "Reuben," she said, rubbing his shoulder, "you're no more a demon than I am."

He buried his face in his knee.

"Is that what this is about?" she said.

He moaned. He began grinding his face into his knee.

"You've got powers now?" she said. "Is that what you're saying?"

He sat there, hunkered in the mud. He didn't move.

Porkpie lifted her foot, then reached into her purse for a Kleenex, which she then used to wipe her calf clean. All around, tiny sand crabs, hundreds of them, were rippling along the beach, burrowing into the mud before each wave, then rising in patches as the water receded, only to vanish in the next rolling wave. The sea was quivering, lit up in giant strips by the moon, and in the darkness, the stripped engine hulks farther down the beach rattled with broken bolts and small, shelled creatures.

He began talking, rambling really, not making much sense, lacking the attractive authority she had come to expect. He was simply surly. She nodded at him pleasantly, then saw that his eyes were moving rapidly about, taking in everything, roaming her face. It was an eerie feeling, watching as you were being watched, and she felt as well a momentary flush of indignation that he should watch her with less focus than she watched him. It was as though the pleasing shape of her face was not nearly as interesting as the fact that it was not shaped like anything else. As if she were merely a piece of the puzzle to him, sitting among other puzzle pieces. He then raised his head and stared at her briefly, a look of confusion spreading across his face, as if wondering where he was. Porkpie smiled, but his head dropped heavily onto his arm.

There was a long silence. "Me and Manley," he said at last. "Last year we hitched up to Bangkok. Pussy's fine up there."

Pussy. There were certain words that educated men never actually said in front of women, and, she suspected, certain words they never actually said in front of each other, except as fodder. The word was so bleak and miserable that it could not possibly indicate lust. His entire statement broke with the rules of his grammar and diction, suggesting to her an internal confusion. Certainly the deliberate look on his face, the tense, exaggerated way his expression mimicked calm, was enough to warrant sympathy. It was as though he were hearing the words as he spoke them, unsure of their source. Men like Reuben, she thought, men without apparent ties to home, were essentially conservative, despite their showy bombast and neon lowlifery. They were rule bound and compulsive, and happiest when confronted with limited options. *Pussy,* spoken with a straight face, to her: that was his known world breaking apart. That was a word weighted with grief.

"To continue," she said softly. "There's nothing inhuman about you." She motioned as if to nuzzle his head between her breasts, but there was something like panic in his expression, some darkening of his eyes, that caused her to step back. He didn't want comforting, and he didn't want to hear about her plan. That could wait. He needed pretense now; he needed the illusion that everything was as it had always been. So she summoned a coquettish, mocking tone, and began to banter. She talked quickly, adversarially, looking his way every few sentences, hoping to rouse his head from his arm, hoping to see his mouth pucker belligerently, to hear him howl at her pronouncements in delighted outrage.

"There's a trap in thinking ironically," she said. "Don't you think? At first it can seem a rather clever announcement of poverty and diminished expectations. But that leads you to the next step, doesn't it? Which is to be superior to everything that might move you. You're like a store clerk then, measuring with an accountant's eye from a fund of sustenance, scooping from the great barrel, only the person you're taking the sustenance from is yourself. I think that's awful. Yes, I do."

She spoke more:

"I was thinking that when you've lived in Asia long enough, you begin to dislike the big cities, working with people in suits and ties, because these people, these Asians who have been educated in the West, who have been around white people, are full of hatred toward you. None of this gets expressed, of course. But at least their groveling allows you to spite them without feeling guilty."

And more:

"Do you know what bores me about Americans our age? All that constant nattering about cultural context. It's like they're saying they don't exist until other people exist as well. It's a horrible business. After a point, cultural context means nothing. I say everything that's lovely about being alive can occur only out of context."

He still wasn't moving. His head rested stumpishly on his arm, and then she saw his eyelids flutter. His brow furrowed, but rather than contest her statements he simply brought up his other arm and scratched at his face. He looked at her. For a moment, his expression seemed not to belong to him, but to her own past. Long ago . . . Of course: Chicago. It was Lyle, lost Lyle, sitting on the bed, filling his antique jar with preserving fluid. His lips were moving slightly, and he was staring at the watery container where he had placed remnants of organs: his kidney stone, a mealy chunk of his lower intestine. There he would be, staring with the look Reuben now had. Loss could do that to people. It made them withdrawn and selfish, and sometimes a snake got loose in their blood and slithered all the way up to their heart and squeezed it so tight they burst into tears if you kissed them.

She stared at him a while. Poor Reuben. Some men grew soft with grief, as if overtaken by slumber. They absorbed their grief slowly, and in the end they smiled like patients at the medicine cabinet, embarrassed and even a little relieved that their grief should carry them into a deep narcotic sleep. Not so Reuben. He would turn nasty.

"Reuben, listen to me," she said.

His eyes were closed. He stuck out his hand and swiped in her direction.

She stepped back. "We can talk tomorrow," she said softly. "Just sleep it off, Reuben. You just need some rest." Then she turned and left for the compound, stopping only to wipe her legs clean.

"A bullhorn for Miss Phu," said Gurmit. "This is what you are asking."

"Yes," said Porkpie, blinking. She was not about to be dissuaded, though now that she sat across from him, watching him fold and unfold his hands, she was more nervous than she had anticipated. She looked at his hands a long time. The overhead fluorescent tube was cracked, but the morning light was bright enough that she was sure she wasn't imagining what she saw: his hands really were green. "A shout-spout," she said. "Like the supply boat captain has. What's his name? Skipper Rahim."

"A bullhorn is educational supplies?"

"Oh, yes. Well, let me think." It was hard not to stare at his hands, so she directed her gaze toward the windows, where the light built up against the panes and seeped between the louvers like a gas. "With a bullhorn, we could increase attendance. So yes. Educational supplies." She pointed. "You know, those windows could use a scrubbing."

Gurmit nodded. "So very dirty all the time." He wiggled his fingers back and forth in imitation, she thought, of active bacteria. His fingers made a crinkly noise, like lettuce being shredded, and then Porkpie saw: he was wearing colored latex gloves, the kind Johann sometimes came to dinner with after a day spent developing X rays. There was a rubber band wrapped around the end of the right-hand glove, cinching it tight against his wrist.

"With a bullhorn," he said, "Miss Phu can be heard all through Zone F? All the way down the hill?"

"Farther, I'll bet," said Porkpie. "I was in Zone G once, and I heard Skipper Rahim on that little bullhorn he has. That was clear across the island, almost."

Gurmit was shifting in his chair, and every time he moved, Porkpie found herself glancing at his gloves, wondering at their implication. Perhaps they meant nothing. Perhaps he had been cleaning and had simply forgotten he was wearing them. He might at any second look at what he had on his hands and then utter an embarrassed *bloody hell* and strip the gloves off. But he might not. Who knew with Gurmit? She hardly ever saw him. He stayed holed up in his office all day, and he never joined the staff for dinner.

"Miss Phu deserves so much," said Gurmit softly. His chair creaked as he leaned back.

"Yes, she does. She works hard."

"She is having such a small voice, isn't it?" said Gurmit. "So polite."

"All the Viets seem polite to me," said Porkpie. "You know, sometimes I almost wish I weren't staff. I wish the Viets weren't afraid to rub us the wrong way."

He nodded. "Yes. We are doing such a good job of wrong-rubbing ourselves, isn't it?"

His tone was so flat, Porkpie was relieved to see a slight smile on his face. He looked haggard. He hardly moved his eyes at all, and when he did, they glistened with a yellowish jelly. His white safari suit was pressed, but Porkpie's gaze was drawn to the line of pens sticking out of his breast pocket. They were coated in a flaky white film. She had to stare at the film for a moment before she realized that she was looking at hundreds of teeth marks. He had been gnawing his pens.

"If we are going to talk," Gurmit said, "then we are needing a requisition form."

He pushed back his chair and stepped over to one of his file drawers and started rummaging through it. Porkpie looked around. The office smelled of sweat, and in the seeping light, she saw the smoky swirls of recently disturbed dust. If indeed Gurmit had been cleaning before she arrived, then he had done a terrible job. One side of the office was littered with jumbled MRCS boxes, marked in felt pen with incomprehensible codes and abbreviations. His row of file cabinets were in disarray. One of the handles hung by a single screw; there were splotches on the drawers, as if someone had shaken ink onto the metal. On the floor were mounds of manila envelopes and refugee files. His desk map of Bidong was stained with coffee and tea rings, and when she leaned forward, she saw streaks of dried Wite-Out covering the spot on the map where his office would have been.

Along the far wall was his engraved table plank. She imagined Gurmit dragging it from place to place, redecorating it, positioning it just so, like an accent piece. It seemed different somehow, less garish than she had remembered. He had, certainly, removed several strands of pearl lights from its decorations. The lights were apparently unplugged; the wire looped around the wood like a thin vine. The garland of bulbs at the top had been removed as well, replaced by a small strip of masking tape, which lifted up a solitary bulb the distance of a finger from the winding cord. And before, hadn't there been messy melted candles on the floor, stuck to tinfoil? Now, two square ration tins nudged the base of the plank; she could see four black candlewicks, symmetrically positioned, peeking out over the tops.

There seemed nothing wild or exotic about the plank now. It had, in fact, a decidedly domesticated air, like some small potted tree, one rough with bark and dotted with twinkly blooms no bigger than raisins. She smiled. Perhaps that was what happened when you felt you actually belonged on Bidong. Things didn't surprise you as much. You were calm. You saw things clearly.

She looked now at Gurmit. The man needed to leave. He needed to rest up in Kuala Trengganu. He stared at each file in the drawer as if he had never seen files before. His face was tight, his shoulders were hunched, and he hardly blinked at all. She imagined him turning and staring at her as if she were just an anonymous confluence of clothes and flesh, then taking out a pen and gnawing at it distractedly, until his jaw got sore.

"Gurmit, I'm afraid I have to ask," Porkpie said. "I can't help but wonder about your gloves."

Gurmit shut the file drawer and returned to his chair, holding a folder that bulged with forms. He raised his eyebrows. "Is nothing," he said, paging through the folder. "With this mud and rain, we are having many germs on Bidong. So very dirty, isn't it? I ask myself, 'Do I wish to be running to the washing room all the day? Or do I wear gloves to protect myself?' My job, you know, with all these forms and such . . . I cannot smudge them all the time, and I cannot be smudged all the time in return."

"So," she said brightly. She could not think of how to respond. "You've been spring cleaning," she continued. "Out with the old, in with new."

"Dirty," he said, raising his head. "I cannot be touching dirtiness all the time. Do you understand?"

"Yes," she nodded. "I'm sorry. I'm disturbing your work."

Gurmit went back to his folder. He was so unreadable. Her first day on Bidong, he couldn't get enough of touching things. Now he acted as if he wanted to run everything through disinfectant.

"Well, what do you say?" said Porkpie. "You think Zone F can get a bullhorn?"

"Not for certain." He pulled out what appeared to be a requisition form, then looked up. "Task Force Chief Ahmed must approve."

"Ahmed," she said. She could not get a clear picture of the man. The last time she saw him, he had been sitting in a straight-backed chair outside the Task Force barracks, hooting at some joke. His shirt had been unbuttoned, and he had startled her by pulling up his T-shirt and slapping a riff on his fat belly, as if it were a drum.

"Really," she said. "Is this a security matter? Just for a bullhorn?"

"Yes-*lah!*" The anger in his voice startled her. "For a bullhorn. Are you not reading the newspapers? With the staff workers, do you not . . ." He raised one of his gloved hands and waved it in the general direction of the UN compound.

"Yes, of course," she said, nodding vigorously. "I've heard rumors."

Apparently she had said the right thing. His expression softened. "The prime minister is under so much pressure now," he said softly, opening the top drawer of his desk. "You have seen?" He pulled out an article clipped from the *New Straits Times.* "From last week. I am receiving newspapers from Captain Rahim, straight from Kuala Trengganu." Gurmit laid the article in front of her. "Task Force is thinking many scenarios now," he said. "If a riot is here, yes? A bullhorn in the wrong hands . . . very dangerous. Is security concern. So close now to Year Five, yes?"

Porkpie scanned the article quickly. Under a photo of a crowded boat at sea, the headline read, "Vietnamese Attacked on Kota Bharu Beach."

Porkpie pointed to a paragraph. "OK. OK," she said. "I didn't know it was escalating. I hadn't heard about . . . what's it say? 'Severe consequences' if the West doesn't take more Viets. We're so isolated here, you know? We're the last to hear."

"It happens so fast," he said. He clapped his gloves together in demonstration.

"I understand," she said. "Yes, I can see that security might be a problem. But look, I can have Miss Phu check the bullhorn out. Under my supervision only."

"Cannot," he said, and then he pulled at his gloves, drawing them tighter around his fingers. "As I am saying, this is security concern. When there is security concern, Ahmed is very strict. Too many thiefs, isn't it? Too many chances for mistake."

"Yes, I see. Well, let me ask you. Do you, personally, think we can get a bullhorn?"

"Perhaps. Ahmed must say."

"Miss Phu would love it so much," she sighed. She shook her head. "All these regulations."

"Must have regulations," he said sharply. The anger had returned to his voice. "Is my job, yes? Administration. Many forms. Policy. Not silly-*lah*. No regulations, no order. If no order, then . . ." He drew a finger all the way across his neck.

"You're scaring me, Gurmit," she said.

You're scaring me. She had simply blurted the words out, not really sure if she meant them. But she was glad she had spoken. Gurmit seemed surprised, as if she had just yelled in his ear. For the first time since she had sat down, she had the sense he was actually looking at her.

"Of course regulations aren't silly," Porkpie said quickly. She leaned forward and lifted her hand, as if to touch him. "That isn't what I meant."

His reaction was baffling. He brought his hands up to his face and buried his face in his gloves. He closed his eyes. She thought she heard him whimper.

Alarmed, Porkpie put her hand on his arm. "Really. That's not what I meant." She paused. The conversation had taken a wrong turn somewhere. She had said nothing offensive, yet here Gurmit was, shrinking into himself. "It's just that there's so much to get used to. I didn't even acknowledge that I was here, I mean, really here, until yesterday. I think the best of you, personally. The very best."

He opened his eyes. "Thank you," he said softly. He cleared his throat. "I tell you frankly . . . this rain." He gestured to the window.

"Yes, it's depressing."

They sat a moment in silence. Porkpie slowly removed her hand from Gurmit's arm and nestled back into her chair. Gurmit looked down at his requisition form, running his finger slowly down the margins.

"Gurmit," said Porkpie, "the bullhorn is such a lovely idea. Just imagine. Miss Phu can sing her praise songs. It'll be such a boost for her, and we might get some more children up to the primary school. Imagine if more people could hear her. Why, it would be like . . . Well, I don't know." Her eyes fell on the plank. "It would be like everyone could see that plank you have in the corner. It means so much to you, but only you see it, you know? I mean, imagine." She held her arms wide. "What if everyone saw? That's what it would be like for her. Everyone would pay attention."

He didn't react at first. His finger stopped moving. Then he clenched his jaws together and stood.

"Yes," he said, walking over to the plank. He grabbed the wood with both hands.

"You'll do it? You'll ask Ahmed?"

"Imagine if more people . . ."

"That's right," said Porkpie, rising from her chair. "That would be lovely. They could all hear. I know you agree with me, Gurmit."

"Reuben Gill," said Gurmit, turning to face her. He seemed excited. "He is sub-engineer, isn't it?"

"Right."

"He is very good with concrete."

"Well, that's what I hear."

"So then," he said, leaning the plank back against the wall. "Bloody hell, yes. You are friends with Reuben Gill."

"I'm not sure what you're getting at."

Gurmit returned to his chair and picked up the requisition form. "I am saying I can talk to Ahmed. He can yell bloody hell at me all he wants. I can make him agree. Oh, yes. But you are friends with Reuben Gill, isn't it?"

"I like him better than anyone. Really."

"Then I will ask Ahmed, and you can ask Reuben Gill." He smiled broadly. He shook the form. "Yes. Reuben Gill can walk with me to Zone F. With the plank, isn't it? Hey? With the plank. He can treat with shellac for the rain. He can pour concrete. Make a frame."

"I'm afraid I don't follow."

"You are seeing this plank?" he said, pointing. "You are looking, isn't it?"

"I am."

"And what if you are looking up at Zone F, and you see this?"

"Are you saying . . . what? You mean like for a monument?"

"Bloody hell," he said, smiling. "Everyone can see, yes? A monument."

She looked out the window, then stood.

This piece of wood, a monument. It was an odd notion, silly even, but the more she thought about the implications, the more sense the monument made. Gurmit, herself, Reuben: as triangles went, it wasn't a bad arrangement. It had an air of the fantastical that thrilled her. And it would give her everything. It had already stirred mushroomy Gurmit to life. Turning now, she saw him smile at her beautifully, revealing high, burnished cheekbones and bright teeth. For herself, just imagining a bullhorn in Miss Phu's hands gave her a sense of giddy high seriousness. With Gurmit's help, she could help Miss Phu sing.

And Reuben. If Reuben could turn the plank into a monument, he might get what he needed: exertion, the exercise of competence, a public display of muscular goodness. He would be up in Zone F, with Miss Phu. Miss Phu would see him with Gurmit. She would see Reuben working to honor the name engraved in the plank. She might sing to him. He might talk to her. They might all sit down in the primary school and drink some lemongrass tea and talk into the afternoon.

Yes. The bullhorn, the plank, the three of them working together. She gave silent praise to the bonds of complicity. The arrangement was marvelous, her course of action clear. Bringing a finger up to her head, she traced a path from the top of her skull all the way to her left ear, etching with a fingernail an approximation of a generous and powerful line of thought, one flowing and direct, clear of doubt.

"Gurmit," she said, sticking out her hand. "We're partners in crime."

"No! Not crime. Do not say."

"It's just an Americanism. Sorry. What I mean is, I agree. We're in it together. I'd be happy to ask."

"And I," he said.

They shook. His gloves were sticky on her hand. She felt his heart pounding through the material.

Then she was off. At the gate, she turned to wave to Gurmit, and he waved back, standing outside the door. "Bloody hell," he was saying, nodding. "Bloody hell, yes."

She felt so energetic and happy, she had to stop by the notice board to get control of her face. She couldn't stop smiling. She formulated a Porkpie pledge: *A Porkpie is strong and powerful. A Porkpie shall lead. A Porkpie shall not fail.* She waved to everyone she knew, and even when she stumbled on the footpath, falling to one knee, she simply shrugged and pulled herself up, not bothering to wipe her legs clean with tissue.

"Where's Reuben?" she asked Manley.

Manley was marking student exercise books on his bungalow porch. "Hey, you ought to know," he said.

"No, I don't. I need to talk to him."

"What do you do to him, anyway? You got him all fucked up now."

"Manley, please. Do you know where he is?"

"Hey, he doesn't listen to me now. I sure didn't fuck him up."

She put her hand on his arm. "Manley," she said. "I'm not sleeping with him."

He backed away. He closed the exercise book. "Hey, I didn't say that. Why are you saying that? I'm just saying he's my buddy, and he's fucked. You ask Ralph. He's inside. He'll tell you."

"I'm right here," said Ralph, stepping out the door. He was shaking his head. "He's fucked, all right."

Ralph told her. In the morning, he said, he had walked with Reuben and a crew of workmen over to Zone D. Reuben looked hung over; he shambled; he snapped at a noodle seller and wouldn't hitch up his pants when his tool belt sagged. They passed over the Zone D sewage canal, one at a time, bouncing across the plank, and one of the workmen, struggling to keep his balance, had dropped a box of mechanical parts into the stinking canal mess.

"I told everyone, 'Just forget it,'" said Ralph. He pushed up his glasses. "I mean, it's like sacrificing a pawn, isn't it? No big deal."

But Reuben, he said, took off his tool belt. Reuben, he said, walked to the bank of the canal and started pacing back and forth, looking into the mucky water. He started *growling,* Ralph said, or at least started saying something that sounded like growling. He snapped his waders tight. He took a cigar out of his pocket and laid it on the ground. And then he waded in. He took a small step, then a big step, and then there he was, plopping himself into the mess. A crowd gathered immediately, men, women, kids, all rushing out of their shelters, oohing and ahhing in disgust and amazement. He waded in muck up to his waist, and then he held his hand over the black ooze and, fingers twitching, closed his eyes as if in a trance and stuck his arm all the way in and plucked the items from the bottom.

"X-ray vision," said Ralph, taking off his glasses. "Show the man an arse, he'll tell you what's in it."

"Hey," said Manley. "Show some sympathy, man."

"All right," said Ralph. "How he found that stuff, I don't know. Bugger me. Those canals are pitch black."

"He's fucked," said Manley.

"What's this about sympathy, hey bugger?"

"He talks to the wrong people," said Manley. He glanced up at Porkpie. "That's why he's fucked. Only reason, I say."

"Where is he?" Porkpie said. "Please tell me. Right now."

"Zone C, Lady Porkpie," said Manley, opening another exercise book. "Garbage detail. Maybe you can lure him into the shower, huh?"

So she left the two men, pausing only to turn around and call out: "I've got nothing more to say to you, Manley."

And then Porkpie was out the gate, walking quickly along the muddy beach, searching the wall of garbage for a sign of Reuben. She found him working at the far end of the beach, oiled in sweat, crushing an empty ration carton under the soles of his rubber waders. She put a Kleenex to her nose. He stank to high heaven. The men in the Viet work crew nearby squinted at her, then went back to shoveling garbage into giant wicker baskets. Reuben was stripped to the waist. Even before she spoke, she couldn't keep her eyes off his expanse of chest and belly. There was so much of Reuben exposed, so much unwashed skin inches away from her face, so much limp body hair, that she at first couldn't believe it was really him. Strips of seaweed were plastered on his back, and the matted, corkscrewing hair ridging the top of his belt buckle seemed to her eyes soggy and dank, like sod. Dark clods clung to his pants.

She explained the plan. She spoke quickly, loudly, laying out exactly what she wanted him to do. "Say yes, Reuben," she said. "Think of what you could do." Then she waited.

He continued crushing ration cartons.

"I'm worried about you, Reuben."

He yelled at the work crew in a distracted, dreamy kind of way, shouting something about hard work, but his voice was unconvincing.

She asked him again. "Reuben," she said. "Sub-engineer Reuben Gill." She removed the Kleenex from her face and mashed it into her hand. She threw the tissue at his feet, and then she breathed deeply. She gagged. Her feet were planted in a long stretch of brown, sinking through the crust into something lumpy and soft. "Do it, and you'll exorcise your demon," she said, raising her foot and kicking a ration carton. "All right? That's why you should do it. Get rid of the demon. Redeem yourself."

He reached into his pocket and pulled out a packet of Kleenex. "Here," he said, handing it over. He watched her blow her nose.

"OK," he said then. "Count me in."

"Then take a bucket bath," she said firmly. "Clean yourself up. Stop moping. We've got work to do."

14

It was impossible to tell if the Vietnamese women milling around the Task Force compound were whores or simply refugee clerks, though why Task Force would need so many clerks was a question well worth considering. Gurmit, searching for Task Force Chief Ahmed, now considered the question. He paused at the rusting concertina wire, considering, then set his face with a firm expression and entered the compound. Apparently, the Vietnamese girls and boys sitting on soft drink cases outside the barracks door had not considered the question. They were no more than teenagers, vigorous and long-haired, and their casual and untroubled demeanor caused Gurmit to raise his arms and for a long, tense moment keep his gloved hands wavering in the air, poised as if to descend either in blessing or punishment. *Look around you!* he thought. *Look! Look!* But he kept the words silent. Gurmit, ascending the Task Force porch, planted his foot on the first step. No one was paying attention. The teenagers jabbered, idly kicking their sandals against the soft drink boxes. Gurmit nodded in their direction, but the teenagers started squabbling over a cassette tape. A boy in sunglasses, leaning against the door frame, gestured toward Gurmit's gloves, then slowly moved out of the way.

The door was open, and inside it was dark and uninviting, and very noisy. Gurmit, now stooping to remove his shoes, gasped: the boy in sunglasses laid a hand on his arm. "Smoke, man?" the boy said, revealing a dragon tattoo on his wrist. He shook an open pack of Marlboros in Gurmit's face. Gurmit shook his head and stepped quietly inside.

It was a poor beginning, but Gurmit was not about to turn around. The bullhorn. He must get the bullhorn from Ahmed, even though he, Gurmit Singh, would have to enter where he did not belong to ask for it. The building was long and narrow—double-tiered bunks were jammed up against the windows—and as Gurmit stood blinking by a bunk, straightening the jacket of his safari suit, he said hello to all the Task Force men squatting on the floor. They were playing cards. One of the men looked past him and made rude kissing noises at someone outside. The boy in the sunglasses brushed past, holding out a sweating bottle of Fanta for the squatting Malay. On the bunks to either side, Task Force men in singlets and sarongs were sleeping or smoking or listening to cassette players pressed against their ears.

Vietnamese women walked about carrying folders, most dressed in loose black pants and white blouses, though one, much taller than the others, had bushy, teased hair and wore a tight red dress held up with spaghetti straps. She carried what appeared to be a spittoon. Gurmit stared: she was walking toward him. Her dress was stained and shiny, and there were bruises on her neck. She stopped in front of him and rubbed the spittoon against his thigh, uncomfortably near his crotch. Gurmit looked at her in confusion, then cleared his throat, preparing to spit into the silver vessel. She jerked the spittoon away and shook it. It rattled with coins. The woman's face was hard and thin, and when she saw Gurmit's expression, she stepped back and looked at him appraisingly. A man on a nearby bunk laughed. "I not whore," she said. Her face darkened. "I singer. Very famous. Fuck you, man. I famous." She rattled her coins sharply and walked on.

No, he did not belong in the Task Force barracks, yet the very fact that he had entered was enough to keep him walking deeper into its dark confines. Deeper, he thought. There was respect to be gained in entering where you do not belong, and Gurmit noted with increasing satisfaction that each and every face he passed did not smile his way or shout out in greeting. Deep into the lion's den walked Gurmit Singh, hair cropped and without turban, but still very much a Singh, which, as even the most ignorant Malay guard must have known, meant "lion" in Hindi.

The air was gummy, thick with grease and stale cigarettes, and Gurmit, proceeding slowly, walked as through fog. The passageway was straight as a nave, and after passing a particularly brutal or unwelcoming face, Gurmit touched the rubber tips of his thumb and forefinger together, confirming, as if pressing a clicker, his safe arrival into ever more threatening levels of the barracks. He passed a mound of military-issue cans that leaked mysterious fluids. He passed a man scraping mud from a Muslim prayer mat with a bayonet. He passed terrible weapons. Stacked against a footlocker were black-barreled rifles. The guns smelled of rot—their canvas-lined shoulder straps were damp and frayed—and Gurmit nearly exclaimed in relief when he saw that the barrels had been covered with caps.

There, at the very end of the barracks, was Chief Ahmed. The chief, consulting with a skinny Vietnamese man, sat behind an overflowing desk, which was at the center of a circle of smaller desks, each occupied by pairs of young Vietnamese women, sitting shoulder to shoulder. The women were busy reading from stacks of mail, stopping every few moments to draw black lines in Magic Marker across selected letters. Ringing the desks were stuffed mailbags, and every so often one of the women would call over a Malay sergeant, who with much frowning and grunting looked at proffered letters and either handed them back or placed them in a large wire basket hanging from the wall.

"*Allah-mak,*" said Ahmed, gesturing toward Gurmit. "Our Indian friend. You have crawled out from your office." The chief said something to the Vietnamese man sitting at his side, and the man immediately leaped from his chair and raced over to one of the smaller desks, where he conversed briefly with one of the women before grabbing a large, steaming thermos. "Come, come," said Ahmed, waving Gurmit over. "I have something to show you."

It was an encouraging sign. Too, there were fresh curry stains on Ahmed's shirt. The chief had apparently eaten heartily. His face was sleepy and relaxed.

Gurmit sat down slowly, summoning a grave tone. "And I am here," Gurmit said, "because of a matter of some importance which I am wanting to discuss with you."

"Oooh-*lah!*" said Ahmed, pointing. "You are washing dishes now."

Gurmit looked at his gloves. "No," he said. "I am wearing because of too many germs. How to keep clean on Bidong?"

"Doctor Gurmit," said Ahmed, laughing. "Bidong surgeon, yes?" He indicated the skinny man who had previously occupied Gurmit's seat.

"I bam-bam this fellow tomorrow, yes? Send him to you for patching." The man, rubbing his hands on the thermos, stood beside the chief and giggled.

"No bam-bam," said Gurmit quickly.

"Joking-*lah*!" said Ahmed. "This fellow, he knows what is a joke. Tell our Indian friend your funny story, Mr. Thich."

Mr. Thich cupped the thermos firmly between his hands and swallowed several times, as if dislodging something caught in his throat.

"Waiting," said Ahmed, looking up in irritation. He pulled out a cup from behind some folders.

"Thirsty, Mr. Ahmed," said the man.

"Funny story first," said Ahmed, wiggling the cup. "Then hot tea for you."

Mr. Thich was so thin that his Adam's apple stuck out like a knuckle, and as Mr. Thich continued swallowing, Gurmit briefly entertained notions of an even thinner Mr. Thich trapped inside the slight figure in front of him, struggling to free his hand from the man's vocal cords.

"Before the communists take over my country," said Mr. Thich, rasping, "I am a member of the Association of Fathers of the Republic. Vinh Loi province, yeah? We play dominoes, drink some tea. No politic. Sometime we carry the banners when Saigon government come to visit. But when communists win, we change our name to the Association of Lucky Seven-Spots. We want to show communists we are only playing dominoes and drinking tea. After one year, food is very scarce, so we must fill up our stomachs on water. Yeah. So now we still play dominoes and drink tea, but between ourselves we are the Association of Water-Loving Fathers. Then some members try to escape Vietnam. We still play dominoes and drink tea, but now we are the Association of Leaky-Boat Families. Our name is very famous in Vietnam. Everyone thinks how funny we are, changing our name all the time."

"And now on Bidong?" said Ahmed, yanking the man's T-shirt.

"Now when people are accepted to America, they make a joke. They play dominoes, drink some tea. Have a party. They say to everyone, 'Today, I am a member of the Association of Hamburger Eaters.' Yeah."

"Hamburger," said Ahmed, winking to Gurmit knowingly. "You see? Americans eat the hamburger. These fellows here, when they say they are a member, they mean they are going to where people love the hamburger. Funny, yes?" He closed his eyes in pleasure, then handed the cup to Mr. Thich. "Drink now!" he said.

Mr. Thich unscrewed the top to the thermos and poured liquid into the cup. He tipped his head back and drank greedily. A brown rivulet raced down his neck.

"Is like . . . how do you say?" said Mr. Thich, lowering his cup. "Is like a code. Yeah. In letters to Vietnam, people are writing, 'In two weeks, I become a member of the Association of Hamburger Eaters.'"

"Letters to Vietnam?" said Gurmit. "From Bidong? How can? Cannot send letters to Vietnam from Malaysia."

"Think-*lah*!" said Ahmed. "These fellows send letters from Bidong to families in America, yes? Families in America know the code too. So the family in America sends another letter to the family in Vietnam, telling Vietnam family when are the refugees on Bidong going to America."

"Very bad to do," said Mr. Thich, disapproving. He slurped his tea noisily, prompting Ahmed to snap his fingers. Mr. Thich looked up from his cup and apologized.

"Yes," said Ahmed. "Then the family in Vietnam thinks, 'Oh, boat people very lucky. Wait only six months on Bidong, then go to America. OK, now I try myself.' So more people leave. More refugees coming."

"We must find letters with the code," said Mr. Thich, nodding toward the mail bags. "Destroy them."

Gurmit looked. The young women at the desks were quickly slicing envelopes open, then settling into reading, furiously crossing out lines with squeaking Magic Markers.

"Very bad to write the letters," said Mr. Thich, smiling at Ahmed. He again brought the cup to his lips and began slurping.

Gurmit scowled. It seemed a sordid business, reading your countrymen's letters, deleting their words. It seemed the work of a coward. Mr. Thich was drinking quickly, and as the huge knuckle in his neck slid up and down, Gurmit thought: Yes. There was another Mr. Thich trapped inside, another truer, nobler Mr. Thich, a man squirming in someone else's organs and bones, laying a knuckle hard against the throat of his tormentor. Why, if you gave Mr. Thich a gallon of tea, he'd still be thirsty. The real Mr. Thich would be drinking inside, feeling the liquid dribble down his knuckle and into his waiting mouth.

"That is not all," said Ahmed, leaning forward. "These letters, sometimes they tell where is Bidong. They tell where is Kuala Trengganu. They tell what is the best route to sail, how many police on Bidong. Dangerous informations." Ahmed leaned back suddenly and tapped the thermos. "Drink more, Mr. Thich. Drink noisy, yes? Turn around and do not listen. Noisy, yes?"

"Thank you, Mr. Ahmed," said Mr. Thich. He poured another cup and turned around. He sipped so loudly that he sounded, Gurmit thought, like a vacuum cleaner shutting off and on. Two women at a nearby desk began laughing.

Ahmed whispered: "Too many dangerous informations in letters. What if trouble comes? Bad things. I tell you, Gurmit. Maybe bad things coming, yes?"

"What are you saying?" asked Gurmit. But he knew. He didn't know what specifically Ahmed had to tell, but he knew what Ahmed meant. Something was tearing. Hundreds of miles away, powerful men were hearing a sound.

"I am saying: think, Gurmit." Ahmed motioned Gurmit closer. "When refugee boats come close to the mainland, we stop them, yes? Causing very much tension on Bidong. Some boats get through, we let them stay here. But what if refugees demand more? What if terrorists land in Kuala Trengganu? Gangsters? Communists-*lah*? What if these fellows talk lies to white-bastard newspaper? Year Five is coming, my friend. Think: Year Five."

The women with the squeaking Magic Markers slowed in their duties. Even with Ahmed blocking much of his view, Gurmit could see the women sitting erect, alert and quiet, straining to hear what Ahmed was saying. It didn't seem possible that they could hear anything more than a buzz. Mr. Thich, diligently slurping, was sucking in so much air that he began to hiccup; at the other end of the barracks, people were slapping down cards, dropping things, talking at the top of their lungs. But still the women stiffened, tilting slightly in their chairs, leaning into the buzzing coming from Ahmed, as if pulled by some magnetic force. Ahmed, whispering, hunched forward. His gut pressed against his shirt. His eyes were bright with excitement.

"What if refugees take hostages?" Ahmed said.

"Please," said Gurmit.

"What if fight us?"

"Cannot listen." Gurmit shook his head.

"What if attack navy patrol?"

"No more," whispered Gurmit. *Dirtiness. Filth.*

"So many possibilities," Ahmed said. "What if emergency here? What if Kuala Trengganu say to carry out certain orders? What if Rangers must come?"

It was too much. The women with the Magic Markers boldly put down their letters and stared. Mr. Thich began to swish his cup, and though his back was still to them, he looked over his shoulder and caught Gurmit's eye. Buzz, Ahmed was saying. Surely they could hear no more than that. Buzz. Buzz. Could they sense the danger behind Ahmed's coiled posture? His mouth was set tight. The words came out hard and clipped, so close to Gurmit's face that the air was sour with curry. How could Ahmed bear to say such things in front of these people? How could he let such words escape?

Look around you, thought Gurmit. Look. You must look.

"A bullhorn is making such happiness," Gurmit said suddenly. His hand was raised, and the green glove seemed bright as metal. When had he raised it? He paused, recalling what he had just said. There was no response. Ahmed drew back in his chair; he had a puzzled expression.

"Yes. I am asking for a bullhorn, you see," said Gurmit. "Everyone is now listening. That is good. I am wanting everyone to hear. I am speaking."

Gurmit rose. Miss Porkpie needed a bullhorn, he said. Miss Porkpie wanted to lend it to one of her teachers who sang to the children. Praise songs to education. Hopeful songs. And if this woman sang, he said, if she sang with a bullhorn from the top of Zone F, then all the people who lived down the hill would lift their heads and hear her voice and see the monument that he, Gurmit Singh, was going to erect from simple wood to honor a deceased refugee, a Mr. Nguyen Van Trinh, a man whose life had not only ended but disappeared, unmourned and unremembered.

"Sit down, Gurmit," Ahmed said.

Everyone was staring.

"Drink, Mr. Thich," said Ahmed. "You girls. Yes, at the desk. You. Work now. Chop-chop." He clapped his hands.

Gurmit sat. Mr. Thich began slurping. The women picked up their letters and sent their Magic Markers squeaking across the pages.

What had he done? It was as though there were two of him sitting on the chair, the Gurmit Singh who had just spoken and the Gurmit Singh who had listened to himself speak. There was a momentary struggle, a sensation of hovering, but Gurmit Singh the warrior, son of Gopal Singh, stared down Gurmit Singh the weak and deceitful. His body trembled. Bloody hell. Turmoil, confusion, bitter accusation. Silently he sat, skirmishing with himself. Then it was over. He shook with victory. He, the Gurmit Singh he knew himself to be, sat in the chair, awaiting Ahmed's response. He, Gurmit Singh, would get the bullhorn. Ahmed could bloody hell go to hell. If Ahmed wanted to fight, then Ahmed had bloody hell be ready.

"*Allah-mak,*" whispered Ahmed. He picked up a folder, then put it down. "Gurmit, you are creating disturbance."

The reprimand pleased Gurmit enormously. Disturbance! Yes, he would disturb. Yes, he would not sit with folded hands.

"I am only speaking what I have come to say," he said.

"Miss Porkpie wants a bullhorn," said Ahmed. "This is what you are saying."

"The American," Gurmit nodded fiercely. "Miss Porkpie."

"Yes-*lah*. I know. Miss Porkpie." Ahmed reached over to a folder and pulled out a form.

"We are wanting—"

"Yes, yes. Can have."

"We are wanting a bullhorn," said Gurmit.

"Can have-*lah*. I am saying already."

"You are saying we can have a bullhorn?"

"Yes."

Gurmit frowned. "For Zone F," he said.

"Zone F. I get for you today."

"Today?"

"Today."

"Bloody good," said Gurmit, but he could not keep the surprise out of his voice.

Ahmed began laughing. "You are not expecting so easy, yes? *Allah-mak,* Gurmit. You are creating disturbance, but you are not allowing me to finish. I have something to show you, yes? Did I not say I had something to show you?"

What Ahmed showed Gurmit, at least as Gurmit later explained it to Porkpie, had been like a curry puff: all flake and fluff on the outside; mysterious, hot spice on the inside. The police chief had opened his desk drawer and withdrawn a letter full of the stamps and imprints used by the prime minister's Bureau of Refugee Affairs. "Just arrived," said Ahmed. The whole letter was only one short paragraph, but Ahmed rapped the lines with his finger anyway, then slid the letter across the desk to Gurmit. The wording was stuffy and vague, but the message seemed clear enough. The Bureau of Refugee Affairs enjoined Task Force—*enjoined,* thought Gurmit, searching his memory: the word made you sit up in your chair—enjoined Task Force to extend every courtesy to the white UN bastards. But, continued the letter, the office also wished Task Force to ensure that the self-same bastards do nothing that might be deemed offensive by the residents of Kuala Trengganu.

Gurmit had been disappointed. The letter sounded like bureaucratic throat-clearing—a mildly harrumphing tone; mushy, undigested content. Even the exciting term "white bastards" was a late addition inserted by Ahmed, who grew impatient with Gurmit's painstaking reading and, snatching the letter from his hand, proceeded to read it aloud. But the more Gurmit thought about the message, the more difficulty he had in divining its actual meaning. Ahmed held forth with a thoughtful, whispered summary of the main difficulties. Several phrases in particular, Ahmed said, proved troublesome. What white bastard actions, for example, might be "deemed offensive by the residents of Kuala Trengganu"? Some were apparent. Wearing short-shorts. Drinking alcohol on the bungalow porches. Mailing letters for refugees without first giving the mail to Task Force for clearance. Fucking in public. Interfering with Task Force affairs. Kissing with open mouths. Fighting each other. Using bad language. Discussing Malaysia's "Chinese problem." But what about showing disrespect to the Koran? To the royal family of Trengganu State, or to the government of Malaysia? Criticizing its policies? Stirring up discontent among the refugees?

And the intention behind "extend every courtesy" was not so clear, either. The phrase itself had a white bastard ring to it. Long before the years of British colonization, said Ahmed, and even after the recent exportation of ill-mannered American TV shows such as *Kojak* and *Charlie's Angels,* the Malay race had extended courtesy to others as a matter of course. Courtesy was integral to Malay culture. Was not *"Awak kurang ajar"*—You were not brought up right—the most severe of Malay insults? Did not the British, in their condescending way, call Malays "nature's gentlemen"? As a *bumiputera,* said Ahmed, as a "son of the soil," a Malay descendant of Malaysia's ancient and rightful owners, he had no need to make special efforts in regards to courtesy. It was the white bastards who needed to make a special effort. Except for Reuben Gill, they wouldn't even say hello, and their women didn't even try to keep their bra straps from showing. The hypocrisy made him sick, especially in light of the white bastards' vain and arrogant idea of courtesy toward Malays. With noticeable irritation, he wagged his head and imitated a man he called Johnny Long-Nose. "Please, so kind," he said, smiling insanely, "thank you please, you brown pile of shit."

Further, Ahmed asked, was it necessary to say that Task Force should "ensure" against the white bastards' offensiveness? Had Task Force not always done so? Parameters had been established nearly from the beginning. No physical punishment for UN workers, no searching of their rooms. The usual method was to forward complaints to the appropriate agencies. The extreme mode of control, though it had never been used, was to refuse to renew the offending white bastard's camp pass, which not by coincidence required renewal every three months. Presumably, if the offense were severe enough, the offender could be hustled to the supply boat and sent packing to Kuala Trengganu, never to return again. But, again, there had never been a need for it. Was there now the presumption that there would be? *Allah-mak!* cried Ahmed, and then he yelled at Mr. Thich, who was spilling tea on the floor.

Back in Porkpie's room, the proper reading of the message was a matter of some debate. "It's telling Task Force to extend a hand whenever possible," said Porkpie. "Like, for example, to lend us a cast-off bullhorn"—she indicated the chipped white-and-blue bullhorn lying on her bunk—"without reference to any large-scale security problems. But be vigilant in enforcing smaller ones."

"That is perhaps the meaning," said Gurmit.

"Hell," said Reuben, pacing. "That's not what it means. It means give us enough rope to hang ourselves with, and then hang us when we take it."

"Such considerations have not been mentioned by Ahmed," said Gurmit. "But that is also possible."

"Of course they haven't been mentioned by Ahmed," said Reuben. "That's the whole point of not coming out and saying what you mean. That's what makes it a curry puff."

"I did not say it *was* a curry puff. A curry puff would be most delicious to eat. We are not eating. The letter is sharing similar properties, that is all."

"Oh Christ." Reuben threw up his hands.

"Ahmed himself is not knowing the specific meaning."

"Surely he asked," said Porkpie.

"Yes-*lah*. In Kuala Trengganu, they tell him the letter means what it means. They tell him to interpret at his discretion."

"Why didn't they just say, 'Smack 'em, but smile when you do it'?" said Reuben.

"Reuben," said Porkpie, "we have the bullhorn." She smiled at the object; it was so scratched and forlorn that she stooped to fluff the pillow on which it rested. Reuben snorted. "Let's focus on the positives," she said. "Such as this bullhorn. How about it?"

But Reuben was not about to leave the issue alone. "They're waiting for a screw-up."

"I tell you frankly," said Gurmit. "There is very much disagreement in Kuala Lumpur about what to do with refugees. No one wants the blame, everyone wants the reward. No one is sure of the outcome. Is no unity, isn't it? That is why the message is so not precise."

"Yes," said Porkpie. "That's right."

"What's right?" said Reuben. "Plain English."

"It's like clouds forming, right?" said Porkpie. "Before they form, all you see is stuff swirling around. For a time, anything's possible. All that stuff can go into any number of shapes, but somehow it chooses to go one particular shape, and before you know it, you've got a certain type of cloud. So that's what this message is. It's stuff floating around."

Reuben stuffed his hands deep into his jeans pockets. "Shit from shinola," he said angrily. "Shit from shinola, shit from shinola." He yanked his hands out so violently that he brought the white pouches of his pockets along with them, and though his hands kept going, the pouches stopped at his belt and poofed into two tiny parachutes that showered the floor with small coins, rubber washers, a cigar wrapper, and wads of lint and pocket crumbs. "That's cloud stuff," he said. "Right on the floor. It's shit is what it is. It's not stuff. A lot you know."

"It is confusion," said Gurmit, waggling his gloves. "But no one will say it is confused."

"That's right. When all that stuff turns into a cloud," said Porkpie, "then people will say, 'See? I *told* you it would be cloud A and not cloud B.' When in fact it was just a bunch of stuff floating around and could have gone either way."

Gurmit nodded. "A man is praising his chicken only after seeing the egg. My father is saying this."

"Enough out of you two," said Reuben, grimacing. "I got questions. I got one for you, Gurmit." He stuck out an arm and pointed an accusing finger. "Answer this. Why did Ahmed show you the letter?"

"I am not understanding."

"Why you? Why did Ahmed show the letter to you instead of us? Why did Ahmed show it to you at all?"

"Reuben, honestly," said Porkpie.

"This is a matter which is not so full of suspicions," said Gurmit. He raised a finger. "I am the administration chief. Are you forgetting? I am having the position. I am the proper liaison between Task Force and UN staff here. And I am not wearing, forgive me for saying, the white bastard skin which is so very covered with hair."

"Watch it. Just watch it, now. What the hell's gotten into you?"

"Boys!" said Porkpie. "Please. That's enough. We have the bullhorn. We have the cement and equipment things, right Reuben? We have the plank. Let's just keep the message in mind and complete our plan."

Reuben didn't seem to be listening. He leaned against the wall and looked up at the ceiling. "He showed you the letter because he wants to warn us. That's why. But he doesn't want us to get mad at him for anything. He's staying in the background. Out of sight, out of mind. He's warning us through a proxy. Through you, Gurmit. That's why he showed you the letter."

"Reuben, that's uncomfortably close to paranoia," said Porkpie, but Reuben's angry expression caused her to wave her hand in surrender. "Sorry," she said. "I withdraw the comment."

"They're up to something," said Reuben.

"Regardless," said Porkpie. "We've made our bed. Now we sleep in it."

Gurmit stirred. "There is no one feeling tired," he said.

"Oh Gurmit," she said. She couldn't keep the frustration out of her voice. There was much work to be done—so many names, so much complication!—and if Reuben and Gurmit didn't stop talking, they were never going to finish it.

"Oh Gurmit," she said again. "Oh Reuben. I have you two to thank for so much."

It was an inspired comment, disarming and sly, and though she was pleased to compliment her partners, she was pleased more by the compliment's effect on them. The words gave Reuben and Gurmit pause. They stood there as if hearing their names spoken in a crowd, shifting their gaze to some peripheral point, ears alert and eager, their mouths suddenly stilled.

"Reuben," she said, seizing her chance. "Perhaps you could check over the bullhorn's little motor." She tapped the pillow lightly with her palm. "It seemed to screech a lot when I tested it. The button seems sticky, too. And Gurmit, perhaps you might run over and inform Manley and Sally of our new arrival time for Zone F. Now, really," she said, mumbling her words. "Both of you. I've got some figuring to do."

The mumbling was for Gurmit's benefit, as well as for Reuben's. Mumbling implied self-consciousness, and self-consciousness implied that she knew Gurmit to be better qualified for planning the operation. He was, after all, the pen-and-clipboard man. He had argued the point earlier, clasping the tiny ornamental Sikh sword at the end of his keychain and going on about honor. But she had won him over in the end. The monument plank, she said: what did he think might happen to the plank if something went wrong? What did he think Task Force might do if he were viewed as the leader? In demonstration she held up a pencil and snapped it in two. She saw his gloves move, and she feared for a moment that he was going to grab her arm. Instead, he bent down. He picked up the broken half, then gently plucked the other half out of her hand and cradled the pieces in his gloves. His eyes were closed; his lips moved, as if in recitation.

"You have looked around you," he said a moment later. "You are good to have looked." And then he reached into his suit pocket and pulled out one of his chewed pens. "Please to take," he said. "For figuring the plan."

Mumbling also implied girlish uncertainty, which, though a demeaning masquerade, seemed to be the only state of mind that Reuben would allow her to exhibit. Anything else, he carped and criticized. But his mood was understandable. He was on the eve of driving away a demon. She could see it in his hard stare. He had, as well, insisted upon using military time. Zero seven hundred tomorrow, he said: that's seven in the A.M. to civilians. Zero seven hundred was P-hour, *P* for plank. Finished by zero nine hundred.

The language was not as silly as it had seemed at first. The whole undertaking had, in fact, grown extraordinarily complicated. Now Ahmed would be coming, as would Sally and Manley, as would thirty new refugee arrivals. And there were still supplies to obtain, refugee groups to contact, items to be delivered, and tests to be conducted.

The lists of names and figures and times wouldn't stay within the margins of her booklet. On one page was a long list of Vietnamese men and women, all new arrivals to Bidong, assigned by the camp committee to live in Zone F. Thanks to Sally and Manley, they were also going to be tested for their English level tomorrow, up in the primary school. She traced her finger up and down the page. Yes. There were thirty entries, all complete strangers, their names thick and dusty on the cheap paper. Thirty adults. Would the primary school be big enough? Would any require special care? Any screamers or comatose old women? How long would testing take? So many unknowns . . . She panicked momentarily, imagining tiny puffs of cloud stuff rising up around her.

She checked her Times list. At twenty hundred hours tonight, Reuben and an interpreter would approach Mr. Tan in the Loudspeaker Division and ask him to broadcast, every hour on the hour, that the Zone F primary school would be closed to students tomorrow. Miss Phu would be visited in person at twenty-one hundred and informed that a special ceremony and gift-giving would be conducted at the school at zero nine hundred hours. But no one was to tell her why.

Porkpie was making things happen in her mind, scribbling, unscribbling, saying yes, saying no. If only she saw clearly enough, if only her mind tunneled straight enough through the cloud stuff, then tomorrow morning would be beautiful. She held the exercise booklet to her lips and kissed the cover. Its thin pages, its scrawled lists, its blotchy ink marks: these were her instruments of clarity, her articles of faith. There were so many practical considerations, so many problems to figure out. How, for example, could she get her two partners to stop sniping at each other? Gurmit, searching now for his umbrella, wondered aloud why he should be expected to go out and tell Sally and Manley the time to arrive in Zone F; was Reuben not able to walk in the rain to say the same thing? Reuben called Gurmit a dandy. He put down his screwdriver and asked why in the hell should he have to lug the plank, three bags of cement, two shovels, wood strips, buckets, trowels, and a jigger up to Zone F by himself. Gurmit, he said, could be his packhorse. Gurmit protested. Pointing to his clothes, Gurmit noted with a raised voice the impossibility of carrying heavy objects up the hill in all this mud and remaining clean. He insisted that his safari suit be spotless for the monument ceremony.

"What ceremony?" said Porkpie, waving her exercise booklet at him. Gurmit reached into his breast pocket and pulled out a folded sheet of yellow paper. A short speech, he announced. He was going to say a few words, no more. People would clap. He would pass out sweets to the children. A silent moment would be observed.

She sighed. There was only one solution: get Reuben a Vietnamese assistant. Someone who would simply do what Reuben said, someone who did not dress in a white safari suit. Mr. Luc, she suggested. Reuben grunted his approval. Porkpie rubbed her forehead. She looked hard at the page, at all that blank space. She flattened the booklet with her palm. The paper gave way, and her pen pressed resolutely onto the page, and she willed the cloud stuff to go away. She sketched a picture of Mr. Luc's moving jaw in the margins of her booklet, to remind herself to ask him.

A commotion broke out near the door. Reuben, seated, started jabbing at Gurmit with the screwdriver. The bullhorn lay exposed on the desk, its metallic insides hanging from wires. "Don't poke me with that," Reuben said. He meant Gurmit's umbrella.

"Accident," said Gurmit, retreating. He grasped the doorknob with his free hand. "Accident only. I am leaving."

"So leave," Reuben said.

"I leave for finding Sally and Manley," he said, turning to Porkpie. "Because I am causing you much trouble with the ceremony, isn't it?" He nodded curtly and backed out the door, keeping the snout of the umbrella aimed at Reuben. But no sooner had the snout disappeared out the door than it knocked the door open and charged back in, its metal tip trailing a shaft of nylon sheeting that suddenly blossomed behind it like a lizard's hood. "Look who is arriving," said Gurmit, a soli-

tary line of rainwater dripping down his face. Then: "Bloody hell umbrella." He smoothed the material down, keeping one eye on Reuben.
"The two for whom I am searching are coming up the steps."

In walked Sally and Manley, both carrying thick sheets of plastic
over their heads. Their rubber boots were coated in creamy, pale mud.

"My umbrella is broken," said Gurmit.

"Enough yapping," said Reuben, rapping the screwdriver on the
desk. "I'm working here."

"Did you say 'here'?" said Manley. He pushed his hair back from his
forehead. "Listen up. I made a proverb about here."

"Manley," said Reuben sharply.

"No, really. It's short. Really." Manley grabbed the plastic roll with
one hand and thrust the crinkling sheet up to his chin. "Wise man
beard," he said. "OK, here goes." He held out his free arm, as if pointing to something in the distance. "If I were Chinese," he said, shaking
his beard, "I'd say I'm here because this is where I'm supposed to be. If
Malay, because this is where I am. If Indian, no offense Gurmit—"

"My umbrella," said Gurmit. Its metal wings rippled like spider
legs. "How to stay clean outside?"

"If Indian," Manley continued, "because this is the scheme of
things. If white, because this is where I want to be. If Vietnamese, because this is where I've been put."

"Speaking of which," said Sally, rolling her eyes. She held out a
sheet of paper for Porkpie. "I gave you the wrong Viet list before. Those
were departures from Zone F. Here are the arrivals."

"I ain't no asshole," said Manley. He was staring at Reuben. "I got
things to say."

"Manley," said Reuben, holding the screwdriver like a knife. "I'll
stick this in your gut if you don't shut up."

Sally put the paper on the table. "It's not like I'm the only one to
ever make a mistake around here."

"No more!" shouted Porkpie, rattling her exercise booklet. "All of
you. Stop it."

Then all you could hear was the sound of breathing.

15

The evening rain stopped even before the generators shut down, and in the cool night air a thin crust formed on the mud, a crust so shiny and crisp that Porkpie, marching up the Zone F hill at zero six-thirty the next morning, pictured herself skating, her body magical and weightless, floating over her shoes like a balloon. Pausing, Porkpie almost cried out in delight. The horizon was an orange band, and arcing over her head were clouds that hung in mounds, like turned dirt. Bidong stirred below. Clattering pots echoed up the hill in waves. Tin roofs shined through the palms, and all along the shoreline the sand was the color of peaches. In back of the hospital, a troop of Bidong Boy Scouts burned the night's harvest, tossing in rats that had bothered women in the maternity ward, where the scent of blood and milk issued as from a bakery, circulated out the windows by rows of churning ceiling fans. A man in a white doctor's coat stood beside them, stacking vials and bottles into a giant Styrofoam cooler.

There are moments, she thought, when you feel so alive that your heart starts to shake, uncontrollable, thumping in its cage as if it could smell the air and see the earth gliding by under your feet. Porkpie climbed with ease. Off to the side of the footpath, she saw an old woman squatting behind a pail of brown water, washing cups. The woman's teeth were black with betel-nut stains, and when the woman looked up, the skin hanging under her chin jiggled. "*Chao ba,*" said Porkpie, "Good morning," and the words came out so bright that the woman laughed, raising a wet green cup in greeting.

Strapped to Porkpie's back was a wicker basket in which she had placed her exercise booklet and, on top of that, the bullhorn, wrapped in a damp wool blanket. The wicker strap pinched her neck, but Porkpie, sliding a bit, her hands skimming the mud, praised the sensation, indulging herself with fanciful images of a sharp steel hook lifting her upward by the scruff of the neck. The plan will work, she thought. I will make this work. She had slept fitfully during the night, tossing in her bunk, but she had awakened so buoyant from a now-forgotten dream that when she saw a rat sniffing at her suitcase, she picked up the screwdriver Reuben had left on the table and flung it at the rodent with the force of a Major League fastball. She felt powerful. She put on her flats and her favorite dress, and left her rain slicker on the hanger. It wouldn't rain until the afternoon. Not today it wouldn't.

At the top of the hill, she heard murmuring coming from the primary school. She stopped. It was Sally and Manley. "Hello, how are you?" they were saying. "What is your name?" Whining Vietnamese voices answered. Over on the mud flat, Reuben and Mr. Luc had already begun work. Reuben was pouring a bag of cement into a wheelbarrow, shaking out the remains by snapping the bag as if it were a rug. Mr. Luc, in running shorts, knelt in a leveled, rectangular depression in the mud, hammering in wood strips along the edges of the rectangle. That was to be the foundation. Behind the men were boxes and sacks containing crusted tools and buckets. The plank lay propped against the largest box, wrapped tightly in a canvas tarp studded with metal eyelets and dangling ropes.

"Hello, Reuben," she said, wiping sweat from her face. "Hello to you, Mr. Luc." Mr. Luc, looking up, appeared to be on the verge of standing. "That's OK, Mr. Luc," she said, waving him down. "No need. No need."

"I got work to do," said Reuben. He picked through a box, removing a trenching shovel.

"Working, Mr. Reuben!" said Mr. Luc, raising his head.

"I'm not talking to you," said Reuben, and then Mr. Luc, realizing his mistake, resumed kneeling. His jaw made a noise.

It was hard not to feel bad for Mr. Luc. Reuben must have been riding him hard all morning. But surely even Mr. Luc saw that Reuben meant nothing personal by his snapping and snarling. If you looked hard enough, which Porkpie now did, you could see Reuben burrowing in on himself. He moved stiffly. His lips curled in over his teeth; his fingers kept balling up, like claws retracting; even the folds of skin over his nostrils were drawn in, like flaps. He was wound tight, ready to explode.

"Can you do something for me?" she said.

Reuben stirred the cement with the shovel handle.

She placed her basket on the ground. "I was thinking," she said, unraveling the blanket. She removed her exercise book. The bullhorn, its handle still nestled in the blanket, looked bulbous and poached, like a baby's head. "It doesn't have to be me giving the bullhorn to Miss Phu," she said, holding the exercise book to her breast. "Why don't you do it? Maybe you could give it to her after the plank ceremony. I'll just watch from the primary school."

She walked away. She didn't wait for him for acknowledge her gesture because she knew he wouldn't. But the stirring noises stopped. She could sense him staring at the basket. She thought: Joy is clarity, joy is powerful and strong.

She swept aside the clear plastic sheet and entered the primary school. The new arrivals were sitting very still on the benches. Most were older women. Their graying hair was done up in buns, and they all wore collarless Vietnamese blouses, marking them as peasants. They looked worried. One woman cradled her hand in her other hand, rocking it like a baby; she raised it to her lips and kissed the dark spot where Medical had pricked her skin and squeezed her blood into a shiny glass tube. Squatting in back was Sally, hunkered down next to a young girl with a large "Translator-English" tag pinned to her sweatshirt. Sally waved.

"Hello, everyone," Porkpie said, grinning. Some of the new arrivals smiled back and nodded extravagantly.

"Hey, this ain't a chirp-along." It was Manley. She hadn't seen him. He was standing next to the blackboard with his back to everyone, frowning at her, a large rock in his hand. She looked. He was in the middle of hammering a long length of yellow yarn from one corner of the room to the other.

"There you are," said Sally, swaying down the aisle. She motioned for the translator to follow, then stuffed her hands into her overalls pockets. "I've been stalling for ten minutes," she said. "We need the roll sheet. You did bring the list, didn't you?"

"I've got the whole morning mapped out, right here," said Porkpie, patting her exercise booklet. She couldn't get the grin off her face, even when one of the new arrivals leaned to the side and quietly vomited. It was over in a second, and then the woman righted herself and dabbed at her mouth with her wrists.

"She nervous," said the translator. The other arrivals tittered, then fell back into silence.

"Here we go again," said Sally, looking pained. "Miss Ba," she said softly to the translator. "Please tell them that we're just testing to find out what class level to put them in. This has nothing to do with getting off Bidong sooner. The results will not, repeat, will not affect their re-settlement status. High score, low score. Doesn't make any difference."

"Relief workers Number One," added Manley, talking to the trans-lator. "UN very good." He tossed the rock aside, apparently finished, and began counting small squares of construction paper stacked on the teacher's desk. Behind him, the yarn sagged like a clothesline, looped around large nails sticking out of the corner joists.

While the translator talked, pausing occasionally to address Sally— "I tell them no worry," the girl kept saying—Sally took the exercise book from Porkpie's hand and began checking the roll list against the stack of ID cards on the teacher's desk. Porkpie, humming, looked through the plastic sheet covering the entrance. The plastic made the people outside waver like watercolors, and even the little pockets of gawkers that had begun to form seemed foggy, a bit uncertain in com-position, as if the borders of their arms and legs were being pressed by moister, more fluid splotches. She saw Miss Phu, standing with her arms crossed, watching the men pour cement. Nearby was Ahmed, walking around with his truncheon dangling from his belt. At his side was a tall Malay man wearing a green Task Force poncho; the poncho stretched high over his back, tapering to a pointed cone. Porkpie tapped the plastic with her finger, dispersing the moisture, and looked again. The Malay man turned; Ahmed brushed at something on the man's back, and the material stretched just enough to expose the cone's form. It was a rifle.

She stopped humming, but everyone in the class was too busy to notice. Manley was stringing up his construction paper squares, at-taching them with clothespins to the sagging yarn. Sally, fidgeting, was talking loudly to the translator, who shouted out instructions to the arrivals. The translator made chopping motions with her hands, and the arrivals immediately formed into two groups, one squatting in front of the sagging yarn, the other sitting on the benches in back of the class, with their faces to the tarp wall.

Porkpie cleared her throat, preparing to speak, but Sally caught her eye and held up her hand, signaling "wait." Porkpie looked again through the plastic. She saw Reuben and Mr. Luc stand the tarp-covered plank into the wet cement, then attach the cords on the tarp to stakes driven into the outlying mud. Off to the right, she thought she saw Gurmit's white safari suit. Yes. It was Gurmit, striding quickly behind a line of young men, making shooing motions to someone she couldn't see. The young men suddenly parted, and Gurmit, his hair slicked with oil, struggled forward, vainly attempting to shove a boy away from his leg. It was the orphan. The crazy boy in the underpants. The boy was clawing at Gurmit's pants pocket, reaching in with his muddy hands and pulling out bright yellow candies, stuffing them into his mouth. Gurmit, pushing now, stumbled. Gurmit fell to one knee, but the boy held on, running one hand down Gurmit's jacket until his fingers clutched the insides of a breast pocket. With the other hand, the boy lunged after falling candies, sticking them, cellophane and all, into his mouth. Gurmit yelled something, she couldn't hear what, but the young men came swarming to his aid, yanking at the boy's arms and legs. Gurmit scrambled up, dripping mud. One of the men raised his arm as if to strike the boy, but then Miss Phu, trotting, began waving her arms around. The men drew back, and Miss Phu bent over the boy and began to stroke his back, calming him, petting him up and down his spine.

"Hey, we could use some help here," said Manley.

"Outside," Porkpie said stupidly.

"Yeah, well, we need some help inside."

Porkpie looked around. Sally sat on a bench in the back row, talking to one of the women; the rest of the group waited a few rows away, pretending not to listen. *Where are you from?* Sally said, speaking slowly. *What is your occupation? Describe your village. No understand? OK, what do you do in the morning?*

"When she's done with mama-san back there," said Manley, "Sally wants us to do the rest of her group. We got two tests going. Sally's doing speaking skills back there, and I'm seeing if they can read and write up here." He motioned toward the front, where the other group of arrivals squatted under the blackboard, writing on notebook sheets. They kept looking up at the paper squares hanging from the yarn.

"The alphabet," Porkpie said, pointing. On each square was a letter, written in large script in Magic Marker.

"You sure?" said Manley. "Look again."

Porkpie said, "Did you know there's a Task Force man walking around outside with a gun?"

"So don't fuck with him."

What is your favorite food? No? OK, if you had a million dollars, what would you do? You understand?

"Manley," said Porkpie, looking again at the squares. "One of the letters is missing. There's no *L*."

"Hey, that's right. There's no *L*. Now you're seeing. The big genius." The alphabet string, he said, only looked like it made sense. The test was his own invention. No matter how many times you told them, he said, new arrivals wouldn't believe that their English scores didn't mean anything. They were convinced that if they scored poorly, no country would want their ignorant hides. So they lied through their teeth. They lied about their past, and they lied about what they did, and they lied about who they were, and they lied about their language skills.

"I had the translator ask them," Manley said. "They all said they could read and write."

"They're all writing," said Porkpie, pointing. "No one's lying." The translator, holding a large stopwatch, picked her way carefully between the squatting figures.

"Hey, that's the beauty of the test," said Manley. "The liars just *think* they're getting away with it. See, I have everyone sit down with a pencil and paper. Then the translator tells them to write out the letters they see. Just the letters they see. I give them five minutes. Now, the ones that actually know the alphabet are going to think they're looking at the alphabet, right? They're going to look real quick, just like you did, and they're gonna say 'Hey, that's the goddamn alphabet.' So they're gonna stop looking and just write the alphabet, right? They're gonna put that *L* in there. But the illiterates, the lying ones anyway, hey, they're gonna be looking at each letter. They're gonna copy down what they actually see because they don't have a picture of the real alphabet in their heads. Right? You see? And they're *not* gonna put the *L* in, because it ain't there."

Manley was talking fast, pushing the hair back from his eyes. He was trying not to smile, but his teeth kept showing.

Do you like hot food? Yes. Make your tongue burn. Hot. Do you like to eat hot things?

"So all I have to do," said Manley, "is look at their papers. If there's no *L,* I know they can't really read and write. If there is an *L,* I know they can."

Porkpie frowned.

"You get it? If you fail, you pass. If you pass, you fail. Hey, it's like . . . Hey . . ." He held up his hand and closed his fist. "It's like, if you know the system, you fuck up. You put in the *L.* And if you don't fuck up, then you're a goddamn liar."

"Gurmit fell outside," Porkpie said, stepping back. She wanted to leave; she wanted to throw the plastic sheet aside and run out. "He got all muddy."

"Who cares?"

"He didn't want to get muddy."

"Who cares?" said Manley. "I'm talking about testing. We got work to do."

"Oh, but this . . ." She didn't know how to finish.

"You got something to say? I worked hard on that test."

"Manley, it's so ugly."

He snapped his jaw shut and turned on his heel.

"Don't be angry," Porkpie said.

He hesitated. She was sure he was going to wheel around and say something. But instead he started clapping his hands and advanced toward the arrivals in the front. "Finish now, finish," he said to the squatting figures. His tone was so sharp that everyone looked up. "Miss Ba, collect their papers. Let's go. Come on. Time's up."

"Well, it certainly is," said Sally, hurrying down the aisle. "I think you went a little overtime." She shook her hand at Miss Ba, who thrust the notebook sheets at her. "Now look, Porkpie, you need to get some practice with our speaking skills test. You can't just be teaching children your whole time here. I'm going to look these papers over, and you and Manley can test the rest of my bunch." She nodded toward the back of the room.

"Let's go, Porky-san," said Manley, walking past.

"Go, go," said Sally, scooping Porkpie's elbow in her sheaf of note-book paper. "They're going to be ready outside pretty soon. We need to do some work in here first."

So Porkpie followed Manley to the back of the room. The arrivals chattered a little in Vietnamese, leaning over and whispering into each other's ears, their eyes following the new testers. Manley didn't look at her. He sat on the bench in the last row and patted the space beside him, signaling Porkpie to sit. Then he gestured for the next woman in line to sit on the bench in the next row. *Where are you from?* he said, facing her. His voice was gruff. He tapped out a beat with his finger, rapping it on the bench. *What is your occupation? Describe your village.*

Porkpie called the next woman forward.

"Hello," Porkpie said. "How are you?"

"I'm fine," said the woman, blinking. She had iron-gray hair and a soft, round face. Her hands were cupped in her lap, as if she were hold-ing a small bird.

"Where are you from?"

"I'm from Da Lat. It is a beautiful town. So many plum and mango."

"Do you like plum and mango?"

"Yes. I eat them on the picnic," she said, and then she looked down at her hands. "For you," the woman said suddenly. "Thank you for help-ing the Vietnam people." She uncupped her hands, sliding the top one away as if it were connected by a hinge, and revealed what she had been holding. It was a boat, carved from a single stick of chalk. It had a wheelhouse and a raised prow; at the back was a tiny nub, the propeller.

Porkpie cupped her palms together, and the woman, blinking hard, gently placed the powdery object in Porkpie's hands.

"Manley," Porkpie said. She turned toward him, cupping the ob-ject. It tickled her palm. She held it up for Manley to see. The boat was light as a flower. "Please don't be mad at me this morning," she whis-pered. "Look how beautiful."

Manley didn't reply. He scratched his chin, rubbing the small whiskers with the back of his hand. Then he leaned over and spoke into Porkpie's ear. "This is a test. Come on. They like to talk about their kids. Ask her how many children she has."

Porkpie turned back. "How many children do you have?" she asked.

The woman looked at her for a moment, then down at the ground.

Manley nudged her. "Ask her again," he whispered. The way he said it, she could tell his heart was beating fast. "This group's tired," he said. "Six weeks at sea, I've seen their records." His eyes roamed her face. He didn't blink. "Ask again," he said in a quavering voice. "That's what you should say."

She looked at him quizzically. "Just say it," he said.

Porkpie turned to the woman.

"Come on," Manley said.

"How many children do you have?" Porkpie asked.

The woman's mouth opened, and then her shoulders started shaking. "I have four," she said then, but her voice was going up and down. She brought her hands to her neck, as if to hold her head in place. "Thai pirate kill one. They take my son. They . . ." Her mouth opened and shut, then opened again. Her chin crinkled.

Porkpie reached out to touch her, but the woman drew away.

"Oh no," Porkpie whispered, withdrawing her hand. "I didn't mean to ask . . . I didn't know." She turned suddenly, cradling the boat on her knees. "Manley," she hissed. She balled her hand into a fist. If there was even a trace of satisfaction on his face, she would strike him.

He was staring past the woman in front of him, past the row of arrivals behind her. He gave no indication of having heard, though there was no way he could not have. A pretense. He knew. And still he made her ask the question. His expression was impenetrable. He looked how Porkpie imagined him looking alone in his room, a small man sitting upright on his bed, just letting the moments build and fall, completely still.

The woman from Da Lat regained control of her face. She sat blinking, hands on her knees, looking at the ground. Behind her, the other arrivals sat stiffly, occasionally shifting their heads, looking around warily, like patients in a waiting room. *What is your favorite food?* said Manley, abruptly. *Uh-huh. OK. Yes. If you had a million dollars, what would you do?* Up front, Miss Ba stripped the alphabet squares from the yarn. Sally was bending down, holding one of the notebook sheets in front of someone's face; she tapped the paper with her fingernail.

None of it seemed possible. For a moment, Porkpie wondered if she had simply hallucinated. She rose then. She could not sit by Manley one more second. She placed the chalk boat on the bench and stood. She walked over to the entryway and leaned against the entrance post, facing out, and, breathing deeply, slowly, traced her finger up and down the plastic sheet. It was hard to see what was going on outside. She squinted. The crowd seemed to have grown. She thought she saw Ralph. He was squatting in the mud, playing chess with a bare-backed man. The board and pieces lay on a cardboard strip, and the men flicked out moves as if swatting flies. Gurmit stood nearby, wiping his ruined suit with a rag. And there was Ahmed, talking to the guard in the poncho. They were circling the crowd, watching. Ahmed held his truncheon against his leg, and the truncheon stopped moving.

The man with the poncho stopped and pointed. Porkpie followed his finger and saw some Vietnamese security yanking on the cords and ropes around the plank tarp. The tarp, stretched tight against the top of the plank, billowed at the bottom, like a skirt. It was hard to see, but the plank seemed to be leaning to one side. The men were trying to straighten it. Reuben, towering over everyone, pushed some of the men aside. He leaned across the foundation and unhooked the rope wrapped around the top of the tarp, providing slack. Kicking the bullhorn basket aside, he unhooked another rope. He hefted the tarp over to the other side and, while the men holding ropes pulled the tarp free, he grabbed the plank with both hands and began to wiggle it into alignment. From inside the primary school, the name engraved at the top looked like a stain.

She couldn't see a thing.

Porkpie threw aside the plastic, then stepped outside, holding her arms out wide to balance herself, and sloshed toward the crowd. She waved some children out of the way. She could see better already. She saw Gurmit walk over to the boy in the underpants and yell something at him. The boy was cradled in Miss Phu's arms like a pet. Miss Phu started stroking the boy's legs, while Gurmit, wiping at his lapels, turned away. The boy looked up, watching Reuben rock the plank back and forth, and then he suddenly broke free from Miss Phu's arms. He began running toward the cement. He pointed to the name on the plank. He yelled something in Vietnamese, over and over, and then the crowd moved forward all at once. Everyone started talking, holding on to the shoulders of the person in front.

"What's happening?" asked Porkpie. She began trotting.

She saw Miss Phu turn to Gurmit and shout something into his ears. Gurmit put his hands to his head and fell to his knees. What had

Miss Phu told him? What had he heard? Gurmit rocked a bit, and then he tumbled toward the wicker basket. He grabbed the bullhorn, and as he did, the boy in the underpants, still shouting, stepped onto the wet cement. Reuben picked the boy up by the arm and threw him clear. The boy started wailing then. He balled his hands into fists and began striking his head, pounding with so much force he made himself cry out.

Gurmit had the bullhorn to his lips. He was yards from the plank. He shook his head. "Enough," he shouted into the bullhorn. The sound was piercing; it was tinny and full of static, and it seemed to ripple through the crowd. "Enough," Gurmit shouted at the plank. "I have done so much. No more."

Porkpie, running now, losing one of her flats, called out, "What's happening?" but the crowd was swelling quickly. People were running in from behind her and leaping up over the crest of the trail. Ralph's chess pieces were scattered like glass. She could see the cone of the Task Force man's poncho off to the right, wiggling over the crowd.

"Miss Phu," said Porkpie, grabbing the woman's arm. "What's happening?"

She could see Reuben wrestling with Gurmit for the bullhorn. The looks on their faces were terrible. The bullhorn started screeching, and then Reuben had Gurmit down on the ground, his knee grinding into the man's chest. "Stop it," Reuben shouted, waving the bullhorn over Gurmit's head. "Stop it. I'll ram this down your throat."

"Miss Phu, what's happening?"

"That boy," Miss Phu howled. "He say his name is Duoc. He say he the nephew of Nguyen Van Trinh." She pointed. "Now so much fighting."

16

Ahmed sent notice to the Task Force office in Kuala Treng-ganu regarding the behavior displayed at the Zone F plank ceremony by the troublemaking white bastards and the un-reliable administration chief. There had been injuries to Gurmit Singh, cuts and bruises about his face and arms, inflicted during a struggle over a security item, a bullhorn, by Reuben Gill of UNHCR, who, de-spite injuries about his back and neck, failed to obey a lawful order to stop fighting, issued by himself, Bidong Island Task Force Chief Ahmed bin Mohari, and his colleague, Corporal Zainal bin Puteh. There had been, as well, a reckless and negligent promotion of the cer-emony by another UNHCR representative, Bobbi Porkpie Sortini, who, as the event's organizational head and program planner, bore full re-sponsibility for the unfortunate and entirely preventable events occur-ring in full view of numerous illegal alien Vietnamese children.

In itself, reported Ahmed in elegant, classically perfumed Malay, in itself the fighting was not especially surprising, given that the white bas-tards were known to consume alcohol, in direct violation of Task Force regulations, and given that their general disposition toward Malaysians, including unreliable Malaysian Indian Sikhs, tended toward the con-tentious. What was surprising was that they had exhibited their disre-gard for Task Force authority in such a public and dramatic fashion, potentially undermining the spirit of cooperation et cetera, et cetera existing between the illegal alien Vietnamese and the Task Force. The white bastards had been forewarned. So, too, had Gurmit Singh, but Gurmit Singh was, as reported, unreliable and, shall he say, possessed of an overly delicate and somewhat jiggly constitution, evidence for which, to mention but the most recent example, was provided by Gurmit Singh's somewhat mawkish and even tearful post-altercation wiping of mud from the underpants of an otherwise naked illegal alien Vietnamese boy. The white bastards, on the other hand, were grossly willful, in the manner of spoiled children. They were unable to control their urges. They had ferocious imaginations, and, also in the manner of spoiled children, they were surprised by their own cruelty and repentant only insofar as the threat of punishment focused their attention.

Conclusions . . . here one must pause, wrote Ahmed; here one must measure immediate consequence against potential effect. Ahmed, himself, lingered for some time over his conclusions, staring at the typewriter, measuring. His fingers, impatient and idle, typed errant letters, breaking his concentration and leading to several muttering searches for a full bottle of Wite-Out. Three conclusions, he wrote at last, were perhaps to be drawn from the unfortunate incident in Zone F.

First—and he, Ahmed bin Mohari, wished no more than to provide for consideration the limited perspective afforded by his humble yet necessary office—first, it was his belief that the chaos and violence of the incident was of sufficient power, both as a tool of edification and as a means of clarification, to impress itself on the jiggly constitution of the Malaysian Red Crescent Society Administration Chief Gurmit Singh, and thereby to still it. Second, it was his belief that the incident was of sufficient outrage to warrant the immediate and permanent removal from the island of the two UNHCR representatives, Reuben Gill and Bobbi Porkpie Sortini. The fight, though of brief duration, had been furious and injurious; the aforementioned bullhorn had been utilized as an offensive weapon; and numerous illegal alien Vietnamese had been encouraged to act in such as manner as to require their immediate dispersal from the site of the incident.

Yet his was but a small lens through which to view the horizon; perhaps the distant raft was really a reef, the dark cloud a swarm of locusts, the incident of which he spoke a matter of mere local importance. In matters of interpretation he, Ahmed bin Mohari, readily acceded to the judgment of the honorable officers of the Kuala Trengganu Task Force office, in consultation with the Bureau of Refugee Affairs, and he would with respect and alacrity bring his evaluation of the incident into conformity with any definitional reappraisals said officers should please to make. But let it be said that he, Ahmed bin Mohari—and would the honorable officers of the Kuala Trengganu office please forgive his presumption for saying so—let it be said that he remained alert to the, shall he say, dynamic nature of relations existing among the various government and white bastard organizations. Let it be said that he, Ahmed bin Mohari, though a simple warrior, did with happy reverence desire, as did the honorable officers in Kuala Trengganu, the continued goodwill of the white bastard organizations until such time as circumstances associated with the upcoming passage of the present year into the new year might irrevocably change.

Third, it was most certainly to be concluded from the aforementioned incident in Zone F that the Bidong Island Task Force detachment retained an unquestioned position of authority regarding island security. Were the situation to deteriorate, he, Ahmed bin Mohari, would of course not hesitate in requesting assistance from his brothers in the 171st Ranger Battalion, Sultan's Division, bivouacked on the sacred soil of the State of Trengganu. At the current time, however, and praise Allah for His merciful guidance and protection, assistance was most assuredly not required. The aforementioned incident in Zone F pointed not toward assistance but toward a renewed and clear-sighted apprehension of the white bastards' nature, which, to return to a point previously raised, inclined them toward a certain, shall he say, unappreciativeness toward the hospitality shown them by the residents of the State of Trengganu, upon whose graces and forbearance the continued successful operation of the camp of course depended.

As to whether such unappreciativeness should lead to a more rigorous application of established security policies, it was not for him, Ahmed bin Mohari, to say. Certainly it *could* lead to a more rigorous application, especially—and, again, would the honorable officers of the Kuala Trengganu office please forgive his appearance of presumptuousness—especially were the Bidong Island Task Force to receive priority material support in regard to the still-undelivered flame thrower, the missing four hundred meters of concertina wire, the twenty bent and worthless hand-grenade pins, the promised five M-16s with automatic fire-control feeder belts, and the possibility of preemptive enforcement of the previously established no-alcohol policy. Certainly the application of discretionary rigor was something for the Kuala Trengganu office to consider, and of such consideration he, Ahmed bin Mohari, speaking on behalf on the entire Bidong Task Force detachment, et cetera, et cetera, was respectfully and patently grateful.

The *orang putehs,* Ahmed thought, depositing the letter into the supply-boat mailbag. The white people were not grateful for his restraint toward them. He shook his head in momentary indignation. Did they not comprehend that with each passing day, the Rangers of the 171st Royal Trengganu Battalion, Sultan's Division, inched closer? That white bastard arrogance only made their arrival more likely? Did they not know that actions had consequences?

The response from the Kuala Trengganu office was, by Bidong standards, nearly instantaneous, and even before Ahmed put down the wireless, he was damning the honorable officers of Kuala Trengganu for the task they wished him to carry out that very day. Idiots! At what point would they cease to wring their hands? How long must he shout before they heard? He had no stomach for enduring white bastard mocking, yet that was what his misguided brothers on the mainland apparently now wished for him to endure. Ahmed rose and kicked his chair. Then he sat down again and, exhaling audibly, began thumbing through his files, wondering where the stupid girl from Vung Tau had put the forms he now needed to give to Bobbi Porkpie Sortini and Reuben Gill.

Reuben Gill was in no condition to receive forms from anyone. He was standing stripped to the waist in front of the mirror of the washing-up shed, worrying over things that were all competing for his attention at the same time. He was worried about the consequences of fighting with Gurmit. He was worried that Doctor Johansson would try to remove him from Bidong, and he was worried that the doctor might succeed, despite the approach of Year Five, when budgets would change, alliances shift, and policies dissolve.

He turned and twisted first one way, then the other. What he saw in the mirror was also a worry, but a foggy kind of worry, one that seemed vague and vast, and one he could not bring into focus without again hearing the sound of Miss Phu's voice. In the mirror he saw swollen, spidery contusions at the top of his spine, spreading in tissuey abandon clear across to his shoulders. He had sustained the injuries during the fight, and now the swelling had grown so bad he could hardly move his shoulders. The swelling seemed to adhere to his neck like an infant; tenacious ridges, long as fingers, rode his bones and joints. He checked his eyes and scalp. He held out his arms and opened and closed his hands, wincing at the stiffness and ache stretching all the way down to the bottom of his spine. Bruises, swelling, contusions . . . he could examine his injuries all day, but no matter what terms he used, he could not forget the words Miss Phu had used. In the melee Gurmit had fought well, striking him repeatedly with the bullhorn, and by the time Ahmed and Corporal Zainal pulled him from Gurmit, his back and neck had begun to swell. He stripped off his shirt. And then Miss Phu—it was certainly her voice, there could be no mistake—had pointed at him and said the words.

He stared at the mirror, then put his fingers to his brow and frowned like a mentalist. Think straight, he ordered. But he couldn't.

Johann, entering the shed with a hand towel and a toothbrush, said, "Got yourself a nasty bruise there." He feinted and weaved a bit, then pretended to slap his toothbrush around. "Sugar Ray Reuben," said Johann. "I heard, man. TKO, round one. Gurmit the Lion hits the deck."

Reuben slipped his wadded T-shirt on over his head.

Johann began brushing his teeth. "I just wanted to know about the swelling."

"Shut up," said Reuben.

Johann froze. He slowly put his toothbrush into his washing-up cup and slurped water from the faucet. Then he cleared his throat. "Have you had it checked?"

Reuben leaned over and knocked Johann's toothbrush cup off the sink.

He waded through the mud without his waders, back to his bungalow, where he opened the top of his blueprint tube and withdrew his secret cache of Johnnie Walker and drank straight from the bottle. He ignored the shouts of his Sanitation Division crew chiefs, calling from outside the wire, requesting consultation and signatures. He drank. He puffed on a Thai cigar, trying to smoke his worries away.

Around lunch, he began swabbing the contusions along his back with Johnnie Walker–soaked cotton balls. He pressed his fingers into the tender ridges—were the ridges so long an hour ago? so mushy?—feeling for a pulse, and then he lanced a spot just to the left of his spine, jabbing it with his pocketknife. He saw his own dark blood. He sat on his bunk and drank some more Johnnie Walker. He lay on his stomach and listened to his heart beating against the mattress. Think straight, man, he thought. But clarity would not come. Only confusion. Only empty displays of strength. He crushed his pillow. He broke a cup in two. He lay with his face hovering over the mattress, his face a furrowed mask, its weight supported through the efforts of his tongue, which now quivered with exertion, stiff and determined, rising like a post from the surface of his bedding.

Maybe, he thought, his tongue collapsing, just maybe . . . Maybe what he needed was a few days off Bidong. It was almost December. Nothing drastic would happen before the new year. He had leave time coming. A couple of days relaxing, playing darts with Cowboy Lim. Just drinking beer and Remy Martin V.S.O.P., wobbling on a bar stool. Then a trip to the Bamboo Club, a late-night climb up the narrow stairs, through the bead door, into the mirrored room where the girls sat clinking their plastic number tags like dominoes. A short couple of days, just to regroup. A few days to clear his head and think straight.

There was a knock at the door.

It was Ahmed, scowling under his bus-driver's hat. He presented a piece of paper, holding it out in obvious distaste, with the tips of his fingers.

"Boo," Reuben said.

"Kuala Trengganu Task Force office wishes you to visit a medical doctor in Kuala Trengganu," said Ahmed, speaking Malay. He stiffened. "You have been drinking alcohol?" he said, making a face.

Reuben, unsteady on his feet, leaned against the door frame. "No. Australian aftershave."

Ahmed adjusted his hat and, blinking hard, handed Reuben the paper. It was a medical form. "Sila-kan," Ahmed said, speaking rapidly in Malay. "Please to have certified on this form that your recent actions in Zone F have been caused by your own free will and not by deficiencies in electrolytes or other health matters."

Reuben held the form to his face.

"Fighting in Zone F," Ahmed said, switching to English. "Very bad. Look please at the orders." He jabbed at the paper with his finger. "There. You see? Paragraph three. Kuala Trengganu office cannot believe. Very shock. You very lucky they allow you back onto Bidong." He raised his eyebrows. "Miss Porkpie will accompany. Same-same examination."

"She didn't fight."

"No. But she is the leader, isn't it?"

Reuben stared dumbly.

"Is Kuala Trengganu orders," said Ahmed firmly. "You very lucky."

"Gurmit coming? I'm not taking a boat with him."

"Recovering in hospital. He is not foreigner, isn't it? Different circumstance."

They stood a moment in the doorway, trying not to look at each other.

Ahmed reached into his pocket and pulled out a pack of Camels. "No argument-*lah*," said Ahmed, pointing at Reuben with a cigarette. "Orders." He reached into his pocket and withdrew a lighter, which he flicked open without looking. The flame was so big Reuben heard its gassy exhaust.

Reuben reached out with a brotherly hand and laid it on Ahmed's shoulder. Ahmed jerked his head back; his cigarette rose like a lance, its burning tip bright with fire.

Reuben said, "Yes. I'll leave this afternoon."

He closed the door on Ahmed's startled face.

Yes. He could go with Porkpie and hitch a ride with Skipper Rahim on the afternoon run. He could have the stupid form filled out, sure. He could let Task Force amass their documentation, their stupid mounds of evidence and contempt. He'd have himself a short vacation. Just until all his worries stopped making noise in his head. He heaved his duffel bag onto his bed. A few days. Just until the swelling went down. Just until he knew for sure that when he woke up some fine morning in the new year, stretching, smelly breathed, he could look in the mirror and see Reuben Gill, Bidong sub-engineer. Just until he could reach behind to rub his neck and not hear Miss Phu say that he was rubbing the folded wings of a demon.

The Year Five

17

The swelling went down, the noise in his head trailed off to a murmer. Bidong was a fever, and the fever finally broke at Cowboy Lim's after sessions of beer and Chinaman jokes and white bastard roughhousing; and there when he needed more was the chummy smell of Remy Martin V.S.O.P. on the bar stools; and Number Nineteen in the back room of the Bamboo Club, a beautiful girl; and a post-coital tumble down the cement stairs; and Mrs. Lim's medicinal hot pack and plates of chilied hog snouts. A colonial wet dream, Porkpie said sourly, and he raised a glass to her severe expression and patted the stool next to him, bidding her come, but she wouldn't. She said good-night and went up the stairs and locked her door. An improvement, he winked to Cowboy Lim. At least she was speaking to him. On the boat trip over . . . How long ago? It was still December, but seemed like ages. How long had they been here? Cowboy Lim didn't care. OK, OK, neither did he.

On the boat trip over from Bidong she had waved him away. Her shoulders shook; she was crying. Then they had walked in silence into the heart of town, medical forms sticking out of their pockets, dogged every step of the way by taxis. The drivers honked and rolled down their windows and made kissing noises, then pointed to the empty passenger seats. A schoolbus of white-shirted Malay boys passed by, and waving schoolboy arms exploded out the windows. "*Matsalleh! Matsalleh!*" the boys cried. "White people!" One boy made an obscene gesture with his forefinger, jabbing it into the curled palm of his other hand. "Oh my darling!" the boy yelled. "I fucking you! Oh my darling, I fucking you!"

Even then, she wouldn't speak. She walked slowly, hardly moving her eyes, and when clouds burst, sending everyone racing for the store-front awnings, she continued down the street at her funereal pace. "Here's the doctor," he shouted from the sidewalk, pointing, but she kept on walking, then turned and said to him: "Later, all right? Later." All through the doctor's exam he was tense with worries, lifting here, bending there, and then he found himself worrying about her as well, and then he knew he had to leave for Cowboy Lim's that very minute and erase all the worries from his head. The Malay doctor quickly confirmed on the medical form that, save for the swelling, Reuben Gill was healthy for a man who drank too much and weighed too much and smoked too much. Into Reuben's arms the doctor shoved a can of pink granules said to aid in electrolyte retention, along with several tubes of ointment and an X ray of Reuben's back and shoulders, shot from a humming camera.

He went directly to Cowboy Lim's. He threw the doctor's things into the waste bin and downed a beer with a trembling hand, then dropped the bottle, empty now, quite by accident onto the floor.

"Clumsy dog dick!" Mrs. Lim yelled.

"White bastard fool," Cowboy Lim roared, and threw a bar rag at him.

He cleaned the mess. He scooped the shards into a pile and put the rag to his nose and breathed in its sweet, welcoming odor. "Another beer," he shouted, and he drank with Cowboy Lim through the day and talked as if he had never left town.

"Because I don't want to tell you about Bidong, that's why," said Reuben, around dinner.

"Why you not want?"

"Forget Bidong."

"To Malaysia, then," said Cowboy Lim, raising his drink for a toast. They clinked glasses. That was what made Cowboy Lim such a good companion. He allowed you secrets. He knew there were things that burrowed so deep in your chest you had to let them slumber.

Now the Peace Corps, said Reuben: if Lim wanted to hear about *that*, he'd be happy to oblige. OK, then. Back in those days, said Reuben, warming to the ease, he slogged through mucky outbacks with a mosquito fogger, handing out pamphlets on hygiene. In the swamps, cradling his fogger in his lap, he saw the pink eyes of rats staring down from the rafters of houses. When he moved, the jungle paths moved with him, alive with leeches. People squatted in the road, smoking pipes and hawking, posed as if in defecation. The old Malay men had skin tough as hides, but they were limber as garden hoses. The tropical heat was a tongue in his ear, licking all day, and he sweltered so much he swore hands were pressed to his body. Chinese men in singlets spat on the floor and laughed like jackals. All of it was arousing. After a rain, the slick tires piled in the streets smelled like hothouse sex. So did the food. Some days he was blue flame. In dreams he walked around with his body turned smelly-side out. He couldn't even breathe without thinking of the odor of open-heart surgery, or food rotting in a pail. The women flirted outrageously, the stars were in the wrong place, and bird spiders laid egg sacs the texture of sponges in his hair.

It had all been so simple. He had a lean-to in the jungle. His needs were basic. Once he had worked out a list of the one hundred words he would need to know to fulfill his needs. The rest was gratuitous grunting. The list was something of a revelation: with one hundred words you could eat, sleep, screw, and take the bus.

There were secret moments as well, moments for which the biggest dictionary was insufficient. He remembered nights when he dragged his box of empty Johnnie Walkers from under the bed and lined up the bottles. He sang, tapping the glass like a xylophonist with the handle of a machete. He played the Stones and Creedence, and stared out the window at the sea hibiscus and elephant palm. The leaves shimmered in the dark, and then the whirring began. There were the small cries of prey, the rustle of hunting rodents. He would sit in a bubble of lamplight, his hands huge in the shadow, a bowl of noodles warm at his side, and a great whoosh would rise from his gut, like a wind, and sometimes his fingers tightened around the handle and sent the machete down hard against a bottle. There would be a sharp noise, a hard thunk against the floorboards, and then silence. Just like that, no longer than it takes to snap a finger, the banyan swamp would fall quiet as a forest of mushrooms. Outside, the plants and trees stopped whirring, like mechanical contrivances clicking off. His chest swayed to the pumping of his heart. His arms twitched, and he felt his lips swell with blood. Then he heard it: a clicking from somewhere inside his body, cartilage rubbing together, tiny bones speaking, knocking like a chick against a shell. As if something were trying to come out. As if something were inside him. It was the most wonderful sound he had ever heard. He wept in joy some nights, it was so wonderful. He ran to the door and kicked it open and yelled into the darkness, *Kiss me,* because if he didn't yell he would be alone in the jungle with the rats scrabbling across his roof and the leeches inching up the lean-to steps, and his spirit would float up through the holes in the tarp when he slept and he would awake puny and oppressed.

Kiss me, he would shout, opening his arms and stumbling down the steps. *Oh yeah. Come on.* Into the elephant palm he said, *Kiss me,* and something did.

Some mornings he taught the words to boys and girls in filthy swamp villages. Their faces lit up in pleasure. *Kiss me,* the boys said. *Kiss me,* the girls said. They chased each other around sewer grates heaped in a pile. They laughed and nudged each other, but Reuben knew what they were thinking. They stared at this giant white stranger and imagined in the lank palms around them the cavernous avenues of New York, where the movies at the town Lido Cinema showed frothy love on every street corner, under the buzz of airplanes, in screeching taxis and blizzards of confetti. The words weren't words. They were magic. You said *Kiss me* and something did, only it wasn't really a kiss, it was something like a kiss, something fleeting and sudden, something that made you think of a bird flying over the ocean. Sky above, water below. Just flying. Something so beautiful you dropped to your knees, and when you dropped to your knees because it was so beautiful, all you saw was just some raggedy-ass bird flying over the water. Like a kiss. Just some greasy lips until they touched you. And when they touched you, when they touched you . . .

He wasn't sure when Porkpie sat down by him. She was speaking softly. She said she wasn't sure of anything anymore. She said she couldn't even see straight. After she left him outside the doctor's, she said, she had taken a trishaw around town, just circling. She saw a Chinese woman standing on a corner, carrying a full-sized car over her head. The woman bore the load effortlessly. The trishaw driver didn't register the least bit of surprise, and as they drew closer to the woman, it became apparent that the car was constructed entirely of tissue-thin paper and strips of bamboo. But why would this woman stand on a corner holding an effigy of a car over her head? She had a bored expression. Her hair was spiky with tiny rollers, as if she had just come from a beauty shop. She was chewing something. Carrying this car was not for her an extraordinary occurrence. Perhaps her paper car was to be burned at a pyre, trailing the soul of a loved one into the next world? That seemed most likely. The Chinese were forever reducing the world to paper and then setting flame to it. But as the trishaw sped on past the woman, that idea gave way to doubt: perhaps, Porkpie thought, perhaps she was just imagining things. The pewter works she thought she had seen behind the woman turned out to be bird cages; the burlap sack revealed itself to be a beggar in rags, scratching his knees with a pie pan.

Then, after going to her exam, she had herself driven around some more, down a stretch of road past the statue of the leatherback turtle. The paved road changed to dirt. Shop houses gave way to palm and jungly undergrowth; the sun dipped down behind her, and just like that, the sky was no longer spongy and streaked with strands of brilliance but hollow and dark. The driver leaned forward, off his bicycle seat, grunting with exertion. The sole of his foot, rising from his sandal, was pale as a Filipino's. She tried to imagine herself back in the Philippines. Had night been like this? Her life in the Philippines seemed so very long ago. She could not picture herself there. The wheels of the trishaw crackled over plastic bags and dried foliage. Seeing became difficult; she leaned her head against the carriage frame. The Muslim call to prayer floated in the breeze. A woman in a white chador, billowing down her body like a sail, stood by a crumbly wall, clucking at something, her face pressing out from the round cloth hole as if from a porthole. Porkpie felt the wheels of the trishaw ride over cans and pebbles. To either side, she sensed hulking shapes; she smelled tamarind and chilies; she could see nothing. There was hissing, as if snakes were about. Then the whole road was suddenly illuminated with the glare of hurricane lamps, as if on signal, and in their halos appeared giant racks of what looked to be strips of meat, rack after rack of meat. She saw women stand briefly in the halos, touching the meat, arranging, then stepping outside the halo, their forms nearly invisible. And then to her astonishment she saw the meat was not meat at all, but purses hanging by their straps. She was in a night market, and women were selling purses. Rack upon rack of brown purses. No one said a word. There was just the grunting of the driver and the women's hands slapping at the racks.

"You got some vacation," said Reuben. "All right."

She shook her head and said call it what it was. What she did all day was fulfill her destiny. She went to dress shops and shoe shops and stood in the air conditioning at the Hung Fatt emporium. She stopped off at Bangles Restaurant, where a shop clerk had told her one could order a banana split, and then she gobbled down the concoction of currants, heavy cream, and nuts the Indian waiter had with a grave and fearful expression placed in front of her. She went to the waterfront and watched a shadow-puppet performance, oohing when the elderly Australians oohed, then tittered afterward when the musicians mingled with the audience and let them blow on their exotic brass instruments. She took another trishaw around Kuala Trengganu and returned with cheap pamphlets on the Reclining Buddha of Trengganu State, the Trengganu Weavers' Guild, Kite-Fighting Villages Just Miles from You, Giant Top Spinning as Performed by Ancient Practitioners, and the Leatherback Sea Turtle Museum and Gift Shoppe.

She said she was just a tourist. She said her soul was so empty and small it floated like a child's balloon. Stick it with a pin and you wouldn't even hear a pop.

She drank glass after glass of gin and tonic. "On Bidong," she said, "none of us really loves the Viets."

"Have another drink, why don't you?" said Reuben.

"Not truly. We just like how they make us feel. Like we're powerful."

"Come on."

"And they don't love us."

"Stop it with that kind of talk," Reuben said.

"And that's OK. That really is. Because we're not really even there. I never was, anyway."

"You're talking bullshit."

"It's not us the Viets care about. It's what we represent. We're symbols. We're the future, come to visit. And we're the past. We bullied them in Vietnam, and we can bully them now. We have so much power." She downed her drink, almost falling off her stool. "We do things to them we don't even realize. It's not about love. It's about power."

"You're not talking sense."

"And we don't care about them. Not really. We need them. We like their helplessness. It makes us feel good. We're not even flesh and blood. We're just self-important. We're just liars."

"Stop beating yourself up," Reuben said.

"We're dangerous." She stood up.

"Come back here," he said. But she walked away. She moved unsteadily from the bar, her shoes squeaking on the wood floor, and rested her hand on the banister of the stairs. Then up she went, rising with great effort, her hair limp and dull, up the stairs and to her room.

She wouldn't talk to him the next day, or the next. He caught sight of her once, riding in the back of a trishaw, staring off into space.

In December there was Christmas and also Tet to prepare for, but no one on Bidong was thinking of festivals or papier-mâché dragons. No one was hoarding food or paying off debts or making decorations from metal Band-Aid cans. Year Five was coming, but no one wanted to say its name out loud. If you spoke its name, the old people said, the water spirits might hear, and the water that was so dark and so blue would trickle into your dreams and whisper *breathe me, breathe me, breathe me*. The clouds flapped open at night. The rain pounded so hard that children slept under tubs, and in the morning they told their mothers that horses from the Jade Emperor's stables had galloped across their heads. Boys stared at the horizon from the outcrop and the beaches, holding reeds to blow like heralding trumpets. If the Rangers came, they would come soon, in Year Five. They would come from out there, along the horizon, in small Malaysian attack craft, in bristling water, in a bee swarm of engines. Mane of spray, swarm of bees: if the Rangers came, they would come hard and fast, with weapons. The navy would circle the island, towing wrecks. They would circle for weeks, filling the wrecks with Vietnamese, and then the wrecks would be towed from Malaysian waters, and the lines would be cut, and the boat people would sail south, or north, or nowhere at all. If the Rangers came, the water that was so dark and so blue would whisper, and the world would end.

No one knew if the Rangers would come. People listened to their guts. People talked so much the air was heavy with rumors, and the rumors floated like clouds, drifting from shelter to shelter, and when you had enough people together you could see the rumors taking shape, charged with the heat of all those bodies, and always, always someone would say, *There, I can see something there, right there, something hard and true and real.*

In December some people acted like fools. Some people sat on the hospital roof and threatened to leap if the American delegation turned their applications down; when the rain came, they slipped on the tin and tumbled like acrobats into the deep, pillowy mud. A monk threatened self-immolation, dragging a giant jerrican of petrol back and forth along the beach in front of the UN compound until he collapsed from exhaustion.

Some people were wise in the morning but fools at night. In the morning, Mr. Tan of the Loudspeaker Division would quote the words of the famous nineteenth-century essayist Nguyen Duc Dat, who believed one's nature was more important than one's destiny. What comes will come, said Mr. Tan: but what will you do with what comes? Mr. Tan wore wire-rimmed glasses that he cleaned with a special flax cloth. Mr. Tan knew many things, but that didn't stop him from signing off for the night by deriding Singapore's prime minister, Lee Kuan Yew. The cause of Mr. Tan's derision was a short speech delivered by the Singaporean prime minister way back in January. Lee Kuan Yew, referring to Singapore's tow-away policy toward boat people, had said, "You've got to grow calluses on your heart or you just bleed to death." Fancy phrases, Mr. Tan said, using a squeaking, hiccuping kind of Vietnamese reserved for mockery. Beautiful as a tiger. Death disguised as poetry. Calluses wouldn't grow on a heart like that.

His friends warned him against political commentary, but Mr. Tan persisted, philosophical and calm in the morning, mocking and savage at night, until Task Force guards rousted him from sleep early one morning and read to him a verbatim copy of his latest sign-off, translated into Malay. The information is correct, said Mr. Tan, cleaning his glasses, but the interesting question is: *What will happen now?* which, his neighbors later agreed, was both a wise thing and a foolish thing to say. The guards grew ill-tempered. They shaved his head and whacked him with a rattan and paraded him through camp all the way to the Task Force barracks, where they threw him into a chicken-wire enclosure already filled with men found to be engaging in illegal fishing.

The fishermen were honored to have an intellectual squatting miserably alongside them in the chicken-wire enclosure, and they asked him a great many questions, such as: Is it a sign from Heaven that the coral off the beaches has begun to spawn? Is it a sign of renewal that the water has turned milky with coral sperm? that lungfish and blue-striped angel gills swim headlong into the coconut-beard nets? Everyone hated to think of the roaring monsoon waves, of all the lost, creaking boats out in the ocean, but it was December, and if you knew where to look, the fishing was fine, at least until you heard the whispering, at least until you felt the water pulling you in.

In December people went to the fortune-tellers and the card readers and the soothsayer from Pleiku who, for five Malaysian ringgit, would open his battered leather satchel that contained bottled snakes, a pickled bat, cats' paws embalmed in syrupy liquid, and a photograph of his own wife giving suck to a baby monkey. People wanted answers, but no one could answer. In the dreary, gray weather everyone seemed to be walking around with expressions of disappointment and confusion, except when the American or French immigration spooks speed-boated in from Kuala Trengganu and ordered the longshoremen to unload heavy metal file cabinets from the hold of the boat and carry the containers to the interviewing sheds. Then the excitement was so great that people mobbed the file cabinets strapped to the longshoremen's backs. They rubbed the sharp edges and rattled the handles, and the longshoremen fell under the weight and complained to camp security with such passion that the cabinets were accompanied on future trips by truncheon-swinging guards. Inside the cabinets were mysterious official papers, written in a language that no one understood and embossed with delicate designs of eagles and stone columns. The papers declared the will of Heaven. When the Americans and French asked you questions and scribbled on the official papers, you knew that your destiny had been decided. If you were lucky, the papers said you could fly your lucky family across the ocean and live in San Diego or Paris. If you were unlucky, you stayed on Bidong and gnashed your teeth and dragged your children by the hair back to your shelter, where the water sometimes whispered terrible things into your ear.

In the interviewing sheds, parents wore their best shirts and blouses. They put burning embers into coffee jars to iron their clothes, then combed their children's hair and slicked down their babies' heads with cooking oil. They were carried by neighbors to the sheds, riding on their neighbors' clasped hands like mandarins riding in sedans. They memorized amazing English sentences and shouted with much conviction to the startled immigration spooks. "The communists are the evil of this world!" "I would rather live without rice than live with communists!"

"Long live America and France!" "Down with communism!" When they spoke to the interviewers, they twitched. They sat with their hands in their laps and curled up their toes in their flip-flops. They were so nervous that the camp committee petitioned for airline sickness bags to be placed at the back of the interviewing sheds. When they went home, exhausted, their clothes sagging and wet, they wailed to their neighbors, *We must leave soon.*

In December people lit joss sticks and prayed to their ancestors and to Jesus and to Buddha to keep the Rangers away, and despairing young men in running shorts hustled other young men away to cut them for something they did in Vietnam or something they did on the boat journey over, and Saigon bar girls fucked Saigon motorcycle cowboys in perfect, despairing silence, and then they fucked the Malay guards and the French immigration spooks and the American immigration spooks in perfect, despairing chatter. "Now you give me sponsor? Now I can go to Texas?" But there was always another promise to hear, another cock to suck, another hand pushing their heads down into places that smelled like Texas must smell, wild and dank and powerful.

In December smart young students wrote poems in English and taped them to the wire fence around the UN compound:

What the water barge brings in the morning is never enough.
In the heart is an ocean that harbors a grudge against love.

In December everyone was a little crazy. Everyone was a little angry and a little scared.

Inside the UN compound, the white people gathered on Sally's porch and drank lots of Johnnie Walker from Sally's mess-kit cups and spoke out loud about wishing they had something a little stronger to unwind with. Thai stick was best, said Manley: you could ask any taxi driver in Bangkok and he'd hook you up with some sweet weed, cheap.

"Bugger me," said Ralph. "Wish I had me some acid blots."

"I'm a white-powder girl myself," said Sally.

"Hey, bullshit," said Manley. "The only powder you ever got up your nose was pancake mix. Am I right? Huh?"

"OK," said Sally, raising her hands in acknowledgment. "I just snorted once. A long time ago. But if you're going to say bullshit, then I say bullshit to Mr. Acid Blot over here. How about it, Ralph? You ever even *seen* an acid blot? Kind of interferes with your quest for the world chess crown, doesn't it?"

"Bugger me," said Ralph, sticking his finger in his cup. He swished the drink. "Just bugger me."

"You're just a little lamb," said Sally.

"You're the little lamb, missy," said Ralph.

"You're keeping mighty quiet, Johann," said Manley.

"I've been to Amsterdam," said Johann, winking. He picked at sand on his white hospital coat. "They serve you hashish in the drug cafés. It comes in little balls."

"Bugger!" said Ralph, pointing. "You wouldn't know hashish from a turd sample."

They laughed hard, but they weren't really sure what they were laughing about. There was nothing funny about the way their thoughts were racing. It was pleasantly cool on the porch; the mud was turning the texture of Play-Doh. All around the wire fence, people were walking or standing, going about their business. Inside the wire, the relief workers kept drinking and laughing, sneaking glances every now and then at people on the other side. Inside the wire, outside the wire. It made a difference.

Sally said, "I hate this." No one answered. They drank some more and turned up the cassette player. A Task Force guard sauntered by, carrying a crab by the claw. He waved. "Shithead," Sally whispered.

Ralph folded his arms and spat.

"Porch monkey," said Manley.

"Manley, dammit," said Sally.

"Keep focused, Manley," said Ralph. "Don't bring in that kind of language."

"Don't play holy with me," said Manley.

"What's that English drill you have?" asked Johann. "'If you had a million dollars, what would you do?'"

"If I had a million dollars," said Ralph, "I'd buy me some safe passage for these Viets." His cup slipped from his hand. "Oh, bugger," he said. "I spilled."

"You mean buy passage if things get worse," said Sally.

"I mean if the Rangers come," said Ralph.

"If the Rangers come," said Johann, "a million won't make any difference."

"No," said Ralph. He poured himself a new drink. "It won't."

Johann said, "I hear a helicopter will come for us."

"Don't talk about that," Sally said, pouring herself another cup. She looked around. "Is that Gurmit there? With that underpants boy?"

"That's him," said Manley. "You can set your watch by those two. Gurmit's got himself a little shadow."

"A chopper," said Ralph. "Hard to imagine, isn't it?"

Sally waved her hands around. "I said I don't want to talk about that. It makes me feel ashamed." She ran her tongue along the rim of the cup, lapping residue. "Talk about something else. Forget the million. What would you do if your thoughts came true?"

"If I could do anything?" asked Johann. He held the bottle by the neck and took a swig.

"Anything," said Sally.

"If my thoughts came true," said Ralph. "I'd like to see an end to newcomers. Viet *and* staff."

"Speaking of which . . ."

"When are the Yank and the Yankette coming back?"

"Hey," said Manley, frowning. "His name ain't Yank."

Johann stood. Rocking a bit, he held the bottle out and peered into the liquid. "If my thoughts came true," he said, "I'd lead as many Viets as I could to the dock and put them on the supply boat. I'd commandeer the boat and sail it to Kuala Trengganu."

Johann then lowered the bottle and stared out at the dock. A solitary guard was patrolling the area around the pill house, picking up litter. Johann swatted the bottle against his palm. "I'd wave my passport around," he said, shaking the bottle toward the dock. "I'd take one of those UN vans and drive them down to the Kuala Lumpur airport and carry them onto the airplane, man."

Ralph nodded. "If only we could make sure it'll all turn out OK."

"Yes," said Johann. "If only."

"Fuckin' A, yes," said Manley. He curled his fingers into a fist, then pumped his arm up and down.

"This isn't American football," said Ralph sharply.

"Hey," said Manley. He shook his head, then stared down at the painted slats. It got very quiet.

"You think I don't feel nothing?" Manley said, looking up at Ralph.

"He didn't mean it like that, Manley," said Sally.

"You think I don't feel nothing?" he said again. "Fuck you."

"Please watch your mouth."

"Hey, listen to me," said Manley.

"Please don't be objectionable."

Manley threw back his head and with a stiffened, outstretched arm thrust his cup skyward. For a moment, he remained still, the cup held high over his face, but everyone could see the vein on his neck pulsing up and down. He slowly turned his wrist and let the liquid funnel through the air into his open mouth. The ribbon of drink gleamed; it made little splashing noises in his mouth, but Manley, swallowing quickly, didn't spill a drop. He drained the cup and, groaning, let it fall from his hand and clatter on the porch, and then he shook his head convulsively and propelled himself out of his chair. He landed hard on his knees. "You think I don't give a shit?" he said.

"Calm down," said Ralph. "Of course you do."

Manley pushed the hair back from his forehead. He thumped across the porch on his knees all the way to the porch railing, where he dropped to all fours.

"If," Manley said, ramming his skull against the railing.

"My," he said. He rammed again.

"Thoughts," he said, setting a rhythm. His eyes were shut tight. "Came. True . . ."

Johann jumped up. Ralph leaned over in his chair, knocking his drink off the porch. He yanked on Manley's shirt, stretching the material, but Manley kept ramming.

". . . I. Would. Save. Everyone."

"OK, OK," Johann cooed, rubbing Manley's back. "Take it easy. OK."

Sally said, "I hate this."

18

ike I was saying," Reuben continued, but Porkpie appeared to be
so disgusted he knew she wouldn't listen. He had just threatened to toss the visiting British journalist overboard, which, he
noted, at least had the effect of making clear to the fool that regardless
of his profession—he was, he said, a stringer for the *Guardian*—he had
no right to interrupt a conversation and question a bigger man about
the spider monkey straining against the collar of the leash in the bigger
man's hand. The spider monkey was none of the fool's business, a fact
the fool now acknowledged by retreating quickly toward the prow of the
supply boat. "Right," Reuben said, yanking the animal away from
Porkpie's legs. "Like I was saying. You let your mind put the puzzle together, you get the willies. It's like I was saying. You got to get out of
your head for a while. See, feel, smell, taste, whatever. Stop thinking so
much. That's why we got eyes and ears. That's why we got hands and
assholes."

Porkpie looked out into the December waves. The ocean was
rough; whitecaps slapped the hull. Bidong was still fifteen minutes
away, an arched green clump on the horizon. She said, "Did you know
that your jungle junkieisms are getting on my nerves?"

So the hell with her. She was determined to be miserable, and now,
with Bidong so close, he wasn't about to let her talk him into being miserable with her. Not on your life. He had the wind in his face, a meal in
his gut, and Pirate straining at the leash. He was jacked. Oh yes. He
yanked Pirate up by the neck and dangled him there, just for the hell of

it, and then he turned from Porkpie and banged open the side door to the pilothouse, where he crowded Skipper Rahim, sitting quietly on a stool.

"Cannot stay," the skipper said, complaining of allergies to Reuben's stinking *mukah monyet besar,* his big monkey face, and to Reuben's stinking *mukah monyet cacil,* his little monkey face, which referred to Pirate. The skipper's pants were rolled to his knees, allowing him easy access to his bare feet, which, by looping his toes around spokes in the pilot wheel, he had assigned the task of steering the vessel. At the moment, his hands were otherwise occupied, tearing into a smelly durian fruit and tossing bits of the fruit's spiky casing against the pilothouse windshield.

"Working here," said Skipper Rahim, tossing another bit of casing. "You two out." Pirate screeched, them made a short, unsuccessful run at the treasures, gnashing his tiny teeth when Reuben yanked the leash.

"Come on, Rahim," said Reuben. He grabbed hold of the shelf behind the skipper's stool, solidifying his position.

"Big monkey, little monkey," Rahim said, waving his hand under his nose. "Smell too much. Make me sneeze."

"Last I saw, you weren't steering with your nose."

"Out," said Rahim.

Reuben wasn't budging. A small porthole had been hacked into the side door, and looking through the glass Reuben caught a glimpse of Porkpie's new batik skirt, purchased at an Indian shop in Kuala Trengganu, whipping in the wind, threatening any second to flap up to her head. It was pointless talking to her. Being around her turned his thoughts unpleasant. He was jacked, dammit, not morose. He felt more like Reuben Gill, Bidong sub-engineer, than he ever had. Yes. That was it exactly, and to hell with anyone who didn't agree. He yanked again on Pirate's leash—you gonna argue? he whispered—and when the monkey grabbed his arm, he threw the unruly animal hard against the door.

Rahim sneezed, then reached into the mushy durian and extracted a fingerful of pulp. "Leave now," he said. He ate.

Reuben persisted. He wasn't going outside with Porkpie still on deck. The only way he was going outside was if the *Guardian* stringer was in need of another trouncing. He looked out the windshield, scanning for a sign of the man. If the fool knew what was good for him, he'd keep out of sight.

"Tell you what," said Reuben, speaking Malay. He grabbed chattering Pirate by the arm, but the monkey, excited by the durian's outhouse odor, wriggled from Reuben's grasp. "I stay, and you get five ringgit. At the jetty, I'll leave."

"*Sepulah,*" said Rahim. "Ten. Five for each monkey."

"Ten! You're worse than a Chinese banker."

"White bastard-*lah*. First you cheat me, now you insult me."

On they went, haggling and arguing, bouncing roughly through the waves. Bidong drew closer; its matted palms looked spiky, like wet fur. If only he could keep jabbering with Rahim a few minutes longer. If only he could keep Pirate under control a bit longer. If only, really, he could keep the moment intact until they reached Bidong. The scene was a charade, but a glorious one: he, Reuben Gill, Bidong sub-engineer, battling the swarthy skipper inside, eluding a detractor outside, hunting another; he, Reuben Gill, scudding across the ocean, returning stronger than ever, rested, irascible, ready to resume his rightful place.

Whoever that other Reuben Gill had been, the one who had left Bidong, that Reuben Gill had not been jacked, and had therefore not been thinking straight. That Reuben Gill was sorry-assed. That man, that memory, had stepped off the jungle path. He had taken a turn somewhere, into snap vines and creepers and strangler palm, and now his voice was, blessedly, just an echo somewhere, just a scent in the air, a gurgle of water spinning down a drain. Remarkable. The past was a crooked road to the present. One minute you can see around the bend, the next minute you're thrashing in the triple canopy.

Inside the pilothouse, Rahim began flicking Pirate's face with his finger, driving the monkey back, and the boat suddenly dipped into a deep wave trough. The side door flew open. Reuben grabbed the shelf to balance himself, and Rahim began spinning the pilot wheel with his feet. Pirate took his chance. The monkey bolted, screeching loudly, and ran up the baskets of flying fish heaped behind Porkpie.

Reuben swore. He punched the shelf and squeezed through the open door, out into the breeze.

"If you didn't want to talk to me anymore, you could have just said so," said Porkpie.

"I'm after Pirate," he said, eyeing the baskets. "Did you see where he went?" The fish, off-loaded from an iced container early that morning, had been laying in the baskets for hours; jellied slime leaked through the weave.

"That way," she said. She waved her hand up and down the mountainous pile of baskets. "Stuffing himself, probably. I can't understand why you bought the little beast in the first place. He's going to piss on the supplies if you don't catch him."

"Thirty ringgit. He's a good deal."

"And while we're on the subject: Pirate? As in Thai pirates? Nudge nudge, wink wink. Is that supposed to be funny? I'm a little disturbed by the name, I don't mind saying."

"It's not what you think."

"No?" She folded her arms and turned to the railing, watching the waves.

"There's shit," he said, peering into the baskets, "and there's shinola, and what you're—"

"Enough," she snapped. "OK, OK. You're rough and you're tough and you lift tractors before breakfast. Fine." She looked at him for what seemed an inordinate amount of time, taking his measure. Then she just turned and walked toward the prow.

Reuben, shoving baskets aside, watched her walk. Her legs were thin, her breasts a bit on the ration-card side. She had a boyish waist. But he couldn't bring himself to go further in his evaluation. The last time he saw her walk like that, from behind, was on the Zone F hill, when she presented him with the bullhorn to give to Miss Phu. Still . . . she was being so difficult now. It was almost as if she didn't want him to feel better. It was almost as if she wanted to bring him down with her. But he, Reuben Gill, Bidong sub-engineer, would not go down. He shoved a basket so hard one of the fish slid onto the deck.

Damn her. The way she was acting, she wouldn't want to hear that Pirate had actually been her idea. Not that she had suggested his purchase, but that her ranting that first night at Cowboy Lim's had led him a few days later to the livestock market. Pirate. Yes. He, Reuben Gill, Bidong sub-engineer, he of clear sight and clear head, knew what to call the animal. And he was so jacked he could already smell Bidong. Even surrounded by the mountain of rotting fish, he was catching whiffs of the Zone C garbage. He was hearing sounds, too, wonderful sounds that flew over the deep engine noises, sounds like whispering, like a mouth close to his ear, opening its sticky wet lips.

"Hullo then. This yours?"

The British journalist approached slowly, holding an occupied arm well out from his body. Pirate, his arms and legs wrapped tightly around the man's limb, screeched in murderous disapproval. The journalist had ensured the monkey's immobility by wrapping the leash tightly around his other arm.

"Hurts just a bit," the journalist said cheerily, offering his arm to Reuben. "Did you know he bites? But not too bad."

"It's a monkey," said Reuben. He grabbed Pirate roughly by the collar and took the leash. "Monkeys bite until you show them who's boss."

That the journalist was a fool had been apparent the moment he boarded the boat in Kuala Trengganu. He had marched right past Skipper Rahim and gone straight to Reuben. "Got a one-day camp pass," he said briskly, pulling on his shirt to expose the official green Task Force paper stapled to his pocket. "Request permission to come aboard." He was trembling a bit, and he smelled of a peculiar fear that Reuben did not at first recognize as fear because the man's diet of meat made his odor faintly sour. Rahim had stared at the back of the fool's head with undisguised contempt, then began walking over. The journalist was rubbing his fingers briskly on his camera cases and scanning Reuben's face, awaiting permission to board. Reuben said: "You're licking the wrong ass." The man looked at him, ashen-faced, and then Rahim turned the fool around and, jabbing his skipper's hat with his thumb, yelled at him in Malay.

Pirate, protesting loudly, now wriggled his head out from the loosened collar and leaped once again from Reuben's grasp. He bounded up the baskets of fish behind the two men, and Reuben, turning sideways, emerged from the stacks just in time to see the end of Pirate's tail peek out the side door to the pilothouse, which was banging open and shut in time with the waves.

Reuben, entering, saw Rahim scoop the monkey up and hurl him at the windshield. Pirate quickly righted himself and yowled menacingly in the direction of Rahim's durian fruit, which the skipper pressed protectively to his chest. "Allah!" said Rahim, spying Reuben. The skipper gave the pilot wheel a hard spin with his feet. "White bastard monkey," he said, grabbing a pointed steel rod from the shelf behind. "Taking my snack."

"Back off," said Reuben. "That's my damn animal." He lunged for Pirate and caught him by the arm.

"I pay for this durian," Rahim said, waving the steel rod. He disengaged his feet from the pilot wheel then and stood.

"The monkey's worth more, so watch it," said Reuben. "How much you pay for the durian?"

"No white bastard question," said Rahim.

"Steer the boat. What's wrong with you?"

"Cannot tell me," said Rahim, slapping himself on the chest. "I tell you. I am skipper."

From outside came the journalist's voice: "Peace, gentlemen."

Reuben withdrew. He cinched the monkey's collar tight and backed out of the pilothouse, nearly tripping over the anchoring rope coiled to the right of the side door. To his surprise, Reuben saw that the journalist's face was animated, almost jolly, blood rushing to his cheeks. "It's not my business," said the journalist quickly, "but there seemed a great deal of commotion in there. Excuse me, I shouldn't interfere." He lowered his voice. "I thought he called you a white bastard. Is that standard?"

Reuben said nothing. He held Pirate's leash tightly and stared at Bidong. The Zone C garbage quivered with lapping waves; Vietnamese longshoremen were running onto the dock.

"I can see how all this must be a strain for everyone," the journalist said excitedly. He waved his hand at the island. "My god, it stinks." He made a face. The loudspeakers were whining; the high arch of the Zone F hill was orange with mud, and at the very top, next to Porkpie's school, Gurmit's monument pointed into the sky. "How do you get used to it?" the journalist said. Reuben glanced at the man, then turned away. Shrugging, the journalist walked back to the mound of fish baskets, where he grabbed one of the tie-down ropes, steadying himself against the rocking of the gliding boat. The metal deck shuddered with the engine's idle, and the vessel bobbed into a swirling gray pool of oil stretching out from the dock, then bumped against one of the docking tires lashed to a mooring.

Porkpie, clutching her green vinyl travel bag, sidled up to Reuben. "Are you proud of yourself?" she said.

"You mean with him?" said Reuben, motioning toward the journalist.

"Yes, with him. Was rudeness necessary?"

"I don't talk to civilians."

"He was just doing his job."

"He'll get everything wrong."

"You have the answers, of course."

Reuben looked down at her in exasperation, but before he could answer, Skipper Rahim yelled from inside the pilothouse for someone to throw the docking rope to the waiting longshoremen. Reuben, stepping past her, heaved the thick line to a man who tied it to a mooring. Yes, the hell with her. And the hell with the Brit. They were like cawing birds, circling high overhead, at a distance, and they were clever in the manner of thieves, and when he wasn't looking, when his head was turned the wrong way, they came swooping down with their beaks wide open and tried to bore a hole into his head. They wanted inside. They wanted to fill his head with straw and feathers and fly around all day and go *bad, bad, bad*. He, Reuben Gill, Bidong sub-engineer, felt himself go soft with fat in their presence. He felt, by god, when he thought about it hard enough, he even felt a tiny, echoing reoccurrence of *faux* asthma: an unmistakable though minor narrowing of his nasal passages, the smallest hint of swampy leakage into his lungs, an almost imperceptible dryness in his throat. They were trying to unjack him, and he would not allow it. No. Not with all this activity, all this racket.

Everywhere, people were running, heaving boxes and baskets onto their heads, yelling over the loudspeakers and the idling engine. Rahim blew the air horn a few times. All around the boat, kids swam and splashed, floating like corks in the swirling water; the loudspeakers were playing the Good-bye Song, and behind the Task Force pill house at the end of the dock, Reuben could see a line of Viets, travel bags at their feet, waiting to board the boat and sail to Kuala Trengganu and from there to the future. "You two," said Reuben, pointing to his two companions. He shook his head at them, then leaped with Pirate onto the dock and snapped his fingers for one of the longshoremen to go aboard and take his travel bag.

He thought: home. His sandals sank into the wet dock wood, and he had to push his way through the crowd of longshoremen, who were now throwing lumber and boards onto the bobbing vessel and running quickly over the bridges to unload the supplies. To his right, a Task Force guard yelled at a couple of squatting Viets, who without a word leaped up and walked onto the boat. To his left, a girl in a mollusk hat, standing atop an engine hulk, tumbled into the water; a crowd gathered around her, scattering dark schools of fish; the water foamed.

"Hey, Big Bro," shouted Manley, emerging from the crowd at the end of the dock. Manley's shirt was stained; his blond hair needed cutting, and the corner of his lips shook with spit bubbles. "You got a monkey. Damn. A monkey."

Pirate, panicked by all the movement, rushed Manley, but Reuben jerked the animal back so hard that it clawed at its collar.

"His name's Pirate," said Reuben. "Say hello to the little Manley man, Pirate." Pirate screeched.

"It's been crazy here, man."

"All right."

"It's rock and roll, man. Task Force is looking to kick ass. The chicken coop's full of Viets."

Reuben, towering over the crowd, could see the corner of the coop: faces were pressed against the wire. Women, wives probably, squatted in the mud just outside the coop, holding on to the bunched fingers of the occupants. "Good to see you," said Reuben, smiling down at Manley. It was. Reuben then grabbed his friend and hugged him roughly with one arm.

"Hey," said Manley, burying his head in Reuben's chest.

"That Gurmit?" said Reuben, staring over the crowd. "With that kid?"

Reuben could feel Manley's breath seep into his shirt. When Manley pulled away, shaking his hair away from his eyes, there was a sweat stain on Reuben's breast pocket.

"Yeah, Gurmit's into hand holding now. You ought to see—"

"Mr. Reuben." It was Mr. Luc, elbowing his way in from behind. He was fiddling with his jaw, making little popping sounds with his tongue. "You buy a monkey."

"His name's Pirate," said Reuben, turning.

"You say Pirate."

"That's what I said. Pirate."

Mr. Luc frowned. He took his hands away from his jaw and looked Reuben in the eye. "Mr. Reuben," he said. "I think Pirate is not a good name, please. Many boats have been attacked, Mr. Reuben."

"Tell you what. Hold him. Go on, here."

The monkey howled, lunging at the leash.

"Smack him," said Reuben. "Go ahead, smack him one. Teach him who's boss."

Mr. Luc did.

"Harder," said Reuben. "Wale on him. There you go. Smack him hard."

"Hey," said Manley. "What's up with this?"

"Ask Porkpie," said Reuben, shrugging. Pirate clawed at Reuben's leg, seeking refuge. "She could tell you," Reuben said. "We're just goddamn symbols here." Then he yanked Pirate away from Mr. Luc, who kicked the monkey and made it screech.

Only the top of Porkpie's head was visible, borne along by the crowd and equipment streaming off the dock into the sand. Another line of people was headed toward the boat, holding bags over their heads, but then the line broke and someone's bag fell into the water. A ripple went through the crowd. People started shouting. A large wave was sweeping past the dock. It roared into the Zone C garbage, and when it hit, a long, dense section of garbage toppled and plopped onto the beach, splitting cleanly, like a log, spilling squirming gray wads into the mud.

Reuben said, "Did you *see* that?"

But Manley was pointing toward the steps to the dock. "Hey," he said, tapping Reuben. It was the British journalist. Three Task Force guards were hustling the man back onto the dock, toward the supply boat. He was clutching his camera cases tightly against his waist.

"Tell them," the journalist shouted to Reuben. One of the guards was pulling the man by the shirt sleeve.

People shouted: "Journalist." A small man in a white shirt approached the Brit: "Please you save us," he said, clasping his hands together, as if in prayer, but then one of the guards shoved the petitioner away.

"Wait now," the journalist said, turning to the guard on his right. "This big fellow can tell you." The journalist's face was blotched. He spoke rapidly to Reuben. "Look, I've got a day pass. Look. Tell them. It's right here. Signed in Kuala Trengganu."

"You know him?" asked one of the guards in Malay.

"No," said Reuben. "How'd he get a pass?"

"Mistake," said the guard. "Whoever signed it shouldn't have. No journalists."

"Tell them . . . ," said the journalist, thrusting the stapled form into Reuben's face. "Here . . . I've got a pass." His breath was shallow; his knee buckled, and one of the guards yanked him up by the sleeve. Pirate leaped onto the journalist's pants and hung there, howling. Reuben yanked.

"My god," shouted the journalist, and then the guard pulled on the man's sleeve and people cleared out of the way all the way to the boat. The whole time, nobody stopped working. Longshoremen thumped past, carrying bulging boxes on their backs. A boy sped on by holding a jerrican, and the tie-down ropes for the fish baskets, thrown onto the dock planks, twitched underfoot like giant eels.

But Reuben wasn't watching the unloading. He was watching one of the longshoremen lift a basket of fish. The Viet wasn't muscled; he wore silver-rimmed glasses, rare for the laborers. The man let out a yell—"Accident!" he said in English; "Accident!"—and then he carefully dumped most of its contents over the boat railing. Two other men were waiting, standing waist-deep in the water, and they scrambled for the dumped fish, stuffing them under their T-shirts, holding a couple against their sides like loaves of bread, and then they splashed away in opposite directions, lost among the wading children and the boat hulls clogging the water.

Reuben saw the whole thing. So did the Task Force guards. "Wah!" the longshoreman cried again. "Accident!" No one was fooled. People on the beach pointed at the escaping men, and the Task Force guards began yelling into the water. Reuben thrust the leash into Manley's hand and began pushing through the Viets. His sandals stuck in the fish slime, so he kicked them off and shouted for everyone to move. He leaped onto the boat and brought his hand down hard on the longshoreman's shoulder. The man's glasses flew off. Reuben threw him down to the deck, and the basket in the man's hands slid along the wet surface, coming to rest against a wall of thongs tied together with twine. On the dock, the other longshoremen stopped in their tracks, bent under their loads, dripping with fish slime. People stared. The Task Force guards trotted over, but the look they saw on Reuben's face made them draw up short. Reuben was yelling. His red hair shook wildly. The words he spoke were incomprehensible, but his voice was wet and snarling, and the harsh English consonants he spat into the man's face made the man whimper. And then Reuben pulled him up by the arm and began to shake him hard, yelling into his ear, his neck bulging with veins, and he brought his mouth down on the man's shoulder and bit him so hard, the man screamed that his arm had been eaten.

Some longshoremen on the dock began to applaud, saying the American had stopped a thief. They swore at the man for stealing food from their children's mouths, and one ran aboard to deliver a kick. The guards stuck out their truncheons, but they were just going through the motions, and soon the man was rolling on the deck, his hand squeezing his shoulder, still yelling that he had been eaten. One of the guards gave a thumbs up to Reuben, then helped the man up. The two other guards, nodding, clipped their truncheons back onto their belts and, grabbing the man by his elbows, hustled him across the deck and over the planks, clearing a path through the dock. All along the beach, people were applauding. "Thief!" they yelled. "Thief!" Task Force Chief Ahmed came running up from the pill house and began to yank the man toward the Task Force compound, but the two guards said, "No need-*lah*, no need-*lah*," and whispered to Ahmed that there was no need to beat the thief since the white bastard had already scared the man half to death and everyone knew it.

19

You bit him," said Porkpie.

"I bit him," said Reuben. He stood up. He sat down. He stood up again and walked to the frosted window. He cranked the louvers open, then he cranked the louvers closed. He was still very jacked. Window open or window closed? Sit down or stand up? The questions didn't make any sense. Not now.

"Trouble with the Tao," he said suddenly, "is the arithmetic's wrong." Yin and yang, spirit and body, light and dark, male and female, hot and cold, wet and dry: the numbers always added up to two. In fact, the number of natural forces was three. The *gook* on the dock, he said, understood that now.

"*Gook*," said Porkpie. "You actually said *gook*."

"You're not listening," he said.

The Tao was wrong. There were three natural forces. If the number of forces was two, then you wouldn't feel the presence of a third, you wouldn't feel the third sweeping up from your gut, the third force that was like a wind, only it wasn't a wind, it was like the combination of forces one and two, of yin and yang, only what their combination produced was not a product, not a sum, but another force in itself, one that was like a wind but was not a wind, a windlike thing that howled through blood and sinew and heart.

"*Gook*," said Porkpie. "I can't believe you said that."

Yes, yes, *gook*. Was she listening? *Gook*. Sometimes words were wicked and sometimes they just seemed wicked. Look at what they do. *Gook* smelled like your asshole and rammed like your cock and spread like your cunt, so pay attention how about, pay attention because out there, out there somewhere in all that water, there was a war that had washed out into the South China Sea, and it was still alive, and it was headed straight for them. It had a beating heart. It was getting closer, couldn't she see? It was pushing at the wall of garbage on the Zone C beach, it was pushing and pushing and soon, very, very soon, pay attention, soon the war was going to push so hard they'd all be swept away unless someone stood up who was savage and nasty and powerful, powerful, powerful.

"What's wrong with you?" said Porkpie.

"There's nothing wrong with me." He wiped away spit that had pooled at the corner of his lips.

"Well."

"Well."

They looked at each other with jungle-cat eyes, appraising, somewhat formal, wary. Outside, the rain was coming down in dark, straight lines, and the nipa palm on the roofs of the shelters shook and wiggled in the rain and made little crackling noises, like fire. Porkpie took the teapot off her hotplate. She poured herself a cup, then poured Reuben a cup. They sat. They looked at their tea, then they looked at each other some more.

"Well," she said.

"Well," he said.

"Still. You bit that man."

"Something came over me," said Reuben. "From here." He slapped his chest. His heart had stopped racing. He was sitting in a chair. He did not feel like getting up and cranking the window louvers back and forth. He slurped the tea in his cup, then slurped the tea in his saucer. "I had to bite him. Think about it. If I hadn't got to him, what do you think Task Force would have done? They would have kicked the shit out of him and thrown him in the chicken coop. Just for running a fish scam."

"But you *bit* him."

"That's right. I took a chaw. I scared him."

"To the *gook,* you mean," she said.

Reuben leaned forward. His face was flushed and angry. "How else can you do it?"

"So . . . If he's a refugee you can't bite him. If he's a *gook* you can. Is that it?"

"What I did was high drama," said Reuben. He tipped his chair back and rocked on the two wooden legs. "Now, if Task Force gets hold of the guy, then it's the real thing. You see? I *saved* him. I had to bite him to save him from something worse."

She sipped loudly. "As in, 'We had to destroy the village to save it'? Like that?"

"He doesn't get the rattan, he doesn't get a rifle butt in the face, he doesn't get his head shaved, he doesn't get the chicken coop. He just gets a bite. You see?"

"You bit him. You made him bleed."

"Listen to me. Listen. It was the right thing to do. Did you hear the Viets applaud me? They knew what was going on. They're glad to see me get in the action. If you're a Viet, who do you want to see dole out the punishment: the fuckheads with the guns, or scary Mr. Reuben?"

"You're acting like you're a god. Reuben Gill, Bidong sub-engineer, Uncle Sam, and the Great White Father rolled into one."

"That again. We're just symbols, right? Wrong. This mouth took a bite out of an arm. I'm flesh and blood. I'm a big-sized human, that's what I am."

"So that's it. This is all about you."

"No. Listen."

"You're the giant American. Judge and jury. You've got all the cards. The refugees are just the faceless crowd."

"Bullshit. I'm me. I'm Reuben Gill, and I'll stand up for what's right."

"You're self-righteous. You're crazy with power. You want to be Lord."

"Shut up."

"You're a Caliban in Prospero's clothing."

"Symbols again! You want a symbol? I'll show you a symbol. Pirate. Come here, boy. Pirate. Here now."

"I'm not interested."

"Pirate's a good name. Look at this little guy. Look close. A little spider monkey beast. He'd rip your eyes out for a meal. No regret. No remorse."

"Put him down, please."

"Kind of looks a Thai pirate, doesn't he?" Reuben wrapped the leash around his wrist. He stood. He looked down at Pirate, and then he jerked his arm up, lifting Pirate into the air. "That stupid look in his eyes," he said. "The animal face, the human features."

Pirate clutched the collar; he was dangling in the air, shrieking.

"It's like he's human but not human," said Reuben. "Got two eyes, two ears, a nose and mouth. But that's not a face you want to see coming at you on the high seas, is it?"

"Stop it."

"That's what a demon looks like. This."

"Stop it."

Pirate was struggling to breathe. Every time he got his feet or hands around the leash, Reuben reached down with his free hand and knocked them away.

"If I was a Viet," Reuben said, "I'd say, 'Make this demon suffer.' I'd say, 'Swing this demon from a tree.'"

"Don't. For my sake, please. Stop it."

"If I was a Viet I'd say, 'Swing, demon. Swing, you fuck.'"

"Reuben!"

He let go of the leash. Pirate hit the floor, still clutching his collar, and ran behind a chair. "If I was a Viet," said Reuben, "I'd get hold of this Pirate. I'd say, 'Thank you, Mr. Reuben for bringing this symbol.' That's what I'd say. 'Thank you, Mr. Reuben. You brought this symbol here. You are a very powerful man, Mr. Reuben. Thank you.'"

All around the wire of the UN compound the next morning the island was smoking, burning in the rain that fell in a straight line, water and red-hot embers meeting and glowing and rising up in smoke. The incinerator in Zone D spewed black flakes and soot that people let fall on their shoulders because it was said to feel like American snow; the fire pits in the shelters were smoky and warm, and people squatted in the mud to feed the embers with ration cartons and scraps of yellowed newspapers and curling handfuls of hair brought home by children who walked single file to the barbers and squatted by chairs to catch the snippings that fell in bunches, like grass cut by a scythe. All around the wire of the UN compound, smoldering wood was breaking like chalk, and in the clumped ash you could see the dark, wrinkled outlines of bark, the places where the skin of the branches split into islands and the islands split into reefs and the reefs into boulders and the boulders into stones and the stones into nothing at all. The island smoked with great bonfires hissing in the rain, bonfires in Zone C where the rats were the worst, and Zones A and B, and even high up the hill in Zone

F, where the smoke rose in a plume, crackling and sighing overhead, drifting like the faraway cloud of something volcanic. Around the bonfires stood the workmen from the Sanitation Division, some wearing oversized gloves and some wearing British oven mitts decorated with winter scenes, with sleighs and fir trees and hatted snowmen, and the workmen were staring into the hissing fires and holding long staves that they used to spear the clotted hides of dead and dying rats, heaps and heaps of the island's rats, more clotted hides than anyone had ever seen.

The rats had been thrown into heaps after the Night of a Thousand Bricks. Had it been a good thing or had it been a bad thing, this Night of a Thousand Bricks? It had started with announcements on the loudspeakers, then shelter-to-shelter visits from the Sanitation Division crew chiefs, then the forming of groups, then the unfurling of the giant tarp in Zone C, under which lay thousands of neatly stacked bricks, all those bricks stacked in a muddy pit, all those bricks just days away from transformation, days away from becoming an incinerator for Zone C. Was it a good thing to hand all those bricks over to lines of wild-eyed boys, to quiet ARVN sergeants, to hunchbacked grandmothers, to slouching Tongs and tattooed hoodlums? During the Night of a Thousand Bricks, you could hardly wait to hurl your weapon. The loudspeakers played American rock and roll all evening and through the night, and Task Force, curtailing curfew, lent out flashlights and shot off rifles in the air—the sound! how everyone jumped!—and the front door to the hospital remained wide open, flanked by gauze-dispensing Bidong Boy Scouts, just in case unfortunate souls in all those roving bands were bitten by the prey they hunted through the night. During the Night of a Thousand Bricks you could hear the heavy bricks thump into the mud, you could feel the ground under your feet tremble with thumping, you could hear the dying squeals of rats, and the sounds made you happy.

But whether the Night of a Thousand Bricks had been a good thing or a bad thing, no one really knew. Certainly it made your spirit soar, seeing all those heaped snouts and tails and rodent paws; it made you sing through your breakfast. For a while, at least before the survivors deep in the burrows mated themselves strong again, for a while you could eat your noodles and rice without sifting for pellets. You could sleep at night in peace, without fear of their ripping teeth, without feeling their tails slide along your nose. You could walk through the mud freely, without worrying over the bandages and gauze wrapped around your toes and fingers. You could breathe without smelling Mercurochrome and witch hazel wafting from your neighbors' shelter, without waking to their screams.

But now the construction of the incinerator in Zone C was delayed; now maybe it wouldn't even get built. The morning after, the loudspeakers urged everyone to return their bricks to the Zone C pit; the camp committee had even made lists of people who had lined up the previous day to receive their group's brick. All morning, people wandered by and dumped bricks back into the muddy pit. But the tarp had been stolen; there was no order; bricks sank in the mud, and by noon the pit looked like a fantastical mouth sucking the rubble of a city. And not everyone returned their weapons. Not everyone wiped the blood from their bricks. Not everyone took care not to chip the edges.

Also, the cooperation of Task Force was worrisome. There had been rat pogroms before, but never had Task Force curtailed the curfew; never had they lent out flashlights; never had the entire camp been mobilized. And why had the guards shot rifles into the air? To keep everyone awake, the loudspeakers said. For celebration, the loudspeakers said. But the thought that went through your head, even as you were laughing, even as you were pointing with your flashlight—*There! There! Kill it!*—even as you heard the crack of gunfire, you had the sense that if you stopped moving, stopped scanning the darkness for something to kill, if you closed your eyes and lowered your brick, you might sink into the mud and disappear.

So the Night of a Thousand Bricks was full of uncertainty, the way water is full of uncertainty, the way water feels warm like love and cold like death. All you could say for sure was that the giant American, the sub-engineer, had shown himself to be powerful and savage, as powerful and savage as everyone knew he must be, as everyone knew all the white people must be, if only the white people would stop pretending they weren't. The Night of a Thousand Bricks had been Mr. Reuben's idea. The idea burned so hot inside him that if you followed his gaze, if you looked where he was looking, you could almost see the rats already heaped in bloody piles. He had personally unfurled the tarp over the bricks; he had made all his engineering chiefs walk from shelter to shelter, encouraging everyone's participation, and he had argued and argued in Malay with the Task Force chief to pass out flashlights and let the brick throwers hunt for prey after the generators shut down for the night.

The other white people stayed in their compound, drinking on their bungalow porches, but at night, as groups started to stream past the UN wire, hunting, Mr. Reuben stripped off his shirt and left the compound. He moved about the crowds, speaking a strange kind of English, a language no one ever heard in the dark because the white people always stayed inside their compound when the generators started up. He waved his arms around, stirring excitement, his pale white skin a shocking thing to see in the dark, a giant but not a giant, a ghost but not a ghost. He was like the famous baobab tree, people said, the giant tree struck white one night many years ago in the An Loa Valley, during the American war. The baobab tree glowed throughout the valley in a shimmering phosphorescent fire, burning white as chalk, crackling with the souls of the dead rising from the ground, but when the fighting was over, when all the killing was done, the baobab tree was still intact, the only thing standing on the churned and awful ground, and though its bark was smoking, though the tree was hot to the touch, its branches were thick with fruit bats and striped lemurs and great flocks of red-plumed birds that no one had seen for ages.

Mr. Reuben did not shimmer or crackle. Mr. Reuben was only a man, an American. People understood that. But as the night grew blacker and the rats began to smell the blood and race in crazy circles, people did not want only a man, a sub-engineer. People did not want to hear stories about baobab trees. People needed more. They needed to run and scream at the top of their lungs when giant Mr. Reuben drew near, when this pale sweating giant yelled "More, more," hurling his bricks then stomping through the mud and retrieving small dark shapes that he lifted by the tails and tossed into the wicker basket that he carried on his shoulders. There were rumors that he ate one, then rumors that he had stuck his head into his basket and gnashed at the contents until his face was sticky. These were only rumors. But that's what people needed, for that's how people are: shadows frighten us; we look for saviors to bathe the world in blood or to bathe the world in light.

So the American must have eaten a rat, he must have stuck his face into his basket, because if he hadn't, then the mystery of the Night of a Thousand Bricks would only have deepened. No one could stand that.

Not so close to Year Five. Not with the water creeping up the beaches, whispering in everyone's ears. People needed a man who was not a man, a man who heard the water but knew it would not come for him, a man so unlike themselves, a white man, a giant man, a powerful, savage man. In the early morning hours, after the rumors came and went, you could hear Mr. Reuben's name spoken among the roving bands of people, you could hear how he had eaten a rat or maybe many rats, no one knew for sure. You could hear how he had bitten the fish thief, how he had bitten the man so hard that the teeth marks formed a necklace on the thief's ruined arm. *Cai Cay Bi Can,* people called him: the Biting Tree. He was Cai Cay Bi Can because he was strong like a tree and big like a tree, and because he had tasted the flesh of both human and rodent alike. He was Cai Cay Bi Can because he was powerful, neither good nor bad. Powerful. So powerful, he gave you hope. Because power was savage and hard, neither good nor bad, and if in Year Five the world should be covered in water, then only power could save you.

When by mid-afternoon all the heaps had been doused with gasoline and set afire, Vietnamese sanitation crews wandered along the Zone D beach, kicking at the sand for dying stragglers. They moved in a ragged line, working slowly, and every few minutes someone would yell out for a palm frond, then stoop and fold a small form into the green sheet, as if wrapping a package, and toss it into a basket. Their feet made plopping sounds, and in the small holes they left behind, brown water rushed in and foamed to the cusps. People slept. The air was still. The camp was quiet, except for the dull noise outside the hospital. There, a small crowd swarmed past the front entrance, trailing the Biting Tree. Pirate was on his shoulders, gnashing his teeth whenever the crowd drew too close.

Inside the UN compound the relief workers looked out from the wire and spoke in low tones to each other. Porkpie stood by the gate, rocking on her heels and staring at Reuben's approaching form. Sally came up behind her. "He's getting Manley worked up," said Sally, motioning to Reuben. "Can you talk to your friend? Please?"

At dawn, Sally said, Manley had been walking around as if he were on jungle patrol, a large stick slung like a rifle over his shoulder. He saw one of his Zone A teachers and invited the man into his bungalow. Manley saw her in the washing-up shed. He shouted out that they were going to his room. The Viet looked nervous. With the door wide open,

Manley picked up his radio and his spare watch and a pornographic magazine from Thailand. She saw him make the man fondle the objects. He put them in the man's hands and clasped his own hands around the man's. "You like?" he said: "UN Number One." Then he took out a hidden bottle of liquor and shook it, and he said in a loud voice that if Task Force caught any refugees drinking booze, they'd bam-bam them. He said not to worry. He pointed to himself. He said if Task Force came to any Viet hootch and started to bam-bam, the Viets should come to Mr. Manley.

Porkpie wrapped her fingers around a strand of fence wire. Reuben was drawing close, and the crowd behind him was talking so much that the line of Viets on the beach turned their heads and stopped working. Sally yanked on her braid and crinkled her nose.

"Reuben," Porkpie said, nodding to Sally. He slowed. He was sweating; his arms were mottled with dark splotches.

"I don't want to be always snapping at you," she said. He nodded. "But you're carrying this too far."

"Save it," he said, shifting Pirate to his other shoulder.

Manley walked up to the fence and stood next to Sally. "Hey," he said, leaning into the wire. He was carrying a toy telephone. He looked straight at Porkpie and talked into the mouthpiece. "Bellhop, send a girl right up, how about?"

"He teaches English class with it," said Sally, indicating the telephone.

"Operator. Operator," Manley said, slapping the receiver. "Who's on the line?" He dropped to a crouch. "VC on the perimeter. Repeat, Victor Charles. Request napalm strike."

Reuben shook his head. "Don't," he said.

Manley straightened, then began pushing his hair forward. "Hey," he said. "I ain't talking about these guys." His arm swept the air, taking in the sanitation crew on the beach and the crowd standing behind Reuben. "These are good guys. I'm talking about the fuckers who fought them, man."

Reuben shook his head and simply turned around and began walking back toward the hospital. Porkpie stuck out her hand, signaling stop, but he kept going. She stood with Sally and Manley, but when she turned to face them she could think of nothing to say. They didn't seem to notice. They watched the sanitation crew for a moment, then Sally patted Manley's arm. "Just calm down," she said to him, and then they, too, walked away.

Porkpie folded her arms. She went straight to her bungalow and made some lemongrass tea. Rummaging, she found an old *Herald Tribune*. She took out a pen and began filling in the crossword. She sipped her tea. She listened to herself breathe. Floorboards squeaked under her feet; when she shifted in the chair, the vinyl cover sighed; she saw her expression mimicked in the well of her spoon. Sunlight shone through the window brightly, and for a moment Porkpie had the sense that she was transparent. The light seemed to shine all the way through her body. She turned over the crossword. She put down the spoon. Did one simply go from dream to dream, helpless as a doe? Under that thought was another, and she clenched her fists when she acknowledged it. She did not belong on Bidong. She was a little girl at a horrid masquerade ball.

For days the loudspeakers crackled with harried voices requesting security personnel. Looking out from her frosted windows, Porkpie frowned at what she saw and heard. There was lavish indulgence: Women reached into lacquered boxes engraved with swirling dragons and stuck hard candies into their daughters' mouths; fathers tossed Malaysian coins in the air for their sons to catch. Late into the night children chased each other up and down the footpaths, yelling at the top of their lungs. Vicious fights broke out over soccer games. One morning, before she had a chance to brush her teeth, a Task Force guard stood in front of the compound gate and announced through a scratchy bullhorn the latest directive from the Kuala Trengganu Task Force office. She couldn't understand what he was saying. No one could. One by one, the relief workers walked out of their bungalows and read the sign the guard posted by the gate latch.

NO DANCING

NO SHORT-SHORTS

NO WEARING WITHOUT BRASSIERE (FEMALE ONLY)

NO DRINKING OF ALCOHOL

CURFEW 2100 HRS TO 0600 UNLESS EXCEPTION

NO KNIFE, GUN, WEAPONS, SHARP POINTING ROCK

NO FRATERNITY WITH ILLEGAL ALIEN VIETNAMESE (MALE AND FEMALE)

GANJA AND THE ILLEGAL DRUG NOT ALLOWED

"In other words," said Ralph, scratching his beard, "sit tight and hold on."

"This is bad," said Sally. "It really is."

The relief workers looked at each other, then they looked out onto the beach, where dead and gasping fish had been washing up all week for reasons no one could fathom. An oil spill perhaps, Johann had guessed. Or maybe something to do with plankton. Perhaps, Porkpie wondered now, though she kept her opinion to herself, perhaps the fish were an omen—but of what, she resolutely refused to contemplate. She was sure she would not like the answer. Certainly Reuben would have plenty to say about the fish, but she would not ask him. He would simply say something dreadful.

He seemed to be constantly in motion, ordering the Viets around, walking from zone to zone with Pirate on his shoulder. He rough-talked the crew chiefs, and the crew chiefs did not resist. The Sanitation Division built a new longhouse in a day, a record, and they built a new latrine, and they cleared the blockage in the sewage canal in Zone D. The Zone C school got new steps, and the cables for the generator in Zone B were safely tucked into plastic housing that rose high over the footpath. The Biting Tree: Reuben seemed to like the name. People looked where he looked, people followed him on the footpaths, they ran to get him things—crowbars, chainsaw oil, paper sacks bulging with nails, channel locks, lumber sealed with roofing tar. Strangers pressed notes into his hand, messages with their names and boat numbers, and polite Bidong-English requests: "If soon very bad, please do not forgetting me."

The Biting Tree paraded through camp with Pirate on his shoulder, leashed to his wrist. He would stop in the middle of footpaths, wondering aloud if anyone wanted to kick Pirate, or to choke him, or to make him screech. Usually no one did. Usually the translators shouted out the offer to the crowd, and people murmured and looked at each other, and sometimes they ran back into their shelters and brought out women whose faces looked hard and fragile as glass. Sometimes the women just stared, and sometimes they whispered things into their husbands' ears, and sometimes they pushed through the crowd and dangled Pirate in the air. Sometimes they yanked his leash high over their heads and listened to his howls, and then, just for a moment, if you looked just right, then just for a moment you could see their glass faces grow milky and full, the way windows look sometimes, when the morning light glares on the pane and makes you think of someone's eyes.

Sometimes men kicked at Pirate, and sometimes boys ran up to the monkey with sticks and struck him hard, sending him leaping to the top of the Biting Tree's head, where he pulled on his master's flaming red hair and trembled and shrieked.

"That's it," said Sally. "You've crossed the line."

"It's bloody animal abuse, you bugger," said Ralph. "Give me that monkey."

"In Amsterdam," said Johann, "you would go to jail for that."

"Who cares what you think?" said Reuben, stroking Pirate's head. "White boys and girls in the helicopter. *Gooks* in the boats. You act like nothing's going to happen. Business as usual."

Sally yelled in his face. "Don't you say that, Reuben Gill."

Ralph fumbled with his wallet, then withdrew a folded piece of paper with UNHCR letterhead. It was the letter from Doctor Johansson. Ralph's hand was trembling, he was so mad. "You're on probation, you bastard. Bugger me. You bastard." He had to stop to compose himself. Then he resumed. "This letter says if there's a peep from anyone about you, then you're off the island. Well, you bugger, there's going to be more than a peep from me."

"And me," said Sally.

Johann nodded.

"I don't care how long the paperwork takes," said Ralph. "Your arse is off this island."

But the words seemed to mean nothing to him. "Not before it comes," he said, and then he was on his way.

"It?" said Ralph, shouting to Reuben's back. "Bugger. Speak English."

Reuben, walking, pointed toward the water.

He tried visiting with Porkpie, but she waved him away. No farther, she said from her porch, so he stood in the mud and said frightening things. He swore there was something wicked in the air. He sniffed. He stripped off his shirt and his nipples stuck straight out, erect. He swore things were happening to his body. When the air turned hot and dry, his body turned hot and dry, and he had to dunk his T-shirt in a bucket of water and wear it like a bandanna around his steaming face. He got enormous erections, he said, for no reason at all.

"Good night," she said, and turned and slammed her bungalow door.

He made sympathy impossible. He fed Pirate well, stuffing the monkey with bananas and dried coconut, and at night he stroked the animal's furry head and squeezed his tube of Swedish antiseptic cream onto its injuries. But in the morning, when he leashed Pirate to his wrist and paraded him up and down the footpaths, he was gruff and brutal. When Pirate cowered at his approach, he wouldn't acknowledge that the monkey was cowering. He refused to admit that Pirate was screaming when a boy stepped on his tail and made him scream, or when a woman pinched his leg, or when a man with a blackened finger tore off part of his ear.

"I don't know you anymore," Porkpie said one morning in the washing-up shed.

"I'm doing a good thing," said Reuben, hooking Pirate up to the leash. "I told you that." But she had already walked out.

He had his toothbrush in his mouth, flecks of shaving cream still on his face. He watched her walk to the compound gate. He looked at the shape of her legs, the back of her dress, the thin ridge of her shoulders. There by the gate was Miss Phu, waiting for her, holding an empty jar in her hands. Miss Phu saw him looking. She stared back at him, and her expression turned hard.

"Miss Phu," he shouted then. "Hello."

Miss Phu looked away.

"Porkpie," he said, spitting toothpaste. "Miss Phu. Hey. Please." But they ignored him.

He stood at the door of the washing-up shed a long time, watching. Porkpie and Miss Phu were talking. Then Miss Phu's face fell; she looked upset. Porkpie reached out and held Miss Phu's hands. Porkpie seemed to be apologizing for something. Miss Phu smiled briefly and looked at the ground; she withdrew her hand from Porkpie's. Miss Phu left, and Porkpie waved, then stood motionless a long time. The loudspeaker chimed nine o'clock. Heat lightning lit up the horizon. When Porkpie at last lifted the gate latch and entered the compound, she was mumbling to herself.

She saw Reuben. She folded her arms and walked to him. "Did you see that outside?" she snapped, waving behind her.

"Whoa," he said, holding up his hands. Pirate began squawking.

"You shut up," she said. "I've had it. You listen." She pointed at him. "I want you to know what you've done. Miss Phu was out there telling me she had a possibility of getting a sponsor in California. I told her, 'Oh, I don't want you to go.' And she didn't understand me. She thought

I was saying that I wouldn't let her leave this place. She thought I might be that cruel. She thinks we must all be like you now. Monsters." She looked down at the ground, then stared up at him with accusation in her eyes. "There. I said it. I feel better now. Goddamn you."

That afternoon, Reuben put Pirate on his shoulder and leashed the animal to his wrist. Outside the gate, Manley ran up to him. They walked fast, slogging through mud. Manley grunted with the effort, struggling to keep the pace.

"I'm telling you," said Manley. He had a dog-eared paperback in his hand. The cover showed a U.S. Marine charging through tall grass. "If the Rangers come, I know some Viets who are gonna fight. I saw some guys in Zone D counting jerricans. They saw me. Then you know what? They fucking covered the cans with a tarp. They're stockpiling, man. There's *gas* in those things. Flame on."

"It's under control here, Manley."

"Hell it is. You see Ahmed stringing up more wire around the Task Force compound?"

"It's under control."

"No, man. It ain't. No way."

"It is *under control.* You hear me?"

"Hey, some of these Viets might fight, man. I got some books on the subject. I been doing some reading."

"Books."

"Hey, that's right. I read, man." He shook his paperback in Reuben's face. "We got Bao-Ba sects here. We got ARVN paratroops. Almost all these old guys are military. The Chinaboy Tongs are mean fuckers."

"Don't start talking like this, Manley."

Manley waved his hand at the dock. "If I had me a couple .50 calibers, I could set up on Zone D and inside the compound. Nice killing zone, man." He imitated the sound of a machine gun: "brum-brum-brum-brum-brum-brum." His shoulders shook, as if caught in the recoil. "If I had me some .50 calibers, the Rangers couldn't dock. And you know those assholes can't do beach assault. I been reading, man. Malaysian military don't even have landing craft. They gotta use the dock."

"Don't even think about it."

"Hey," Manley said. "You're supposed to be the tough guy. What the hell they calling you now? The Biting Tree? What the hell are you gonna do?"

"You're not being tough, Manley. You're being crazy. Crazy ain't power. Crazy's crazy."

"So walking around with that little punching bag on your shoulder ain't crazy?"

"No."

"Hey, it's crazy."

"Think what you want," said Reuben. "I don't care."

"Hey, OK. OK. So what are you gonna do, tough guy? Huh? What?"

"I don't know. I'll figure it out."

"You'll figure it out."

"I'll figure it out," said Reuben.

"You don't know what you're going to do?"

"Right now, I'm correcting the ledger."

"What the hell is that supposed to mean?"

"It means what it means. I'm correcting the ledger."

"Hey, we're going to Gurmit's office. You're gonna talk to Gurmit. That don't sound like correcting nothing to me."

Correcting the ledger. Reuben turned the words over in his mind. They were dreamy and overheated, but there was something pure about the way they sounded. So yes: correcting the ledger. Entry by entry. Box by box until it came out right.

20

Inside the Administration Office, Gurmit and Duoc sat holding darts on their laps, filling time until Miss Phu returned with the jar of glowing mud. She had, Gurmit felt, been unwise to promise magic to the nephew of Nguyen Van Trinh: Duoc had been so excited at the prospect of seeing mud glow that he was bound to be disappointed when it didn't. But there was no way to take back what Miss Phu had said. All Gurmit could do was keep Duoc occupied until she returned. So he tacked up a dartboard salvaged from the Zone C garbage and cleared out the dart-throwing lane that now whistled with feathered red projectiles. As an activity, darts seemed a brilliant choice. Modest hand movements, a clear objective, an atmosphere of precision: it was just what Duoc needed to calm down. The dart-throwing lane was tidy and unassuming. The entire office, in fact, had never looked better. All the junk and dust had been swept out the door; the long row of file cabinets gleamed with a soft luster, like refrigerators; the MRCS boxes were stacked into sturdy towers in the back corner. Gurmit had even swatted a broom against the rafters, clearing out the cobwebs and wasp mounds, and just minutes ago, searching for the box of darts, he had paused to rub his desk with a kerosene-soaked rag, removing a tea stain. Clarity. Order. That was what the office needed, and that was what he had given it. He only hoped that Miss Phu would follow his example in the future.

"Now here is how you throw the dart," said Gurmit, holding Duoc's wrist. "Flicking. You are knowing, yes? Flicking?"

Duoc stared dumbly at his darts and, petting one, mumbled something back to Gurmit in Vietnamese. Conversation was so difficult. The boy spoke only Vietnamese, he only English and Malay, and he had to admit that even now, after so many months on Bidong, the sound of Vietnamese still reminded him of fowl strutting inside a coop. Words, Gurmit thought, shaking the boy's wrist back and forth in demonstration of flicking: how far words drifted sometimes. We think they are anchors when really they are sails. How vague were words, how they led us into illusion. We talked and talked, and still nobody could hear us. An image came to him then: Miss Phu walking the beach, filling the jar with mud. What outrageous magical words did she think she could say to make the mud glow? What spell? It was hard enough simply to tell Duoc how to flick his wrists.

"Flicking," Gurmit said again. "Must concentrate."

Duoc was grasping his dart as if it were a stick. His fingers coiled around the cone, but despite Gurmit's efforts, the boy did not seem any closer to flicking his wrist than he had been a minute ago. He kept looking out the window slats, watching for Miss Phu.

"Flicking," said Gurmit. "Must focus, isn't it?"

Duoc hurled his dart, which, after a wobbling trajectory, thudded gracelessly onto the floor.

"Flicking," said Gurmit. "Like this." He held his own dart by the fingertips and waggled his wrist back and forth. He flicked. The dart flew forward, arcing gently, and pierced the soft tissue of the dartboard. "Is looking so easy, but is not, yes?"

Duoc, stony faced, leaped from his chair and retrieved his dart. He seemed more interested in waving it up and down than in throwing it. Miss Phu . . . where was she? She was always so good with Duoc, so imaginative and generous in her activities. If only she hadn't promised glowing mud. Duoc wouldn't calm down. The boy kept smiling to himself, looking around occasionally as if to assure himself that the office was still there. To Gurmit, it was a worrisome expression: the eyes greedy and expansive, the face placid and detached. Behind that look, Gurmit knew—how well he knew! how well!—dangerous fantasies could lie in wait.

It seemed to Gurmit, watching Duoc stare, watching Duoc wave the dart, that he could anticipate Duoc's every movement. The left corner of the mouth would rise, like so; the eyes would glance up now—yes, like so—and now the right hand would caress the dart . . . It was like watching a play seen long, long ago, sitting in a chair and suddenly knowing whole chunks of dialogue, envisioning the ripple of an arm— like so!—a dramatic facial expression, a fumbled line. Gurmit shifted in his chair. The boy's actions had been his own, had they not? It was as if, Gurmit thought, rubbing his chin, as if a scene from his own past were being played out in front of his eyes: a figure clutching objects, lost in the enormous landscape of his own mind.

Seeing such things made you aware that you were no longer who you used to be. Certainly he, Gurmit Singh, was no longer *that* Gurmit Singh, that flickering, fantasy-filled Gurmit Singh. Certainly his own life was at last taking shape, drawing together into the true form of Gurmit Singh, son of Gopal Singh. It was as if, before, months ago, weeks ago even, he had been merely a projection of the true Gurmit Singh, an illusion of mass, a hoax. Bloody hell! How vague he had been, how full of foolish notions.

The warrior, the hero, the righteous leader: the titles seemed to him now extravagant and absurd. They were like molted skins on the floor, transparent, ancient debris from which something new had emerged. What had emerged, surprisingly, was smaller, not bigger. But it was solid and lean, compressed and weighty, hard as a cup. What had emerged did not dream of every square foot of Bidong, did not dream of crowds, of the thousands of faces, did not dream of grand gestures. No. In that direction lay illusion. "Praise loss!" he thought now. "Praise suffering!" For only through loss and suffering do we come into understanding. Was it not glory enough to show kindness to the nephew of Nguyen Van Trinh? To sit for hours in the office, caring for this one unruly, difficult boy? The smallest acts were in fact the largest. The carcass of the elephant is carried by the ant, morsel by morsel. The earth is plowed by the worm, grain by grain. By morsels and grains: that was how the true Gurmit Singh would fulfill his destiny. He would sweat and struggle, inch by difficult inch.

The foolish gloves were in his drawer now. They were where they belonged, next to the sponge and scrub brush. One could not sweat or struggle when one was wearing gloves. By morsels and grains we are freed, by morsels and grains we are contaminated. One could never be truly clean. Not entirely. But not clean was different from dirty. Not innocent was different from guilty. He understood that now. He understood because Nguyen Van Trinh's nephew sat in his office, fondling darts. He understood because he wanted Duoc to stay, did he not? He frowned for a moment, summoning emotion, turning the statement over in his mind. Yes. That was true. He wanted Duoc to stay, even though Duoc was filthy and ill-mannered and very, very difficult to be around. Even physically, the boy was unpleasant. The supervisor of the Unaccompanied Minors longhouse had shaved the heads of all the inhabitants, fearing an outbreak of head lice. Snot dripped from Duoc's nose; he kept scratching at his smelly gray underwear, and he wouldn't wear pants or a shirt.

But Gurmit understood now that his true place was next to this boy. Every day, Gurmit filled his pockets with cellophane-wrapped candies and walked through camp to the Unaccompanied Minors longhouse, where he handed out candies to all the other orphans, then squatted in front of Duoc and had a translator ask if he wanted to play with Mr. Gurmit. "Tell him we can play cards," Gurmit would say to the translator. "Or darts. Or Chinese chess. Or we can do the running. Or we can tie strings to flying beetles, isn't it? Have them fly like airplanes. Or we can listen to my cassette player, or paint the watercolor, or eat the very delicious candies. Anything he is wanting to do."

So every day, Gurmit would walk with Duoc hand in hand back to the Administration Office to play card-slapping games, or to slam the drawers of the desk open and shut, or to slide the window louvers in and out, and sometimes to wriggle a glass pane out of the frame, into the mud. He stared at the boy. He fed him candies. He spoke to him in English, and sometimes in Malay. Miss Phu often helped out, rushing down from Zone F to translate Gurmit's questions. "What are you knowing of your uncle?" Gurmit would ask. "Was he a good man? A patient man? A forgiving man? Do you look like him? Are you like him?" But Duoc wouldn't answer. Once, though, he crawled along the floor, pushing piles of dried mud that gathered between the slats, and when he reached the wall he spit into the piles, making them soft. Then he sculpted with his hands, turning the wet mounds around and around, and when they were round as coconuts, he stood and smashed them against his head.

"He say that is his uncle," said Miss Phu, pointing.

"What? Duoc has seen the suicide? Oh dear. Oh bloody hell. Ask him more, Miss Phu. What did he see? What happened?"

But Miss Phu held up her hand. Such questions, she said, made Duoc uncomfortable. Such questions she would not ask, for Duoc did not wish to speak of his uncle. So Gurmit stopped asking. He felt a tingle of shame. He savored the tingle. He felt weak with sensation. He let the tingle work its way into his stomach, and then he apologized to Miss Phu and to Duoc. Praise loss! Praise suffering! The tingle did not consume him. No. Never again. One made mistakes, one righted one-self. One learned. What, really, could Duoc say about his uncle that would be meaningful? What was to be gained by such information? What had happened to Nguyen Van Trinh could not be taken back. What he, Gurmit Singh, had done to Nguyen Van Trinh could not be erased. Nor could his shameful behavior at the Zone F plank ceremony be undone. One could destroy oneself with such knowledge, or one could endure. One could force oneself to see clearly.

What he saw was that he, Gurmit Singh, had to forgive Gurmit Singh. It was not Nguyen Van Trinh who had to forgive. It was he. He had to forgive his own foolishness and, in forgiving, become less fool-ish, morsel by morsel, grain by grain. Illusion was to be excised, vision focused, action moderated. Grasp and reach were to be aligned. One's life, he knew now, had to shrink before it could grow.

But shrinking was not diminishment. No. Shrinking was clarifica-tion. Shrinking was seeing, truly seeing, what needed to be done, not what one desired in one's fantasies. This orphaned boy needed care. When Duoc talked, the sound was loud; when he was quiet, you hardly knew he was alive. The boy grabbed things without asking—pens, paper clips, box flaps—and he flew into rages when you took them back. He picked his scabs and ground the debris between his fingers into a fine powder, which he then sprinkled onto the floor, and once into Gurmit's tea. He ran in circles inside the office, playing tag with imaginary playmates, and when he got breathless, he sat in a chair for a very long time, then cracked open the door and shouted nonsense syl-lables out to passersby. Sometimes he just stared, glum-faced and solemn. Sometimes he cried for no reason at all.

"By morsels and grains," Gurmit said aloud. "That is how we shall meet the future, hey, Duoc?" Duoc began picking off the feathers from one of his darts. Gurmit grabbed the boy's arm and gently coaxed the dart away.

The future. Year Five was the future, and the future was only days away. Perhaps nothing would happen. Perhaps the future would be peaceful. Or perhaps history was about to unfold: hundreds of leaking ships, some sailing toward another future, some toward annihilation. There was nothing one could do about history. When one saw clearly, one knew this. We live by morsels and grains, but history . . . history was a powerful dream, a great, towering wave of dreaming. You couldn't escape it. No. All you could do was ride the dream wave as long as you could before sinking. All you could do was clasp another's hand—and Gurmit now reached down and held Duoc's hand tightly in his own. Clasp just one real hand, feel the skin and blood and bone of a real human hand, because if you did that, you could ride the towering wave a little longer.

Duoc slipped from Gurmit's grasp and rushed to the window to scan the footpath for Miss Phu. Duoc was dreaming of glowing mud. His mind was floating, prey to illusion, prey to voices and monstrous commands. Dream water, thought Gurmit: even into the head of this poor boy, dream water was now leaking, drop by drop.

"Duoc," Gurmit said, but the boy looked past him.

"Duoc," Gurmit said again, but Duoc was still looking past him, toward the door, frowning. There was a cracking sound then. Gurmit turned. It was Reuben Gill at the doorway, knocking and entering in the same motion, advancing across the office with his big face hunched forward, his hair nearly scraping the rafters. That horrible chained monkey was screeching on the American's shoulder, baring teeth. Gurmit pulled Duoc to his side. The boy stiffened, pressing his head into Gurmit's stomach. The boy was awake now, alert and wary. The dream water would stop for a moment. There was this giant to contend with, to mollify, to hiss at. Gurmit shouted at the approaching shape, at this giant man leashed to the prune-faced animal. Only then did Reuben Gill stop. Only then did Reuben Gill speak, and much to Gurmit's surprise the voice that spoke was sheepish and polite. Reuben said he had a favor to ask. A small favor. Reuben cleared his throat; he tucked the flailing monkey under his arm. A favor, he said again. Couldn't Gurmit just ask Miss Phu one small thing?

———

It was a simple request. A shipment of hammocks had just come in; did Miss Phu want Reuben Gill to give her one? Apparently the American would not ask her himself. Apparently there was some distance between the American and Miss Phu, something that went beyond Reuben's behavior up at the Zone F plank ceremony. When Miss Phu returned, holding a jar of plain, dark mud at her side, her face seemed to blanch when Gurmit told her of the American's request. It had seemed harmless enough; Gurmit supposed that Miss Phu would be overjoyed to receive a hammock. Even from Reuben Gill. Even from that unpleasant white bastard.

But she refused. She said, "He very frightening me."

"Frightening you," said Gurmit. "He is behaving poorly at the plank ceremony, Miss Phu. But I am behaving poorly as well, you know. Many people are behaving so poorly that I . . . that I cannot think . . ." He stopped. Miss Phu was too busy to listen.

She put the jar of mud on the desk and said something to Duoc. The boy, obedient, sat in his chair. "Mr. Gurmit," she said, turning the jar around and around. "Mr. Reuben having too much power."

It was a startling statement. Refugees never spoke publicly of power. Not even Miss Phu. One did not take such chances, not when the wrong word in the wrong ear could make you stay on Bidong forever. By morsels and grains, that was how Miss Phu had always spoken.

"He is the Biting Tree," Miss Phu said, tapping the jar. "People are saying this. The Biting Tree. Everyone giving Mr. Reuben the power." Then she whispered: "Year Five is coming, Mr. Gurmit. Everyone wanting him to have the power, but he is too scary, Mr. Gurmit."

Gurmit nodded.

"Year Five," he said. "Yes. I am knowing. And so we are needing to help each other." He looked over at Duoc, fidgeting in front of the dark jar. "So we must let others help us, Miss Phu. Even the scary people. Is only a hammock, isn't it?"

"No, Mr. Gurmit. He too much. I will not accept."

No. Remarkable. She had refused him nothing before. She had always been tireless and cheerful and agreeable. She knew what it was to struggle by morsels and grains. For months she had obeyed his every word. Now she ignored him. Now she refused the simple offer of a hammock.

Was dream water leaking into her head as well? Did she not understand that we must clutch each other's hands tightly? Even Mr. Reuben's hands. Did she not know that if the towering wave came, we could only squeeze and squeeze and not let go?

Miss Phu turned her back to him. She picked up the jar and smelled it. She said something to Duoc, then put the jar under his nose. He sniffed. His eyes were closed. He opened them once, but then Miss Phu spoke to him sharply, and he closed them again and breathed the mud deeply.

She whispered to Gurmit. "I tell him to keeping his eyes closed and smelling the mud. Now, Mr. Gurmit. Please giving me your small flashlight."

Gurmit reached into his breast pocket and took out his penlight, which Miss Phu plucked from his hand. She flicked it on and held the tube behind the jar, bathing the glass in light. She said something to Duoc. The boy opened his eyes, and as he did, Miss Phu brought the jar right up to his eyes and then flicked the penlight off.

"Oooh," said Miss Phu, loudly. She closed her fist, shielding the penlight.

"Oooh," said Gurmit. He brought his hand up to his face, pretending to be blinded by a flash.

But Duoc, blinking slowly, stared hard at the jar. He frowned. He looked angry. He said something that sounded like an accusation, then leaped from his chair and grabbed Miss Phu's fist. He stuck one of his fingers into her closed hand, down to where the penlight was. The jar fell. Mud oozed onto the floor, a dark, pebbly mixture, wet and plain, spilling out, morsel by morsel, grain by grain, spreading like ordinary mud in front of everyone's eyes.

The next day, Duoc refused to follow Gurmit to the Administration Office for games. Duoc shook his head and ducked under the stilts of the Unaccompanied Minors longhouse, where he sat until Gurmit left.

Later, Miss Phu said, "What to do, Mr. Gurmit?" She looked down at the floor. At first Gurmit wasn't sure what she meant. He thought she might be referring to Reuben Gill, who, she reported, had stopped by her shelter, once in the morning and once yesterday evening, laden with small gifts: mango slices, a jar of sesame oil, even a bulging sack of long-stemmed rice. He stood outside her shelter door, trying to peek in, while his horrible monkey wrapped its hands around his ears, screeching at all the passersby. Anything I can do? Reuben kept asking. Anything at all? But Miss Phu stayed inside, keeping quiet until he put the gifts at her door and left.

Miss Phu snapped at Gurmit when he admitted his confusion. "What to do about *Duoc*, Mr. Gurmit," she said. "I talking about Duoc." Gurmit had no answer. He filled his pockets with butterscotch sweets and went to the Unaccompanied Minors longhouse again. He had the supervisor translate: "We can play cards, isn't it? We can draw the pictures. We can open and close the windows. We can sit in the chair with the darts."

"Duoc say," said the supervisor. "He want to see . . . I do not know how to say. The shining mud."

"So I will helping him see it," said Miss Phu severely, back in the Administration Office. She puckered her lips. All over Bidong, she said, people reported fantastical sights. Surely they could think of some way to make Duoc see glowing mud. Gurmit nodded enthusiastically. He ran to his desk drawers and pulled out a notebook full of his recent observations.

"I am writing how much illusion people are now seeing," he said, waving the notebook in front of her.

"I know how much illusion, Mr. Gurmit," she said. But for Gurmit, the recitation of others' foolishness was a source of contentment. He begged her indulgence and read aloud from the page.

People were seeing blood-red petals in the sunrise, he said. Small girls said bits of coral rose clung to the dock at night and shook themselves like dogs. Others saw the souls of ancestors hovering at the corners of their shelters. He said the beaches were reported to be shrinking, eaten away by the tide, and crowds gathered on the Zone C beach to watch the waves rock the wall of garbage as if the wall were a log. Every night you could hear the garbage tumble forward, soggy now as pudding, plopping its way up the beach. Every morning people scanned the horizon for Rangers, and every morning some panicked peasant boy would blow his palm-frond trumpet. There was illusion and foolishness everywhere, he said.

OK, OK, Miss Phu agreed.

But he continued. Task Force guards, he said, hardly ventured out of their compound. They sat on their barracks porch, waiting. Every once in a while one of the men would stand in the middle of the compound and fire off a round into the air, then walk back inside without a word. The white people were waiting, too. They sat on their bungalow porches, drinking, playing board games. Miss Sally had started holding hands with her female teachers, like a Vietnamese. Mr. Manley almost never went to school now. He wore a black T-shirt and black pants; he carried around thin paperbacks on military history and waved them in people's faces. And even when the rain came down hard, you could see him every day at noon, running down the beach one way, then the other, shouting, "Semper Fi! Semper Fi!" which Gurmit believed meant *Together*.

Yes, yes, yes, said Miss Phu wearily: she knew. So making one small boy see glowing mud was not impossible.

Every day Miss Phu went to the longhouse with a new jar of mud. For days she went, and for days she returned to tell Gurmit what had happened. One day she tapped the glass and said, "Yes, yes, I see. Don't you see it, too?" Duoc had screwed up his face and squinted at the jar. He held his fingers to his head, concentrating, and stared at the glass with a mean expression. He got creases on his forehead from looking so hard. He shook the jar with such abandon, his feet slipped out from under him and he began to swear.

Miss Phu bent down, hugging him, but the boy was wooden in her arms. She stroked Duoc's hair. When she was finished, Duoc simply sat on the floor.

But every day, whenever Miss Phu arrived, Duoc would look up and hold his hands out to receive the new jar. He turned the jars around and smelled them and scratched at the glass with his fingernails. He spit into them. He poked a stick into one and stirred the mud around. But still he couldn't see what Miss Phu claimed she saw. She tried every trick she could think of. She brought a 7-Up bottle and had Duoc look through the end. She had him shut his eyes for a long time so that he would see stars when he opened them. She jangled the key ring from Gurmit's office and had Duoc look at the jar in its reflection. She had the supervisor of the longhouse look at the jar with her. "Oooh," the man said, theatrically, "I can see it shine." But Duoc, pressing his nose against the glass, only shook his head.

"Miss Phu," Gurmit said in the office. He held his arms out in exasperation. "Please to stop now. This in not healthy up here, isn't it?" He tapped his head. "We must not let the fantasy control us. We must not allow—"

Miss Phu shook her new jar of mud in his face. She began singing then, swaying the jar back and forth in rhythm with her song, cupping one hand under the jar's bottom and slipping the fingers of her other hand around the rim. She sang loudly, caressing the jar. She looked deeply into the glass, singing with her lips so close to the jar that a patch of condensation began to cloud over the contents. When she was finished, she smiled at Gurmit. "Beautiful thinking OK, Mr. Gurmit," she said. "Fantasy thinking OK sometime, Mr. Gurmit." And then she walked down the Administration Office steps, off to see Duoc once again.

The next day, Miss Phu entered the office, wiping a filled jar with a sock. Her pants were rolled up to her knees; her legs were streaked with mud. She had been unsuccessful with Duoc that morning, she said, but she would try again in the afternoon. She sat down, wiping slowly, gingerly rubbing the rim of the jar. She seemed out of breath. She wiped a little more, then dropped the dirty sock onto the office floor. She closed her eyes.

"Sick?" Gurmit asked.

"Not sick," she said, straightening. "Confusing. In here." She pointed to her heart. Reuben Gill was the trouble, she said. He had stopped by her shelter last night and offered up Pirate. She hadn't understood what he was offering. So he dangled the beast from the leash. Pirate, he said: this is a pirate. A crowd of harsh-sounding boys gathered, laughing and taking wild swings at the choking animal.

"I saying, 'No thank you, Mr. Reuben,'" she said then, speaking loudly. There was anger in her voice. "No thank you, no thank you. No." She placed her jar on the desk. She was trembling. Reuben Gill had stood there a long time, she said, asking, "You sure? Sure?" swinging the shrieking animal like a pendulum.

She fell silent. She placed her arms firmly on the armrests of the chair and looked around, surveying. Everything was still in place. The boxes, the file cabinets, the folders, the desk: all where they should be, all purposeful, all newly dusted. She seemed to relax. The office was so quiet, so tidy. Outside, the rain wasn't letting up. There had been mist earlier, chilling everyone. Ragged streams raced down the gullies, and if the loudspeakers were to be believed, a shelter on the Zone F hill had collapsed during the night, swept into racing water. Earlier, there had been a scare: when the French delegation speed-boated to the dock, the noise of the engine frightened some girls into shouting that the Rangers had come.

Gurmit touched her arm with his fingers. Her skin was cold. He then squatted beside her, resting on one knee, and squeezed her hand. She smiled at him.

"Last night, I wanting to hit the Pirate," she said.

"Miss Phu . . ."

"But I do not," she said. "Is only the monkey, yes please?" She squeezed his hand, and in feeling the pressure returned, Gurmit allowed his eyes to roam over her face.

She slowly withdrew her fingers from his and bent at the waist, rolling her wet pants cuffs down over her shins. There was more to her story about Reuben Gill. Early that morning, she said, the American had stopped by her door, carrying a large washing basin. She brushed at her wet pants, then held her arms out, demonstrating the size of the gift. "Very nice," she said to Gurmit. The basin had been mother of pearl, with blue trim. It looked new. She said she thanked Reuben Gill politely, but refused to take anything he offered.

"But Miss Phu," said Gurmit softly. "Is only a basin. Very useful, I think. He is only wanting to help, isn't it?"

"Not taking from him," said Miss Phu, pressing her lips together.

"Nothing?"

"Nothing, Mr. Gurmit. Because one time . . ." She looked away. "I thinking one time that he is like the demon."

"Oh, Miss Phu." Gurmit rose from his chair. "Please do not say. Miss Phu. Please do not allowing the fantasy up here." He pressed his hands to the sides of his skull. "Is illusion. Is like dreaming. Not good. So dangerous."

She shrugged. She cast a lingering look around the office, then stood. Reaching into the bowl on the desk, she stuffed a handful of peppermint candies into her pocket and, saying good-bye, walked out the door, out to Duoc, holding the jar of mud against her breasts.

But later in the day, Gurmit heard her singing outside. He heard her click the gate latch open, and he heard her saying something in Vietnamese. She swung the office door open. Her hair was wet, and her clothes were dirty, but she was beaming. Behind her was Duoc. The boy was holding a jar of mud tightly in his hand, wiping his nose against the glass. He was creamy with mud; even his shaved head was spattered.

She held a finger up to her lips. "He cannot see the mud glowing. But that OK. Is OK today, I think." She patted the boy's filthy shoulder. "He agreeing to come with me today. Back here." Duoc was wiping his flip-flops on the floor. When he finished, he placed his jar in the corner and folded his arms.

"By morsels and grains, Miss Phu," Gurmit said happily. "That is how we—"

"Oh, Mr. Gurmit," she laughed. "All the time you are saying this. But look how dirty is the boy now. Too many morsels. Too many grains. He must bathing, yes?"

"The bathing wells are very crowded now," said Gurmit. "Maybe tomorrow, hey?"

"Mr. Gurmit," said Miss Phu. She touched Gurmit's arm. "We can go to white people compound. They having a pump."

The UN compound. He hadn't set foot in the place for weeks. It seemed so unwelcoming, what with Ralph and Sally and Johann sitting on their porches all the time, staring at him, whispering.

"No crowd there," Miss Phu said. "They all working now. You can letting us inside."

Miss Phu seemed so happy, it was impossible to refuse her.

Minutes later they all walked down the Administration Office steps and out the gate, headed for the washing-up shed in the UN compound. Gurmit's pants were rolled up to his knees; he carried a large red plastic tub over his head. The mud was soupy from all the rain. Duoc, sloshing, leaped from spot to spot, splattering Miss Phu, who carried a large white towel in one hand and a brush and blue Chinese soap in the other.

Miss Phu was right: the relief workers were all someplace else. Gurmit opened the gate, struggling a moment with the latch, and, waving to a Task Force guard, led Miss Phu and Duoc to the washing-up shed. They walked up the stairs and past the sink basins, then through a latched door in the back of the shed, which opened up to a large concrete pad surrounded by sheets of corrugated tin. There was a chipped red pump in the corner and a clothesline overhead, on which hung someone's forgotten laundry.

Gurmit rolled up his sleeves. He began working the squeaking pump handle, slowly filling the tub with water, while Miss Phu, pausing to drape the towel on the clothesline, bent down beside him and swirled her hand around in the foam. Duoc, prodded by Miss Phu, stepped into the tub and crouched. He tensed his muscles; he stood once to get out of the tub, but Gurmit pressed him down, back into the water, and then Miss Phu began talking into his ear, telling him over and over how new he would feel after a bath.

"Wait," Gurmit said. "Are you hearing?"

Miss Phu lowered her voice. She shook her head and began talking to Duoc again.

There was a creaking sound, like a door being opened, and Gurmit stared at a dark open window of the washing-up shed. Nothing. Miss Phu splashed water on the crouching boy's head and began rubbing the blue bar against his scalp. Gurmit began scrubbing with his fingers. He soaped up Duoc's nubby hair, and Miss Phu gripped the brush firmly and scoured the boy's back. Gurmit, pumping with one hand, rubbed soapy water over Duoc's thigh and calf, then rubbed between the boy's toes with his bare fingers. Miss Phu started singing. She guided Duoc's fingers up to his ears and had him clean the ridges in time with her song. "Wait," said Gurmit, holding up his hand. "Someone is in there, isn't it?" But no sound came from the washing-up shed, so Gurmit cupped his hands, filling them with pump water. The boy stood, and as he did, Gurmit let the water run down from his fingers and over the boy's head, rinsing away the soapy film, streaming down to his underpants, then coursing down his legs and into the bubbly tub.

"Miss Phu," said Gurmit, "turn your back please." Miss Phu did, and then Gurmit pulled the boy's wet underwear all the way down to his feet. Duoc, lathering his hands, soaped his knees, then his thigh, then his tiny sac and penis; foam gathered into a beard and dripped from his anus. Gurmit, grabbing first one of Duoc's ankles, then the other, lifted the boy's feet one by one and slipped the gray underwear off. The fabric was so thin that he felt one of his fingers tearing through, so he laid the underwear against the side of the tub and scrubbed the cloth with his knuckles. Duoc, crouching again, rubbed the bar on his shoulders and arms; he rubbed so hard a scab tore off, and then Gurmit, dunking the underwear into the water, pressed his own finger into the raw patch until Duoc stopped wincing. The tub was overflowing now; the water was frothy and black, and clear bubbles flowed in a line down the cement all the way to the privacy wall, where they disappeared under the tin.

"There," said Gurmit, sliding the towel off the line. He thought he heard rustling from inside the shed, but he didn't look: Miss Phu was growing impatient. "Turn now? Turn now?" she kept asking.

"Almost," said Gurmit. His safari suit was soaked; he draped the towel like a curtain around Duoc's shoulders.

"Please turn," Gurmit said, and she did. Her blouse was dark with water; Gurmit could see the cup of her brassiere rimming the fabric. So beautiful, he thought. He began brushing his jacket, wiping away moisture, to keep his hands occupied.

Miss Phu smiled at him. "Very good," she said, plucking Duoc's underwear from the tub.

Duoc, sneezing once, dried himself. He wrapped the towel around his waist and took the underwear from Miss Phu's hand, slipping first one leg, then the other, into the crotch holes.

Gurmit said, "If only the mud can be made to glow with such easiness."

"Tomorrow," said Miss Phu, looking over at Duoc. "I try again." The boy was still rubbing vigorously, slapping the soles of his feet against the cement.

There was thumping from inside the shed: footsteps. The door swung open. "You want," said a voice, "I can help you do that." And then Reuben Gill appeared in the doorway, holding a toothbrush in his mouth. "You're talking about that mud in a jar, aren't you?" His toothbrush wiggled up and down as he spoke. "I been keeping tabs. I can help you do that."

All you could hear for a moment was Duoc's towel rubbing against his body. Then the boy began speaking excitedly in Vietnamese. Miss Phu started talking to the boy, turning her head away from the shed. She grabbed hold of the towel and began drying Duoc's ears.

"You hear me?" said Reuben, leaning against the door frame.

Gurmit nodded at Reuben. "Miss Phu . . . ," Gurmit said, holding out his hands. She was carrying on a rapid conversation with Duoc. "You are hearing?"

Miss Phu rubbed the towel against Duoc's neck. "Duoc say the Biting Tree can do many things," she said.

"You are hearing what Mr. Reuben says?" said Gurmit.

Miss Phu began rubbing Duoc's back. She rubbed so hard, Duoc stumbled forward. "Duoc say the Biting Tree like a spirit," she said.

Gurmit said, "Are you saying yes, Miss Phu?"

"Duoc say the Biting Tree have magic," she said.

"Miss Phu."

"This boy very crazy."

"Miss Phu!"

She looked Duoc straight in the eyes and rubbed his shoulders fiercely. She was squeezing; her fingers pressed so hard into the towel that Duoc drew his arms together and stepped back. Then she let go. The towel almost dropped from her hands. She looked at Gurmit. "Mr. Gurmit," she said quickly. "You telling Mr. Reuben OK. If he can do, OK. OK. Mr. Gurmit, you telling him."

She clamped her jaw shut then. She rubbed with the towel for a long time. She rubbed Duoc's stomach, his arms, his legs, and between each toe. Duoc stood silently, staring at Reuben. When Reuben, conferring with Gurmit, turned to leave, Duoc started talking quickly to Miss Phu. He kept on talking no matter what Miss Phu said, and he wouldn't be quiet until Gurmit walked them out of the UN compound and onto the footpath.

When Reuben tried to tell Porkpie about their plan that night—she allowed him onto her porch and directed him coldly to sit—she held up her hand and stopped him mid-sentence. "You talked to Miss Phu?" she said, alarm in her voice. "I better not hear you did something beastly. I won't put up with your infantilism any more." She spoke forcefully and smoothly; she made no attempt to hide the fact that she had been practicing for such a conversation. "Because that's what it is. Profound infantilism."

"Let me finish," he said, rising.

"Sit," she ordered. He wouldn't. "OK," she said. "Don't sit. Infantilism. You want to remain outside social convention. It's a conscious choice, fine. It's so typical. You think you're exposing the tyranny behind proper causes and generous opinions, don't you? You think the only way to save yourself from making pacts with liars is to fight everyone every inch of the way, don't you? You don't know how to draw back and examine your actions."

"If you're done," he said, running his hand through his hair, "I've come to give you a chance—"

"I'm not done. And how dare you say you're going to give me a chance."

He sat down, thrusting up his arms in irritation. He said he meant a chance to do something for Miss Phu. She leaned against the porch. She closed her eyes. Then she opened them. "OK," she said. "Talk."

The next morning the five of them climbed the Zone F hill in a wavery line, Gurmit leading, followed by Miss Phu and Duoc, who carried a full jar of mud, holding it out from his body as if it were a candle. Then came Porkpie, dabbing off mud with a tissue every few moments. Reuben, wearing his waders, brought up the rear. On his head was a large, sloshing tub of seawater, which he balanced by clasping the side handles tightly. The tub was covered with layers of tarp lashed with ropes, so that when Reuben slipped in the mud, tipping the tub one way or the other, only a few drops of seawater escaped. The five walked slowly, stumbling on tree roots, sliding into narrow, naked rain gullies. Reuben began swearing. He fell twice, but each time he landed on his knees and struggled up, losing only a few drops. Gurmit wore his white safari suit; his pants were rolled to his knees. Miss Phu, too, had her black pants rolled to her knees, but she wore a pretty pink blouse that she said she had been saving for a special occasion. Duoc, steady in flip-flops, kept wiping his hands on his freshly laundered underwear, and when Porkpie offered him a tissue, he looked at it blankly and tucked part of it into his elastic band, letting it flap at his side like a wing.

Except for Reuben, they were silent as they walked, nodding in quiet greeting to all the people who stood in the open shelters off the trail. Past a snaking water pipe, they had to duck their heads to walk under a clothesline that had been decorated with cardboard letters for Christmas and Tet. Duoc stopped for a moment in front of one shelter, staring at a man constructing a dragon's head from cans of peas, but Miss Phu hurried the boy along by clucking her tongue. It was drizzling. They climbed and climbed, and then, near the crest of the hill, Gurmit turned around and slid down the pathway to help Reuben carry the tub of seawater. Reuben, breathing hard, almost dropped his end, but Gurmit acted quickly and stood underneath the tub, collapsing to his knees, and held the weight until Reuben regained his balance.

They crested the hill. They all wiped mud from their hands with a cloth that Gurmit pulled from his safari jacket. Between loudspeaker announcements, they heard the sounds of chanting coming from the Zone F primary school. "Mrs. Lai teaching now," said Miss Phu. She excused herself and walked across the mud flat to say hello. "Can I go with you?" asked Porkpie. Miss Phu nodded, and while the two women ducked into the school, Reuben and Gurmit dragged the heavy tub to the cement pad of the plank monument, where they untied the ropes. They rested then. Duoc placed the jar of mud next to the tub and squatted. Reuben pulled out a Thai cigar and put it in his mouth, snapping his fingers at Gurmit—"Light? Light?"—who stared at the plank and stroked his hand up and down the grain of the wood.

Gurmit handed Reuben a matchbook. He turned. "OK," Gurmit said. "Here comes Miss Phu and Miss Porkpie." Reuben turned too, then. Porkpie stood behind Miss Phu. He waved, but Porkpie remained by the door. "I'm taking a back seat to this," she said. "I'll just watch."

"Duoc," said Gurmit, placing his hands on the boy's shoulders. Duoc rose. Together, they walked around the monument, front and back. Gurmit hoisted Duoc up, lifting the boy by his torso, high enough for Duoc to run his fingers along his uncle's name and feel the shape of the letters. Nguyen Van Trinh. Duoc traced the name, working his fingers into the gouges, following the trail of each letter, each swirl, each corner and end, and then he let out a small cry. He stuck his fingers into his mouth, as if to cool them down. Gurmit let him down. He reached up and touched the name. Those words. Nguyen Van Trinh. They were warm.

"Let's get going," Reuben said. He threw his cigar into the mud.

"Can start," said Miss Phu.

Gurmit stepped back and stood next to the tub of seawater. Reuben stripped off his T-shirt. He then grabbed the jar of mud and dipped it into the tub, turning the seawater pebbly and dark. Duoc leaped up, alarmed, but Miss Phu put her hand on his shoulder, forcing him down, speaking softly into his ear. Reuben placed his hand over the top of the jar and shook the mud and water hard, and as he shook, he roared like a lion, looking up into the sky. He started speaking. He shouted, "Hocus pocus, shinola on locust," and then he gave the jar to

Gurmit, who, clasping the glass around the bottom, opened his mouth, then closed his mouth. Gurmit shrugged. He opened his mouth again, but he was having trouble speaking.

"Say it," Reuben said. "You got to say it."

"Please no morsel and grain, Mr. Gurmit," said Miss Phu.

Gurmit held the jar out in front of him. He closed his eyes, and then he shouted: "Bloody hell, bloody hell, upon this jar I cast my spell." Reuben roared some more, thrusting his arms straight up and waggling his fingers. He reached out for the jar. Both men held the jar tightly in their hands, Gurmit by the bottom, Reuben by the top. They turned around, shielding the object from Duoc's sight, and shook the jar hard. Dark foam began trickling out between Reuben's fingers. They shook the jar so long that Gurmit's arm began to tremble. Then they stopped. They turned around, facing Duoc, holding the jar out between them. The mud and the seawater was still swirling, and then Miss Phu said to Duoc, "Go look, go look," and when he did, he started to cheer because the mud was glowing now, it was swirling fast, and it was glowing in a faint green light, alive with phosphorescent sea algae. Duoc was talking. He had goose bumps on his arms, and he grabbed Miss Phu's hand and made her look, too, and then she began to cheer as well because the mud was alive with phosphorescent sea algae and glowing for Duoc. Reuben pulled a Malaysian coin from his ear and tossed it high in the air. Duoc was so excited, he started to hiccup and point at the jar that Reuben and Gurmit held between them. Porkpie, walking slowly now across the mud flat, began clapping as she walked.

"Thank you, Mr. Reuben," Miss Phu whispered.

Reuben smiled at her. Words bubbled on his lips, but the sea algae had already started to fade, so he bowed slightly, then turned his back and started shaking the jar again. He shook hard enough to make the algae glow a bit more. Boys along the outcrop began to blow their palm-frond trumpets; some men came running up the crest of the hill.

"They are seeing," said Gurmit, smiling at the running figures. "Everyone is seeing now." He handed the jar to Duoc, then he waved to Porkpie, who, drawing closer, raised her hands over her head and began to clap.

It was a hypnotizing sight, watching Duoc peer into the jar, examining the faintly glowing dots. The rain had picked up, and each time a drop stuck the jar, Duoc wiped away the moisture with his thumb. He held the jar against his cheek for a moment. Slowly, bending to one knee, he placed the fading jar against the base of the plank. People were running by, racing along the perimeter of the mud flat to the outcrop, but Duoc, nodding slightly, ignored them all. Nobody at the plank moved. Duoc rose; he stepped away from the plank, not even turning his head when one of the running man began yelling. Reuben sat hunkered over the tub, quietly stirring the remains. Miss Phu was humming. Gurmit stood on the concrete, staring at the name carved into the wood. They stayed still a long time. They weren't sure how long. They knew only that, for a moment, everything was still. For a moment, no one looked at the people running toward the outcrop, no one leaped when a boy ran up to the plank and made a bleating sound with a palm-frond trumpet.

"Rangers coming," people said. Mane of spray, swarm of bees: on the horizon, rooster tails were shooting high into the air.

Rangers coming.

"Too soon," Gurmit said. "Cannot."

Gurmit felt water leak into his ears. He couldn't hear a thing then. It was a helpless feeling, not being able to hear. He shook his head, but he couldn't make the water go away. The water was cold. It was very cold and very blue, and it was leaking deeper and deeper into his head and it wouldn't stop.

21

Reuben didn't wait for the others. He ran down the Zone F hill, slapping away drooping fronds, his footsteps wide and deep on the muddy trail. He couldn't get a clear view of the ocean. Every few steps the side of the hill would open up, exposing the horizon, and then the picture would turn dark and jumbled, blocked by another tree or bush or blue-tarp shelter. He saw flat, watery patches. Then clouded, blue ones. Then some white with spray, others tassled with foliage. Where were the boats? How many? A rooster tail of spray shot up. Think clear, he ordered. Between the trees: two white plumes. Put the puzzle together. Stumbling, he saw the flash of a hull.

He got the willies then. Children were wandering up and down the trail, crying. A woman stood by a tree, bouncing a plastic pail against her forehead. A mantra: You can't come, you can't come. Put the puzzle together. There were three rooster tails. Three boats. But that made no sense. If the Rangers were going to secure the island, they'd need more than three boatloads. And what had Gurmit said? Too soon? Yes. Year Five was still days away. Nothing could happen before then. Everyone knew it.

Yet the ocean was buzzing. He could hear the engines whine.

He got the willies so bad, he tripped and fell, skidding into the post of a woman's shelter. The woman looked at him hard. She looked at his white skin and his muscles and his tremendous size. She folded her arms, and under her gaze he felt the air turn hot.

"Rangers coming," she said.

In her voice was accusation. Blood rushed to Reuben's face, and on his tongue was the taste of something sharp and bitter, as if a blade were scraping up through his windpipe. He lay in the mud a moment, smelling earth. He got up very slowly. Mud dripped from his arms. He nodded gravely at the woman, and she nodded gravely back.

Rangers coming.

He understood. Whether the puzzle made any sense didn't matter. There was something coming, right now, something terrible screaming toward the island, and if the muddy shape that rose to his feet was the Biting Tree, then he could not tremble with the willies. So he didn't. He stuck his arm in his mouth and sucked on the mud, just to feel the ooze on his tongue. He smacked his fist into his palm. And then he was running again, leaping down the hill, striding the gullies and shelter pegs. He plowed through a clothesline. He twisted his ankle, but he just swore at the top of his lungs and kept on running until he came to the bottom of the hill and ran all the way to Zone C, where he stopped to wipe mud from his shirt and catch his breath. People were jogging in from the tree line, standing so close together that they held on to each other's shoulders. A crowd had gathered around the dock, and, to his right, Reuben saw Task Force guards file by in ones and twos, some still buttoning their shirts and hitching up their sarongs. Patrolling the dock steps, a couple of pill house guards banged their truncheons against the planks, warning the crowd to stay clear of the steps. The shoreline was white with splashing and foam, thick with people pushed from behind into the waves.

One look was all he needed. Three boats skirted the coral. Only three. He had seen others like them before: wide-bottomed fiberglass speedboats with enormous engines in the back; on the prow, a mounted swivel gun. They rode low in the water, and in the spray he could see the outline of the passengers, bristling with antennas and weapons. The boats rounded a finger of land jutting out from Zone F, then seemed to change direction. They veered away from the inlet to Zone C, away from the dock, then slowed to a bubbling whine. A short man in a baseball hat caught Reuben's eye and shouted out to the crowd: "Cai Cay Bi Can. Cai Cay Bi Can." The Biting Tree. People turned. They shouted out questions in Vietnamese. "There's only three," Reuben shouted. "They'd need more. I'm sure. Positive." Nobody could understand.

The boats hovered, rocking in the waves, and then a man in the lead boat leaned over the railing and shouted something through a bullhorn. A flare shot up from the second boat, a fizzing, green ball, and even before the flare began its descent, the lead boat lurched toward the dock, gunning its engine. The two other boats bobbed in the rough water awhile, then began moving in slow, wide circles, taxiing a few hundreds yards out from the inlet.

"They're coming one at a time," said Manley, nudging Reuben from behind. "I told you those assholes can't do beach assault. That's pussy style, what they're doing."

Reuben grunted.

"But they're coming," said Manley. "Oh shit." He ran his hand through his hair. "Oh shit."

Near the dock, the lead boat cut its engines. There were so many people on the beach, no one could move forward or backward. People leaned into each other, whispering and staring. Even from far away, you could see that the deck of the lead boat was jammed with Rangers, sitting in three neat rows. They wore camouflage fatigues and wide, floppy jungle hats. Their boots were covered with webbing, and strapped to their back were bulky packs that dangled canteens and small tools secured with canvas straps.

The vessel was secured to a piling with two tie ropes. On the dock, the Task Force contingent milled around nervously, their movements jerky and rapid. Ahmed, patrolling the receiving area, walked in and out of tight circles of his men, patting their shoulders, then snapped his fingers at some Vietnamese security guards wearing special white bracelets around their wrists. The Viets nodded. They ran in a group toward the boat, squatting over the water to receive the packs and boxes being hefted out of the boats by the Rangers. Someone raced from the pill house with a portable ladder, and then the line of Viet security, shoving packs against the pilings, parted to either side. The Rangers began filing off. They set foot on Bidong one by one, very slowly, checking their footing on the ladder rungs, sometimes pausing halfway up while their companions adjusted their packs or shoved items into the knotted pockets.

The second boat began its approach. Ahmed was shaking hands with one of the Rangers, who threw down his heavy pack and began rummaging through its contents. The crowd was so quiet that Reuben heard individual sounds: the loudspeaker crackling with the Welcome

Song; the waves folding onto the beach, thumping against the wall of garbage; Task Force men banging on the dock steps; the occasional protesting voice, exploding in the air like a rocket, then falling silent.

The first boat, emptied now of its passengers and cargo, pulled into reverse, spraying white water out the back, and the second boat began a slow glide to the dock. Reuben had imagined the scene differently: he had pictured loud voices, screams perhaps, footfalls squishing rapidly in the mud, a gunshot here or there. He had pictured time compressed into vivid, movielike scenes—Rangers fanning out, the snouts of their guns twitching in people's faces; mothers clutching babies; men on their knees, clasping their hands together. It was as if, in imagining, he had already witnessed the arrival of annihilation. In imagining, his heart had raced, his fists had crashed against his door frame. And in looking around, scanning the faces, he had the sense that everyone had already pictured the arrival of the Rangers, that everyone had already seen the scene unfold dramatically, violently, in their heads.

Annihilation: the notion seemed absurd, despite the continued bleating of palm-frond trumpets, despite the steady crash of waves against the beaches, despite the cold drizzle that was running down people's faces and wetting their shirts and blouses. The Rangers were taking their time. Nobody was panicking. Some people in the crowd started jumping up and down, as if at a sporting event, trying to get a better view. Some were even carrying on joking conversations, hee-hawing, revealing lousy teeth. There was something calming about the leisurely pace of the arrival, something soporific, as if a gas were drifting through the crowd, a clear, odorless gas swirling up the dock steps and into the lungs of the Rangers checking their weapons and forming themselves into threes. There was a sense of floating, of being lifted by imperceptible degrees. All of them: Viet, white, and Malaysian, all rising together, weightless and numb.

"Not enough Rangers," Reuben shouted then. "It's OK. It's OK."

People translated. His words traveled through the crowd. A man near the back, smiling now, withdrew some Malaysian coins and gave them to a boy. "7-Up," the man said, and the boy looked at the money and, closing his hands around it, jangled the coins, walking back through the crowd toward the black market tables.

"Hey," said Manley. He grinned. "That's right, Big Bro. There's not enough of them assholes. Hey. All right."

The third boat approached. On the dock, the Task Force guards grew more animated. Some began smoking. One of the guards turned on a cassette player, idly tying a length of wire around the handle, and nodded to the music. Others approached the Rangers timidly, leaning forward and carrying on small conversations. The Rangers ignored them. They talked among themselves, stacking boxes, shaking their legs and stretching. One of them lost his hat, which flew into the water, and some boys splashed over to the object and tossed it back to the squatting soldier. From the beach, everyone saw the Ranger smile in thanks.

"Is OK," people said. "OK. OK."

"There you are," said Porkpie.

Reuben turned. She was approaching from behind, nudging through with her forearms. Gurmit trailed behind her, wiping leaves and twigs from his jacket sleeve. Farther back, squatting by a tree, was Miss Phu, behind Duoc.

On the dock, a man in dress uniform and sunglasses climbed the ladder and walked half the length of the dock. He carried a walking stick. He then turned and shouted something, which caused the soldiers to look up from their packs and buddy up, unstrapping flaps in each other's packs, cinching things. The men shifted some, turning their heads, tightening the line, and then they began marching by twos off the dock, even while the third boat was unloading. They marched in a snaking line, small bristling figures weighted with bloated rucksacks. They marched quickly, past the pill house, then down the dock steps. The crowd rippled like an accordion. A murmer went up. People in back peeled away and began to run toward the tree line.

"Is it OK?" asked Porkpie, straining to see over people's heads.

"Is OK, I think," said Gurmit.

"There's not enough Rangers," said Reuben. "There'd have to be more to sweep the place."

"Reuben, what can you see?" Porkpie asked.

"He said it's OK," said Manley.

"Is OK," said Gurmit.

"Biting Tree," a man said, jogging past. The man didn't finish his sentence: his face went blank and he jogged away, toward the tree line. All around, people were squishing mud, clearing the beach. Someone tripped over a log, swearing, and then a crackle coursed down the beach: a military radio, blaring static. The line of Rangers drew near.

First came the officer with the walking stick and sunglasses, then the soldiers bent under their black-barreled rifles and jiggling field packs. Their sleeves were rolled high, and their arms swelled under the weight of their packs. You could smell the seawater on their boots. Nobody in the crowd said a word. People looked down at the mud as if unsure of their footing, as if the ground were bulging, lifting them to places they did not wish to go. The Rangers marched at a furious pace, clacking with each step, and though their faces were soft and round, they breathed heavily, straining with exertion, and when one of them stumbled, falling to one knee, he glared at the crowd with such fierce irritation that people looked away.

"Bloody hell," Gurmit whispered. He pointed.

"My gosh," said Porkpie. "Reuben. Look. Walking with Ahmed."

"Hey," said Manley. "Bringing up the rear. It's him."

"You," Reuben shouted.

At the end of the line was Doctor Johansson, adjusting a plastic-coated ID tag clipped to his shirt pocket. His pants were wet with spray; his windblown hair gave him an air of distraction. He waved, then tapped Ahmed on the shoulder and jogged over. Ahmed brought a few guards with him, men tapping truncheons onto their palms.

Doctor Johansson's washcloth tongue came out, then slipped back in. The doctor said, "Now stay calm. The Rangers are just here for a safety precaution. That's all. Things are happening tomorrow."

"What's happening tomorrow?" asked Porkpie.

"Christ," the doctor said. "Look at you people."

"She asked you a question," said Reuben.

The doctor's face clouded over. "Reuben Gill. You too, Porkpie. And you, Gurmit." He made shooing motions in Manley's direction. "Not you, Manley. These three only." The rain made the doctor's skin look raw.

"Hey," said Manley, but he stepped aside.

A Ranger carrying a mortar tube walked past. Two more went by, balancing a wooden crate on their shoulders. There was shouting coming from the tree line.

"The paperwork doesn't clear till tomorrow," the doctor said angrily. "So I don't want any nonsense from you three. I don't want a repeat of that fight over the bullhorn. And no damn monkey." The doctor took a step backward and looped his fingers into Ahmed's shoulder epaulet.

His eyes were a series of tics. "Now listen," he said, blinking. "Your contracts have been terminated. As of tomorrow, you three are off the island."

The calming gas that just minutes ago had seemed to envelop everyone now sparked with current, jerking hands against shoulders, pressing fingers to flesh, stirring the mud. People rushed forward, flip-flops tucked safely under their armpits, following the line of Rangers. The doctor fell to one knee, dirtying his pants, and one of the guards, excited by all the movement, brought his truncheon up and yelled, "Ahhh," but Reuben pulled back and held out his hands in a display of contrition. The crowd swept through then, all arms and legs and black running shorts. The doctor went one way, holding tightly on to Ahmed's shirt. Reuben went the other way, quietly surrendering to the fingers and hands pressing against his body. He did not resist. He floated from Porkpie and Gurmit and Manley, grateful to be drifting, lost among faces that would not turn and ask him if he had lunged at the doctor. Certainly he had wanted to lunge at the doctor. His muscles had tightened. His torso had bent. Even his organs seemed to clench; he had felt them ticking against his spine. But even as he felt himself lunge, he had felt himself stop, planting a foot in the mud. Reuben Gill could lunge. The Biting Tree could not. The Biting Tree had responsibilities. He could not do what Reuben Gill wanted to do, because if he did, if he let his fists strike the doctor, then the Task Force guards would pummel him with truncheons, and all his power would be lost, right there, right then, exiled to a locked bungalow or to the Task Force chicken coop or perhaps even thrown aboard one of the idling speedboats.

"*Cai Cay Bi Can,*" people shouted, grabbing his hands.

"Reuben," yelled Manley from a distance. "Hey. Big Bro."

The crowd moved forward in small waves, rippling one way, then another, surging around trees and dipping into troughs. People pushed after the Rangers, following their bootprints, and then young men started to shout because the crowd was growing too big, swollen with people jamming the footpaths. No one could see their feet; no one could stop. Someone passed an infant overhead, from hand to hand, out of the crowd and into a woman's outstretched arms. On the beach people were fleeing, laying their hands on the shoulders of stragglers, pressing against the wall of people. Only a thin line of Task Force guards kept the crowd from pressing into the Rangers. The guards trailed the Rangers, holding on to the canteens dangling from the packs and swinging their truncheons to keep the Vietnamese back. But nobody could stop. People kept streaming in from the beach, running now, emptying the strip of land that was now littered with sandals and cigarettes and bits of gray soppy garbage, stepping high, slipping sometimes in the trampled mud that was dark and filling with water and riddled with holes like the surface of the moon.

Reuben, though, floated the other way, away from the crowd that followed the line of Rangers, caught in a smaller crowd that streamed along the Zone C beach, staggering along the wall of garbage and past the wire fence of the UN compound. "Bloody hell," he heard from behind. He looked, but all he saw were Vietnamese faces tight with strain. He shoved his way to the edge of the crowd and grabbed a fence post. He opened the latch and let himself in, then closed the gate and watched the crowd rush past, and then he walked to his bungalow, where Pirate, chained to the doorknob, cowered at his approach. Reuben left the door open, letting the sounds wash over him. The loudspeakers were blaring now, urging calm; the crowd outside the gate thinned; in the distance, a low murmur, occasional shouts.

Reuben picked up his bunk. He held the bunk by the frame and heaved it crashing against the wall, metal and mattress, spilling everything, because that's what he knew had to happen, that's what he knew he would have to do, if only he could get it done before Doctor Johansson hustled him onto a boat in the morning and the ocean roared in.

"Bloody hell-*lah*," he heard again.

Gurmit was standing in the doorway, breathing hard. The left sleeve of his jacket hung by the shoulder seams, dangling thread.

"You are not hearing my voice? All this way I have been shouting."

"You got something to say?"

Gurmit picked his way over the metal frame. He opened his jacket and pulled out an envelope. "Termination papers," he said sharply, waving the envelope under Reuben's nose. "The doctor is giving."

Reuben nodded.

"Miss Porkpie is very upset-*lah*. She is not wishing to speak to anyone."

"That all you got to say?"

"No," said Gurmit, nudging a pillow out of the way. "I am saying Doctor Johansson is calling a staff meeting in three hours' time."

"That it?"

"That is not it."

Reuben waited.

Gurmit hissed: "I am saying bloody hell."

"Yeah?"

"Yes."

Reuben picked up the mattress then and, grunting, dragged it out the door and heaved it down the porch steps. Pirate began shrieking. Reuben motioned to Gurmit, who then pulled one of the metal bed slats from its socket and tossed it like a javelin through the open door, narrowly missing Reuben's head. Reuben, moving quickly, bounded inside and swept the cups and blueprint tubes from his desk, while Gurmit carried the rest of the bed frame to the door and sent it tumbling off the porch. They threw everything out: magazines, pillows, a chair, sheets, travel bags, the desk, plastic sandals, pens, laundry, baskets, mosquito coils, rat traps, old newspapers. The room was blank and bare. Gurmit, sweating, removed his safari jacket and tossed it to the empty floor. Reuben wiped mud from his face. "Bloody hell then," Reuben said. Gurmit was nodding, even as the shouting started up again somewhere outside. Yes, he said, answering Reuben's question, he still had access to the shortwave. Yes, he still had friends at the Red Crescent office in Kuala Trengganu. Oh yes, those friends would get a message to Reuben's friend. Bloody hell, yes, they would.

Early in the afternoon the rain stopped, and the Rangers began setting up their tents along the Zone D beach, driving the stakes in so far that they ruptured a buried water pipe and had to spend an hour making repairs, which delayed the two corporals assigned to Zone F from carrying out their task. People were already filing into Sally's bungalow, where Doctor Johansson was going to talk. At the other end of the compound, Reuben and Manley leaned against the wire, watching the Rangers shoulder a chainsaw up the Zone F hill.

"You got a plan?" said Manley.

"No."

Manley looked at Reuben out of the corner of his eye. "You lie," he said.

"Drop it."

"So what's the plan?"

"We get on the boat tomorrow and leave."

"Hey, bullshit." Manley drew a circle in the mud with his foot. "I know a guy in Zone D," he said. "Fucker knows mortars. He'll fight." He clenched his fist.

"Stop it with that talk."

"You throw all your stuff out and you tell me you're not planning nothing." Manley gestured to the debris in front of Reuben's bungalow porch.

"Fresh start."

"We can't just do *nothing*."

"Don't involve the Viets," said Reuben.

"Guy up in Zone B was Saigon police. If we get a weapon, he can use it."

"Don't you get it, Manley? Viets fight, they lose. End of story."

"You don't trust me."

Reuben jiggled the wire strands. The two Rangers were halfway up the hill.

"Hey," said Manley.

"Just drop it."

"We gotta do something."

"Don't involve the Viets."

"Guy I know can break the lock on the pill house."

"Damn it, Manley. Keep the Viets out of this."

"Hey," said Manley. He picked at his lip and let his long hair drop over his eyes. "Hey. I know some Viets who *want* to fight."

"Manley, no Viets. Don't you get it? The Viets try something, you think the Rangers are going to hold back? They're licking their chops, Manley. It's only the Viets that are going to get hurt. One of them gets killed, who cares? It's just a *gook*."

"Don't say *gook*."

"*Gook*. Meat. Garbage. I'm trying to make you see, Manley. Rangers'll pick him up and cart him away. Nothing'll change. It's just waste."

From across the compound, Sally called for everyone to file into her bungalow to hear the doctor speak.

Manley squatted, placing his hands over his head. He started moaning.

"Don't stir anyone up," said Reuben. "I mean it."

Manley was rocking, swaying his head as if it were on a swing. "Got to do something," he said softly. He wouldn't shut up. "Got to do something. Got to do something."

Reuben squatted next to him. He put his hand on Manley's shoulder.

"I got to make amends," Manley said, looking at the ground.

"You got to think clear, Manley."

"I got to make amends."

"There's no time for this."

"Got to *do* something."

Reuben pressed his lips close to Manley's ear. "What you got to do," he whispered, "is think clear. This isn't about you. You start stirring things up, Manley, I'll turn on you. I swear I will. You hear?"

Reuben pulled away. *Reuben*, Sally was yelling. *Manley. We're starting.* "Come on," Reuben said, kicking at a box of mosquito coils that had blown over from his bungalow porch. Manley, his back turned, held up an arm and waved for Reuben to go on without him. "Manley," Reuben said, tramping. "I'm sorry. That's just the way it is." But Manley wasn't budging. He stayed squatting along the wire, rocking.

There was a Ranger milling around Sally's steps. When Reuben approached, the man looked up at Sally, nodding in the doorway, then whistled through his teeth, signaling "stop."

"Reuben," said Sally. She leaned over the railing. "Please. Listen to me. Doctor Johansson doesn't want trouble. He'd like you to hear what he has to say, but he wants you to keep your distance." She glanced at the Ranger tapping his rifle butt against his boot. "Insurance," she whispered.

"Cannot go in," said the Ranger.

"No trouble," said Reuben, holding up his hands. "I'll just stand by the door." He walked up the steps. "Nice as pie."

He leaned against the door frame, peering in. Gurmit caught his eye and winked: the message had gone through. There must have been twenty people in the small room, relief workers and staffers from various Kuala Trengganu offices who arrived with the doctor. Cigarette smoke mingled with mud and sweat, drifting toward the door in a sweet cloud. Sally snuggled next to Ralph. Johann had on his light green hospital vest, spattered with dark dots that could have been blood. The Swedes were there, too, sitting in a foursome on Sally's bunk; two of them smoked. They wore shorts, and the hairs on their legs were silky and blond.

Sitting behind Sally's writing desk was the doctor, glancing at his watch. He was jittery, pumping his leg up and down, and he kept sweeping the bare desk with his hand.

"Are we ready?" he asked.

"Ready," said Sally.

The doctor spoke softly. "I can only stay a minute," he said. "I'm sorry. I'll talk in more detail at dinner." He cleared his throat. "I want to begin by apologizing for my dramatic entrance earlier this morning."

"Louder please," said one of the Swedes.

"Yes, louder," nodded the doctor, but he did not raise his voice. "None of us expected such excitement among the refugees. You'll be happy to know there was only one injury. Minor abrasions, that's all. Now I know even one is too many, but that is the nature of the beast. We're dealing with volatile forces. Everyone knows this, yes?" He frowned. "I can assume that, yes? Now the head of the detachment is Colonel Mansoor. He's the fellow in the sunglasses. He assures me his men are professional. Now these are not pleasant times. I'm aware of that. But I assure you that the Ranger detachment is well-led and disciplined."

"Could you speak up?" said Ralph.

The doctor raised his head and looked around, his eyes roaming. "I'm here, on Bidong, right now," he said, "to tell you what I know and what I don't know. I don't have all the answers. This has been a period of great strain for all of us. I know you've worked hard. I know you've put in the hours. God knows you deserve recompense, at least in the form of certainty. I only wish I had some to give you."

"Please to speaking louder," said Gurmit.

"But that is the nature of our situation," said the doctor. "The great French writer Flaubert once said that we are cut from but a thread, yet wish to know the whole cloth. That cloth is not ours to know. I'm here to tell you that. I've been in this business many a year, and I've learned a great many things. I've learned to live without seeing the cloth. Be thankful for the thread, children, because a view of the cloth will cost you dearly. It'll put you in a poorhouse you can't ever leave. Do you understand me?" Blinking, he scanned the room. "Am I clear to everyone?"

"Up the volume, please," said Sally, tapping her ear.

"As you know, time is short," said the doctor. "Year Five is just around the corner, and what's going to happen then is beyond my knowledge and beyond my control. I come to you bearing a handful of threads. Just a few"—he held out his thumb and forefinger, as if measuring—"and they're already getting tangled. Now what's going to happen in Year Five, I don't know. I do not know. That's a cloth that gets dropped on all of us at the same time. There's nothing you or I can do about it. I repeat: nothing. It's out of your hands. It's out of my hands. It's out of Task Force's hands."

He paused then. His chin seem to quiver; he leaned over, plucking a folder from Sally's shelf, and shielded his face with the folder for a moment.

"OK. OK. Please let me continue. What I know is this. I know the Malaysians and UNHCR are going to meet in Kuala Lumpur in the next few days to make a decision. *The* decision. It's all very sudden. It's going to be decisive. My information is that the Rangers here are just going to scope things out. It's just a small contingent. They're just looking around. Checking things. They're going to be searching shelters. They're looking for weapons. Knives, jerricans, things like that. They're going to round some people up. Just a few. Just for questioning.

"These are all contingency measures. Just contingency. In themselves, they aren't significant acts. Now, after the meeting in Kuala Lumpur, something significant will happen. Year Five will reveal itself. It could be that things will continue as usual, at least for another year. There might be a shoot-on-sight policy enacted for new boats coming in. Or . . . I'll be honest with you. The camp might be shut down. Now you know what that would mean. A helicopter would come for you before anything happened. And you know that these people here . . ." He waved his arm toward the window, then brought up his hand to cover his twitching eye.

He stood, pressing his hands onto the desk. "You know if the camp gets shut down, the boat people will be put out to sea. I've been assured it would be humane. The government's already contracted some shipbuilders. They tell me the boats would be seaworthy. They would provide fuel and provisions. Now, children, I've got to believe that. I've got to believe with the weather the way it is . . ."

He sat down. "I just don't know." He grabbed a handful of air and shook it. "None of us knows. But I'll tell you this. Tomorrow morning, we have a window. We have a glimpse into the future. It's a very, very small window. Tomorrow morning, there's going to be two boats coming in. One boat is a delegation from the prime minister's office, plus regional officers. A few people from UNHCR, UNDP, and UNV, too. It's an official visit. Fact-finding and so on. These are the movers and shakers. They're going to be instrumental in whatever decision is made in Kuala Lumpur. Wing Kit Choong, Mr. Ibrahim, Mr. Anand, Mike Petocz, Joseph Michell, Datok Lee . . . all of them. After Bidong, they go to Kuala Lumpur for the meeting. Now the second boat is different. The second boat is for the press corps."

"Did you say press?" said Ralph, leaning forward. "He said press, didn't he?"

"Photographers, too, right?" said Sally. "I've got photos to show. I've got lots of photos."

"Yes," said the doctor. "Press types. Mostly stringers. A fellow from the *Times,* I think. Various Commonwealth papers. The Malaysians want to be straightforward about how the camp is run. They've got nothing to hide. They want no accusations of cover-up. In many ways, Bidong is a model camp."

The doctor held up his fingers and began counting. "One, processing is quick," he said, lowering a finger. "Faster than Singapore or Hong Kong, I'll say that. Two, we have a strong English program. Three, big money's been pumped into the hospital. Four, no backlogs in immigration and screening. That's quite a record, believe me. I could go on." All of his fingers had come down, which seemed to surprise him: he looked at his balled fist and rotated it slowly, then lowered the hand to his lap, where it snuggled into his crotch like a puppy.

"Could you speak up a little?" asked Sally.

"Yes, yes," said Johann, pointing to his ear.

The doctor looked at Sally blankly, and continued. Sally, sighing loudly, cupped her ear.

"The boats arrive at nine in the morning," the doctor said, "and they leave at noon. The delegation and the press corps are going to tour the hospital and the community centers . . . Some of the schools, too, and the camp committee will be putting together a cultural show. Dances and songs, mostly. Plus some gift exchanges. Now, I know everyone wants to influence decisions, and I encourage you to air your views. You have personal knowledge that no one else can have. Stories. Personal reminiscences. I encourage you to share your stories. I encourage you to communicate your concerns in a professional and reasoned manner. Now, there's going to be a special hour set aside for you to meet with one of the UNHCR regional officers. One hour. I've been assured he'll listen. He's a good, good man. They all are. These are good men, children. Keep in mind they're in a difficult situation. Keep in mind they have to make decisions sometimes that they don't want to make."

The doctor's voice began to rise. He pulled a pen out of his shirt pocket and began tapping it against his watch. "You aren't the only ones with difficult jobs. Please keep that in mind when you speak to these men. Please be professional. There are voices out there, children, and they whisper into all of our ears and sometimes they make us do things we don't want to do. But we have to do them. It's the nature of the job, now, isn't it?"

He stood, searching the room. "Gurmit, I tried to keep you here. I really did." The doctor pointed toward the door. "And you, too, Reuben Gill. And Porkpie, too. Is she present? No. I tried. It was so hard. But you have to understand, all the pressure . . . there are so many voices in times like these. They all want something. They all point fingers. I've got . . ."

He sat down again, and as he did, he cupped his hands over his eyes and sighed.

"Are you OK?" asked Sally.

"Yes," he said, straightening. "I'm sorry. I won't burden you with this. Now, I encourage you to talk to the UNHCR officer. And to the press. Most certainly the press. I encourage an active engagement in the process. But I have to caution . . . I have to say . . . We have to present ourselves as professionals. I don't mean to be insulting, but dress neatly, please. These men value professionalism. I'm afraid the moment for emotional appeals has long passed. These men have heard it all. Believe me. They're not likely to be swayed by emotionalism. There are other voices whispering in their ears. Believe me. Hard voices, children."

"You said we can talk to them," said Sally.

"This isn't the Gulag. Of course you can. You can talk to the press, too."

"I, for one," said Ralph, "do not intend to guard my mouth."

"You're free to say whatever you wish. But please keep in mind, these men have other considerations. They have other voices to listen to, Ralph."

"I've got photos," said Sally. "They've got to see pictures of the children."

"By all means, show them pictures."

"I will."

"It's just . . . ," said the doctor. He paused, wiping sweat from his face. "It's almost time for me to meet with the colonel. We want to make sure things go smoothly here tonight. Now, I'm going to leave now, but don't think I'm done listening to you. Oh no. But I have to say, I have to just tell you . . . The men on those boats tomorrow have seen photos. They've heard the personal accounts. I just think . . . it's important to maintain a professional demeanor tomorrow. I just want to caution you. They'll listen, but I just want to say that when they leave, they'll be hearing other voices that are very, very loud. Do you follow me? I'm sorry, but that's just how it is. Now, really, I must . . . I'm afraid I have to leave."

The meeting broke up quickly. Reuben bounded down the steps, avoiding contact with the doctor, who, tapping his watch, promised to answer any questions over dinner. There were protests, and Ralph, raising his arms, began denouncing the Voice of America for broadcasting tide tables in Vietnamese. One of the Swedes nodded. "Yes, and the World Bank, too, is guilty of the improper loan policies," the Swede said. "The problem is American economics." The doctor, carrying a thin briefcase, worked his way to the door, stopping to shake hands. At the doorway, he put his hand over his left eye, which had begun twitching again.

Reuben watched from a distance. The Ranger, walking with the doctor down the steps and into the mud, kept turning his head as if expecting Reuben to charge. Halfway across the compound, the doctor stopped. He reached into his breast pocket and pulled out a pair of glasses. "Up there," he said, addressing Sally. He put on his glasses. "That's the Zone F hill, right? What's that thing sticking out of the ground?"

"The plank monument," said Sally.

"What do you mean?"

"Gurmit's plank. The one he took from the table. It's a monument now."

Doctor Johansson shook his head. "A monument. That's how the table business got resolved. A monument."

Sally stuck out her arm. "Those two men up there. They're cutting it down."

"They're Rangers," said the doctor. He put a hand on Sally's shoulder. "I'm sorry, but that piece of wood has got to go. If we need a chopper, that's where it lands. Right up there."

They watched the plank fall.

"You trying to tell me this is all just contingency?" said Ralph.

"This is what I'm told," said the doctor. "I can only tell you . . . This is what I've heard."

"This gives me the creeps," said Sally.

"I pray that chopper doesn't have to come," said the doctor. "I sincerely pray it doesn't. This whole business. It's been so hard. I've had . . . Damn it, my eye again." He brought his hand up to his face.

"It's just like '72, isn't it?" said Ralph. "Right at the end. Yank Marines on the embassy roof, cutting down the tamarind tree to make room for the choppers."

The two figures on the hill bent at the waist and hoisted the plank up, placing it flat on their heads, and walked toward the outcrop, one in front, one in back. They stood a moment at the edge, then heaved the plank over the side, out over the water below.

"Did you see that?"

"It's just the wind."

"No. It went out too far for just the wind."

"It fluttered some. The gusts are bad there."

"Well, it sure hung up there a long time."

"It did."

"Yes, it did. It surely did."

"Where's Manley going?"

"Manley, come back here."

"Forget him. I'm telling you, the plank flew."

"OK. Don't get in an uproar."

"It's just floating in the water now, anyway."

"I'm telling you, it flew. I saw it."

Everyone fell silent then, watching Manley race down the beach toward Zone F, struggling to keep his feet free of the mud. Reuben opened the gate latch and stepped outside to get a better view. He saw

Manley shuck off his T-shirt. There were people in the way, but Reuben, standing now on an engine hulk, could see Manley running into the tide, slipping off his sandals. Even as Manley began to crouch, wading into the waves, Reuben could see that Manley was too late. Other figures were already splashing into the water farther down the beach. Men with brown arms and legs were climbing atop the coral ringing the Zone F cliff. There were lots of them, Vietnamese men swimming, dragging the plank to shore, figures clad in pants and running shorts, and one thin boy wearing only a pair of gray underpants. But still Manley ran through the surf, waving his arms around, shouting orders that no one understood.

That night Reuben lifted the wire at the back of the UN compound and slipped through, walking in a crouch behind Mr. Luc, who, using a code of his own invention, made popping noises with his jaw whenever he wanted Reuben to stop. They walked along the side of the Zone C footpath, stepping over the stakes and tie-down ropes attached to the shelters, pausing sometimes to raise their fingers to their lips and shush the faces staring out the door flaps. It was dark. Earlier in the evening, a team of Rangers had dragged the petrol from the outdoor lanterns and emptied the fuel into the ocean, along with two pallets, stacked with sloshing jerricans, discovered at the bottom of one of the boarded-up wells in Zone D. There was only the glow of the fire pits to guide them along the footpath, and the camp was quiet, the shelters melding into the darkness, row upon row of shelters humming with whispers. Reuben couldn't see: he grabbed hold of the back of Mr. Luc's shirt and didn't let go. Neither man spoke. The camp was dripping with noisy runoff from the afternoon downpour. Sill, the daypack on Reuben's back rustled too much; he cinched it tighter. He did not carry a flashlight. He wore flip-flops because his waders squeaked, and when the mud sucked one of the sandals from his foot, he did not bother to rummage for it.

They walked a long way, passing silently into Zone D, scanning for patrolling Rangers, and then they walked into brush and dense stands of palm, leaving the footpaths, rising with each step closer to the overgrown crest that Mr. Luc promised would lead to the cleared trails used by black marketeers. The trees rustled with bird spiders and rodents. The men climbed, pushing aside fronds and swollen vines that were heavy as arms; they tripped over the knuckly roots and scratched themselves on the brambles and jagged points of stripped trees. And then they were headed down, holding their arms out like surfers, sliding down boulders and mossy inclines. They began running, unable to slow their progress, and then they felt themselves crash through a wall of foliage. There was goo everywhere, and Reuben, reaching for branches to slow his descent, plunged his hand into something that felt like soft wax, then continued running and sliding, coming to rest only after grabbing hold of Mr. Luc's leg. Mr. Luc was holding tight to a thick vine.

"There," said Mr. Luc, breathing hard. He pointed with his jaw. Reuben, swiping crawling insects from his arm, saw the globes of light, bobbing in the darkness. He heard the water then, too, a rapid gurgling.

"Is here, Mr. Reuben," said Mr. Luc. They brushed themselves, then came to the bottom of the hill. The ground was rocky and slick. Reuben heard voices. Someone ahead was carrying a lit flashlight. Mr. Luc began speaking in Vietnamese, and when the voice answered, Mr. Luc turned and nodded. "We follow the flashlight, Mr. Reuben." All around, Reuben could hear water, but he followed Mr. Luc, who leaped nimbly from boulder to boulder, slipping only once in thick moss. Then the ground seemed to rise: there was a shelf of mud ahead, and Mr. Luc, carrying on a conversation with the man carrying the flashlight, felt his way along the shelf until he came to a length of wood and pulled himself up. Reuben followed. There, lit by a hanging lantern, was a narrow strip of beach running along a small, rocky ledge. Water bubbled up and down the mud. There were four boats visible farther out, dark, rocking shapes illuminated by lanterns. Reuben squinted. To his left were figures wading out in a line.

"Traders here," said Mr. Luc. "But I do not know which one is your boat."

"I don't either," Reuben said. He pulled off his daypack. He stripped off his shirt and, holding the daypack high overhead, stepped into the water. There were clinking sounds around him, iron chains scrapping the hulls of a boat, and in the lantern light, Reuben could see Malay men bending down, handing jugs and cartons of cigarettes from Kuala Trengganu to Vietnamese men who hoisted the items over their heads and waded back to shore.

"White bastard," Reuben heard.

Reuben waded toward the voice. He swayed in the waves, stepping gingerly, following the lantern that was swinging from side to side, marking the position. The hull came into view: a Malay fishing boat, bulging with nets and crane pulleys.

"White bastard." There, leaning over the side, was Cowboy Lim. He waved a lantern with one hand and his Stetson with the other.

"Chinaman," said Reuben, spitting seawater. He clasped Cowboy Lim's hand in greeting.

"Oh-*lah*," said Cowboy Lim. Worry lines creased his face. In the lamplight his skin looked bright as the moon.

A Malay man in the pilothouse stuck his head out the door and revved the boat motor. *Come on,* the man shouted in Malay. *Move it. Give it to him and let's get going.*

"You bring it?" Reuben said.

"Got-*lah*." Cowboy Lim pulled away. He hung the lantern on a metal eyelet and bent down, disappearing for a moment. When he came back up, he was holding a package wrapped in pink raffia string.

Reuben took the package. He ripped away the paper, tossing the strips into the water. Then he zipped the daypack open and placed the object inside. He zipped the pack up.

"You sure you want?" said Cowboy Lim.

"Sure."

"You stay with us. No problem. Can leave now. With me."

"Can't."

"Can."

"Later, huh?" Reuben held the daypack over his head.

The Malay man put the engine into gear. There was no time for more talking, no time to reach up and hold Cowboy Lim by the arm. Reuben, shouting thanks, felt the wake of the boat push him away; he saw the water churn, and then the boat was gone into the night, its lantern extinguished, its motor muted and clanking.

Reuben waded back to shore.

Mr. Luc did not ask what Reuben had received. Mr. Luc was squatting on the beach with a small, shivering man, wet with seawater. Navy patrols were coming, said Mr. Luc, nodding at his informant. Mr. Luc let his gaze rest on the daypack; his jaw jutted out, rotating, and then he leaped up, leading Reuben back toward the mud ledge, and from there across the slick boulders and into the underbrush. The two men slogged their way back up over the hill and through the footpaths.

In Zone B, Mr. Luc said his good-byes and pointed Reuben across a duck walk that led to the main Zone C footpath and then to the UN compound.

Reuben slipped back under the wire. On Sally's porch, white people were drinking and talking softly, staring in the direction of the Ranger tents set up along the Zone D beach. A small lantern hissed on the railing, and in the light Reuben saw Ralph whispering to a small magnetic chessboard, pushing pieces around. Sally, paging through a photo album, sat with Johann and the Swedes. One of the Swedes picked up a bottle and passed it around.

Sally heard Reuben walk past. She called out, "Porkpie's in her room. You might want to . . . I don't know. She won't come out."

"Where's Manley?" asked Reuben.

"Where have you been?" Sally asked. "You're wet."

"Where is he?" asked Reuben.

"We were hoping you might know," said Sally. "He's got a bandanna around his head now. We're worried he might be out there rabble rousing."

"There's Rangers all over," said Ralph, looking up from his board. "Freaking buggers."

"It is the fault of America," said one of the Swedes, taking a swig from the bottle. "They have brought the Rangers here."

"The history is clear," said another Swede.

"History ends tomorrow, I think," said another.

"Stop it," said Sally. She rose from her chair and shoved her photo album in the Swede's face. "Look at the children. Will you please look at the children."

"Freaking liars," said Ralph, scraping a chess piece across the board. "All those buggers coming tomorrow. They'll freaking steal you blind."

Reuben couldn't listen. He looped his hands around the straps of the daypack and without another word walked to Porkpie's bungalow. He knocked on her door, not sure what he wanted to say to her, not even sure if she would listen, but when she answered, her face lit up. They talked awhile, pausing whenever they heard footfalls outside the wire. He told her good-bye. Not yet, she answered: she heard they would be leaving on the press boat, after the journalists piled off. She was looking at him strangely, her eyes roaming his face, and then she touched his arm and said, "You're wet." He nodded. She grabbed his sleeve suddenly and pressed against him, reaching around with one arm and pawing at his daypack.

She slapped the daypack hard. She said, "You could have at least zipped your damn pack up all the way." She shoved him, knocking his arm against the doorjamb. "You left the barrel sticking out."

He put his finger to his lips. They looked at each other a long time. He stripped off the daypack, then reached inside and pulled out the long, black pistol. "No bullets," he said. "Cowboy Lim's trophy piece. It's just a symbol. It's harmless."

"No, it's not," she said. She closed her eyes. "Reuben, tomorrow . . ."

"Yeah."

She clasped her hand over his. He started trembling then. He frowned in surprise and drew away, but she told him to sit down. He did, collapsing onto the chair. She touched his lips, wiping a droplet of water away, and then she whispered into his ear and closed the door. "Yeah," she said, but all he could hear was the sound of zippers and buttons. She kissed him. His tongue darted inside. Their hands were all over each other, and then they were breathing together, and the chair began to squeak back and forth.

22

Through the night it rained, great warm sheets falling on the black muddy pools, water stirring the mud flats, tugging on the posts of the shelters, racing down to the beaches where the tide surged forward and covered the mud with seaweed and tiny gasping fish. In the morning the wall of garbage on the Zone C beach was slick with an oily goo that smelled of seawater, and even the cooking fires along the tree line blistered with the pungent odor of brine. Everything was wet, everything filmy and running with watery colors. There were drowned rats in Zone B floating in the sewage canal, and in Zone F the tarp roof of the primary school had collapsed, ruining the English books stacked on the teacher's desk. Some lean-tos on the Zone F hill had been swept away, carrying panicked families into a flooded gully, but no one had time to rebuild the shelters or petition Supply for fresh blankets, at least not until the two boats arrived. People rose early, even before the loudspeakers thumped on, splashing in the half-light past the Ranger tents to paint welcome banners for the delegation and the journalists.

In the Zone C school, the Bidong Boy Scouts laid out tarp along the benches, cutting streamers, and the Women's Service Committee tacked up material to the blackboard, sewing green dresses for the dancers who were going to perform a Highlands dance for the cultural show. Everyone was nervous. Teams of Rangers poked their guns through the open windows, ordering gawkers to leave, checking camp IDs to make sure that the Boy Scouts were official scouts and not just troublemakers wearing yellow scarves. Down from the tree line, people kept slipping in the goo, but nobody complained or swore because

Rangers were patrolling the dock area and didn't want anyone lolling around or speaking in a loud voice.

Around eight, the approach route from the dock up to the Zone C footpath was cordoned off by Task Force men who planted notched sticks into the mud and strung twine into the grooves. A line of Rangers jogged in from Zone D then. They stood at intervals of twenty paces and cleared the approach route, waving at people walking down from the tree line to stand behind the twine. On the dock, there was much aimless activity. Rangers leaned against the pilings, smoking, checking the IDs of the refugee security men, who went from piling to piling, holding out the plastic cards looped around their necks. By the pill house, a corporal tried to lay yellow tape across the planks, marking off a line, but the wood was so wet and soft that the tape kept peeling off, leading to an outburst by the corporal, who then unstrapped his knife and cut a line across the wood, shouting into a bullhorn that only staff and VIPs could step across.

The dock was quickly becoming crowded. Task Force Chief Ahmed walked up the steps, trailed by ten of his men wearing freshly creased uniforms. Then came Colonel Mansoor, wiping his sunglasses, and a frowning Doctor Johansson, followed by members of the camp committee. Viet security was given push brooms; the men giggled and bowed, then began sweeping the slippery goo off the sides of the dock. Ready, people said. OK-*lah*. Ahmed and Colonel Mansoor checked their clipboards. Doctor Johansson filled out a questionnaire. Everyone was looking out into the ocean, waiting for the morning mist to burn off and reveal the two boats.

What people on the dock didn't see then was Reuben and Porkpie walking up the dock steps, slowly wending their way through a knot of uniformed men. Reuben held his daypack by the straps; Porkpie carried a length of thick wire spooled around her arm. They stopped halfway up the dock, in front of a piling. They didn't move, not even when a Task Force guard tapped his watch and pointed them back toward the pill house. Doctor Johansson, showing the effects of a poor night's sleep, walked by, grinding the heel of his hand into his eyes. The doctor nodded at them grimly, but continued walking to the pill house, tapping a clipboard against his leg.

The doctor conferred with Ahmed by the pill house door, then walked out again. "You can't stand there when the boats arrive, you know," the doctor said, keeping his distance. "You're going to have to wait with your luggage back by the pill house."

Reuben nodded.

"Uh-huh," said Porkpie, but she didn't move.

"Where are your bags?" the doctor asked. His washcloth tongue slipped in and out, but then he turned: Colonel Mansoor was gesturing to him by a piling, calling for assistance in deciphering the list of certified journalists.

On the beach, people kept streaming in from the tree line, leaning over the twine fence to better see the activities on the dock. Members of the camp committee shooed some Boy Scouts away, and with much grave effort stuck long poles into the mud and unfurled the banners:

Bidong Island Refugees Welcome Delegation and Journalists
Happy Coming 1980 to the UN and Malaysia Who Save the Boat People
Please to Saving Boat People

"Boats coming," shouted a Ranger. There was much movement then. Uniformed men jogged up the dock steps. One of the Task Force guards, trying to climb atop a piling, slipped in some goo behind Reuben and Porkpie. He looked around angrily, shouting for someone to come and sweep the mess, but no sooner did men with push brooms bolt from the pill house than they slowed to a crawl, unable to maneuver around Gurmit, who was proceeding at a stately pace toward the two Americans.

"Gurmit," Reuben nodded.

Gurmit nodded back. His safari suit was torn, and he was wearing a large naval captain's hat, resplendent with a gold-leaf bill. He turned sideways, moving aside for the push broom men, and pressed the cap down firmly on his head.

"Captain Gurmit," said Porkpie.

All around them, men were jogging and slipping, crowding the end of the dock to watch the approaching boats. Then there was no movement: Gurmit, Porkpie, and Reuben stood quietly, shifting their feet on the broad dock planks, alone now, well behind the men at the end of the dock, well in front of the men still standing by the pill house. For a moment, there was only the waves gulping and rising beneath them, only a solitary shout of *Cai Cay Bi Can*, Biting Tree, carrying forward

from the crowd, the words knifing into Reuben's ear, the words pleading and fearful, cutting into the stillness in a way Reuben had never
heard them before. He looked toward the beach. It was Mr. Luc, waving a shirt over his head, pointing. In front of the pill house, something
was happening. Guards were filing out the door, staring at the crowd.
Two Rangers walked slowly down the dock steps.

Then he saw. Standing in the middle of the approach route was
Manley, dressed only in running shorts and flip-flops. Pirate dangled
from the leash in his hand. The monkey was strangling, kicking its feet
and arms, and Manley, yelling now, walked back and forth in front of
the crowd, holding the leash at arm's length. "This is a pirate," he was
shouting. "This is a pirate." The approaching Rangers gestured to the
crowd. People obeyed, stepping back from the twine fence. Manley,
turning, watched the Rangers draw near, then began jogging down the
length of the cordoned area, shouting at the flailing monkey.

"No, Reuben," said Porkpie. She squeezed his hand tightly. "You've
got to stay."

The two Rangers pointed their weapons straight in the air and signaled for calm by waving them up and down. No one in the crowd
moved. Manley reached down, prying a stone from the mud, and, yanking on the leash, brought the stone down hard on the monkey's head.
"Do it," he shouted, looking up at the crowd. "Come on. Come on."

The monkey leaped away then, freed of Manley's grasp, but Manley grabbed the trailing leash and brought the stone down hard again.
The monkey staggered forward, grasping a woman's leg, but again Manley grabbed the leash and pulled Pirate toward him. He dropped to one
knee and brought his stone down again, and then the monkey was still,
sprawled in the mud. Manley stood. People in the crowd pointed at
Manley and shook their heads dramatically from side to side, addressing the Rangers. Manley turned to the Rangers. He slapped his naked
chest, but the Rangers were scanning the crowd, watching for movement. One of the Rangers walked up and poked the monkey with the
snout of his weapon. He started talking to Manley, but Manley turned
and calmly stepped back over the twine fence. He raised his arms again
and shouted, but no one looked at him. The Rangers just watched.
They talked together, then waved to the dock, and when two more
Rangers trotted down the steps, Manley suddenly turned and jogged
back toward the tree line, pushing through the silent crowd.

Task Force Chief Ahmed, watching Manley disappear up the foot-path, walked slowly back from the end of the dock. He stopped in front of Gurmit and snapped his fingers.

"Must go now," he said. "You three go waiting back there." The two boats were clearly visible. You could see men holding on to the railings.

"No," said Reuben, shaking his daypack.

Ahmed frowned. He clapped his hands at a nearby corporal, then walked toward the dock steps, shooing away some Viet security men.

Porkpie unraveled the wire spooled around her arm. She threaded one end through a belt loop in Reuben's pants, then around his waist, then pulled the stiff wire toward herself and spooled a length around her own waist. There were yards of it left, but when she began wrapping the slack around herself, Gurmit leaned over and yanked the wire out of her hand.

"Are you sure?" Porkpie said.

"Sure," said Gurmit. Lifting up his safari jacket, he threaded the wire through one of his belt loops, then around his waist. He handed the remaining wire to Reuben, who, leaning into the piling behind him, looped the wire around it, cinching the strands so tight they cut grooves into the wood. He did this three times, then raveled the wire into a knot and bent the remaining length down, where it disappeared into the water. He yanked: the wire was ungiving, stiff and wavery as an umbilical cord.

Ahmed returned, clipboard in hand. "Boats arriving," he said. "You must go now."

"No," said Reuben.

Ahmed grabbed Gurmit by the arm. The Task Force chief pulled on him, but Gurmit, wincing as the wire cut into his skin, remained in place.

"Wire," said Ahmed dumbly. He looked out at the approaching boats, then began pacing. He slapped the clipboard with his hand. "Must go now."

"No," said Reuben.

Ahmed stepped back, considering. He walked quickly to the end of the dock and stood next to Colonel Mansoor, gesturing. The colonel turned around, then both men trotted back and looked at the wire. The colonel ripped off his sunglasses. "I am warning," he said.

Porkpie shifted, grabbing Reuben's wrist. "My knees," she whispered, dipping slightly. Gurmit put his hand under her armpit and yanked her straight.

Ahmed whispered something into the colonel's ear, and then the two of them left, striding side by side toward the pill house. They brushed aside a guard and descended the steps. There was noise coming from the crowd now, some shouts, but nobody could see well enough to figure out what was happening. Out in the water, the boats blew their air horns, causing a stir at the end of the dock, but Reuben kept his eyes on the beach.

Up came Sally and Ralph, followed by the colonel, rapping a walking stick against his palm. "What are you doing?" asked Sally. She was breathing hard. Her hands were stuck so deeply into her overalls that Reuben could see the imprint of her knuckles sticking out from her thighs. Ralph kept turning around, glancing at the colonel and stroking his beard.

"Making a scene," said Porkpie.

"You have to leave now. The delegation's almost here."

"No," said Reuben.

"Cannot," said Gurmit.

A couple of Rangers sauntered over. One touched the wire with the barrel of his gun.

Sally whispered, "Are you trying to get people hurt?"

There was no response.

"Are you rabble rousing the refugees? What do you think—"

"No Viets," said Reuben. "There's no Viets involved. Just us."

The colonel spoke: "Off now." He grabbed hold of Sally's arm, then Ralph's, and pushed them away. A Task Force guard hustled them down the steps.

Doctor Johansson ran up. Some more Rangers walked over, fingering triggers.

"Leave," the doctor said, his eye twitching. "Don't do this. You damn ideologues."

"This is our war," said Reuben.

"There's no goddamn war. What's wrong with you? There's no war."

"There is," said Porkpie.

The doctor whispered. "Stop it. You're going to get hurt. The colonel's military." He put his hand on Porkpie's shoulder. "Don't listen to Reuben." He snapped his fingers at her. "This is a prison camp.

Military jurisdiction. Your passport protects you just so far. Are you listening?"

"There's press coming," said Reuben.

The doctor grabbed Reuben's shirt and yanked. "Is that it? You *want* to get hurt?"

"*Gook* blood don't matter to them. Ours does."

"Stop this."

"We get hurt, it's front-page news," said Reuben.

The doctor curled his hand into a fist and pressed his knuckles into the side of his head. He hissed: "Don't you think Bidong's already been decided? Think."

"Our blood matters," Reuben said.

The doctor slapped him hard in the face.

Porkpie began to cry then. Her chin was tucked into her chest, and her head jerked forward twice. She wiped her eyes. She hiccuped. "OK," she said, clasping one of the straps on Reuben's daypack. "I'm OK now."

"Yes, yes," said Gurmit, squeezing her hand.

More Rangers jogged over, circling. They stood shoulder to shoulder, blocking the view from the beach and the water. The doctor said, "Do you want me to get on my knees and beg? Is that what you want?" He fell to his knees and clasped his hands together. "Did you want to see this?" He held his arms out wide. "Please leave." His face was dripping sweat.

"Come on over here," shouted Ralph from the beach.

"Quickly," said Sally.

"Damn you," said the doctor, rising. "Oh Christ. Please. The boats are here. Get off the dock."

The press boat was chugging into the inlet, rocking wildly, and behind them was a UN speedboat, jammed with brown men and white men in safari suits.

"Leave now," said the colonel. He drew back his walking stick and struck Reuben expertly in the ribs. One of his men lifted his gun, then put it back down.

"Please, no violence," said Doctor Johansson. The press boat was at the end of the dock. A pair of Rangers clamped the portable ladder onto the dock; the loudspeakers came on, blaring the Welcome Song.

Reuben, groaning, dropped to one knee and held the daypack tightly against his chest. "I've got you," said Porkpie, pulling on his sleeve; Gurmit dropped to one knee as well, leaning over and yanking on Reuben's collar, helping him to his feet.

"Take them off," said the colonel. "Quickly." Three Rangers, shouldering their rifles, pressed against Reuben and surged forward. The wire held. "Get cutters," the colonel barked: "Go, go." One of the Rangers broke from the group and began running toward the beach, while another knocked Gurmit's hat off and grabbed him by the hair. A rifle butt swung down. Then another. Reuben, swinging hard, freed his arm. He unzipped his daypack.

"Take it out," Gurmit said.

"Hurry," whispered Porkpie.

There was a clinking sound, then a flash of black, and then the pistol was in Reuben's hand and he was waving it over his head, yelling now, calling to the men climbing up the portable ladder.

A Ranger pushed the barrel of his rifle into Reuben's stomach. The other men stumbled back, shouting threats, and leveled their weapons.

Porkpie cupped her hands to her face.

"Drop it, Reuben," said Doctor Johansson. "Please."

"I will fire," shouted the colonel. "Drop it. I will fire."

They all felt it then, a luffing, everyone on the dock swaying to the cresting water that smacked against the underside of the dock, spurting up through the cracks and goo. There was noise, too, a blaring air horn, the loudspeaker tape, the crowd, the circle of shouting Rangers, all the sounds roaring, tingling up people's spines, and for a moment you could feel yourself rising, shoes and cameras and push brooms rising with you, imperceptibly it seemed, imperceptible because everything was rising, lifted together into the air, and then everything was falling, all falling together, and then perfectly still, as if nothing had risen at all, as if everyone on the dock had been looking at the Zone F hill all along, watching with their mind's eye the small whirling movements up on the rocks. The delegation men were looking up, and the journalists were looking up, aiming their cameras, staring at the edge of the Zone F hill, where Manley stood on the slippery outcrop, holding out the plank and shouting. He was waving the plank from side to side, holding one end like a signalman waving a flag, screaming something toward the dock.

No one could hear what he was saying, but the journalists were pointing, and the men from the speedboat were shielding their eyes from the glare, holding their hands like visors, pressing the sides of the palms to their heads, staring at the tiny white figure high up on the outcrop waving the cumbersome plank. Each time he waved he stumbled a little, lifted by the force of the weight, stumbling first one way, then the other. There was nothing anyone could do. People stared and pointed, but no one said a word because there was nothing anyone could say when Manley waved the plank out toward the ocean and soared into the air, soaring and falling all at once, soaring with his arms outstretched, clutching the plank, then plunging into the water, where he vanished without a sound.

23

The day of the new year came and went, at least the day of the Western new year came and went, the day of the lunar new year still being subject in the city of Kuala Trengganu to much preparatory purchasing of firecrackers, glutinous sweets, and papier-mâché. But the day of the Western new year, assigned by the Malaysian government and the UN agencies as the administrative demarcation between past and present, came and went much as the previous days had come and gone, and much as the following week then came and went, day after day coming and going, days arranging themselves into patterns of payment and debt and brief flurries of rage that boats from Vietnam should still be scuttling on the beaches of the east coast of Malaysia. Malaysia was not a gutter, stated a January 2 editorial in the Malay-language newspaper *Berita Harian,* from which the cataclysmic human wave erupting from the cataclysmic human fire of Vietnam could be indefinitely funneled. But for at least another year it would. At least for another year the boats would steer by the lights of the Dutch oil rigs hundreds of kilometers from shore, and shippers would instruct their freighter captains to bypass swamped wooden craft, and Thai demons would board the crowded decks as if in a dream, though the dreaming was hard and true and real. At least for another year the folders in the refugee files would be covered in yellow stickers that bristled as if in a dream with the letters *RPM,* Rape Pillage Murder, which were letters that were hard and true and real but sounded like dreaming when you said them.

In Year Five there would be no history. There would be only the water whispering in your ears.

Still, it was a surprise to everyone in Kuala Trengganu that Porkpie, who wondered for a moment if she was actually saying the words, insisted on the beachfront Seven Wings Yellow Swallow Restaurant, whose dining area rose on pilings over the ocean, as the venue for the farewell luncheon. The luncheon had been the doctor's idea. After everything that had happened, the doctor said, it was time to call a truce. Out of respect for Manley, if for nothing else, he said. Before they all went their separate ways.

Porkpie was the first to agree to the luncheon. Then Gurmit agreed, after first borrowing money from Porkpie for the purchase of new clothing. Reuben, grumbling, called in his acceptance from Cowboy Lim's bar phone. But when the doctor made clear his preference for the Tin Mine Room of the Hotel Kuala Trengganu as the luncheon's venue, Porkpie unexpectedly put her face directly in the doctor's line of vision and squinted horribly, displaying sufficient physical evidence to remind the doctor that it was she, and not he, who had been struck in the face with the butt of a Ranger's automatic weapon and was therefore to be listened to until some as-yet undetermined date. No, she said, not really sure what she was going to say next. We're going to the Seven Wings Yellow Swallow Restaurant.

The doctor asked her what she knew about the place.

You could hear the water from there, she said, sounding more mysterious than she had intended.

Reuben, she knew, would find an ocean-side venue agreeable, as would Gurmit. Both men had already evinced a preference for seafood on Bidong, as well as for the curried prawns served during one of their various heated exit interviews with representatives of the Bureau of Refugee Affairs, MRCS, Malaysian Armed Forces Police, Special Branch, UNV, UNHCR, and with the head of Malaysian Prison Systems. Too, the doctor had called the luncheon-planning meeting for precisely the time Reuben and Gurmit were due in the examination room of the Kuala Trengganu general hospital to have their dressings rewrapped, which seemed to Porkpie a deliberate attempt on the doctor's part to preemptively cull two-thirds of the opposition he suspected might be mounted against his luncheon decisions. So, partly on principle, and partly for reasons she could not fathom, she thrust her bloated cheek across his desk and demanded to eat at a restaurant overlooking the water. Yet even as she fingered the creeping bruise that spread all the way to her lips, she felt a bit silly arguing over venue. It seemed a trivial and mean-spirited thing to argue over. She could not keep out of her movements a certain hesitation, even as she rose to insist on a restaurant near the water, delivering her demands urgently, speaking with a kind of disembodied woodenness, like a student actor reading a script. The doctor acquiesced readily; the secretary promised to phone the guests immediately. The matter was settled.

As it turned out, the Seven Wings Yellow Swallow Restaurant was an excellent venue for a group luncheon, serving a wide range of clay-pot seafood dishes, shelled baby-crab soup, and fried clam noodles reputed by the Kuala Trengganu Businessman's Association to rival any found in Malaysia. The air was cool and heady, freshened by the ocean breeze that poured in freely through the far wall, which was in fact not a wall but a reinforced wire-mesh enclosure on which patrons could lean and see a tiny stretch of beach below and sometimes feel misty spray floating up from the ocean. The dining area was spacious, the Chinese waiters voluble English speakers, and the tables generously apportioned with spice trays, silver-handled chopsticks, and glass water pitchers cut into the approximate shape of resting swallows. For the luncheon, the proprietor had covered a long banquet table with an embroidered linen tablecloth and shoved it against the wire meshing, which, bending slightly, gave the appearance of having stopped the table from hurtling out into the surf.

Porkpie arrived late, noting with relief that the doctor had already occupied the head of the table and filled all but three seats at the far end with secretaries, squat Malay and Chinese officials with some vague relation to the UN office, and four American newcomers, all of whom were to ship out to Bidong as teachers as soon as their camp passes cleared. Perfect. She would be able to sit near the water, with Reuben and Gurmit. Reuben, she announced to the doctor, would be along shortly, after his visit to Immigration, where he hoped to secure a resident alien card. No need to shout, the doctor said, smiling. She did not believe herself to be shouting, and she was surprised to discover that no one else found the restaurant noisy. Gurmit had gone shopping, she said then, lowering her volume. He was due any minute.

But you don't hear that racket? she said. Really? The ocean's so loud today.

She took her seat next to the newcomers, shaking hands, introducing herself, all the while sweeping her hair forward to cover up the unsightly swelling on her face. Sorry, she said, apologizing for holding up the luncheon, which was, after all, partly in her honor. But a moment later she mumbled. "No, I'm not sorry," and then she looked at the newcomers' expressions to see if they thought she sounded as far away as she felt. She could not get her final hour on Bidong out of her mind. Sorry or not sorry? She was sorry for Manley, yes. But was she sorry for what they had done? It seemed a question directed toward some part of herself she could not reach. Not yet, anyway. In her mind she was floating, drifting as if circling an anchor, waiting for a time when the events of the past week would stop replaying in her mind, when people would stop yelling at her for what she had done, or shaking her hand for what she had done, or looking deeply into her eyes to see how she felt about what she had done.

"Porkpie," one of the newcomers said. He looked at her thoughtfully. "Is that Irish?"

"No," she said. "Just exuberance."

The man nodded, then turned to the woman to his right. "Did I hear you say you were Peace Corps Thailand?" he asked. "Did you learn straight Thai or one of the hill tribe dialects?"

The newcomers began talking among themselves, describing their old Peace Corps posting sites and telling anecdotes about outhouses. Porkpie sipped a glass of tea. So she had failed to make an impression on them. How strange it all seemed, sitting in this open-air restaurant talking with strangers, waiting for strangers to feed her. How strange it was to say *exuberance* and almost start crying.

The doctor was standing over her then, resting a hand on her shoulder. "They're flying Manley's remains home tomorrow morning," he said. "I thought you'd like to know."

"Thank you," she said. "Yes."

"The mud flats on Zone F are going to be filled in so people can't slip again."

"Who said he slipped?" she said.

The doctor nodded. "You're right. No one can really know. I retract the implication. But look," he said, rubbing her arm. "Before we get started with the food and all, I feel I have to say this." He paused. "Before you leave for Chicago. I feel I have a responsibility. I honestly don't think what happened . . . I think the delegates would have voted the same, regardless. I honestly do." He began to whisper. "I don't say this to be cruel. I have to say this. I want to be honest with you . . ." He stopped. His face was creased with frowns, and his left eye began twitching. "I say this out of respect for you and Gurmit and Reuben. And Manley, yes. Certainly Manley, accident or not. But I honestly don't think you or anyone else affected the decision. I think that's presumptuous to think otherwise. I think all you can say is this was a terrible price for a maybe."

She nodded. "You're right."

"I hope I'm not. For Manley's sake, I want to be wrong."

She closed her eyes, feigning contemplation, waiting for his hand to lift from her shoulder. He was lying, of course. He hoped he was right. But maintaining the illusion was important to him, that was clear, and in watching him walk slowly away, covering his twitching left eye, she sensed how easy it would have been to have reduced him to tears. It would have been equally easy to make him smile. Accuse him or thank him. Nod in agreement or scream in his face. The choices seemed arbitrary. They were all possible, all fully formed, their contours known, all lying in wait, all easy as picking up a fork or a chopstick or a napkin. They were all lies.

By the time Reuben and Gurmit walked in, the waiters had filled the table with steaming platters. There was Chinese sausage peeking out of a flaky golden batter, a dish of peppers and eggplant stuffed with pounded fish, several bowls of onions, garlic, and green herbs simmered in fish broth. There were giant bowls of yellow fried rice, mounds of beef garlanded with pale lettuce, glazed diced chicken, serving boats overflowing with lemon sauce, thick chilied soups, tendrils of octopus, sizzling dark-brown chunks of pork, giant mushrooms rising over a bed of leeks and bamboo shoots, ginger and tamarind beef, rose-colored lobsters, giant golden prawns curled like question marks, small jars of chili powder, soy sauce, prawn paste, green chilies in oil, platter after platter filling the table, wedged side by side among the flatware and tureens of green tea.

Reuben sat across from her, scratching under his arm cast, groaning slightly as he eased himself down. Gurmit, turbaned in gauze, was slowed by a momentary dizzy spell and relegated to the remaining seat next to the wire mesh. He propped his enormous shopping bag against the baseboard. Neither man introduced himself to anyone, even when Doctor Johansson shouted, "There they are. Our three farewellers. Say hello to our new volunteers, farewellers." Reuben and Gurmit looked at the doctor blankly. There was an unmistakable moment of tension at the table. The newcomers smiled brightly, and the Malay and Chinese officials frowned, and Doctor Johansson suddenly turned his attention to the lobster, which he proclaimed the largest he had ever seen. "Eat," said the doctor, swooping his hands into the air. "Don't be shy. We'll skip the speeches for now and go straight for the main attraction. Come on now. Everyone."

Gurmit spooned rice onto Porkpie's plate, then a small mound onto his own. Reuben took a prawn. "You know," Reuben whispered. "I don't have much appetite today. I feel sick as hell."

Porkpie looked out the wire mesh. On the strip of beach below, she saw two children, a boy and a girl, walking toward a giant black piling. The boy had one hand around the handlebars of a clunky bicycle, cutting a tire rut into the sand. The girl, flouncing her dress, carried a paper sack. The children were talking loudly, pushing each other and laughing. Porkpie smiled down at them, but they were staring out into the waves.

Everyone else at the table began eating, dishing huge mounds of rice onto their plates. They dipped into pork and beef and vegetables, their chopsticks darting from dish to dish, stacking so much food onto their plates that sauces began to drip over the sides. They were all reaching, arms and hands crossing into latticework patterns. There were chopsticks and forks clacking against plates and much commentary devoted to a green striped bowl that steamed with a deep red soup and smelled of shellfish or possibly eel or even tubers marinated in pepper and coriander. There was loud talk and boisterous joking, and one of the waiters, sensing distance between the three injured diners and the other guests, enlivened the meal by bringing out a cassette player and sliding in a tape of Chinese rock songs.

"I hear the Vietnamese go more for sentimental music," said one of the newcomers, addressing Reuben. "That so?"

Reuben looked at the man evenly, then turned away. He tapped Gurmit's shopping bag. "What you got in here?"

Gurmit opened his bag. Inside was a spatula, a metal bowl made in Korea, a pair of sturdy Bata sandals, a set of pens, a small inflatable dinosaur, and a plastic sleeve containing three pairs of boy's underwear.

"For Miss Phu and Duoc," said Gurmit.

"How? . . ." said Porkpie.

Gurmit waved his hand dismissively. "I am having friends still in Red Crescent Society. Supply room. They can make special deliveries, isn't it?"

Porkpie smiled. "Would you mind if I did some shopping, too? And then gave it to you for special delivery?"

"Yeah," said Reuben. He scratched at his cast. "Me, too."

Gurmit nodded.

"Maybe a soccer ball," Reuben said.

"Maybe some blouses would be nice," Porkpie said. "They were getting so frayed on her."

"Maybe a washbasin," said Reuben.

"Yes," said Porkpie. "And maybe some mantles for her lantern. Maybe lots of things."

The three began talking to each other then, mostly about supplies, making lists of items they'd like to load aboard a black market boat. They talked about Sally and Ralph and how they never saw the Swedes. They talked about the primary school and the English texts. They talked about the leaking ceiling in the community center and the chainsaws that kept stalling and the wall of garbage on Zone C and the terrible coffee in the staff eating hut and the mud and the beaches and the loudspeakers.

Outside, the girl was holding the boy's bicycle now, just standing in the sand, looking out past the piling. Porkpie, warming to the conversation, poked Reuben's cast with her fork, joshing, and glanced around for the boy. She poured herself some more tea. Reuben called for beer, and then Gurmit snapped his fingers at one of the newcomers, asking if he would please pass over the vegetable plate. Porkpie leaned back, clearing a path for the newcomer man to hand over the dish. She saw the boy then. He was walking backward out of the water, dripping, his trunks stuck to his legs, dragging something long and narrow.

She sipped her tea, staring, and then the boy turned, revealing a weathered length of wood, bleached the color of highway stones by the sun and water. Whether it was the plank, Porkpie couldn't say. Certainly

it was the right length and thickness. Certainly the grain looked the same, given allowances for the effects of seawater and sun. But she would have to see the other side to be sure. She would have to see if there was a name.

She nudged Gurmit. He turned his head toward the window, and Reuben did, too, bringing a beer bottle to his lips and sucking, then slowly putting the bottle back on the table.

"Is it?" she said.

Reuben shrugged.

"Maybe," said Gurmit.

The girl squatted in the sand. She opened her paper sack and took out something bound in plastic wrap while the boy stood the board on end. He turned the board around, examining. Porkpie squinted. No name. It was simply a board, and the boy laid it down lengthwise at his feet. The girl stripped away the wrap and laid the plastic like a table-cloth on the wood, smoothing the wrinkles and bubbles with her hand, and then she laid food on the wood. There was a small red rambutan fruit, and in a green packet was a white ball of rice. The boy looked on, sweeping away sand. There was no ceremony: the children simply began eating, scooping their hands into the rice, putting their fingers to their lips, and then the boy, his fingers sticky with grains, reached up and idly sounded the bicycle bell, *brrng-chung, brrng-chung,* while the girl peeled away the rambutan skin with her teeth. Porkpie, putting down her tea, stiffened suddenly, her ears back like a cat's. She listened very hard. "You hear?" she said. She slowly pushed back her chair and sat very still, alert and silent, listening. She heard the water and the roaring and the voices carrying in the air. She heard something that sounded like dreaming sounds, something hard and true and real. She stood then, very quietly, staring out the wire mesh, her shoulders straight back, and then Gurmit stood, and then Reuben, the three of them scraping their chairs on the cement floor, standing, their eyes hardly moving, even as everyone put down their forks and chopsticks and stopped eating. She looked down the long table then, at all the questioning faces, and she said to them, "Stand." All of you, she said. Right now. On your feet. Stand.

About the Author

Paul Eggers was born in 1953 in East St. Louis, Illinois. The son of a U.S. Air Force sergeant, he traveled extensively as a child and later, upon graduating with a B.A. from the University of Washington, joined the Peace Corps in 1976. He taught English in Malaysia for two years, and, in 1980, he returned to Southeast Asia for another two years, this time as a relief worker for the United Nations High Commission for Refugees, teaching English in refugee camps in the Philippines and Malaysia, including the island of Bidong.

Upon returning to the U.S., Eggers completed an M.A. in English from Pennsylvania State University, then left to teach for a year in Burundi, Africa. Back in the U.S. again, he worked as a technical writer and editor, employed at various times by Microsoft, Boeing, and a nationally distributed chess magazine, where, as a ranked chess master, he was an associate editor.

He received his Ph.D. in English from the University of Nebraska–Lincoln in 1996 and currently teaches there. His fiction has appeared in *Granta*, the *Quarterly*, and other literary journals; he was the 1995 winner of the *Quarterly West* Best Novella competition, judged by Jane Smiley. Currently, Eggers is working on his second novel. He and his wife, Ellen, live in Lincoln, Nebraska.